WHITE AS FROST

THE DARKWOOD TRILOGY
BOOK ONE

WHITE AS FROST

USA TODAY BESTSELLING AUTHOR
ANTHEA SHARP

Cover by Mulan Jiang. Map by Sarah Kellington. Professional editing by LHTemple and Editing720.

Fiddlehead Press
63 Via Pico Plaza #234
San Clemente, CA 92672

ISBN 9781680131437 (hardcover)

Subjects: Siblings - Young Adult Fiction / Fairy Tale & Folklore Adaptations - Young Adult Fiction / Royalty - Young Adult Fiction / Coming of Age Fantasy - Fiction

Visit www.antheasharp.com and join her newsletter for a FREE STORY, plus find out about upcoming releases and reader perks.

QUALITY CONTROL

We care about producing error-free books. If you discover a typo or formatting issue, please contact antheasharp@hotmail so that it may be corrected.

Don't miss the previous Darkwood-set books, ELFHAME, HAWTHORNE, and RAINE, available in print and ebook at all online booksellers.

DEDICATION

For the seekers and dreamers,
your magic is out there, waiting...

And for Sophia, who has always believed.

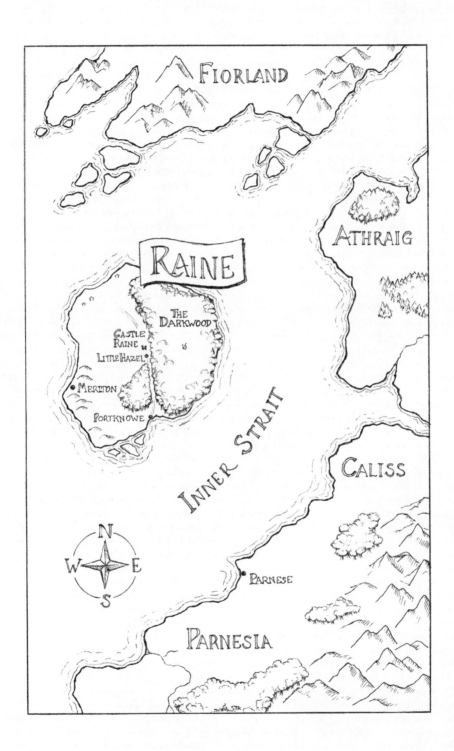

PART I

CHAPTER 1

When I was thirteen years old, I came to live in the castle beside the Darkwood.

"What a lucky girl you are," my mother said as the velvet-lined coach jolted down the road. "Not everyone gets to live in a castle and call themselves a princess."

I wanted neither of those things, and considered myself most *un*lucky to be torn away from my friends in the bright city of Parnese. They were the closest thing I had to family.

Except for Mama—but I knew better than to expect warmth and sympathy from her. She had always been my mother, of course, yet she'd never seemed terribly interested in fulfilling that role. Despite hazy memories of her affection when I was younger, it had taken me a long while to realize that most other mothers behaved very differently toward their children.

Because there's something wrong with you.

I slammed the door shut on that insidious voice. For as long as I could remember, it had whispered in my ear—part of me, and yet separate. It encouraged me to disobey, it confirmed my deepest fears, and sometimes it seemed the truest thing in my world.

Most of the time I could ignore it, shove it back into the deepest part of my mind and pretend there was not a wicked little voice living inside me, pushing me to say and do reckless things. The journey made it harder, without my books and companions to divert me. But I did not want to disappoint Mama when I was presented to her new husband. With a sigh, I twined my fingers together.

The inexpertly sewn seam on my left glove caught against my skirts, and I glanced down at it with a grimace. All my left-handed gloves had to be modified to fit my disfigured pinky finger, which was missing the top two joints from a long-ago accident.

We hadn't the money to hire a seamstress, and so I adapted my gloves myself. Most of the time the clumsy work didn't bother me overmuch, but now, on the way to meet a king, I felt suddenly self-conscious about my flaw.

Stubby pinky or no, there was little I could do about my maimed finger. I pulled my gaze from my imperfect hand and stared out the window. I hoped we would arrive soon.

Or never...

The encroaching branches of the evergreens lining the narrow road made the air thick and shadowed, the trees a dark wall unbroken except for the high-banked road cutting through. Every time I looked at the forest, the branches seemed to be moving—beckoning to me with their restless limbs.

"Stop squinting at the scenery, Rosaline, and pay attention," Mama said, for the hundredth time. "When we arrive at Castle Raine, make sure to stand up straight and greet your new father properly."

"I won't call him Papa," I said stubbornly.

I'd never had a father, and had no interest in acquiring one at this late stage. And even if I did, there was no use in it. If Mama did not love me enough, what hope was there that some strange king would be any different?

"Why must you be so difficult?" Mama brought a perfectly manicured hand up to her cheek and let out a sigh. "Very well. You may call him Lord Raine."

I gave her a grudging nod. Growing up on the outskirts of the court in Parnese, I understood that protocol must be followed. Even though

Mama was the old queen's distant cousin, she was only allowed to address the dowager as "Your Highness," which I thought rather stuffy. Then again, the rules of the adult world often seemed foolish to me.

The closer we came to the castle, the more Mama chattered on, her voice full of nervous faux-cheer.

"You must be kind to his daughter, as well. You're of an age, so I expect you to become fast friends. Despite the tales..." She trailed off, but now my attention was caught.

"What tales?" This was the first I'd heard that anything in our new life might be out of the ordinary. Despite myself, my interest was piqued.

From the moment Mama had announced that she'd wed the King of Raine and we would be following him across the Outer Strait to dwell with him in his castle, I'd resolved to enjoy no part of it.

The sea crossing had not been so bad, though, especially when a trio of dolphins leaped and played in the sailing ship's wake. Unlike Mama, I was not confined to the cabin by seasickness. I explored the ship, managing not to fall overboard or become tangled in the ropes scattered about the deck.

On the second day, the coast of Raine appeared, black against the horizon. I hung on the rails and watched, unwillingly eager for a first glimpse of my new home.

What I saw did not look promising. We were headed for a tiny harbor flanked by stark cliffs streaked with white. Lonely seabirds cried and wheeled in the gray, misty air. The only spot of color was a yellow coach awaiting our arrival. After debarking from the ship, we were whisked into the vehicle so quickly I only caught a glimpse of the surroundings: stone buildings, wet thatch, and dour-faced people garbed in homespun cloth.

The Kingdom of Raine was altogether unpromising—except for this new bit of information Mama had just let slip. Was there a child as wayward as myself living in the castle? I leaned forward on the plush seat and asked again.

"What tales of his daughter, Mama? Please tell me."

My mother bit her lip, a shadow of worry crossing her face.

"Promise me you won't be afraid of her. The two of you are to be sisters, after all."

Behind my stubborn resolve to dislike Raine and everyone in it, I could not help a glimmer of hope that the king's daughter and I would become friends. If I must leave my companions behind, perhaps a new one waited for me in Raine. And I had no fear that Mama would come to love that other girl better than me. My mother always loved herself best of all.

"What's so bad about the princess?" I asked. "Does she set things on fire, or misbehave, or torment the servants?"

"There are stories." Mama looked out the window, as if she did not want to see my face as she spoke. "Some say an ancient, terrible magic lurks in her eyes."

Magic. The one thing in the world that could transform an ordinary girl into someone special. Someone worthy of being loved. I shivered, my left pinky throbbing slightly. The trees leaned over the road, listening.

"What magic?" I asked softly. "Is there actual, true sorcery in Raine?"

The question stretched out, a thin silver strand looping around and around me until I felt encased in its web. Then it began to squeeze, and I gasped as the air left my lungs.

"Mama!" I cried, though it came out more as a wheeze. "I can't breathe."

Her eyes wide with alarm, my mother shrieked at the driver to stop the coach. Dizzily, I slid off the seat and crumpled to the floor. From this vantage point, my cheek resting on the rough carpet, I absently noticed its pattern: an interlocking design of green and black ferns.

"Help her," Mama commanded when the coachman opened the door. "My daughter has fainted."

I wanted to argue that this was far more than a simple faint, but I couldn't find the breath to form words.

"Yes, mistress," the man said. "We must bring her outside, where there's more air."

He hoisted me up like a sack of onions and deposited me on the embankment beside the road. Which was also carpeted with ferns, though these ones danced faintly in the breeze.

It occurred to me, in a distant, drowning way, that I was dying. I was sorry that I'd never see my friends again. And I was sorry that I would never meet the mysterious girl who lived in Castle Raine.

My eyelids fluttered shut.

Between one heartbeat and the next, there was a great roaring and rustle of leaves. I managed to open my eyes in time to see a huge, hairy beast leap over me. Its muzzle was flecked with spittle, and its long claws dug into the earth right beside my head. Dirt sprayed, stinging my cheek and landing on my lips.

The bear—for that was what the huge animal was—turned its head and regarded me from its dark, amber-flecked eye. The musky smell of earth and blood whispered in the air. My heart thundered, either with its last beating, or its first.

The soft fur of the creature's underbelly brushed my outstretched arm. Strangely unafraid, I waited for it to open its jaws and devour me. I was dimly aware of my mother wailing in terror, of the coachman's shouts.

The bear's face came closer to mine, and closer, until its wet nose touched my cheek. I was too amazed to be scared—or maybe my mind was already numb, falling into the shadows. Then the bear gathered itself. As quickly as it had appeared, it leaped away, back into the dark forest.

For a long moment, everything was utterly still. Even the branches stopped their ceaseless gesturing.

The world ticked into motion once more. I drew in a deep, ragged breath, inhaling the rank smell of the bear still hanging in the air. The air burned my lungs, which had nearly forgotten how to breathe. With the back of one shaky hand, I wiped the trace of dampness from my cheek. Above me, the trees seemed to whisper among themselves.

"Heavens." Mama sank down into the crushed bracken at my side, her face pale beneath her powder. "How very dreadful. First you faint, and then that creature nearly mauls you. I am thankful beyond words that he was frightened off."

She drew a violet-scented fan from her reticule and began to wave it, alternating between wafting air at my face and her own. The vigorousness of her movement was the only outward sign of her agitation. The last trace of bear was overwhelmed with the cloying smell of violets. So quickly was our sudden adventure erased.

As usual, my own perception of events was quite different from my mother's. In retrospect, it seemed clear that the bear had broken the strange spell intent on suffocating me.

How or why it had known to do such a thing was a mystery—but I was quickly coming to suspect that Raine was full of such mysteries.

The bear, I was quite certain, had saved my life. I was not comfortable owing such a debt to a wild creature of the woods, as it did not seem like a thing I could ever repay. But perhaps such things didn't matter to bears. Even magical ones.

"We'd best keep moving," the coachman said, casting a nervous look at the shadows beneath the trees.

"Of course." Mama waited for him to offer his hand, then took it and stepped daintily up into the coach.

I stood and brushed crushed ferns from my skirt, then climbed awkwardly into the vehicle. My breath still came a bit short as I settled onto the seat.

Right before the door closed, I leaned forward, searching the forest for a large, dark shape. Nothing moved in the maze of evergreens, but I could not dispel the sensation that I was being watched.

Had I truly almost died? Already the sharp, panicked memory was receding, blunting, until it seemed that perhaps I'd only grown short of breath, after all. My left hand ached.

I was still trying to sort out what had happened an hour later, when the coach wheels clattered over cobblestones. The shadow of an iron-spiked portcullis fell over the road. We drove beneath it, past thick stone walls reaching high to either side, and at last arrived in the courtyard entry of Castle Raine.

CHAPTER 2

The coach came to a halt before Castle Raine's front steps, which were flanked by ivy-covered stone walls beneath the pewter sky. My skirt was still marked with green smears from the crushed ferns, and I hoped the king wouldn't notice. Mama had said nothing for the remainder of the journey, only worried at her handkerchief and spent the time glancing between me and the endless forest outside.

As soon as the coachman opened the door, I jumped from my seat and down from the coach, which was overfull of my mother's fretful, unsaid words.

Feet planted on the blue-gray cobblestones, I took a deep breath. The air smelled of horses and damp and wood smoke. My gaze went to the man and girl waiting at the top of the dozen hewn stone steps leading to an impressive arched entryway. The two of them seemed to tower above me, the castle rising steeply at their backs as if to say *keep out*.

The man—the king, judging by the gold circlet on his brow and his cloak of rich blue velvet—gave me a quick nod. His stern eyes were set in a face that seemed chiseled from stone, and I was glad his attention didn't linger on me. After that brief glance, he focused on the door of the coach, where Mama had yet to emerge.

His daughter, however, looked right at me, her stare so dark and intense I felt it down to the soles of my feet.

We were too far away for me to determine if strange magic lurked in her eyes, but even without that knowledge, I had to admit she was a trifle alarming. Not just in the fierceness of her gaze, but in her entire demeanor. Her skin held a strange pallor, so white it looked as though she'd used a whole tin of rice powder on her cheeks—but her paleness was natural, not artificial.

In contrast, her lips were shockingly red, a deep scarlet as though smeared with fresh blood. For a moment I wondered if she'd been eating pomegranate seeds. But no, this color, too, was a natural part of her.

Her long hair, the deep black of a raven's wing, was pulled back from her face. In addition to her strange coloring, she had high cheekbones and slightly tilted eyes. I could not tell if she was pretty, or hideous, or merely the strangest girl I had ever seen.

"Tobin!" my mother cried as she stepped out of the coach.

Lifting her skirts, she rushed up the steps in a froth of lace and lavender silk. I followed, far less gracefully.

"Welcome, my dear," the king said.

He opened his arms and let Mama throw herself into his embrace. I glanced to one side. It was uncomfortable to see my mother being affectionate with a man. She kissed him upon the lips, then drew back, turning to the girl at the king's side.

"And this is your daughter, Neeve?" Mama asked.

"Yes," the king said.

"What a pretty thing you are," my mother said, her voice ringing false to my ears. "I am so delighted to join your family. I've brought you a sister. Come, Rose." She beckoned me to join her at the top of the stairs.

"I don't want a pretend mother. Or a false sister." The girl's voice was cold as ice, and I hesitated, one foot on the top flagstone.

This princess seemed free to voice the kinds of thoughts I'd always worked hard to keep to myself. I didn't know if I admired or hated her for it.

"Neeve." Her father's voice was cold. "We have spoken of this."

Resentment flashed across her face, but she bowed her head, as if in agreement. I could see the gleam of her eyes, though, and there was nothing dutiful in their expression.

"This is Rosaline," my mother said, hauling me up to stand before her.

"Lord Raine." I gave him my best court curtsey, only wobbling a tiny bit. "Miss Neeve."

I curtseyed to her, too, but she seemed to take no notice, and certainly didn't return the favor. Either we would become friends, or the bitterest of enemies.

I hoped it would be the former, and resolved to do what I could to win this strange princess over. Life trapped in this dreary castle was going to be hard enough as it was.

Lord Raine gave me a tight smile, then held his arm out to my mother. "Come. Your rooms are ready. I'll have the servants bring your things and help you settle in."

"That would be lovely. Let me tell you about our journey..." My mother launched into a stream of inconsequential chatter, and Neeve and I fell into step behind them.

The great iron-bound doors of the castle swung open, like a beast parting its jaws, and I couldn't help but shiver as we passed over the threshold. It was no warmer inside the stone walls than it had been outside in the mist-laden air. Our footsteps echoed through the great hall.

Empty fireplaces stood on either side of the long room, and the walls were draped with dark tapestries full of figures clashing in scenes I couldn't quite make out. Neeve walked like a shadow beside me. In the dimness of the room, her dark cloak and hair made it seem as though her face was floating in midair, a disembodied specter of a girl.

"We'll need more candles in here," my mother said. "Is it always so chilly in the summer?"

"I do not spend much time in the great hall," Lord Raine replied. "But you may do as you see fit. You are now the lady of the castle."

Neeve let out an annoyed huff, and I slanted a quick, sideways glance at her. Two spots of color stood on her cheeks, as bright as if they'd been painted there. I found this evidence of emotion reassuring. She was, indeed, made of flesh and blood and not a ghost girl.

Not that I'd really thought so, although according to Mama my imagination was ever my downfall. It seemed our mysterious new home would give me ample opportunity to exercise it. *There are secrets here,* the voice inside me whispered. *You must discover everything you can.*

Lord Raine led us up a wide, curving staircase. The treads were worn in the middle with shallow depressions, and I wondered how many pairs of feet had trodden up and down over the centuries. I had not thought the castle would be so old. In truth, I had not really thought about the castle at all, and Mama had been no help.

Two months ago, she'd swept into the airy parlor of our apartments in Parnese and announced that she'd just married a king. Despite my abundance of questions, she would say little about him, or the country we would be going to, or even her reasons for marrying him.

"Darling, isn't it wonderful?" she'd said. "Now go and think about what gowns you want to bring with you. I'm told the weather in Raine is cooler than here, so plan accordingly."

Always annoyingly vague, Mama had outdone herself this time. Though perhaps she'd known little more than I about the kingdom we were about to call home. After several evasions, I'd stopped questioning aloud, though the need for answers still gnawed at me.

Now that we were here, perhaps I'd finally learn *why.* My mother was impulsive and self-serving, but marrying a king and whisking us off to the far corner of the map was a bit extreme, even for her.

Lord Raine led us down a chilly hallway. Oil sconces lining the walls cast flickering shadows, and my heart beat fast, half with fear, half with excitement. I snuck another glance at Neeve pacing beside me, but her pale face was unreadable. The notion that we might be friends shriveled a little more, but I was determined to try.

"Here are your rooms, Arabelle," the king said, halting before a wooden door carved with stags. "I hope you find them comfortable."

"Of course I will." Mama opened the door.

I peered around her to see a small parlor with a fire crackling on the hearth. The bedroom lay beyond, a huge four-poster bed hung with tapestries visible through the half-open door. A hulking wardrobe on the far wall was framed by windows that looked out upon gray skies and dark evergreens.

I wondered if there was anything *but* trees in the whole kingdom.

The king turned to his daughter.

"Take Rosaline to the east wing," he said.

"I'm not to be near Mama?" I asked, suddenly bereft.

I'd not fully considered what it meant, now that my mother was married. I was no longer a priority in her life—not that she'd ever treated me as much of one, leaving me mostly to my own devices. But still, my rooms had always adjoined hers, and I was not yet so grown that I welcomed her absence. She had ever been there for me, in her own distant way.

This, though, I had not foreseen.

"Now, now." Mama patted my shoulder. "It's time for you to be more independent, Rose. Follow Neeve, and I'll see you at dinner."

More independent? I scowled at my mother. More abandoned, it felt like.

Seeing my face, Mama relented slightly. She bent and laid a perfumed kiss on my cheek. "I'll come and visit your rooms this evening, shall I? You can show me everything."

I gave her a short nod, then turned on my heel and trudged to where Neeve was waiting. Without a word, she led me around the corner. We traversed two more long corridors before she finally halted in front of a door carved with twining roses.

"Here," she said, then turned away.

"Wait." I caught her sleeve, not wanting to be alone. "Are your rooms nearby?"

Her dark gaze met mine, the nearby sconce pricking twin flames in her eyes.

"Two doors down," she finally said, grudging me the information.

I let go of her and she stepped out of reach, still regarding me.

"Why don't you come in?" I turned the wrought-iron handle.

"I've seen them," she said, her voice cool. "I'm acquainted with every room in the castle."

"Then you could be my guide." I gave her a tentative smile, which was not returned. "At least show me a *few* things. Is there a water closet nearby, a bathing room? What do I need to know?"

She let out a wintry sigh. "Very well."

I felt like I'd won a small victory. Befriending Neeve seemed a daunting task—and a worthy enough one to quiet my wicked voice. Besides, I hadn't seen any other alternative to utter loneliness. But perhaps the castle servants had children—provided my new status allowed me to make their acquaintance.

I'd always had playmates and confidantes, met while running about in the park or splashing in the lazy bend of the river. It was a simple thing for me to make friends, and I loved my companions dearly, especially laughing Paulette and clever Marco. We'd wept bitter tears when we parted, and I promised to return as soon as I came of age and could direct my own future.

Run away, my little voice had suggested. *Stay in Parnese and let your mother go to Raine without you.*

Had I been few years older, I might have done that very thing—but she was still my family, and I'd seen what had happened to orphans on the street. It was not a good life.

With Neeve at my shoulder, I pushed the door open to see my new accommodations.

Like my mother's rooms, my suite consisted of a sitting area and a bedroom beyond. A coal fire smoldered in the hearth in the front room, which also held two chairs, a small table, a writing desk, and an empty set of shelves, presumably waiting for me to put my things upon them.

True to the carvings on the door, the rooms inside were decorated with a rose theme. Someone had no doubt thought it amusing to put me in this suite, but I didn't mind—especially as the flower motif wasn't overly fussy. Indeed, I doubted anything in Castle Raine could be frivolous. The weight of the stones would smother anything too gaudy, and the cool, musty air would do the rest.

"This is pleasant," I said, filling the silence. It was plain that Neeve wasn't going to say much of anything. "I like the green carpet, especially. Let's go see the bedroom."

I pushed open the connecting door, glad to find several large windows along the far wall. The lack of light in the corridors made me uncomfortable.

A four-poster bed, smaller than the one in Mama's rooms, dominated one side of the bedroom. Dusky pink curtains were drawn back, revealing snowy linens and a duvet covered with a pattern of embroidered leaves. At the foot of the bed stood a large wooden chest, and to the side was a table holding a washbasin and pitcher. Across the room, a wardrobe took up most of the far wall. The mirror in the door gave back a wavery reflection of two girls—one pale-faced and inky-haired with a red slash of a mouth, the other with sun-bronzed skin and kinky red-gold hair whose lips seemed the palest rose in comparison.

"We're the same height," I observed, pleased at the notion.

Neeve's eye's narrowed. "We have nothing in common. Don't make the mistake of thinking so, *etrannach*."

"Don't call me names." I swung about to face her, hands fisted on my hips. "Take it back, whatever you said."

She blinked at me, a flash of surprise crossing her face. Likely she was unused to being challenged—but I refused to simply stand there and let her call me something filthy.

"It only means foreigner." Her tone was less sharp, and I guessed it was as close to an apology as I would get.

"Still." I unclenched my hands and smoothed my skirts. "I'm to live here now."

"Yes." She did not sound glad of the fact.

Her gaze went to my left hand, and I belatedly realized I'd just revealed my flaw.

"What's wrong with your finger?" she asked. Yet another demonstration that she wasn't overly concerned with politeness.

In a way, her candor was refreshing. If she didn't want to pretend to ignore my too-short finger, then I wouldn't have to try to conceal it. I stripped off my gloves and held out my left hand for her inspection.

"I'm missing parts of it." I wiggled my pinky at her.

She looked at the stub, her expression as still as glass. "Were you born that way?"

"No. When I was seven, there was an accident."

"What happened?"

I pressed my lips together. "I don't remember, and Mama won't talk about it. But it doesn't matter. I can still use my hand without any problems."

The arrival of two servants carrying my trunks interrupted our conversation. As I directed them to set the luggage beside the wardrobe, Neeve took the opportunity to sidle to the door.

"I'll show you to the dining room when it's time for dinner," she said.

Without waiting for a reply, she was gone. I tried not to let her abrupt departure bother me.

"Sorche will be up soon to help you unpack," one of the servants said.

"I don't know who that is," I said forlornly.

The man straightened and gave me a look of rough sympathy. "She's to be your maid. Don't fret, youngling. She's a kind girl, if a bit untried."

I'd never had a maid. Even if this one wasn't very skilled, at least she would be someone to talk to.

"Thank you." I nodded at the servant.

With a quick bow, he and the other man left. They gently shut the door behind them, and I was alone. How I yearned for my friends. Instead I was stuck in a set of rooms far away from Mama, my only prospect for a companion a strange, sharp-edged girl who didn't seem to like me at all.

With a heavy heart, I went to the window and perched on the window seat, cushioned in green velvet. At least I had a view of the sky and forest. I leaned my forehead against the cool glass and sighed. My breath made a mist, blurring the scene outside.

Something moved in the deep shadows, and I sat up, scrubbing the glass clear with my sleeve. Had that been the outline of an animal skulking through the woods, or a cloaked figure?

Heart thumping in my chest, I scanned the evergreens and ferny underbrush. Small white flowers starred the mosses, and I noticed that the forest stopped several yards from the castle walls, as if something invisible kept it at bay.

For several long minutes I stared at the Darkwood, but nothing else stirred except the restless wind in the branches.

CHAPTER 3

A s promised, Neeve came to show me to the dining room. At first I had not known what the strange, mournful clang was that had echoed down the halls, until she came to fetch me.

"Dinner," she said when I opened the door to her knock. Then her dark eyes looked me up and down and her lips thinned the slightest bit.

I returned her look, wary.

"Don't you dress for dinner here?" I asked. I couldn't help but notice she was wearing the same drab gown as before.

"I don't." She turned and, without waiting for me to follow, went down the cool, shadowy corridor.

I pulled my door shut with a thud and hurried after. The gold silk skirts I wore made whispering sounds with each quick footstep. At least Mama would be pleased that I'd changed from my stained traveling clothes into something more suitable for dining with a king.

My new maid, Sorche, had seemed to think it a good idea as well. Or maybe she'd just wanted to please me by agreeing with whatever I said. She seemed attentive, and was younger than I'd expected. When they'd told me I was to have my own maid, I'd expected a matron, not a girl only a handful of years older than myself.

Unfortunately, she refused to answer any of my questions, only bobbing curtseys and murmuring, "That's not for me to say, miss."

After three different attempts to pry information from her about the castle and its inhabitants, I gave up and simply let Sorche braid my hair.

"They won't stay," I warned her as she pinned the half-dozen red braids in an intricate pattern around my head. "In no time, it'll be nothing but frizz and tangles."

I wasn't worried about having a perfect coiffure, although I often wished my hair were better behaved. What did concern me, though, was how to make Neeve like me. It was a new experience, being disliked on sight, and one I did not enjoy.

"What are your hobbies?" I asked Neeve when I finally caught up to her, halfway down the hallway.

"Hobbies?" She sent me a disdainful look.

"Reading?" I asked, trying to guess what she might enjoy. "I imagine the castle must have a nice library. I prefer tales of adventure, mostly. What do you like to read?"

"I don't."

"What?" I stopped in the middle of the hall and stared at her. "You don't know how to *read?*"

Apprehension knotted in my lungs. What strange, primitive place had I come to?

She turned on me, eyes sparking with temper. "Of course I know how to read, idiot. I simply said I don't like to."

"Oh." I trailed behind her for a moment, wondering if I should apologize, or if the fact that she'd called me *idiot* made us even.

Even, I decided, increasing my pace until I walked beside her once more.

"Then what do you *like* to do?" I tried again.

"What does it matter to you what I like, or don't like?" She didn't bother looking at me when she spoke.

"I'm just— I want to be friends."

I felt prickly. No one had ever asked me to explain myself. It was as though Neeve operated by her own set of rules, and making friends wasn't anywhere near the front of that list. Possibly not even on it at all.

She made no reply, and for a few minutes I was silenced. We walked on, the emptiness underscored by the clack of her boot heels and the shush of my slippers. As we went down the stairs—a different staircase than the one we'd ascended when I first arrived—Neeve gave my satin footwear a scornful look.

"You call those shoes?" she asked.

"They're the fashion in Parnese," I said.

"They're silly. All those laces and tassels. It's a wonder you haven't tripped."

I did stumble, then, as though her words had tangled about my feet. I grabbed the railing to keep from tumbling down the stairs and gave her a sharp look.

Her dark eyes met mine, calm and revealing nothing. We stared at one another for a moment, and then she turned and gracefully continued down the stairs. She had an odd way of moving, almost as if she were floating through the world and not truly connected to it.

Mindful of my feet, I followed, but at the bottom of the staircase I stopped. Three different hallways led off, identical stone corridors, just like the ones upstairs. And though I'd defended my footwear, it was true that thin satin slippers were not, perhaps, the best choice in this drafty old castle. Already my feet were chilled from walking over the cold floors.

"How far away is the dining room?" I demanded. Had Neeve been leading me in circles all this time? Somehow, it wouldn't surprise me.

"There." She gestured to the right-hand hall.

Midway down the dim corridor a pair of double doors stood open, a liveried servant standing at attention before them. He kept his eyes fixed on the air above our heads as we approached, then stood aside to let us enter.

A long table covered by a white tablecloth ran the length of the room. Neeve and I stood at the bottom, and it seemed to me that the head was very far away. There were no flowers, no bright runners; only a few candles in dull metal holders to light the expanse of pale linen. The ceiling overhead stretched away into the shadows.

Windows ran along one side of the room, covered by dark blue curtains. I hoped they'd be open during daylight meals, otherwise the room would be so dark and dreary I feared I might permanently lose my appetite.

There was no one else there, although I made a quick tally of the chairs. Eleven, five ranged down either side of the table and a tall, ornate armchair at the head that was surely the king's. A few more empty chairs lined the walls on either side of the room, looking like strange, spindly creatures in the flickering candlelight.

At home—our old home—Mama and I had eaten at a small wooden table in our apartments. Sometimes my friends would join us, or hers would, in which case we'd put in the single leaf and squeeze about the edges. Or we'd take our plates into the sunny salon and, mindful of spills, eat our dinner there. Our cook and maid didn't seem to mind.

I hadn't been deemed old enough to attend formal dinners at the palace itself, and only once had I eaten there, in a smaller dining room. Mama had taken me to see the old queen when I turned six, and I recalled that she'd coached me for weeks about the proper uses of the various forks and spoons, and how to drape the napkin across my lap, just so.

I forgot all of it, of course, but I remember the old queen laughing, the wrinkles on her face deepening as she showed her amusement at something I'd said. It must not have been too mortifying, for Mama had patted my hand and told me I was a clever girl.

Now, though, faced with the long expanse of table, I felt suddenly six years old again. Generally the prospect of dinner with nine strangers wouldn't trouble me overmuch, but it had been a long and taxing day. If I could, I'd go back to my rooms and take my meal there on a tray.

But that would be rude, and besides, I had no notion how to get back to my suite. I might starve to death wandering the halls before I ever found it.

"How many people will be dining?" I asked, trying to mask my worry.

"I don't know." Neeve sounded sublimely unconcerned. "Sometimes my father's advisors join him at mealtimes, sometimes not. There are always places set for them, regardless."

"His Royal Majesty, King Tobin of Raine," the servant announced, as if the room were full of nobility instead of just two girls hovering at the end of the table. "Accompanied by Queen Arabelle."

Neeve shot me a narrow-eyed glare as we hurried out of the way, as if it were my fault my mother had married her father. I wrinkled my nose at her. Certainly I had nothing to do with it. I'd rather be back home in Parnese.

The king strode in, Mama on his arm. She looked so beautiful that for a moment I nearly forgave her. The candlelight made her golden hair shine and sparked bright darts from the diamond crown she wore. My full skirts and fancy slippers paled in comparison to her gown, the gauzy overskirt sewn with winking gems.

Even Neeve seemed impressed, at least for a moment. She blinked, wide-eyed, before the shutters of her thoughts slammed closed once more and I could no longer read her expression.

I made a low curtsey. After a moment's hesitation, Neeve bowed too. Though not quite so low. She was a full-blood princess, after all.

"Hello, girls," Mama said.

I wasn't sure how I felt about being put into the same category as Neeve. Mama and I had always been the pair, unless I was off with my friends. My heart twisted as I realized that she would now be fixed on her new husband, and on being the queen.

"Punctual," the king said, with an approving nod that encompassed both myself and Neeve.

He escorted Mama to the head of the table. There was an awkward moment when Neeve went to take the chair on Lord Raine's right, just as he pulled it out for my mother.

The king cleared his throat and his daughter leaped back, two spots of color staining her cheeks. She came around the table and perched on the chair to his left. I took the seat below hers, facing an empty place. Or possibly a stranger, if one of the king's advisors made an appearance.

"It will be just family this evening," Lord Raine said, as if reading my thoughts.

"These people are *not* my family," Neeve muttered.

Either the king did not hear, or he chose to ignore her words. He raised his hand, signaling for the servant to bring wine.

It was a subdued dinner. The king and Mama put their heads close and murmured together for much of the meal, leaving Neeve and I to one another's company. I'd already learned she didn't respond well to questions, but I still could not help trying.

"Do you have any pets?"

"Except for horses, animals dislike me." She took a bite of meat.

It didn't surprise me in the least. I imagined that most creatures, humans included, did not take well to her prickly nature. I decided not to tell her about the menagerie I'd befriended over the years. Though none of those creatures had included horses. To be honest, though I'd ridden once or twice, I found horses rather intimidating. They were so very large, after all.

"Music, perhaps?" I gave her a hopeful look. "You play an instrument, or sing?"

In truth, I could not imagine this pale, contained girl actually opening her mouth wide enough to let a melody come out.

The look she gave me was condescending. "*You* sing, I suppose."

"I do! I love all the popular ballads, as well as the classical—"

"I'm not interested in music."

I set down my fork and stared at her, feeling the heat in my eyes. "Besides being rude to other people, is there anything you *are* interested in?"

Her gaze flicked to mine, then away. The telltale red spots bloomed on her cheeks—not as fiercely as when the king had given away her seat at his right hand, but enough so that I knew my words had met their mark.

"Herbalism," she said.

I suspected it was as much of an answer as I was going to get. At least it was better than nothing.

"Finally," I said. "Do you make tisanes and sachets and the like? I do love the smell of lavender."

"It's too wet and dark here for lavender."

Of course. I should have guessed that nothing so pleasant as lavender would actually grow in the climate of Raine.

"What do you do during your days?" I asked. "Other than study herbalism."

"I have tutorials in the mornings," she said.

"On what subjects?" For once, she was answering my questions, and I'd keep them coming until she stopped.

Besides, I was interested to know what my life in the castle would be like. I'd attended the school for nobles' children in Parnese, where we studied languages, history, politics, art, music, culinary appreciation... anything and everything that might be useful for a courtier.

"Math," Neeve said. "Geography. The history of Raine."

The king glanced over, our conversation obviously catching his attention. "Rosaline, we expect you will join Neeve at her studies. Have you been to school? Are you accustomed to lessons?"

"Yes, my lord," I said meekly, though his words stung my pride.

I was not some unschooled street urchin. In fact, I'd wager that my education so far had been superior to whatever Neeve had learned in this provincial backwater of a kingdom. I kept my eyes lowered, however, showing no sign of my thoughts. One of my best subjects last year had been diplomacy—perhaps because I'd struggled to master my wicked voice for so many years. I'd taken the lessons in subtlety to heart, especially where adults were concerned.

"Good," Lord Raine said. "We will expect you to join my daughter in the classroom promptly at eight."

"In the morning?" I slanted a glance at Mama. That seemed like a most uncivilized hour to begin lessons. "After breakfast?"

"We eat during lessons," Neeve said. "Miss Groves always begins with a lecture, so there's time for a meal. The servants bring up trays from the kitchens."

"Oh." I was accustomed to lying abed until nearly nine, then taking a cup of milky tea and hurrying off to school, which began at half past.

"That's settled." The king gave me a nod, then turned back to conversing with my mother.

I looked at Neeve, my appetite fleeing as a terrible thought occurred to me. "You don't have lessons all *afternoon* as well?"

One corner of her red lips twitched, as if she sensed my horror and was amused by it.

"No," she said. "You can do whatever you like after lunch."

Also served in the schoolroom, I guessed.

"What do *you* do?" Perhaps I'd join Neeve. At least for the first few afternoons, until I understood the lay of the castle better, and what my options might be.

Her expression went blank again. "It's none of your business."

I blinked at her a moment, then gathered my wits. "Very well."

What a strange girl she was, and so cold. I'd heard that her name meant *snow* in Raine's ancient language, and that fact did not surprise me in the least.

But if Neeve did not want me to find out what she did each afternoon, she'd just guaranteed that I'd do my best to discover it. I didn't like being told no, especially not by someone my own age who thought herself so much better than me.

One of my classes had introduced the art of skullduggery. I wasn't as good at sneaking about as I was at diplomacy, but I knew how to drape a cloak to blend into the shadows and how to trail someone while keeping my own steps silent.

Whatever Neeve was up to the next afternoon, I was determined to follow her and find out.

CHAPTER 4

Despite the early hour and the dry topics, lessons the next morning were not quite as dreadful as I'd imagined. Miss Groves was a good enough teacher to make even the history of Raine interesting.

"Rosaline, is it?" She pushed up her glasses and gave me a matter-of-fact look. Her hair was grayish brown; her eyes were the same. She was one of those perplexing people whose age was difficult to determine; I could not tell if she were younger than Mama or much, much older.

"Yes, Miss Groves," I said. "Though I prefer Rose."

"You do?" Neeve glanced at me, as though the idea of a short name had never crossed her mind.

I supposed, since her name was already short, it hadn't. I tilted my head, considering. One could condense Neeve down to Nee. Somehow, the thought of anyone calling her Nee was quite ridiculous. Which was why, I thought, I might be tempted to do so—after we'd gotten to know one another a bit more.

"What do you know of Raine, Rose?" Miss Groves fixed me with an encouraging look.

"It's an island," I began, feeling suddenly unprepared.

Neeve let out a snort. "That's obvious."

"If you would let Rose continue," Miss Groves said mildly.

"It has a cooler, wetter climate than the rest of the Continent, being located to the north and west."

Neeve rolled her eyes, but refrained from saying anything.

"It... Um." I scrambled to recall the tiny bit of history we'd touched on in my previous classes. In the grand capital of Parnese, anything not on the Continent was considered barely worth studying.

"It is known for the production of *bellarmes*, an herb used in expensive creams which supposedly restore the complexion," I said triumphantly, glad to have recalled something of substance. "My mother has some, I think."

"A waste," Neeve said, her mouth pinching together. "Here in Raine, we call it *nirwen*, and it has more uses than you know."

"I don't care what you do with some provincial herb," I said, tired of her scorn.

Miss Groves gave me a look over the top of her spectacles. "I encourage you not to dismiss information out of hand, Rose. It behooves us all to keep an open mind in the pursuit of education."

"I'm sorry, Miss Groves," I said, chastened. Though I was not sorry for the flash of temper I'd sparked in Neeve's eyes. I preferred her anger to her disdain.

"The plant of which we speak," the teacher continued, "is, as Neeve said, useful as more than just an ingredient in beauty creams. Known in an even older tongue as *cailindeora*, it has other restorative powers. A small amount is a valuable addition to any apothecary's store, though if used in too large a dose, or too frequently, the effects can prove toxic."

"If it's so special, why don't the Parnesians use it more often?" I asked.

"It is a rare herb," Miss Groves said. "It cannot be cultivated, and we prefer to keep most of what is harvested here in Raine, selling only a small amount to the Continent. Now, Neeve, what else do we export?"

"Amber," my stepsister answered. "And aromatic woods."

"Again, both in small quantities." Miss Groves gave me a slight smile. "Raine is not a particularly powerful country, economically or politically. Why do you think that is?"

"It's too isolated," I said. "And not largely populated. There seem to be more trees here than people."

Miss Groves looked amused.

"Our trees are better company than most humans," Neeve declared, which was an odd thing to say.

I glanced out the window. The schoolroom was located in one of the turrets and had curved windows on three sides. The north and west windows looked out on forest, while the south held a view of the castle courtyard and the road beyond. From this height, I could glimpse a village just off the main road, tucked back into the trees.

"I want to know more of the Darkwood," I said, my gaze still fixed outside. A wind stirred the feathery tops of the evergreens, which seemed to stretch forever into the distance. "Is the castle located in the very center of it?"

Neeve laughed, a hard, icy sound. "Hardly. We're just on the outskirts. If you ever reach the center of the Darkwood, you'll know it."

"What's so special about the forest, then?" I turned to her. "We have woods in Parnese, you know."

Of course I was baiting her. It was clear there was something out of the ordinary about the mysterious forest that covered most of Raine. Something magical, though I was hesitant to say that word out loud—especially after what had happened to me in the forest the day before.

Magic.

In Parnese, such talk was heretical. While it was acknowledged that sorcerous powers existed, only the priests were permitted to wield the blessings of the Twin Gods.

My stomach twisted with the memory of what had happened to my mother's friend, Ser Pietro—a merry fellow who could make tiny flames dance at the ends of his fingertips. He would come to Mama's dinner parties and entertain everyone by spinning illusions of birds made out of fire.

"Be careful," my mother had said, frowning at him. "The priests do not like anyone but themselves to show such powers. I hear they are proposing laws—"

"You worry too much," Pietro had said, waving his hand at her. "The infighting among the followers of the Twin Gods is notorious, and nothing for us to concern ourselves over. Those foolish laws will never pass."

As it turned out, however, he had been wrong. The balance of power shifted radically within the temple, and decrees had gone out under the authority of the Parnesian high court. All those with sorcerous ability were required to report to the temple. Those who did not would be hunted down.

Pietro went into hiding, but a few months later he was found. Mama wept bitterly at the news.

"They mean to make an example of him," she'd said. "I cannot let him die all alone."

I had not understood what she meant, or why she took me to the main square in front of the temple of the Twin Gods so early in the morning.

Despite the hour, there was already a crowd. Mama pushed through the throng, forcing us to the very front. I didn't know why a wooden platform had been built at the base of the stairs leading to the temple, or why dry kindling was stacked all about it.

"Bringing a child?" the woman next to us said, with a glance at me. "How old is your girl?"

"Seven," my mother answered, her face turned toward the temple. "She must see what the priests can do."

"Old enough to know the truth, aye." The woman nodded. "A pious woman, you are. Walk in the light."

My mother returned the ritual gesture of the Twin Gods: two fingers laid against her upraised palm. I blinked to see it, but said nothing of my confusion. As far as I knew, we were not worshippers.

The sun rose higher in the sky. Finally, a group of red-cowled priests descended the stairs, a prisoner in their midst. Pietro.

I leaned forward, and my mother gripped my shoulder hard, in warning.

"Be quiet," she murmured. "Whatever happens, say nothing."

Behind the group walked a tall figure, all in scarlet. Galtus Celcio was his name—spoken in fearful whispers—Warder of the red priests. His hair was red, too, darker than mine, and smooth, as though it had been oiled. My mother stifled a small gasp when she saw him, and flipped my hood up to cover my hair.

I glanced at her in surprise and saw that she'd drawn her scarf up around her head. Hand still clenched on my shoulder, she pulled us back a pace. Two men surged forward, eager to take our places at the front.

We were still close enough to watch as the priests chained Pietro to the platform. To hear the condemnation of his powers. And to shiver in fear as the warder lifted his hands in the air, called upon the Twin Gods, and brought down a column of flame to engulf Pietro.

Everything burned.

His hair, his clothing. His flesh.

I turned and hid my face in Mama's skirts, crying and choking, but she did not turn away. She watched her friend as the fire consumed him, and I finally understood what she had meant. I had no doubt Pietro knew she was there, in the crowd. Perhaps his last sight had been of her, silent and powerless, but present, witness to his suffering. So that he would not die alone, surrounded by enemies.

I shuddered at the memory. The intervening years had not blunted it.

And yet, despite the horror of what had happened, I became fascinated by all thoughts of magic. I had seen sorcery with my own eyes. Magic existed in the world, not just in the pages of the books I read. *If you had powers,* my voice suggested, *you would be special. Worthy. Your mother would love you.*

I scoffed at the notion, but could not quiet my curiosity. Over the next few years, I hunted down anything I could on the subject of sorcery; a perilous undertaking in a city where possession of such things was a death sentence.

Still, I'd found bits here and pieces there, cobbling together a few rudimentary spells and attempting them in my room late at night, after I was certain Mama was asleep. Something inside me was certain if only I tried hard enough that I, too, could work magic.

Nothing ever happened—except that Mama finally discovered me. Pale with anger, she'd gathered my notes and thrown them all into the fire.

"No!" I reached my hand out to try to rescue the papers, but she slapped it away.

"Never, ever attempt such things," she cried, her eyes glittering with tears of rage. "Never! Don't you remember Pietro?"

"Yes, Mama." I blinked back tears as all my hard work, my scavenging and spending precious hoarded coin, burned to ash. I felt hollow inside. Even though I'd never managed to produce even the smallest spark of sorcery, it had seemed possible.

Now, though, all that was gone. I was nothing but an ordinary girl, without even the pretense of power.

"You endanger us both." She took hold of my shoulders, her nails pricking through the cotton of my nightgown. "If you ever bring a hint of sorcery into this house again, you will be banished from it. Forever. Do you understand? We could *die*."

Her breath was hot with panic.

Ashamed, I hung my head. "I didn't think—"

"You have more sense that that, Rose." Mama's voice turned pleading. "You are growing up—why, next year you'll be fourteen. Promise me you'll stop this dangerous interest in sorcery. Promise!"

She gave me a little shake, and I realized in surprise that I was only a hand span shorter than she was. It had been that long since she'd stood so close.

"I promise," I said, and I'd meant it. No matter what the little voice might tell me to do.

Only a few months later, she'd wed the King of Raine.

Now here we were, in a land where magic shimmered like a promise just inside the shadow of the Darkwood. I could feel my old yearning spring up, my fierce desire to discover everything I could about sorcery burning hot and insistent inside me.

Outside the turret window the trees swayed, their feathery green boughs beckoning.

"The Darkwood is ancient," Miss Groves said to me. "There are many stories surrounding it. I will give you a history to read, if you like."

Neeve shot the teacher a glance. "Those are just fables and children's tales," she said. Despite the mocking words, her voice was serious.

"If Rose is to live here, she ought to know something of it," Miss Groves said. "Now, let us turn to mathematics. Rose, do you know your multiplication?"

I did, well enough to satisfy Miss Groves, and so we moved on from the subject of the Darkwood and into the far less interesting realm of numerations. For the rest of the morning we worked sums, until the small pendulum clock on one of the bookshelves dinged a dozen times.

"Lunch," Miss Groves announced, closing her textbook. "Tidy up, the both of you."

There was a washbasin and ewer on a stand in one corner of the schoolroom. I let Neeve go first.

"Is lunch served in here every day?" I asked Miss Groves, already tired of the gray stone walls and view of the overcast sky.

My heart yearned for the sunny streets of Parnese and my cheerful companions, for days spent splashing in the fountains and darting about the colorful marketplaces near our apartments.

"Every day that we have classes, yes," Miss Groves said.

I shot a look at Neeve, still at the washbasin, then leaned forward.

"Are there any other children here?" I asked in a low voice. "Someone I could be friends with?"

Sympathy flashed through the teacher's eyes. "I'm afraid not. Perhaps in the village, but you'll have little call to go there."

The schoolroom door swung open to admit two maids carrying trays. Our lunch had arrived. Dutifully, I traded places with Neeve and washed my face and hands. The pitcher teetered as I set it back on the stand, and I caught it before it smashed on the floor.

It reminded me of the countless plates and cups I'd accidentally dropped, back in Parnese, and homesickness stabbed through me.

What was Mama doing today? It was strange not to take breakfast with her. She had briefly looked in on me after dinner the previous night—and if that meal was any indication, we wouldn't be returning to the quiet suppers we'd shared in Parnese. I tried to tell myself I didn't miss her, but there was no denying the hollow ache just under my ribs.

Trying to ignore the feeling, I sat down beside Neeve and began spooning up mouthfuls of broth. At least the food was good; the soup flavorful and rich with vegetables, the bread still warm from the oven, with plenty of creamy golden butter to slather upon it.

"Do have some carrots, Neeve," the teacher said.

I glanced over to see that my stepsister had fished out every scrap of meat from her bowl and sipped up only the broth, leaving all her vegetables behind.

With a look of distaste, Neeve lifted a carrot to her mouth and chewed it. Slowly.

Miss Groves' mouth firmed, but she said nothing more, only turned to me.

"Have you been shown the library yet?" she asked.

I shook my head, unwilling to answer through a mouthful of bread, though my interest leaped at the words like a starving dog for a bone.

"I will take you down to it," the teacher said.

I swallowed my bite. "I'd like that very much."

Giving Miss Groves a genuine smile, I scraped the last bite of vegetables from the bottom of my bowl.

I *did* want to see the library—though the timing was not the best, since I'd planned to follow Neeve after lunch.

Ah well. Perhaps Miss Groves would simply show me the library and leave me to myself. In which case, I'd know where to find it and could return later. After I stalked Neeve.

CHAPTER 5

Miss Groves led me down the winding turret stairs, past the corridor leading to my rooms, then through a series of hallways.

"The library entrance is on the bottom floor of Castle Raine," she said. "But as you will see, the room itself takes up three stories. Here we are."

She paused beside another of the castle's dark, ornate doors. This one, most appropriately, had an open book carved in the center.

"Is it ever locked?" I asked, keeping in mind my plan to return later.

"I believe the steward closes it up at night, along with the other rooms that contain items of value."

I nodded, then followed her into the cavernous library. Once over the threshold, I halted, eyes wide. Much to my delight, the library was nothing like I'd expected.

The walls were granite, true, but clad in shelves lined with books, so that only a glimpse of hard stone remained. Colorful rugs carpeted the floor and, best of all, tall windows lined the room, letting in columns of light. At last, I'd found someplace in this dreary pile of stone that felt—almost—like home.

"It's so much brighter in here," I said, making for a shaft of pale sunshine.

"The library is so big," Miss Groves said, "it's essential to have enough light to read all the titles." She gestured to the iron chandeliers overhead, the candles carefully enclosed in glass cups. "In the winter, the lamps are lit every afternoon at sundown."

I turned to her. "It truly gets dark that early?"

"Yes. You must recall that we are much farther north than Parnese. But summer has just begun, so there's no need to fret. In six months, you'll have accustomed yourself to Raine, and all of this will be less strange."

I wasn't so certain. I didn't think I'd ever feel as though I belonged in this dreary land Mama had dragged us to.

Stuffing back my longing for Parnese, I glanced about the huge room. At least I had a library to explore.

"Where are the tales of adventure?" I asked.

That earned me a smile from Miss Groves. "This way."

I followed her, taking note of the number of shelves we passed. Surely somewhere in this vast library would be books pertaining to sorcery, too—and Raine seemed to have no priests intent on erasing all knowledge of magic outside of their own temple. My heart jumped at the thought. Perhaps I'd be able to continue my illicit studies, though I would have to take care that Mama did not discover me again.

At the ninth bay of bookshelves, we halted.

"Here." Miss Groves nodded to the brightly lettered spines. "The tales of adventure you requested. And next door—history."

She moved down one more bank of books, clearly expecting me to follow. With a regretful glance at the titles in front of me, I moved on.

As if sensing my reluctance, Miss Groves raised her eyebrows. "Do bear in mind, Rose, that there is plenty of adventure and excitement to be found in the past." She pulled a book from the stacks. "This is the history of Raine I promised you. Study it well."

She placed the book in my hands. It was heavy, the green leather binding dark with age. Faded gold lettering stared up at me from the cover. *Raine: A Complete History*.

"How could it be complete?" I asked.

"A good question," she said. "I'm glad to see you have a curious mind. To answer your question: every two years the historians add to the book, bringing it as up to date as possible."

"So Mama and I won't be in it." I flipped to the back to see dozens of blank pages awaiting the newest events of the kingdom.

"Not yet. This winter, I believe."

I closed the thick tome, wondering what the historians would say about me and my mother. And how long our story might last in the great book of the kingdom. And how many pages might come after, until we were buried under the weight of the future.

It was an unsettling thought, and I shivered.

Miss Groves put a warm hand on my shoulder. "Go ahead and choose another book, and then I'll take you back to the east wing."

Although I wanted to linger over my choices, I scanned the books of adventure and grabbed a thin, red-bound book called *Miss Fortune and the Swamp of Sorrows*. A promising enough title, and I wanted to try to intercept Neeve. The enticements of the library would have to wait.

As Miss Groves bade me farewell outside my rooms, Neeve's door opened. Her pale face peered into the hall.

"Hello, Neeve," Miss Groves said. "Are you going out, as usual?"

Neeve's eyes narrowed, and she glanced at me. I pretended to take no notice of the teacher's words.

"Thank you for showing me the library," I said to Miss Groves. "I can hardly wait to spend all afternoon reading."

Neeve's frown smoothed.

"I hope you learn a great deal," Miss Groves said, an undercurrent of amusement in her voice. "Good day, Rose."

I bobbed the teacher a short curtsey, careful not to look at Neeve, then went into my rooms and shut the door behind me. Quick as a blink, I set the books on the low table in the sitting area and hurried to fetch my boots. Judging from Miss Groves' words, my stepsister was headed outside, and my indoor slippers wouldn't do.

I pulled on my boots and grabbed my belt pouch. It contained a few useful items, including the small pair of scissors that were the closest thing I had to a weapon. If Neeve was going into the forest, I didn't want to be entirely unprepared. I fastened the pouch at my waist, then slung my cloak over my shoulders and hastened to the door.

It was difficult to hear anything out in the hallway through the thick wood. Carefully, I pressed down the handle and cracked the door open the tiniest bit—just in time to see Neeve sweep past. The black of her cloak blended with the shadows.

Heart thudding, I waited a handful of seconds then slipped out of my room. The latch snicked shut behind me, but Neeve didn't seem to hear. Already she was disappearing around the corner.

Keeping to my toes and summoning everything I'd learned of stealth, I hurried after.

Despite my skullduggery lessons, it was difficult to follow my stepsister. She moved quickly through the cold corridors, her form almost invisible in the flickering light of the few sconces. Twice I thought I'd lost her at a branching in the halls, and simply had to guess, biting my lip with worry until I caught sight of her dark form ahead.

By the time she reached a small door at the end of a narrow hall-way, my breath was coming fast and sweat dampened my forehead. I hung back as Neeve opened the door, the wan light of the overcast sun silhouetting her dark figure. As my quarry slipped outside, a puff of air reached down the corridor, smelling of wet and green.

I caught the door just before it closed and eased gently around it, keeping my stepsister in sight. Even though the day was cool compared to Parnese, it was wonderful to be outside. A faint trill of birdsong reached my ears.

Now that we were out of the stone hallways of Castle Raine, I found it easier to follow Neeve. She slowed, but there was plenty of cover I could duck behind: a crumbling stone wall, a large hedge, a flowering bush whose thorns pricked through my cloak.

I tried to pay attention to the route she wove through the gardens, for we were still inside the high granite walls enclosing the back of the castle. Perhaps my stepsister had spoken the truth, and had an herb patch tucked away where she would dig in the ground until the light faded.

It was a disappointing thought. I'd been so certain she was up to something illicit and exciting. Something worth skulking after her to discover.

As I hid behind a statue of a cloaked maiden, Neeve went to a small shed tucked up against the wall. Beside the shed was, to my dismay, a small garden holding what I could only guess were herbs.

Drat it.

Folding my arms, I leaned against the back of the statue. I supposed I'd wait for a short while and watch my stepsister garden before slipping back to my rooms. Hopefully, the book Miss Groves had given me would prove more entertaining than this jaunt into the gardens. And if not, perhaps I could begin my hunt in the library for the tomes of magic I hoped it contained.

Neeve emerged from the shed, holding a trowel and a hoe. I frowned in disappointment.

She went back into the small structure, and I sighed and rested my head against the statue's elbow. I should leave while Neeve was occupied, but I wasn't ready to close myself within the oppressive walls of Castle Raine quite yet. Surely she'd turn her back at some point. Or, if she didn't, I could go on hands and knees and hope she wouldn't spot me crawling away along the path.

I could see the tops of the tallest trees above the wall girdling the castle. The wind sighed through the evergreens. A single black-winged bird took flight, drifting silently into the silvery air.

It took me far too long to realize that Neeve hadn't emerged from the garden shed. What was she doing in there? I peered around the statue, listening, but no sound came from the little building.

Swallowing past the dryness in my throat, I left the shelter of the stone maiden behind and crept forward. At any moment I was certain Neeve would fling the door open, spots of color high on her cheeks, and denounce me as a sneak and a spy. Twice I darted for cover behind the nearby hedge, but nothing happened.

The door did not open.

Heart beating like a flutter of wings, I came right up to the shed and put my ear to the crack between the door and the jamb.

Silence.

Willing my hand to steadiness, I caught the weathered wood and pulled the door open, just far enough that I could peek inside.

A stack of clay pots and a dirt-encrusted shovel met my gaze. With a steadying breath, I pulled the door wider. More tools and a bench. Bundles of herbs hung from the ceiling, emitting a faint, minty aroma.

And that was all.

No scowling black-haired maiden waited inside to scold me with a tongue of ice.

I didn't know how she had managed to escape the windowless shed without my seeing her, but Neeve was gone.

CHAPTER 6

My stepsister had simply disappeared from the middle of the shed. My heart surged with excitement. Something mysterious *was* going on at Castle Raine—and it most certainly had to do with Neeve.

I stepped inside, wrinkling my nose at the smell of drying herbs, then turned in a slow circle. Had she left by magic? There was no evidence of anything out of the ordinary, no half-burned candles or sigils inscribed on the floor.

The floor...

I bent to take a closer look. A barely visible scratch ran along the scuffed boards from the back wall, arcing out to my left. Very like the mark a door would make as it swung open and shut.

Triumphantly, I straightened and went to the wall. It was hard to make out details in the dim light filtering into the shed, much less try to locate a hidden door. Using my fingertips as well as my eyes, I was finally able to find the thin cracks revealing the outline of a door. It was lower and smaller than I'd expected. I'd have to duck to go through.

But how to open it?

I brushed my hands up and down the nearly invisible seams, but encountered no handle, no latch, nothing that might trigger the door to swing wide. The clay pots on the bench squatted there smugly, and a bit of breeze stirred the herbs overhead. Dry stalks rubbed together like the edge of mocking laughter. *Think, Rose.*

The door swung open from the right, as the scrape on the floor showed. Therefore, the latch must be on the right-hand side of the shed. Somewhere. And probably not too far away from the door itself.

Moments later, I found a lever hidden in the shadows under the bench. I pulled it, grinning with satisfaction at my own cleverness as the little door popped open.

Behind it was another door, this one much older, set into the stone wall surrounding the castle. Whoever had built the shed, they'd constructed it to back up against this door, hiding it from view. It had a proper latch, well oiled, that lifted soundlessly at my touch.

The door swung open, and a gust of moist air rich with the scent of evergreens swirled about me. Ten paces ahead, across a moat of unmown grass, stood the forbidding trees of the Darkwood.

There was no sign of Neeve.

Of course not—I'd spent too long trying to figure out the secret door, and she'd gotten too far ahead. But I could still see traces of where she'd gone, the grasses flattened beneath her feet, marking a track into the forest.

Without a moment's hesitation, I ducked out of the shed, closed both doors behind me, and followed the faint trail.

The grass gave way to ferns and moss as I entered the shadows of the trees. I was relieved to find that the forest was not as murky as it appeared from the outside. Light filtered through the boughs, giving a silver-green hue to the trees and thick-leaved shrubs.

Just inside the perimeter of the Darkwood, I paused. I don't know what I was expecting: a magical bear to come roaring out of the forest, or the sound of distant bells. Instead there was only a feeling of *depth*, as though time moved at a different pace here beneath the trees.

I pulled in a breath of green-scented air, my excitement blunted by a strange sense of calm. The breeze found me again, tugging at my hair. I cast about for signs of Neeve's passage, glad to see the beginning of a narrow path a few paces ahead. Perhaps it had been made by creatures traversing the woods, but I would wager that Neeve's feet had trodden it recently.

None of my lessons had included woodcraft, as Parnese was a bustling city and not a quiet forest, but skullduggery had included the art of tracking. As it turned out, it was far simpler to follow bent stalks and crushed leaves than try to make out footprints on a dusty city street.

The path meandered through the trees. I placed my hand on the rough bark of an evergreen as I passed, wondering if the tree could feel my touch in return.

Oh, but that was a silly notion. The forest was alive, yes, but not in any sentient way.

Birds darted through the trees, chirping, and a huge dragonfly whirred past, close enough to startle me. A loud chittering from overhead caused my heart to lurch, until I saw the small, furry creature with a brush of a tail scolding me from a nearby branch.

There were no buildings, no roads. And no sign of my stepsister.

Still, I pressed on, trying to hasten my steps without tripping over exposed roots or snarling my cloak in the bushes. After some time, the little trail branched. I paused, the sound of my breathing loud in the still air.

Had Neeve gone to the right, or to the left? The helpful signs of broken twigs and folded leaves had disappeared, leaving me to guess at the proper direction. Maybe if I went partway down each path, I'd see signs of her passing.

I started down the left-hand path. It seemed undisturbed, and after a short time I halted and turned back around.

The right-hand branch seemed equally untraveled, and I wondered if I'd missed a turnoff earlier. I'd been too immersed in looking about the forest to notice where Neeve had stepped off the trail. If she had.

It seemed foolish to retrace my steps, so I continued on the path. A low bush snagged the hem of my cloak. I pulled the fabric free, eyeing the red berries gleaming beneath the prickle-edged leaves. In case I was ever lost in the forest, I supposed I would have to try to forage for food, though I had no way to tell if the berries were poisonous.

My stepsister would know, having grown up in the forest. I'd have to subtly quiz her about her knowledge of herbs and plants without raising her already suspicious nature. Or perhaps the great library in the castle held a book that could help me. *Edible Plants of Raine* or some such.

Not that I was planning to get lost in the forest any time soon.

As long as I stayed on the path, it would be simple enough to retrace my steps. In fact, having found no trace of Neeve's passage, I was ready to do that very thing. What had started as a promising adventure had turned to nothing except a walk in the woods.

I turned to head back toward the castle, when something that sounded like a cry for help filtered through the dark trees behind me. Heart thumping, I pivoted and stared into the woods. Maybe the sound had merely been the scraping of branches together or the screech of a bird.

The wind stirred the boughs, shaking soft sighs from the trees surrounding me. Faint sunlight dappled the path. And then I heard it again—unmistakable this time.

"Help!" The high-pitched voice sounded desperate.

It must be my stepsister. I picked up my skirts in both hands and began to run toward the voice, thankful for the sturdy boots encasing my feet. A thin branch whipped across my cheek, stinging tears from my eyes, but I kept on. What better way to convince Neeve to befriend me than to save her?

"Where are you?" I called, chest heaving with my panting breath.

"Here!" The voice lay ahead and somewhat to the left of the trail.

Hoping I wouldn't go too far astray, I jumped into the tangled underbrush. The moss was soft under my feet, and I stumbled over hidden hummocks and dips. At last I came to a clearing formed where a huge evergreen had, at some point in the past, crashed to the ground.

The tree had fallen years ago, judging by the thick crust of moss and ferns growing atop its prone length. I let out a relieved breath that I would not have to extract Neeve from beneath it.

"Are you here?" I called softly.

"Of course I am." The voice did not belong to Neeve, after all. It was raspy and even more ill-humored than my stepsister's.

Biting my lip, I took a small step backward. My gaze swept the clearing, but I could see no sign of the speaker. Perhaps I should not have raced away from the path quite so quickly without considering the consequences.

The bracken beside the prone tree thrashed wildly.

"Stop standing there like a fool and help me," the voice said.

Whoever was trapped in the underbrush, they were smaller than I. Still, that did not make them harmless.

I moved forward, scooping up a broken-off branch along the way to use as a club. The scissors in my belt pouch seemed quite inadequate. Next time I ventured into the Darkwood, I'd bring a knife.

When I came to where the bushes rustled, I reached out the tip of the branch to nudge the leaves aside.

A hairy, bearded creature glared up at me, scarlet sparks in his eyes. He wore a soiled red tunic and a little brown hat that came to a point at the top of his head. His clawed hands were wrapped around his long beard, the end of which was somehow trapped inside the tree trunk.

"What *are* you?" I asked, taking a tighter grip on my makeshift club. Never in my life had I seen such a strange little being—or even imagined such a thing existed outside the pages of a storybook.

"I could ask the same, milk face," the creature said, tugging at its beard. "Stop staring like an ugly fool and free me."

"But... however did you get into such a mess?"

"A mess? Why you useless lump of dough! Isn't it plain to see, tangle-head?"

The creature looked so ludicrous hopping back and forth with its beard stuck fast, and spewing insults like a gutter rat, that I couldn't help laughing.

He stopped his struggles for a moment to give me a scathing look.

"Stupid goose. I was trying to split the tree for a bit of firewood, but my wedge slipped and the wood closed again, so quickly it trapped my beautiful beard. As anyone with a bit of sense could see, lack-wit. Quickly, now, get me free."

He shot a glance over his shoulder at the thick trees. The shadows beneath seemed darker in contrast to the clearing where we stood, and I shivered, wondering what he was afraid of.

"Is something coming?" I asked, my amusement suddenly gone.

The creature made a face. "Let me go, and I'll tell you."

Hoping he would not bite or scratch me, I set my branch down and knelt beside the tree trunk, close by the little fellow. He smelled like old mushrooms and dirt, and I wrinkled my nose. Reaching over his head, I took the raspy tangle of its beard in both hands and pulled.

"Aiee! Are you trying to rip the hairs from my face?"

"I'm trying to help," I replied. "What an ungrateful thing you are. Maybe I should just leave you here."

"No." His eyes widened, then narrowed in a sly look. "I'll give you gold if you get me free."

"I don't care about that." I dusted off my hands and studied the smooth wood enclosing the end of the creature's beard.

There was no crack in the tree that I could pry open, and pulling the beard free wasn't working.

After a moment's thought, the solution was clear—my scissors. I opened the pouch at my waist and pulled them out. Before the creature could protest or fling any more insults at me, I snipped the thick brush of hair binding it to the tree.

He tumbled backward into the brush, wailing.

"Ow—my precious beard! Bad luck to you, for cutting off such a handsome piece."

I frowned as I tucked the scissors away. It would have been nice to at least have some small word of thanks. Instead, the little creature scrabbled in the loam and snatched up a bag that had been hidden in the underbrush. Clawed fingers tight about its belongings, it turned its back on me and began to scuttle off.

"Wait," I called. "You promised to tell me what was coming."

It turned, scarlet sparks in its eyes. "Boglins."

"What do you mean..." My words trailed off as the creature rushed into the forest and was gone.

The breeze turned cold, and a faint rasping sound whispered through the Darkwood. Strange shapes moved in the dimness under the trees.

Panic tightening my throat, I whirled about in the direction I'd come, and ran.

CHAPTER 7

I crashed through the underbrush, my cloak flying behind me. Rustling noises scraped the shadows, getting closer. I'd left my makeshift club behind, abandoned beside the tree trunk, and there was no time to snatch up another.

If I reached the path, would I be able to run fast enough to break free of the forest before whatever was chasing me caught up? But where was the path?

There was no trace of it—only the forest stretching around me in all directions, a black and forbidding wall. Panic burned in my chest and I could scarcely draw a breath.

A sudden dip, hidden by a screen of ferns, sent me sprawling. I scrambled onto my knees, and suddenly the *things* were there, all around me. The boglins.

They looked like figures made of sticks and leaves; harmless enough, until one leaped upon my arm and bit me with sharp, serrated teeth.

"Get off!" I staggered to my feet, knocking the creature away.

The other boglins hemmed me in. I could feel them quivering, preparing to throw themselves on me, devour me with their pointed little mouths. Nothing would be left except my bones and a few strands of frizzled red hair.

Terror roiled through me. When I'd gone into the forest, I'd never expected to be *eaten* by it.

Mama would never know what became of me. Fleetingly, I wondered how long her grief would last. A year? A month?

Then the boglins leaped, a flurry of biting edges. I screamed and threw up my arms to cover my face.

"*Daro!*" someone shouted. The sound tore through the air and ripped the creatures from me.

Hard upon that came a blast of icy white light that sent the boglins fleeing, like so many leaves blown before the storm.

Blinking, I turned to see two figures coming through the trees. The shorter one was Neeve, her red mouth set in a furious line. At her side strode a young man.

He was dressed in fluttering clothes the colors of the forest—green and gray, with a deep green cloak clasped at his throat and tall boots reaching to his knees. His dark hair fell long down his back but was braided in front, away from his face.

That face... I stared openly. He shared the same pale skin as Neeve, the same dark eyes and high cheekbones, but there was something unutterably foreign about his features. He turned his head to look at my stepsister, and I saw the pointed tip of his ear poking from beneath his hair.

Pointed ears? I sucked in an amazed breath. Surely he had stepped from the pages of myth and mystery. I nearly expected the air to shimmer silver about him as he walked, his long-legged, graceful stride keeping pace with Neeve's quick steps.

"What are you doing here?" my stepsister demanded as she and her companion halted before me.

Heat rushed into my cheeks. Drat it—I was supposed to be rescuing *her*, not the other way around. Not only must I admit I'd followed her, but I'd gotten into serious trouble, too. It was beyond humiliating.

Deflecting her question, I turned to the young man beside her.

"Thank you," I said, certain it had been his magic that had chased the boglins away.

He blinked and stepped back a pace, shooting another glance at Neeve.

The angry light in her eyes increased as she glared at me. "Who are you talking to? There's no one here but the two of us."

"You can't see him?" I looked at the man again. No, I was not hallucinating. He stood there, clear as day.

"Are you fevered?" Neeve reached a hand out and placed it on my forehead. Her fingers were cold.

"No." I pushed her hand away.

"You've taken a knock to the head," she said. "Stupid of you, to wander alone about the Darkwood. I'll get you back to the castle, where the infirmarian can tend to you."

"I did not hit my head," I said. "Other than a few bites, I'm perfectly fine. What were those things? Those boglins?"

She gave me a sharp look. The supposedly invisible man beside her crossed his arms, the grimness about his mouth and eyes easing into curiosity.

"I've never heard of such a thing," she said.

"You're lying. I can hear it in your voice." I glanced at the fellow once more. "Can you really not see him?"

She shook her head, nostrils flaring.

"It's no use, Neeve," he said, his voice low and melodic. "The girl's as stubborn as you are. We might as well admit I'm here."

"I can hear you, you know." I looked straight at him. "There's no point trying to deceive me—I'll just keep following Neeve into the forest until I find out what's going on."

"I can make you stop." Neeve's fingers twitched.

"No." The young man set his hand over hers. "There is a reason she was able to follow you, though we may not know what that reason is. The Darkwood has spoken."

"It has?" I found my voice and cocked my head, hearing only the sound of wind through the trees.

A faint smile lifted the corner of the young man's mouth. "The forest does not speak in a language mortals can hear."

"Then you're not human?" I'd guessed it, of course, from the ears and strange set of his features.

He did not answer—but then, he didn't need to. A renewed surge of excitement tingled through me at this further proof that the Darkwood was full of extraordinary things.

"My name is Thorne." He made me a bow that could rival any of the courtiers of Parnese.

"I'm Rose," I said, my heart thudding as I dropped him my best curtsey.

He nodded, as if he'd known that already. Which he probably had. I looked at Neeve.

"Are you going to tell me about those boglins now?" I asked.

"They're harmless." She did not bother to hide the scorn in her voice.

"They attacked me!"

"The creatures of the Darkwood can sense fear," Thorne said, his voice gentle. "To Neeve, the boglins pose no threat. But to those who are afraid, they can inflict much harm. Tell me, how did you know to name them?"

"I came upon a strange little creature with its beard trapped in a tree. It was most rude and ungrateful, even after I freed it."

"About this tall?" Thorne held his hand just above his knee. "Hairy, with reddish eyes?"

I nodded. "Exactly."

"A hobnie," Neeve said, the usual disdain in her voice. "They do nothing but complain and dig in the dirt."

Thorne turned a reproving look on her. "Every creature in the Darkwood has its place. Even the hobnies, who unearth gems and gold from hidden places, so that you might sport lovely jewelry. Do not speak ill of them."

Red spots rose in her cheeks, and she looked more contrite than I'd ever seen her. Whoever this Thorne was, he held a position of high respect in Neeve's secret world.

"It sounds as though you met Cancrach," he said, turning to me. "He is the most ill-tempered of the seven hobnies who inhabit the Darkwood. Though none of them are particularly polite."

Neeve looked as though she'd like to further air her low opinion of the hobnies and was biting her tongue to keep from saying anything more.

"Where are you from?" I asked Thorne. "Surely you don't live at the castle?"

"No." A spark of amusement flashed, a gold speck in his dark eyes.

I had the strangest notion that I'd met him before. But that was impossible. I would certainly have remembered such an extraordinary person. I blinked away the thought.

"You didn't answer my question," I pointed out.

"I did not." His expression grew serious. "But we must speak of weightier things. Such as the fact that you should not be wandering unescorted about the forest."

"You never should have followed me," Neeve said accusingly.

Thorne turned to her. "And you should have used more caution. You've grown careless, Neeve. What if someone other than Rose had seen you?"

"As a matter of fact," I said, "I didn't actually see her."

Why I was jumping to Neeve's defense, I had no idea. Maybe it was the genuine hurt in her eyes, which pulled reluctant sympathy from me. I knew what it was to be chastised for very little reason. Or none at all.

One of Thorne's elegantly arched brows rose, and I thought it was unfair of him, a boy, to have such lovely eyebrows.

"I tracked her," I explained. "I never actually *saw* her go into the woods. I figured out where she'd gone and discovered the secret door all on my own."

"That was clever," Neeve said grudgingly.

"Regardless." Thorne gave me a pointed look. "You must promise not to come into the Darkwood again, Rose."

I laughed at him. "Truly? I won't promise that. This is the most interesting day I've had in ages."

I waved my hand at the sunbeams straggling between the tall trees, the sifted shadows deeper in. The smell of pine and cedar tickled my nose and the boughs rustled softly overhead, underlying the bright chirps of the birds. Already I was in love with the Darkwood—with its mystery and magic, its promises and shrouded secrets.

"It's dangerous." Thorne's voice was low. "There are worse things in the forest than boglins. Things that truly do pose a threat. Things that could hurt you—badly."

"Or even kill you," Neeve added, sounding a little too happy at the thought. So much for our tentative truce.

I scowled at her. "*You* come here. Every day, I'd wager."

"I'm a—"

"Neeve has certain protections," Thorne said, cutting off whatever she was about to say.

"Well, can't I have them too?" I felt suddenly like the youngest of the group, desperate to tag along and knowing that I'd be left behind.

"You can't." Neeve gave me a superior look.

"I'll just keep following you, then." I hated the petulant edge to my voice, but I couldn't help it. "You can't make me stop."

"Oh, but we can." Neeve glanced at her companion. "Take her memories away. Erase her curiosity about the Darkwood."

The birds stopped chirping and flitting, and I folded my arms about myself. I could think of nothing worse than someone meddling about with my mind. Changing my memories. A chill shuddered down my spine.

"That's dark magic," I whispered.

"It is not light," Thorne agreed.

He studied me for several moments, and I felt as though my very soul was being weighed in the shadowy depths of his eyes. I held his gaze for as long as I could before looking away, into the rising mist between the trees.

"No," he said at last. "I believe you came into the Darkwood for a reason. I will not interfere with your free will."

I drew in a shaky breath and felt as though all the blood in my body was suddenly freed to race hot and headlong through my veins.

Neeve took a step forward. "But—"

"No argument," Thorne said.

"I won't tell anyone about it," I said. "Or about you, or anything I see in the Darkwood. I promise."

He regarded me for a long moment, his dark eyes thoughtful. "I will take your promise. But it must be more than simply your word. Do you agree to a binding vow?"

"You'll perform the binding ceremony?" Neeve gave him a look. "On her?"

Her tone suggested I was not nearly important enough for such a thing.

"I will," he replied gravely. "On all of us together, for there is power in threes. Rose, will you say yes? You must be a willing participant."

My pulse jumped, fear and excitement tangling in my stomach. What was this binding ceremony? More magic? If so, I'd give anything to see it. And honestly, I didn't think I could say no. After all, he had the power to erase my memories if I didn't comply—and I had no wish to test him.

"Do I have any other choice?"

"Not really." His mouth twisted ruefully. "I'm sorry."

I nodded once. "Then I agree to it."

A length of leafy vine appeared in his hands. "Don't be afraid. This won't hurt. Neeve, take her hand."

With a look that could freeze fire, my stepsister faced me and grabbed my left hand. My pinky throbbed, the stub aching. The rising mist curled in tendrils about our feet, and the forest sounds were suddenly muffled, as though we stood one step removed from the world. Clasping our hands palm to palm, elbows touching, Neeve raised our arms into the air.

Thorne gently pushed down our sleeves and placed his cool hand over both of ours. The three of us stood so close together I imagined I could hear their hearts beating, even as my pulse raced where our arms met, skin to skin.

Starting at our elbows, Thorne used his free hand to wind the vine up, binding his own arm alongside ours. As he encircled our clasped hands, he chanted—the syllables low and liquid in a language I could not even begin to recognize.

"*Erynvanda,*" he said, "*thurin din gleinaethl.*"

When he reached our fingertips, he released the vine. The glossy green leaves tightened, pulling the three of us closer together, and a sharp prick on the inside of my wrist made me gasp in startled pain.

Neeve glared at me. "Quiet."

"Rose," Thorne said, his voice suddenly deep and resonant, "do you promise to speak no word of what you encounter within the Darkwood?"

"I promise. I'll say nothing."

The pain echoed through my left hand. Blood trickled from my wrist, tracing a scarlet line down my arm. I tugged, but the vines holding us together were unyielding.

"Be still," my stepsister hissed.

She was bleeding, too, a bright ruby drop sliding down her pale skin. My blood seemed thick and dull in comparison, especially when I noticed the silvery trail marking Thorne's skin. He didn't even bleed like a human.

Neeve's eyes widened in surprise when she noticed he was bleeding, too. Perhaps that wasn't a normal part of the ceremony. The drop on his arm looked like a faceted jewel, flecked with gold, blue, green...

I looked up at him, our gazes locking. What *was* he? Questions crowded my mouth, but my throat was too dry to give them voice. The air of the Darkwood pressed down upon us, heavy with watching. Waiting.

Without taking his eyes from mine, Thorne chanted a few more words. I felt each syllable vibrate through me, though I had no idea what was being said. The blood itched as it slowly dripped down my arm.

Thorne glanced at Neeve. "Now."

"*Asa,*" she said.

He nodded at me, his eyebrow lifting. "You too, Rose."

"*Asa.*" I tried to give the word the same lift and turn as Neeve. It sounded clumsy in my mouth.

At the point of my elbow, our three drops of blood met.

"*Naechant,*" Thorne said, his voice low.

Agony lanced through my arm, running from my maimed finger down to my elbow, and I cried out as a blinding flare of light filled the misty air. For a confused instant I wondered if we had been struck by a bolt of lightning.

But no, this was magic—this ringing in my ears, this scorching on my skin. The taste of gold and cedar on my tongue.

The vine wrapping our arms disappeared, and I felt my knees buckle. Before I collapsed completely, Thorne caught me. As though I were nothing more than a bundle of cloth, he laid me on the loamy soil. The tree branches waved overhead. The mist was gone, as if I'd imagined it.

I did not, however, imagine the blaze of pain at my elbow. Shakily, I raised my left arm. Inscribed on the tender skin just inside my elbow was a small green leaf on a twisted stem, imprinted as though I'd visited a tattooist and had it inked there.

"You said it wouldn't hurt," I said accusingly.

"It wasn't supposed to," Thorne said, apology in his voice. "I did not expect quite that result."

I licked my thumb and rubbed at the leaf, wincing. It didn't smudge at all.

"It's permanent," Thorne said, offering me a hand up. "A reminder of the vow you made."

I took his hand. His clasp was cool and strong as he helped me to my feet.

"Is it magic?" I asked, glancing once more at the mark upon my arm. How could it be anything else?

A shadow flitted through his eyes.

"Yes." He did not elaborate.

"If you try to speak the secrets of the Darkwood, it will bind your tongue with bitterness," Neeve said.

"No wonder you always sound so sour," I said. "How many leaves do you have on your arm?"

"Idiot."

"Peace." Thorne held up his hand. "Rose, you are bound to preserve the secrets of the Darkwood now."

"I understand," I said, though I had the uncomfortable suspicion I didn't know the full of it.

"Tomorrow afternoon, you'll accompany Neeve into the forest."

"What?" Neeve shot him a surprised, unhappy look. "I thought we'd be rid of her now."

Thorne raised his brows. "Don't wish your new sister harm. Remember, the forest can read your intent."

She flushed. "Rose is *not* my sister."

"Her mother and your father are handfasted. That makes you family, whether you like it or not. And"—he gestured to the mark on my elbow—"you are now bound by blood. Any malice you direct to her will return to you threefold. Remember your lessons."

Mouth set, Neeve glared at him. "Very well. Though I don't understand why you're making such a fuss over her."

Expression thoughtful, Thorne turned his gaze on me. His dark eyes were flecked with amber sparks, like motes of sun glimmering at the bottom of a deep pool.

"I am not exactly certain, myself," he said. "But the Darkwood has made its intentions clear. Whether or not we understand the reasons why..." He ended with a shrug.

"But you're *Galadhir*." For once, Neeve sounded uncertain. It was a pleasant reminder that, despite her high-handed ways, we were the same age. "Don't you know what the forest wants of her?"

"I'm young yet in my duties," he replied, which was really no answer at all.

"How old are you?" The question blurted out of me, but I didn't feel unduly embarrassed.

I wanted to know, and with the strange cast to his features it was impossible to even guess. In some ways, Thorne seemed of an age with myself and Neeve, and yet he was as tall as any adult. And he had a title of some sort. *Galadhir*, Neeve had called him—whatever that meant. I made a note to ask her about it later.

"I am older than you think," he said, lightly amused. "Now, the two of you must go before your presence in the castle is missed."

The path I had searched for earlier in my flight from the boglins suddenly appeared beneath our feet.

Neeve let out a displeased huff and set off, not bothering to bid farewell to Thorne. Or wait for me. I rubbed the sore spot at my elbow and glanced at him—this strange, fascinating young man who spoke for the forest and performed magic with the wave of a hand.

"Don't worry," he said, his voice unexpectedly gentle. "Despite Neeve's manner, you're not unwelcome in the Darkwood. I've seen to it that your presence here will be accepted."

Not unwelcome. That didn't exactly mean I was safe, but I didn't want to quibble with him. Especially as my stepsister was quickly disappearing between the tall tree trunks.

"If you say so." I bit my lip, wishing there was time to voice all my questions. Wishing I could spend another hour or seventeen in his presence.

"I do say so. Now go." He gestured after Neeve. "We'll meet again."

I certainly hoped so.

I caught up to my stepsister, then paused and glanced over my shoulder. Thorne stood where we'd left him. He gazed after us, his expression troubled, and lifted one hand in farewell.

"Are you coming?" Neeve asked me sharply.

"Yes."

I followed her over a fallen log, the path twisted, and when I looked behind me again, Thorne was gone.

At the castle, Neeve slipped away from me without a backward glance. All through dinner she continued to act as if she couldn't see me. Since Mama and the king treated me the same—if less coldly—I asked to be excused before dessert. I meant to stop at the library to look for any reference to the word *Galadhir*, but suddenly the adventures of the day overtook me. I stumbled to my room, fell into bed, and didn't rouse until Sorche woke me for lessons the next morning.

CHAPTER 8

All morning, Neeve continued to treat me as if I was invisible until finally, as we left the schoolroom after lunch, she glanced at me.

"I suppose you're excited about going back into the forest today," she said, a resentful edge in her voice.

"Yes." Adventure and magic to stir my blood? She couldn't keep me away. Besides, Thorne had commanded I come.

As if sensing my determination, she lifted one shoulder in grudging acknowledgement. "Very well. Follow me."

Instead of slipping out through the secret door in the garden shed, however, she led me down into the cellars below the kitchen.

As we navigated the clammy darkness by the light of her single candle, I recalled the old ballads I'd heard about murderous sisters. Was she planning to kill me and leave my bones to rot in some unused storeroom?

I bit my tongue and followed her, wishing again for a knife at my belt. When we returned, I vowed I'd detour through the kitchens and help myself to a small blade.

A bit of cobweb brushed my cheek, and I yelped. Ahead of me, Neeve let out a low laugh.

"You'll have to be braver than that," she said. "The Darkwood holds terrors you can't imagine."

I thought of the horror of Ser Pietro's burning. "You have no idea what I have seen."

Something in my tone made her pause. She turned to face me, candle lifted, and studied my face.

"Perhaps there is more to you than I thought," she said after a moment.

I wiped the sticky strands of web from my cheek and scowled at her. "No matter how magical the Darkwood might be, there's a wider world out there, you know."

"I know it well." A shadow crossed her expression.

Her words surprised me. "I thought you'd never left Raine."

"I haven't." She pivoted again, her movements sharp, and continued on.

I hurried to catch up. It hadn't occurred to me that Neeve might feel as imprisoned within the castle as I did. Maybe I wasn't the only girl trapped in the kingdom. I blinked at the notion that we might have that in common.

Just when I was certain we'd never emerge, Neeve turned a corner that ended in a crumbling stair. As I ascended behind her, the ceiling lowered over our heads until we were both crouching. I tried to still my racing heart at the feeling of being imprisoned beneath the earth.

My stepsister pulled back a bolt overhead and threw open a trap-door. Light and air rushed in. I sucked in a greedy breath, the smell of warm grass tickling my nose.

"Shh." Neeve jerked her head at me and gracefully stepped out of the cramped stairwell.

I scrambled to follow, unsurprised to see that we'd emerged outside the castle walls. How many secret exits did Castle Raine hold? This one seemed to emerge in the middle of a thicket.

Quietly, Neeve lowered the door behind me, and then we pushed through the underbrush toward the beckoning edge of the Darkwood.

I was delighted see Thorne waiting for us in the shadow of a tall cedar, shrouded in his dark green cloak. His gold-flecked dark eyes rested on me a moment, and then he turned to Neeve.

"I've business to attend to today," he said. "Watch over Rose."

My heart fell, and Neeve scowled at him.

"I'm not her nursemaid," she said.

The forest shivered, like the hide of a great beast troubled by biting gnats, and Thorne glanced up to the tops of the swaying trees. "I must be off. *Namarie.*"

Quiet as a breath of air, he turned and was gone. I squinted, trying to make out his figure moving between the trees, but there was nothing but a lazy moth fluttering through the shafts of sunlight.

"I wish you'd never come here," Neeve said to me.

"I wish the same," I replied. "But we can't do anything about it. Couldn't you at least try to be civil?"

I'd given up any notion that we could be friends.

Neeve was too prickly, too strange. And, truthfully, far too full of herself to make a pleasant companion. But she was better than nothing. I, at least, was willing to make some effort.

She looked at me a long moment, and I couldn't tell what thoughts moved in the darkness of her eyes. Finally her mouth twisted slightly—not into her usual scowl, but the barest smile of apology.

"I'll show you the stream," she said.

She led me along another of the narrow trails that wove through the forest. It seemed we were angling away from the castle, to the north and east, but I couldn't be sure. Without being able to see the sun, my usual sense of direction was bewildered.

Set me down in the streets of Parnese, and I could unerringly find my way about the city. But the Darkwood was all trees and rustling shadows and confusion. I hated being so dependent on Neeve, but I would bear it for the sake of finding out everything I could about the magic of the forest.

I heard the water before we came to it, a merry burbling that seemed more suited to a sunny hillside than the depths of the forest.

"Is there anything I should know?" I asked.

Neeve slanted me a look. "Know?"

"Yes." Stopping, I planted my fists on my hips. "Is there a water creature living in the depths that will pull me in and eat me if I dabble my fingers in the deepest pools? Is the water poisonous, for that matter? Will it turn me to stone if I drink it?"

"You have the strangest notions," she said with a dismissive turn of her head.

"I do not." My temper rose, despite my resolution to keep it leashed. I waved my arm in a circle. "This isn't an ordinary forest. Don't try to pretend otherwise."

She blinked at me, her expression softening. "I suppose you're right. I'm not used to having anyone who understands. Besides Thorne."

There was an undercurrent of loneliness in her voice, barely audible, but I heard it. Perhaps because it mirrored my own.

"I understand," I said. "Well, a little."

There was so much in Raine that was overwhelmingly strange, the Darkwood most of all. But my stepsister maybe wasn't quite the puzzle I'd first thought her.

"To answer your question," Neeve said, "no, there's nothing dangerous about the stream. The water is perfectly fine to drink, and the creatures that dwell there are of no concern to us."

"Good. Then lead on."

As I followed her through a leaf-trembling glade, I couldn't help the smile spreading over my face. After years of reading about adventure, *yearning* for it, I was finally inside the pages of a storybook; a tale of princesses and magic and an enchanted forest full of strange creatures. And a mysterious foreign prince—though I still had no idea what Thorne's title might mean, or what he actually was.

We brushed past ferns and bushes holding clusters of blue-black berries. The lilt of the stream grew louder, and I saw the bright glint of water ahead.

The path led to the edge of the water, then continued on the other side. The stream itself was too wide to step over easily, though I'd be able to jump it with only a slight danger of getting my feet wet.

Water-slicked stones glowed brown and pink beside the stream. The sky overhead was open, revealing white scuds of clouds against the blue, though I still couldn't tell the direction of the sun.

"Come." Neeve turned to the right, following the line of the stream.

I hopped over a green plant trailing into the water, and followed. It soon became clear we were headed toward a huge, pale boulder at the edge of the bank.

Neeve scrambled up the rock face easily enough, but it took me longer to find hand and footholds. Panting slightly, I gained the top of the boulder. Neeve sat quietly looking out over the stream and small meadow beyond, her arms looped about her updrawn knees. I brushed a few twigs and pine needles off the rock and settled beside her.

The faint chirping of birds blended with the sunlight, and the breeze sighed, low and peaceful through the trees. Unusual for me, I didn't feel any need to speak. Neeve, of course, seldom seemed inclined to conversation. She combed her fingers through her hair, then parted it in small sections and began to weave intricate braids, nimble fingers flashing pale against the dark silk. My own hair would never fall into such sleek coils, of course, but was ever a stubborn, fuzzy mass.

The silence between us was contented, and my hope rekindled that she and I could be, if not friends, then at least allies.

After a time I lay back on the stone, tucking my hands under my head and shifting until I found a place that was not too knobbly. I closed my eyes, grateful for the warmth on my face. For the first time, I felt like I might, perhaps, be able to call this new place home.

Lulled by the quiet babble of the stream below, I dozed. Memories of Parnese moved through my thoughts, already hazy and gold-tinged, as if seen through a sheet of amber-tinted glass. Besides my friends, I missed the delicate pastries studded with raspberries, the bustling street markets, the sound of bells in the air, morning and night, as the churches of the Twin Gods called their congregations to worship.

I don't know how much time passed, but something brought me alert, heart racing and senses sharp. I opened my eyes and made to sit up, but Neeve's outstretched hand stopped me.

"Slowly," she said, her voice a bare whisper of sound.

Moving with care, I came up on my elbows, then followed her gaze to the meadow across the stream.

A stag stood there. But not any stag. To call it such a thing was insulting, like saying the sun was a candle flame in the sky.

This creature was majestic, as pale as frost. The seven-pointed antlers rising from its brow shone, and it was so bright it nearly hurt my eyes to look upon. I squinted, feeling my heartbeat pound through me.

"What is it?" I whispered.

"The White Hart." Neeve's voice was a thread, barely audible above the burble of the stream. "I've only seen it once before."

She sounded awed, and I was glad to know that in this, at least, we felt the same.

As if sensing our regard, the stag lifted its head. The forest stilled, the breeze falling to nothing. Even the merry singing of the water seemed muted.

Then, with a powerful leap, the white stag bounded back into the trees. It sped away from us, a spark of light disappearing into the dark until it was just a memory. I blinked, the afterimage of blazing antlers scribed against the back of my eyelids.

Neeve let out her breath. "It is a good portent."

I was glad that seeing something so brilliantly beautiful as the White Hart didn't mean imminent death and destruction. Perhaps I could find out more about it in the history book Miss Groves had given me from the library. And if not that title, then surely the library held some other tome about the strange and wondrous creatures of the Darkwood. I resolved to catch up on my reading that night, after dinner.

"Come." The cool briskness had returned to Neeve's voice. "We must return to the castle."

She slid gracefully down from the boulder we'd been sitting on. I followed, managing to crash into the underbrush, which earned me an exasperated glance. Ignoring her, I brushed the broken leaves and twigs from my skirt.

Instead of returning the way we'd come, she led me along a small track paralleling the stream. We hadn't gone very far when a shrill call for help pierced the air. It sounded very like the cries of the hobnie I'd rescued the day before, and I shot Neeve a glance.

"Do you hear that?"

"Of course I do." She sounded annoyed. "And it's directly in our way."

We rounded a stand of willows to see something jumping along beside the stream bank. A hobnie, as I'd guessed, though this one wore a blue cap and did not look quite as peevish as the one I'd encountered previously.

"Where are you going, hobnie?" Neeve asked. "I thought your kind disliked the water."

"Foolish girl," the hobnie snapped, still hopping along. "Can't you see yonder fish is trying to pull me in and drown me?"

It waved toward the stream, where a large trout was, indeed, pulling the hobnie along. Apparently the little fellow had been fishing, and the line had gotten tangled up in his beard. When he'd finally hooked a trout, he'd been forced to leap along the bank in its wake.

The trout gave a splashing dive, and the hobnie was pulled almost into the water.

He grabbed onto the rushes on the bank, screeching, "Help me, you useless creatures!"

I rushed forward and took hold of the fishing line, but it was too thin to grasp properly. Wrinkling my nose at the earthy smell of the hobnie, I took him by the shoulders to keep him from being towed into the water.

Neeve picked at the line twined in his beard with a look of distaste. "No use," she said. "It's quite tangled."

The hobnie scowled at her. "What good are you, then, you oaf?"

It seemed my scissors would be the solution once more. I let go of the hobnie, ignoring his cries of dismay that he was in imminent danger of drowning, and rummaged in my belt pouch.

A snip later, and the hobnie was free. Instead of thanks, however, he gave me a red-eyed glare.

"There's my dinner gone, and half my beautiful beard as well, you great lunking toadstool." Then he yawned mightily, showing blackened, stumpy teeth, and, without another word, turned his back on us and scuttled away along the stream bank.

"Those creatures are very rude," I said, tucking my scissors away.

Neeve shrugged. "They're hobnies. They don't much care for humans—or anything other than their own kind."

"I met a different one yesterday, didn't I?" I asked.

"Yes." Neeve tilted her head, as though listening to something. "I believe this one was Codlatach. Not that it matters."

Nothing much seemed to matter to Neeve, I thought, following her down the trail once more. She was a bit like the hobnies that way, caring nothing for any creature other than her own kind. Whatever kind that might be.

We stepped into the shadows under the trees, leaving the tinkling stream behind, and I pondered on that question. What *was* Neeve? Was she even fully human?

It was a discomfiting question, and I shivered. Her father, King Tobin, seemed quite mortal... but perhaps her mother had not been.

Thorne wasn't human, that much was obvious, and he shared similarities with Neeve: the pale skin and dark eyes, the sharp cheekbones and graceful build. Though in his case those things were much more pronounced. Not to mention the pointed ears.

And the magic.

I wanted to ask my stepsister about her origins, but I knew she wouldn't tell me anything. It was too soon, despite the few adventures we'd shared, and I didn't want to squander any goodwill I might have earned.

And so, although it went against my nature, I bit my tongue on my questions.

We emerged from the shelter of the trees. I wanted nothing more than to stay in the Darkwood, but the castle rose before us, gray and dreary, promising another awkward dinner. Neeve and I clearly couldn't discuss the events of the afternoon in front of Lord Raine and my mother—even if they were too engrossed in each other to pay us much heed.

At least this time I knew better than to wear one of my ornate Parnesian gowns. And I'd take a shawl. By the end of dinner the night before, I'd been chilled to the bone.

"Will we see Thorne tomorrow?" I asked as we stepped out of the last shadows of the woods.

"I don't know." Neeve's tone was short.

"But—"

"Don't speak of him." She rounded on me. "Only in the Darkwood, and then, only sparingly. He has other duties, you know."

Her expression implied that Thorne was far too important for the likes of me.

I shrugged as if I didn't care, but her words stung.

"It's not like I could speak, even if I wanted to, remember?" I pulled up my sleeve, showing the leaf tattoo on my inner arm. "This is supposed to ensure my silence, isn't it?"

"It will not keep you from speaking," she said. "Not entirely. But the words will taste most unpleasant. Thorne was too kind to bind your tongue altogether. Though he ought to have done so."

I had no reply to that.

We came into the castle grounds through a door beside the kitchen gardens. Without a word, Neeve led me into the maze of the castle, until at last we reached the corridor housing our rooms. Finally, just outside my door, she paused.

"Do you think you can make your way to the dining hall by yourself tonight?" she asked. There was no kindness in her voice, only the edge of mockery, as if I was a baby that must be led about by the hand.

I wanted to spite her and say yes, then stay in my rooms and sulk all through dinner—but that would earn me a strong reprimand from my mother. And who knew what kind of punishment it might merit from Lord Raine. He didn't seem a cruel man, but he was certainly one who would not tolerate disobedience.

"No," I said, though I hated to admit it.

Neeve let out an impatient breath. "Very well. I'll meet you here when the dinner gong sounds."

Nose in the air, she turned and strode away toward her rooms.

"If it's that much trouble, you could draw me a map!" I called after her.

The thud of her door shutting was her only reply, not that I'd expected anything more.

With a sigh, I went into my rooms. Neeve had not been quite so dreadful while we were in the forest.

I went into my bedroom and stood beside the windows, where the light was strong. Once again, I pulled up my sleeve. The leaf embossed on my skin didn't hurt at all when I ran my fingers over it.

I wondered what would happen if I tried to speak to Sorche. What did Neeve mean, the words would *taste most unpleasant*? Would my tongue sting, as if pricked by nettles? Would I stutter and fall into a faint?

Or would nothing happen at all? The ritual in the forest could have been an empty threat—merely an elaborate display meant to keep me quiet.

Try it, and see what happens, the wicked voice inside me urged. *See if the magic is real.*

Very well, I would. As soon as Sorche came to help me wash up for dinner, I'd casually mention a few of the things I'd seen that afternoon in the Darkwood.

CHAPTER 9

"I think she is beginning to mend." The voice, though I didn't recognize it, roused me from foggy, half-waking dreams.

I blinked, trying to clear my thoughts of shadowy trees and leaping white deer. Above me, the rose-colored curtains of my bed came into focus. Sitting beside my bed was a gray-haired man I did not know, and behind him my mother hovered, her hands fluttering with worry.

"Mama?" I asked, my throat dry as parchment.

"Oh, my darling!" She rushed forward and bent to kiss my cheek. "We were so worried we'd lost you."

"What... happened?" I had a dim memory of Sorche coming into my rooms, of me rising to tell her about the Darkwood—and then a blinding sheet of blue fire slamming across all my senses.

Oh, I'd been a fool to test magic I knew nothing about. Once again, my wicked little voice had led me into too much trouble. I resolved not to listen to it again.

The man, whom I took to be a doctor of some kind, gave me a grave look. "I believe that your constitution, still taxed by travel, was not able to withstand one of the simple illnesses present here in Raine.

You have been abed and mostly unconscious for three days. It was all we could do to force a bit of broth into you."

That would explain the stiffness in my body and my raging thirst.

"Water?" I croaked hopefully.

Mama lifted a glass beside the bed and held it to my lips. I was able to prop myself up on shaking elbows and drink greedily, uncaring that half the liquid sloshed onto my nightgown. My skin felt like a parched desert that welcomed any extra moisture.

When the glass was empty, I sagged back down onto the pillows, exhaustion pulling at me to come back into the blackness.

"Is she awake?" Neeve's voice came from my bedroom doorway, more subdued than I'd ever heard her.

"She is, thank the Twin Gods," Mama said. "Come and say hello."

My stepsister approached warily, coming to stand on the other side of the bed.

"I'm sorry you've been unwell," she said, her dark gaze fixed on mine. "The doctor says you had an unusually severe reaction to something here in Raine." She paused, eyebrows arching slightly for emphasis.

Judging by the look on her face, she'd guessed what had happened, and hadn't expected such a violent response to the binding magic. I hoped she felt guilty for her part in it, for it seemed she had not been entirely truthful about its effects. What I'd experienced went far beyond sour-tasting words.

"I see," I said, my voice still hoarse.

At least Thorne hadn't set a fatal trap for me. Had he known this would happen? Somehow, I suspected not, though it still didn't excuse my own foolishness in pushing the limits of the binding. I let out a ragged, weary breath.

"You're healing." The doctor stood and gave me a brisk nod. "Now that you're awake and in full possession of your faculties, I have every confidence you'll be on your feet within a day or two."

Mama took my limp hand and gave it a gentle squeeze. For the moment, it seemed that she truly did care for me. In her eyes I saw the echo of old fear, and I recalled that she'd almost lost me to illness once before, when I was seven—though I remembered almost nothing of that time.

"Rest now," she said. "I'll have the servants bring you some broth and bread a bit later. We don't want to overtax you."

I nodded weakly, then glanced once more at Neeve.

"I'll visit you later," she said.

I supposed I should be glad that the dreadful workings of the binding vow had at least resulted in Neeve talking to me, but I was suddenly too tired to care about anything other than sleep.

WHEN I NEXT AWOKE, evening had fallen. The curtains had not yet been drawn, and I could see a spattering of stars in the gray-black sky. Light from my sitting room threw a golden rectangle through the doorway into the bedroom.

"Hello?" I said, my throat still sore.

"Oh, miss," Sorche called from the other room. "I'll be right there."

A few moments later she entered, a candle in one hand and a small, covered tray of food in the other. She lit the lamp beside my bed, then helped me sit up and placed the tray upon my lap.

"It's a bit of soup and bread," she said, lifting the cover. "I can help you, if you like?"

"I can manage." At least, I hoped so. I didn't want her to feed me as though I were nothing more than an infant.

"I'm that glad to see you recovering," she said. "You gave me such a fright. I thought you'd dropped dead at my feet. It was dreadful."

"No doubt." I managed to bring a spoonful of soup to my mouth and slurp it up. "I'm sorry."

"It wasn't your fault," she said. "Your poor foreign blood was infected—leastwise, that's what the doctor said."

Oh, my blood had indeed been infected. By magic.

I took a bite of the soft bread and chewed it slowly, thinking. The next time I saw Thorne, I had a few hard questions for him about the binding spell he'd set upon me.

It took me some time to finish my meal. By the time Sorche gathered up the empty bowl and crumb-filled plate, I was tired again. But not too tired to bid the maid open the door when a soft knock sounded.

It was, as I'd guessed, Neeve. She came gracefully up to the bed.

"Are you feeling better?" she asked.

"A bit." I nodded at the chair the doctor had occupied. "Sit down."

I didn't want her towering over me any more than was necessary.

"Right then," Sorche said. "I'll just take these down to the kitchen, since Miss Neeve is here to sit with you."

As soon as she'd gone, I gave my stepsister a penetrating look.

"Did you know that would happen?" I asked. "Are you and Thorne trying to hurt me?"

"No," she said, a trace of heat in her voice. "The vow was only supposed to make your mouth pucker and give you a prickle over your body. Nothing like what happened. Thorne is a protector. He does not injure if he can help it."

"I'd like to hear him say so."

Neeve crossed her arms. "It's your own fault. If you hadn't tried to say something to your maid, you wouldn't be here now. I knew we couldn't trust you with Raine's secrets, and you've proven me right."

She glared at me, lying beneath the covers, and the truth of her words deflated my anger. I had to admit I hadn't shown myself to be particularly worthy of Thorne's trust.

"Very well." I picked at the few crumbs scattered on the bedcover. "I promise I won't say anything ever again. But I still want to go back into the Darkwood."

"Yes, you must. Thorne wants to see you, to make sure you haven't taken any lasting harm."

"*Lasting* harm? That's wonderful." I frowned at her. "Will he be able to tell if I have?"

"Of course. He's *Galadhir*."

"Whatever that means."

"It means he watches over the Darkwood. Tends to its needs."

I raised my brows. "What *needs* might a forest have, then?"

"The other day, when he left us, he went to protect a stand of trees from woodcutters. And to protect the woodcutters, as well. The Dark-wood doesn't like humans venturing too deep."

I thought once more of the suffocation that had beset me on the journey to the castle. "What about traveling the roads?"

"Less dangerous. But if the Darkwood senses a threat, it takes action."

I wasn't ready to tell her about the attack on me, or the bear that had come to my rescue. Not yet, anyway. She had so many secrets, I needed some of my own to hold onto in turn. Besides, how could I, just a girl from Parnese, be seen as a threat to the mighty forest? It made no sense.

Maybe Thorne could help answer that question as well.

"Did you tell him that we saw the deer?" I asked. "The White Hart?"

"He knew. He knows everything that happens in the forest."

"But what did it mean?"

"He wouldn't say." She didn't sound happy about it.

Sorche bustled back into my rooms, and the chance for further conversation between myself and Neeve was gone. Just as well. I could feel exhaustion pulling my eyelids down.

"Rest well," Neeve said softly, rising.

Or maybe I'd only imagined she said it.

CHAPTER 10

Over a week passed before I felt well enough to return with Neeve to the Darkwood. The only good thing about spending so much time abed was that I'd been able to read half of the *Complete History of Raine* that Miss Groves had given me.

I still felt woefully uninformed about the Darkwood, however. The book seemed to dance around the subject of the forest, alluding to strange alliances and mysterious happenings in the vaguest of terms. It was quite annoying.

The one thing I did discover was that the flower called *nirwen* actually grew deep in the wood. Which made sense, I supposed, since it was reputed to have potent properties. And apparently it bloomed infrequently, so it was no wonder the country didn't export a great deal of it. Either way, I wouldn't want to be the one sent into the heart of the Darkwood to pick some herb.

I wondered what Thorne, and the forest, thought of such incursions. But that was the least of my questions when Neeve and I stepped into the welcoming shadows of the trees and found him waiting.

I opened my mouth to accuse him of nearly killing me, but he spoke first.

"My deepest apologies, Rose," he said. "When we performed the binding spell, there were certain... unpredictable elements I should have heeded."

Neeve gave him a sharp look. "Your blood?"

"Yes." He turned his troubled gaze to her. "You've minded your studies well, Neeve. The magic we performed should not have affected me. The fact that a drop of my blood mingled with both of yours was of more significance than I wanted to admit."

Neeve nodded gravely. "The *Galadhir* is not meant to bleed."

"What does it mean?" I asked.

He looked back at me, gold lights glinting in his dark eyes. "It means that you are of importance, in some way I have yet to determine. And that, perhaps, you have a touch of magic in your own blood, Rose."

"What, her?" Neeve let out a snort. "She's just a girl from Parnese. How could she have anything of the sort?"

I wondered the same myself—not that I'd ever voice it aloud. Still, the possibility hummed through me, vibrating down to my bones. Was it true? Could I have some special power, unknown until now?

It seemed impossible, yet my heart leaped at the thought that my wildest hopes might come true.

"Humans don't have magic," Neeve said.

"That's not entirely correct." Thorne gave her a quelling look. "There are been instances of humans with powers. Not many, I admit. But you know it is not impossible."

"Humans *can* have magic," I said. "I knew a sorcerer in Parnese that could create images out of flame."

I couldn't keep the quaver of memory from my voice, and Thorne gave me a penetrating look.

"What happened to him?" he asked.

"He was... burned alive by the red priests." I swallowed back bile, trying not to recall the horrible smell of scorched flesh.

"How barbaric!" Neeve looked shocked. "Why would your people do such a thing?"

"They're not *my* people. It's the priests of the Twin Gods, hunting down anyone that might carry even a hint of sorcery."

Thorne's eyebrows drew together. "That is troubling. Tell me, Rose, how do you suppose they are going about finding such people? It takes magic to sense magic, you know."

"It does?" I stared at him. "Do you mean that the priests of the Twin Gods are actually sorcerers themselves?"

"Of course not," Neeve said. "There can't be a whole sect of magic users running about the Continent."

The wind stirred the branches over our heads, as if in agreement.

"It does seem unlikely," Thorne said. "But perhaps there only needs to be one. A powerful sorcerer could craft magic-sensing trinkets that could be used by those without powers of their own."

"But why?" I asked. "That can't have anything to do with us."

Thorne's gaze stabbed through me. Like an unwary moth skewered by a pin, I flinched from the intensity in his eyes.

"Think, Rose. It concerns you quite directly, if you carry magic in your blood."

"We're far from Parnese," I said. "Surely nothing can happen to me here, even if I do have... magic."

I still couldn't credit the idea, no matter how much I might wish to.

"Not that you do," Neeve said. It seemed she could not imagine it, either.

"We will have to discover if Rose does, or if she does not." Thorne's brows knitted together.

"Another spell?' I gulped back the sourness of fear. It was clear the magic of the Darkwood did not agree with me, and I was not eager to experience its effects again.

To my relief, he shook his head. "No. We'll go visit the *cailleach*."

Neeve frowned at him. "Would she be able to tell?"

"Who or what is the kyle-ya?" I asked. It was growing wearisome, being the only one of our trio who knew absolutely nothing.

"The people in the village call her the herbwife," Neeve said. "But she's much more than that."

"We get to go to the village?" At last, I'd meet some of the people that dwelt outside the dreary walls of Castle Raine.

"No," Neeve said, squelching my rising anticipation. "She lives in the forest a short distance from Little Hazel."

Thorne glanced up at the bit of sky visible through the trees. "We have enough time this afternoon to pay her a visit. Come."

A shiver of excitement ran down my back as I followed. Whoever this herbwife was, she clearly had power. Magic. And if she did, then perhaps I might, too.

CHAPTER 11

As Thorne led the way through the Darkwood, a path seemed to open beneath his feet. Birds chirped in greeting as he passed, and a thick carpet of loam cushioned our steps. Ferns glowed emerald in shafts of light breaking through the evergreens, and three-petaled white flowers shone like little stars beside trunks shaggy with moss.

He and Neeve moved gracefully, and I trailed in their wake, ungainly and sticky with sweat. Branches that seemed to sway aside at their passage returned to slap me on the arms and legs, suddenly sprouting thorns. Once I ran face-first into the clinging strands of a spider web, though Neeve had walked that way just moments before.

A cloud of gnats found me as we traveled, the cloud about my head growing with each minute. One or two managed to land on my neck and deliver an itchy sting.

"Ow!" I tried to wave the buzzing gnats away.

Thorne stopped and turned, his eyes narrowing as he took in my state: hands scratched by twigs, the remains of spider web in my hair, and the gnats bedeviling me.

"*Daro,*" he said, his voice rich with a quiet authority that belied his years.

The cloud of bothersome insects whirled away, and Thorne stepped lightly to my side.

"You ought to have said something." He took my hands and inspected the scratches. "The forest shouldn't be resisting your passage."

"I don't think it likes me." I looked ruefully down at the thin red welts on my skin.

"I will speak to it," he said.

The words were laughable—he would *speak* to the forest, as though it were an unruly pet that needed chastising? And yet I had no doubt he would. I just hoped the Darkwood would care to listen.

"Here." Cradling my hand in his, he drew his long index finger down the scratches marring my skin. They did not heal completely beneath his touch, but coolness followed, the welts subsiding as the redness faded.

When both my abraded hands had been tended to, he set his fingertip lightly to the bites on my neck. I tried not to hold my breath at his nearness. It felt very much like the moment I saw the White Hart, the air trembling, a sense of magic sifting down like silver from the stars.

"Hurry up," Neeve said, sounding cross.

"Take the lead," Thorne said. "You know the way well enough. I'll watch over Rose."

Neeve sent me a quick scowl, as though jealous of Thorne's attention, then turned and continued down the trail.

Conscious of his presence at my back, I tried to walk more elegantly, though it was difficult to feel graceful with my hair a frizz about my face and my neck damp with perspiration. At least the branches had ceased whipping me, and the gnats seemed gone for good.

Before long the trees thinned, changing from evergreens to white-barked birch. Swaths of blue flowers filled a glade ahead, and at the far edge stood a thatched cottage with whitewashed walls. A low fence surrounded a garden full of flowers and herbs. I recognized a few of them, including—to my surprise—a small patch of purple-headed blooms on long stems.

Neeve pushed open the garden gate, then waited for Thorne and me to join her.

"I thought you said lavender doesn't grow here," I said to her. What else had she lied to me about?

"It doesn't." There was no remorse in her black eyes.

"What's that, then?" I pointed to the patch.

"Lavender." Thorne set a quelling hand on my shoulder. "But things bloom in the *cailleach*'s garden that you can find no place else. Neeve is correct—this herb does not grow in Raine."

"Except here." I glanced at the silvery-leaved shrub.

The top half-door of the cottage swung open, and a white-haired woman looked out, leaning her elbows on the bottom sill. Eyes as blue as the sky regarded us from her crease-lined face.

"Good day to you," she said with a genial smile. "Neeve, of course, is here frequently, but it's not often I have a visit from you, Thorne Windrift. Is all well within the wood?"

"Well enough." Thorne stepped forward and made her a slight bow. "We've come to ask you a favor, Mistress Ainya."

"Concerning this girl, no doubt." The herbwife nodded at me. "I'm thinking you're wise to worry, *Galadhir*."

"I'm Rose," I said, tired of people talking around me all the time, as if I wasn't standing right in front of them. "And why should he be worried?"

Mistress Ainya smiled at me, her eyes crinkling. "Because, even from here, I sense something strange about you."

"Something strange? Like what?" Did I dare to hope it was magic, hiding just under my skin?

"Come in, all of you," she said, avoiding my question. "I've a kettle on the hob."

She stepped back and swung open the bottom half of the door. As we obediently filed past her, I realized she was tiny—smaller even than Neeve and me. The force of her personality had made her seem much bigger.

The inside of the cottage was small and tidy, the slate floor swept clean and an array of copper pans gleaming over the fireplace. Our hostess ushered us to a small table with four chairs crowded around it.

I took a seat, with Thorne on one side and Neeve at the other. Bunches of dried herbs hung from the ceiling, which put me in mind of the shed where I'd discovered the secret door through the wall.

I glanced at Neeve. "Are you her apprentice?"

The herbwife let out a cackle of laughter. "A clever one you are, Rose. Aye, Neeve studies herbalism with me once a week. Would you all like a cup of tea?"

Without waiting for an answer, she bustled to her counter and filled a stout brown teapot with herbs. When she poured the boiling water over, a delicious aroma filled the cottage—sweet and comforting, with a hint of spice.

"What are you brewing there?" Thorne asked. Mostly to be polite, I guessed, for he did not sound the least bit worried that the herbwife was planning to poison us.

Mistress Ainya raised her brows at Neeve, who proceeded to name a list of ingredients. Chamomile I knew, and anise, but beyond that, the rest of the herbs were unfamiliar to me.

"Now, Rose," the *cailleach* said, setting a mug of tea before me, "tell me about yourself."

I gave her my brief history, including the fact that my mother had married the king. When I finished, she nodded.

"So you've no notion who your father is?" she asked.

"None at all. Not that it's ever bothered me." I'd never seen the point of pining for an absent father—not when my own mother was absent enough all on her own.

Speaking about Parnese, however, had roused the hollow ache of homesickness. Had Marco and Pauline forgotten me already, carrying on with their lives beneath the warm, dry sun?

I took a sip of tea, trying to cover the sudden loneliness I felt. The taste of flowers and warmth soothed me somewhat, blunting the twist of loneliness that curled in my belly.

"What did you mean, earlier?" Thorne asked the *cailleach*. "When you said there's a strangeness about Rose?"

"Well now." Mistress Ainya looked at me, her mouth squinching up. "It seems there's something upon you, girl. A touch of power, perhaps, but only a trace, and nothing like I've ever seen."

"Magic?" I whispered, my heart hammering suddenly inside my chest.

I wanted it to be true, and yet hearing her imply it frightened me. I was safe from the Twin Gods' priests here in Raine, but the memory of Pietro's death still echoed through my bones.

"How can we tell?" Thorne asked, an undercurrent of urgency in his voice. "The forest is not easy with her presence."

"Hmm." Mistress Ainya gave me a penetrating stare. "May I touch you, Rose?"

I nodded mutely, heartbeat hammering in my ears.

The *cailleach* stood and rounded the table. She set her wizened hands on my shoulders, and I tensed.

"Breathe, lass," she said.

I tried to relax, the scents of herbs filling my nose. Surely Thorne would not let the herbwife harm me.

A faint tickling sensation moved over my skin, and I tried not to squirm. A few moments later, Mistress Ainya lifted her hands and went back to her place.

"Well then." She sat, her bright gaze upon me. "You're a puzzle, make no mistake."

Thorne leaned forward. "What did you sense?"

"'Tis not entirely clear," the herbwife said, still looking at me. "There is some power surrounding you, Rose—but whether it's inside you, or you cast a resonance because you are the harbinger of some great event, I can't be sure."

I swallowed in confusion. "What does that mean?"

"Fate casts a shadow," Mistress Ainya said. "Thorne's people use Oracles and prophecy to read those shadows. Very few can interpret the signs. I, myself, am not skilled enough to tell you whether what I sense upon you is the power of destiny, or if you indeed carry magic in your blood."

Disappointed, I balled my hands in my lap, the stub of my pinky curled against my left palm. "How do we find out?"

I'd far prefer to have magic—no matter how dangerous—than simply be some pawn of fate.

"Over time it should become clear," the herbwife said. "If you have power, it will unfurl by the time you reach eighteen years of age."

"Eighteen?" I all but wailed the word. "That's ages from now."

Mistress Ainya's expression softened with sympathy. "Aye—but it may well show sooner. I, myself, came into my power, small as it is, at fourteen."

Somewhat mollified, I blew out a breath. I'd be fourteen on my next birthday. Surely I could wait that long.

"Can we do nothing in the meantime?" Thorne asked. His pale fist was clenched upon the table.

The herbwife let out one of her cackling laughs. "Well of course you can! Rose can learn enough to be prepared, if the magic comes upon her. And if it does not..." She lifted her bony shoulders in a shrug.

"If it doesn't..." I swallowed back the bitter thought of disappointment. "Then what am I?"

"Trouble." Mistress Ainya's expression was suddenly quite serious. "Trouble like a cold gale brewing on the sea, and make no mistake. Whatever's to come, I fear you're at the very heart of the storm."

CHAPTER 12

Despite Mistress Ainya's foreboding words, nothing dreadful came to pass in the weeks that followed our visit to her cottage.

As promised, I began taking lessons with her. My afternoons alternated between roaming the Darkwood with Neeve and Thorne, and spending time in the *cailleach*'s sunny cottage. Once a week, Neeve accompanied me to continue her own study of herbalism.

I did not enjoy those lessons nearly as much, and so shirked my reading—perhaps more than I should.

"Which is better for headaches, Rose?" Mistress Ainya asked as we sat outside in her fragrant garden. "Tansy, rue, or willow?"

Drat. Instead of studying the herbal she'd sent home with me, I'd devoured the latest volume in the Red Rohan series—a thrilling set of adventure books I'd recently discovered in Castle Raine's library.

"Um... tansy?" I guessed.

Neeve let out a mocking snort, not even looking up from where she was plaiting lavender stalks together.

"No." Mistress Ainya sounded disappointed. "It is willow. You would brew a tisane from the bark. Did you not even glance at your herbal?"

Shame made me reply too hotly. "I don't see what memorizing useless facts about plants has to do with magic. My lessons so far seem an utter waste of time."

The herbwife's blue eyes were shadowed as she looked at me, and I was sorry for my outburst. But still, there was truth in it. Why wasn't I learning something interesting, like how to chant spells or create magical trinkets? So far, all Mistress Ainya had showed me was how to keep the iron cookpot at an even boil so our soup did not scorch, how to tie rushes into a broom, and the proper way to keep mice out of the larder.

"Patience," she said, her voice weary. "Ah, I am too old for the temper of red-headed children. If you don't like it, Rose, you are free to leave."

Those last words doused the fire of my anger, leaving behind only a dissatisfaction that scratched at the back of my neck.

"I didn't mean it," I said, going to kneel beside her. "Truly. It's just..."

Neeve set aside her beautifully braided lavender and gave me a long look.

"When I first apprenticed with Mistress Ainya," my stepsister said, "she did not even allow me to take the herbal back to the castle. I had to study it here, in addition to my other lessons. You're luckier than you know, Rose."

I glanced down at the fine black dirt under my knees. The smell of thyme and rosemary pricked my nose, and the low, steady humming of bees filled the bushes around us. No matter what lessons humans learned, or didn't learn, they kept on with their work, unconcerned.

"I'll try and do better," I said, looking up at Mistress Ainya. "I promise."

"See that you do." The *cailleach* set her wrinkled hand on my head. "Now, since you did not bother to study your herbal, you may sweep out the cottage with the broom you made the other day."

"Yes, mistress." I rose, brushed the soil from my skirts, and went into Mistress Ainya's small home.

My broom was a clumsy thing, but it did well enough. Soon I had swept up a pile of crumbled bits of herbs that had fallen from the ceiling, a few dried peas that had spilled from the container, and plenty of dirt tracked in from the garden. I gently pushed it all to the threshold, then nudged it outside, depositing the pile to the side of the flagstone walk.

"Thank you," Mistress Ainya said. "That will do. But bring me one of the peas you swept up."

I leaned my broom beside the door, then fished a pea out of the dirt and brought it to where the herbwife sat. She held out her hand, and I deposited the pea in her seamed palm.

"Neeve, you too," she called.

On the far side of the garden, my stepsister left off snipping leaves off the sage and came to stand beside me.

"My magic works with physical objects," Mistress Ainya said. "I cannot create something from thin air, nor can I work with ephemeral thoughts. It is a power grounded by what I can touch, and taste, and feel."

I leaned forward, trying to absorb every word and commit it to memory. Even Neeve seemed interested, her customary mask of indifference gone.

"Everything holds the energy of what it was, what it is now, and what it might be." The *cailleach* lifted her hand, the hard pea rolling in her palm. "Those three states represent all possibilities. Tell me, Rose, what am I holding?"

"It's a pea." I stared at it, trying to recall what the herbwife had said. *What it was, what it is, what it might be.* "It, um, it was a live plant one time. And I suppose it will turn back into dirt. Is that the three things?"

Mistress Ainya cocked her head. "A creditable first try. Neeve?"

My stepsister shot our teacher a quick glance, then looked at the pea. "Living essence, now stored and dormant, waiting to grow or be consumed."

"Excellent." The *cailleach* closed her hand. "The pea is potential, Rose. It is life, and death."

She opened her fingers and the pea was gone. A crisp white blossom lay in its place.

I pulled in my breath, excitement tingling over my skin. *Magic.*

"It is growth and decay." She closed her hand then opened it again to reveal the pea. "Most of all, it is energy."

She stared at the little green ball in her palm. A heartbeat later, it burst into flame. I tried not to jump back at the sight. The fire burned quick and bright, and in another few seconds there was only a smear of ash in Mistress Ainya's hand.

"Did it burn you?" I whispered, shivering at the echo of flame, the distant memory of Ser Pietro's screams. "How did you do that?"

"By knowing that I could." She brushed her palm against her skirts. "You will come to learn the shape of things, Rose, and what might be done. But you must never, ever, perform magic on a living creature."

I shot a glance at Neeve, and thought of the leaf tattooed on my arm. "Thorne did."

Mistress Ainya leaned forward and took my hands. "His magic is not human magic. Promise me, Rose."

"I promise," I said, looking straight into her eyes. This time, I vowed, I would keep my word and not let my worst impulses get the better of me.

"Good." The *cailleach* gave my hands a squeeze and let me go. "Now, make me a cup of tea, and then the two of you may go. Magic is tiring work, and I'm not as young as I once was."

Our teacher was soon settled in the sunniest patch of her garden with a mug of mint and chamomile tea. Neeve and I bade her farewell, and then my stepsister led me into the forest once more.

I was beginning to know the path back to Castle Raine: the white-barked trees, the trail through the ferns, the left-hand branching at the mossy stump. When she took the turn to the right instead, I frowned.

"Where are we going?" I asked.

"We don't have to return to the castle just yet," she said, not answering my question.

"Will we see Thorne?" My spirits lifted at the thought.

Neeve made no answer, and I had no choice but to follow her straight-backed figure deeper into the Darkwood. At least I was reasonably sure she wasn't planning to lead me into danger and abandon me. Even if she wanted to, both Thorne and Mistress Ainya would disapprove.

Still, as we entered a shadowy, whispering grove of hemlock trees, a shiver went down my back. The sky was barely visible through the dark tapestry of branches. Somewhere overhead, a raven let out a loud caw, startling me.

Something glimmered ahead of us, and as we drew closer I saw there was a small pool in the center of the grove. It was scarcely bigger than my bathing tub at the castle, and perfectly round. No stream fed it, no trickle exited. The surface of the pool was as unmoving as a burnished silver coin.

"What is it?" I asked softly.

"Airgid Tarn," Neeve answered, just as quietly. "Now, be still."

She went to her knees at the edge of the pool, facing the calm water. I knelt on the soft, damp moss beside her and held my breath in anticipation. Whatever Neeve was about to do, I had no doubt it would be out of the ordinary. I only hoped it wouldn't hurt.

CHAPTER 13

Kneeling beside the pond, Neeve raised her hands overhead and spoke one of those strange, twisty words I'd heard Thorne utter. A speck of glowing blue light hovered at her fingertips, no bigger than a firefly. I stared up at it and felt my eyes widen. Could Mistress Ainya do such things? Somehow, I thought not.

"*Caladlim,*" Neeve said again.

The spark grew and brightened until it was the size of a small plum. Azure light reflected on the surface of the tarn. Neeve lowered her hands, but the glowing ball remained suspended, hovering over her head.

I wondered if that was the end of the magical demonstration, for it seemed clear my stepsister had brought me here in order to show off her own abilities. Especially because I knew nothing, and could no more light a pea on fire with my thoughts than fly to the stars.

Neeve was not finished, however. She waved one hand over the water and spoke another word, then leaned forward, staring intently at the surface.

Was my stepsister summoning some creature up from the depths? I forced myself not to scoot away from the edge.

"Look," she said.

I did, and saw our two faces reflected side by side. Her skin seemed pale as milk beneath her night-black hair. In contrast, my own hair was unruly fire, my complexion bronzed by the sun. We were as different as night and day.

The silver water shimmered. Our reflections wavered, then elongated into two standing figures. Neeve wore a gown of silver, and I of gold. In the strange mirror of the water, we turned to face one another. Neeve held an icy sword wreathed in blue flame. She lifted it to strike at me, but I threw up my hands, red fire lashing from my fingertips. The fire touched the sword, there was a flash of light, and our reflections disappeared. Dry-mouthed, I stared at the water.

"What was that?" I whispered.

"Wait." She waved her hand again across the surface.

Another image wavered there—a star-shaped flower, five petals scribed in yellow light. Bright flashes streaked through the blossom, and the surface of the pond wavered. I glanced up, startled to see that the flying sparks were actually reflections in the water from three small golden balls of light whirling in the air over our heads. Something fluttered within each glowing sphere. I squinted, trying to see more clearly, but the lights swept up into the black branches of the trees and disappeared.

When I looked back down at the pond, the flower was gone. Only Neeve's pale face and my own astonished one gazed back at us. And a third figure, dark brows drawn into a frown beneath the hood of his green cloak.

"Hello, Thorne," Neeve said to his reflection.

I swiveled to see him standing just behind us, arms crossed. He did not seem pleased.

"What do you think you were doing?" His words were directed at Neeve. "You know better than to attempt scrying without me."

She slowly stood, then turned to face him. I scrambled to my feet as well, suddenly worried for my stepsister. It was not a comfortable thing, to see Thorne angry.

"I ask your forgiveness," Neeve said.

Thorne shook his head, his expression unforgiving. "Why did you attempt such a thing?"

She clenched her hands and stared down at the mosses beneath our feet. Surely admitting she was trying to show off was not an answer she wanted to give.

"I asked her to," I said impetuously. "I asked if she might show me some of her magic. Mistress Ainya set a pea on fire."

One eyebrow going up, Thorne transferred his piercing gaze to me. "Is that so?"

"Yes." At least, the part about the pea.

He regarded me steadily, as if seeking the truth in my eyes. I refused to drop my gaze, though prickles ran up and down my spine with the effort. After a long moment, he turned back to Neeve.

"Did you see anything?" he asked.

"Yes." Her voice was low. "We saw the blossom of the *nirwen*."

"Both of you?" He sounded surprised.

I nodded. "That was after the images where we were..." I glanced at my stepsister. "Were we fighting against each other?"

"I don't know."

"Describe what you saw," Thorne said. "Every detail."

Between the two of us, Neeve and I tried to explain the images: our gowns of silver and gold, our weapons clashing. As we spoke, the mirrored stillness of the pond shivered as though stirred by the kiss of a breeze, though the air was still.

"And when your flame met Neeve's sword, then what?" Thorne asked me.

"We told you. There was a bright flash of light and then the water cleared."

"And then the *nirwen* came," Neeve said.

"And the flying lights," I added.

"Flying lights?" Thorne gave me a sharp look.

"Three of them. They disappeared into the trees." I gestured above our heads. "What does it all mean?"

"I cannot say." His tone was stern.

"Cannot, or will not?" Neeve asked. "What good are you as a teacher if you won't help me interpret my scrying?"

He let out a heavy breath, the uncertainty in his eyes making him seem suddenly quite young. "In truth, I'm not sure of the exact meanings. I'll have to consult those with more experience."

Who? I went up on my toes. Where were the others of his kind? Did they all dwell within the Darkwood? Why was Thorne the only one I'd ever seen?

The questions burned my tongue, but it knew that the more I asked, the warier he would become. My best course was to draw no attention to the pieces of information he let slip.

"What do *you* think, about what we saw in the water?" I finally asked. It seemed the safest course.

"I can only say that your destinies seem entwined," he replied.

I had guessed as much, myself.

"What about the flower?"

He shook his head. Frowning, I turned to Neeve and gave her a pointed look. She owed me, after all, for lying on her behalf.

"Perhaps Rose should come along when the next harvest is due," Neeve said.

"No." Thorne's expression returned to one of hard certainty. "Absolutely not."

Another raven swept overhead, cawing hoarsely. Its reflection was a black shadow in the silver eye of the pond.

Neeve glanced up. "We ought to return to the castle. Dusk is falling."

It was true. The shadows beneath the hemlocks gathered more thickly, and the sky was smudged with gray.

"Who are you going to ask about the vision?" Despite my earlier resolution to remain quiet, I tossed the question at Thorne.

"Someone who can give me answers," he said, his expression hooded.

"Mistress Ainya?"

"She knows nothing of this type of magic," Neeve said.

Thorne gave her a stern look, and she closed her mouth quickly. Drat it.

Silently, we filed out of the grove. At the fork in the path, Thorne halted.

"I'll leave you here," he said. "Farewell."

Before we could respond, he was gone, melted into the embrace of the Darkwood. I was certain he was off to consult with his mysterious sources, and wished rather desperately to follow. But it was growing dark, and Neeve gave me a sharp look, as if she could read my thoughts.

With a sigh, I followed her back toward the castle.

Yet it seemed our adventures that day were not at an end. Before we had gone much farther, a high-pitched cry for help made us both stop and stare into the dimming forest.

"It's another of those annoying little hobnies," Neeve said dismissively.

"We should go help." After all, we'd aided two of the creatures already.

Another yell sounded, closer this time. Without waiting to see if my stepsister would follow, I darted off the path in the direction of that panicked cry.

CHAPTER 14

"Wait!" Neeve called after me, but I paid no heed.

I dashed through the underbrush at the fringe of the forest, to see one of the bearded little men running straight toward me. He zigged and zagged through the meadow ahead, trying to outrun a huge, dark-winged eagle.

The raptor kept pace easily, extending its sharp claws. I watched in horror as the eagle caught the hobnie by his long beard and hoisted him into the air.

"Help me!" the little man screeched, his red eyes bright with panic.

As the bird flew past, I leaped and caught a handful of the hobnie's tattered brown tunic. I held fast, but I was not strong enough to pull him out of the eagle's clutches.

A pair of pale hands joined mine. Together, Neeve and I tugged with all our might. I let go of the hobnie's tunic and managed to catch one of his arms. His screeching increased.

"Must my limbs be torn off, as well as my beard?" he cried. "What ugly, clumsy creatures you are. Can you not be more careful?"

With a last wrench, my stepsister and I pulled the little creature free. The eagle gave a screeching cry and sheared off. I could see the glint of its eye fixed upon us, even as it climbed higher into the sky.

"Ungainly girls, to abuse me so." The hobnie rolled out of our hands, then snatched up his greenish cap from where it had fallen on the ground and jammed it on his head.

"You should be grateful," I began, irritated by the creature's manner, when a sharp cry sounded over our heads.

"It's coming back!" The hobnie threw his arms about my knees. "Save me!"

I looked up to see the dark arrow of the eagle pointed at us, fierce of beak and claw. My first impulse was to run for the cover of the trees, but the panicked hobnie would not let go of my skirts.

Neeve lifted her hands. A momentary blue fire outlined her finger-tips, then faded.

"*Daro*," she said urgently, her face strained. Nothing happened.

The eagle plummeted toward us. I covered my head with my arms and peeked out from between my elbows. Just as the bird was about to rake us with its extended talons, a mighty roar shook the trees.

With a squawk, the eagle veered away. The wind of its passage whipped my hair into my eyes. I pushed it impatiently away in time to see the bird fly away over the treetops.

"Run!" the hobnie cried, letting go of me. "Or have you escaped the eagle only to be dinner for a hungry bear?"

He suited action to words, scurrying away through the tall meadow grass.

I looked at Neeve. "Are we really about to be eaten by a bear?"

"No." She looked down at her hands and gave them a quick shake.

"What happened to your magic?"

She let out a sigh. "I used up my wellspring of power by scrying in the pool."

"What?" I stared at her, aghast. "You won't be able to do magic again?"

No wonder Thorne had been so angry.

"Of course I'll be able to do magic again." She narrowed her eyes at me. "My power is not gone. It's only depleted for a short time."

"Oh." I thought on her words for a moment. "What is a wellspring? Do I have one too? How do I fill it with power?"

She lifted her nose in the air. "You don't have one."

I wasn't entirely sure she was right. I must have *something*, for both Thorne and Mistress Ainya seemed to think so. Although it seemed I must wait until I turned fourteen to find out.

"What about the bear?" I glanced back over my shoulder at the shadows beneath the tall evergreens. "Are there many in the Darkwood?"

"We ought to get back to the castle," Neeve said, ignoring my question.

I had been on the verge of finally telling her about my encounter with the bear while journeying to Castle Raine, but irritation stifled the words. If she didn't want to tell me anything of interest, I'd gladly return the favor.

I trailed Neeve through the grasses and up to the small door in the castle wall. Behind me lay the Darkwood, huge and breathing softly like some untamed animal—and full of secrets I feared I'd never discover.

PART II

CHAPTER 15

The rest of the summer passed quickly, filled with morning lessons from Miss Groves and sunny afternoons spent with Mistress Ainya. Neeve and I continued to roam the Darkwood, and had another encounter with an ill-tempered hobnie in need of rescue.

We were sitting in the meadow where we'd seen the White Hart. My fingers were busy braiding stalks of yarrow into a flower crown. Ostensibly, Neeve was doing the same, but she'd set her flowers aside and was staring moodily at the tall cedars at the edge of the clearing.

"What is it?" I asked. "Is something there? Is it Thorne?"

Sometimes—not often enough for my liking—the *Galadhir* accompanied us on our rambles through the Darkwood. I loved those afternoons, when he would pluck handfuls of ripe berries for us, or point out the delicate tangles of birds' nests hidden high in the branches.

Neeve shook her head. "Nothing. At least, nothing out of the ordinary."

I regarded her a moment. It wasn't the first time a melancholy mood had overtaken my stepsister when we were in the forest. I wondered if it was because she missed her time alone in the Darkwood, or whether my presence kept Thorne away. But I didn't particularly want to know the answer, so I didn't ask.

The dusty-sweet smell of the bruised stems hovered around us as I went back to making my flower crown. The intermittent sun warmed my back, in between puffs of clouds floating through the pale blue sky, and a soft breeze pulled a frizz of red curls from my plaited hair, the strands tickling my cheek. Impatiently, I swiped my hair back.

Neeve suddenly stood. "Do you hear that?"

I jammed the completed crown on my head, the stems slightly itchy on my scalp, and rose. "What? No."

Even as I said the words, I heard it—a high-pitched cry for help.

"Another hobnie?" I asked.

"Likely." She brushed seed-heads from her skirts. "Let's go see what trouble this one has gotten into."

I followed as she strode through the small meadow. "I thought you didn't like helping the hobnies. They annoy you."

"Many things annoy me." She threw me a glance over her shoulder, making it clear she included me among them. "But that doesn't mean I won't give my aid when needed. Besides, whenever we help one, it owes us a favor—which is not a bad thing. Magical creatures take their debts seriously."

Was Thorne such a creature, and what debt did he owe to Neeve? So many questions needing answers. It occurred to me that maybe the hobnie would tell me, in return for its rescue.

Neeve led me deeper into the trees and to a rocky ravine, while the cries for assistance grew louder.

"We're coming!" I called, partially to quiet the creature.

"Your laggardly ways will be the death of me," it screeched in return. "Hurry, you useless imbecile!"

Neeve's lips pressed into a frown at the insult, but she didn't halt. A moment later, we rounded a jagged outcropping of granite to find the hobnie pinned to the ground by a huge chunk of rock that had fallen, or perhaps rolled, onto his disheveled beard. His dingy mustard-colored hat had fallen off and his feet had dug ruts into the earth from his efforts to free himself.

"It's the whey-faced children," he said crossly. "You took your time in coming."

"You hardly seem in danger of imminent death," Neeve said, glancing about. "Is something menacing you?"

Eyes wide, I turned in a slow circle, but there didn't seem to be any sharp-beaked hawks or dangerous bears lurking in the underbrush.

"I'd perish of starvation soon enough," the hobnie grumbled. "Now, roll that rock away so I might be about my business."

Neeve and I set our shoulders to the stone, but it didn't budge. Of course not—I'd come to understand how such things worked in the Darkwood. Opening the pouch at my belt, I pulled out my scissors.

At the sight, the little hobnie began to shriek.

"Nooo! Do not shave me as you have my brethren! Come, you weaklings, put your backs into it, and have mercy on my beautiful long beard."

I shook my head at him. "We've done our best. That stone isn't moving, no matter how hard we push."

"If you don't let Rose snip off the end of your beard then you can stay here until you starve," Neeve added.

The hobnie wailed and drummed his arms and legs on the ground. Ignoring his caterwauls, I bent and snipped the end of his beard. He instantly sprang to his feet and glared at me, his red eyes sparking with anger.

"Wretched little mortal," he said. "I'd be glad never to see your hideous face again."

He scooped up his hat and thrust it atop his head, then grabbed the lumpy bag he'd abandoned during the course of his tantrum.

"Wait," I said as he turned to stomp away. "I wanted to ask you—"

"No questions." He scowled so fiercely his face turned into nothing but creases, then scurried away before I could catch his arm.

Annoyed, I watched the bushes close about him. Once he was gone, I looked at Neeve.

"What did he mean, no questions? I can't ask the hobnies anything?"

"You can try," she said. "But they only answer once, if at all."

So much for my plan to glean information from the grumpy little creatures.

"Then what good are their debts?" I asked.

She gave me an arch look. "You simply must be persistent with them. But it's time we went back to the castle."

The trees around us swayed, as if in agreement, and I let out a sigh. The hobnie was gone now, and I certainly didn't know how to find him. And Neeve was right, we ought to be returning. I could never tell how many hours we'd spent in the Darkwood, but she always seemed to know.

"I don't suppose we'll see Thorne today?" I asked, a bit hopelessly.

"No." She glanced into the green-edged shadows. "You pestered him so much last time, I don't know when he'll seek out our company again."

"That's not fair! It's not my fault if he has other things to do." Though I winced at the thought she might be right.

I *had* kept asking whether I had a wellspring of magic, like Neeve. To my regret, he'd finally told me I did not, in fact, possess one.

"Your power," he said, "if indeed you have any, comes from the ability to focus your mind and truly *see into* the things around you. Is Mistress Ainya not teaching you thus?"

"She is, I think." I'd let out a sigh. "But I'd rather have blue fire shoot from my hands than have to sort out a bucket of beans and lentils. What's the use of that?"

So far, my efforts had only resulted in haphazard piles of legumes on Mistress Ainya's table. I'd carelessly knocked the corner when rising, scattering lentils and beans to the far corners of the cottage. After sweeping them up, I'd been forced to begin all over again. It seemed I was rather a hopeless student, after all.

"Don't worry." Thorne had rested his hand on my shoulder a moment, his touch cool and reassuring. "You'll master this in time. Each small step builds to the next."

I'd swallowed my impatience and glanced at Neeve's serene face. It was easy for her—magic seemed to flow in her blood, while I was nothing but a clumsy human.

Still, I persevered, and by the time the golden leaves of the birch trees carpeted the ground, I could sort the lentils and the brown beans apart in less than an hour. More or less.

"Better." Mistress Ainya straightened from inspecting the untidy piles. "You still have a few lentils in the wrong place. Try once more."

She waved her hand, and the legumes whirled together, pouring back into the bucket in an undifferentiated stream. I sighed, and started over. Again.

Dinner that night at the castle was a rich lentil stew, but I couldn't bring myself to eat much of it. Each bite tasted like failure in my mouth.

The days shortened, and a chilly rain began drizzling out of a perpetually clouded sky. The onset of winter in Raine was a dreary affair, indeed—made worse by the fact that the lessons with Mistress Ainya had ended for the season.

"We'll resume in the spring," she'd said, her eyes crinkling in a smile. "Don't fret, Rose. The winter will pass quickly enough."

It didn't, though. Even rambling with Neeve in the wet forest did little to lift my spirits. We had only a handful of hours, at most, before the sun set behind the lid of gray clouds overhead. Damp gloom lay thickly beneath the trees. No more hobnies appeared to revile us, and even Thorne seemed quiet and distant.

"Winter is upon us," he said one afternoon, as we sheltered from the rain beneath the thick canopy of a cedar tree. "While I'm gone, the two of you must remain inside the castle."

He waved his hand, banishing the illusion of a butterfly he'd been causing to flit through the air.

"You're leaving?" I asked with a stab of dismay.

Neeve shot him a glance. "A little rain won't bother me. I'm perfectly safe on my own in the Darkwood."

"You are," he said. "But Rose is not."

My stepsister glared at me. "Then I'll come alone."

"You can't leave me behind," I replied hotly.

"No," Thorne said. "I don't trust you to be sensible about this, Rose. And I dare not set an enchantment upon you, after what happened last time. So, both of you are forbidden from the forest until I return."

Neeve looked furious, but I ignored her and turned to Thorne. "Where are you going?"

"I have duties to attend to," he said evasively.

"Where?"

"Must you constantly annoy Thorne with your questions?" Neeve jumped to her feet. "I wish you'd go back where you came from, and never return."

She stalked away, her black cloak swirling with the force of her footsteps. I curled into myself, feeling as though I'd breathed in a mouthful of rain.

"Why does she have to be so unkind?" I asked.

Thorne let out a low breath. "It is difficult for her."

"For *her*?" The first edge of temper heated my face. I preferred it to sorrow. "I never asked for this. I never wanted to come to this dreary country anyway. I hate it here."

"Do you?" His eyes were sad. "I never told you about the meaning of Neeve's scrying that day you both saw the images in Airgid Tarn."

"No." I folded my arms. "You didn't."

He glanced into the trees, where Neeve's form was a sulky shadow, then back at me. "You're not here by accident, Rose. Your fate is bound up with the Darkwood in some manner, and with your stepsister as well."

I thought back to the glowing vision: the sight of Neeve and I facing one another in what had looked like battle.

"Will we have to fight one another?" It wasn't a pleasant thought.

"Perhaps." His mouth tightened. "But scrying is not always literal. The two of you might end up at odds, without coming to magical blows."

"So you think I have magic?" I unfolded my arms and leaned toward him. "Is that what the scrying meant?"

He sighed. "I told you, the meanings are not always clear."

"Well, that's no help." A fat drop of water landed on my cheek from the rain-drenched branches overhead. I brushed it away and scowled up at the sky. "Is the sun ever going to come out?"

"It will." He gave me a small smile. "But you won't have to be out in the rain. Spend the next few months cozy beside the fire, reading, and celebrate the turn of the season with joy."

"How do you know I like to sit by the fire and read?" I shot him a suspicious look. "Are you spying on me?"

The faintest flush rose on his high cheekbones. "It is my duty to look after all the creatures of the Darkwood."

"I'm not a creature." And I didn't like being lumped in with the hobnies and boglins, the scolding squirrels and flittering birds.

"You are connected to the future of this place," he said. "And to Neeve."

"Do you spy on her, too?" I glanced at her dim shape, still stalking about beneath the cedar trees.

"She is my charge," he said calmly.

I'd always known Neeve was special to him, and I hated the spur of jealousy kicking my belly. I was special to no one. As the months passed, Mama became even more attentive to the king—and to her own vanity—and did not pay me much heed.

Miss Groves liked me well enough, I thought, but I was no dearer to her than Neeve was. And Mistress Ainya had been Neeve's teacher first. At the *cailleach*'s cottage I always felt like the simpleton, the taga-long, catching any crumbs that might fall my way.

"Don't look so sad." Thorne ruffled my hair. "I'll be back in time for your birthday."

I squinted up at him. "How do you know when it is?"

"I don't know, precisely, but you are a child of the light. I'd guess the day you were born falls soon after the first of May, when the roses are just beginning to bloom."

"It's the ninth of May. Do they even celebrate birthdays here in Raine?"

"Of course we do." Neeve had wandered back over to where we stood. "In fact, *my* birthday is very soon."

If I was a child of the light, as Thorne had said, then of course Neeve was a child of the darkness. It made sense that she was born in the black of winter.

"When is it?" I asked, somewhat reluctantly.

"Next week, before the Yule celebrations begin. Which makes me a half a year older than you." She gave me a superior look.

I did a quick calculation in my head. "It does not! There's only five months between us." More or less.

Very well, *more*, but only by a week or so.

"Speaking of birthdays," Thorne said, "here is your present, Neeve."

He pulled a silk-wrapped bundle out of his pocket and handed it to her.

"Thank you," she said solemnly, and tucked it away into her cloak.

I was burning for her to open it that minute, but clearly she was going to wait.

"Won't people ask where it came from, if you open it with your other presents?" I asked, in a transparent attempt to coax her to reveal it right away.

"No." She gave me a thin-lipped smile. "Your curiosity will have to bide."

If I'd not been there, I suspected she would have opened her present in front of Thorne. But this way she could aggravate me, which she probably enjoyed as much as any gift made of silver or gold.

"You'd best be on your way," Thorne said, tilting his head. "I will see you after the sun's balance swings back into the sky."

Whatever that meant. I held tightly to the thought that it would be before my birthday, at any rate.

"Be well, *Galadhir*," Neeve said, giving him a regal dip of her head. "We shall await your return."

"Princess." He bowed, his cloak swirling.

Sudden grief stung my eyes, and I could not be nearly so poised as my stepsister. First Mistress Ainya, now Thorne. I'd just gotten used to my new life in Raine, and now I was losing everything again. Everything except my stepsister, who I'd trade for Thorne in a heartbeat.

The winter was going to be extremely tedious.

"Goodbye," I said, trying to keep the wretchedness from my voice, and not succeeding.

"Rose." He touched my cheek. "It won't be long."

Then he turned, soft as mist, and strode away into the Darkwood.

CHAPTER 16

Despite my unhappiness at being cooped up in Castle Raine every afternoon, there were some bright spots. Miss Groves pointed me toward several interesting books in the library, and I finally had a chance to explore the halls and winding staircases of the castle to my satisfaction.

I didn't discover anything of great interest in the rooms, but at least I no longer became lost in the dim passageways. There was one parlor filled with dusty musical instruments—including a stringless harp—that I intended to visit again, and a study that held a strange collection of stuffed animal heads on the walls. Their dead glass eyes seemed to watch me, and I left after a brief inspection.

Warned that Neeve's birthday was coming, I made her a painstaking watercolor of a bouquet of lavender. Miss Groves helped, as I did not count painting among my skills. At the end, I had a serviceable enough picture to give Neeve.

My stepsister was still in the habit of coming to fetch me when the dinner gong rang. Since her prickly company was better than nothing, I didn't tell her I could finally find my way down to the dining room without help. She probably knew as much, but as long as neither of us spoke of it, we could continue going down together.

On her birthday, when I opened my door to her knock, I noticed the silver pendant she wore—a circle of twined vines, with tiny red rubies winking in the dim light.

"Is that Thorne's gift?" I asked, closing my door behind me.

"Yes." She glanced over her shoulder, then held the necklace out for my inspection.

I leaned forward to admire it. The rubies sparkled like tiny drops of blood at the ends of delicately spiked silver thorns.

"It's rather gruesome," I said. "Do you like it?"

Offended, she pulled the pendant back. "Of course I do. There is no workmanship to rival that of the dark—that is, the makers of this necklace."

"The dark what?" I stared intently at her, willing her to answer.

"Nothing." She tucked the pendant beneath the neckline of her black velvet dress.

Whatever the dark *something* were, I'd wager my last Parnesian gold coin that Thorne was one of them. And possibly Neeve as well, though the more I learned, the more of a puzzle she became.

"What's that?" She nodded at the wrapped painting tucked under my arm.

"Your birthday present."

She blinked, as though surprised I had a gift for her. "Oh."

The dinner gong sounded again, and we hurried through the halls. The king demanded punctuality, although most nights he completely ignored the presence of two girls at his dinner table. Either his advisors monopolized his attention—which Mama did not like at all—or his new queen did. His daughter was often spoken to as an afterthought, and he almost never had anything to say to me.

Tonight, though, Neeve's presence was the focus of dinner.

The birthday celebration was nothing grand, though the cook had made Neeve's favorite foods and, for once, her father seemed to show an interest in her studies. Mama was at her best, keeping the conversation lively and drawing everyone's participation. It was one of her talents, when she was moved to employ it, and had made her a celebrated hostess back when we lived in Parnese.

I was relieved to see there was a cake for dessert. It tasted almost as good as the confections made by Parnesian bakers—a light almond pastry dusted with sugar and topped with apricot jam.

"And now for the presents," Lord Raine said. "Arabelle, would you like to lead off?"

Mama produced two gifts wrapped in ornate gold paper. They proved to be a bottle of jasmine-scented perfume and scarlet hair ribbons.

"Thank you," Neeve said, though I could tell she had no interest in either smelling like a flowering bush or tying up her long black hair with fancy ribbons.

I gave her my painting, and she seemed to appreciate it well enough. At least she didn't make disparaging comments about the clumsiness of the lines.

"And now for my gift to you," the king said, with a smile.

He clapped his hands twice, and a servant appeared, carrying something bulky covered with a cloth. The man set it on the table in front of Neeve. She stared at it warily, until the servant pulled the cloth off, revealing a beautifully crafted leather saddle.

"Oh," she breathed.

"You are now of an age—and a height—to manage a real horse," Lord Raine said. "No more ponies for you, my girl. It's time to ride as a princess does. Would you like to go down to the stables and see your new mount?"

Neeve nodded, her eyes shining. "That would be the best present in the world."

"Don't catch a chill," my mother said. "I'll send the servants to fetch your cloaks."

"Aren't we going?" I asked her. Although I hadn't been much in the company of horses, I was curious to see Neeve's present.

Mama wrinkled her nose. "If you wish to accompany them to the stables, you may, though I shall stay behind. My lord?"

The king tipped his head. "If Rose wants to come along, she is welcome to do so."

Mama shot me a look, and I dropped Lord Raine a belated curtsey of thanks. Our cloaks were brought, and then we went out into the cold night. The courtyard looked strange in the light of the flickering torches mounted on the walls, and the damp air curled into my lungs, making me want to cough.

It was warmer in the stables, though they stank of manure and wet animals. I followed the king and Neeve a bit warily, peering at the stalls as we went past. Some of the horses watched us go by; some seemed intent on their dinner. Halfway down the long row of stalls, the king halted.

"Her name is Peerless," he said, gesturing to the black mare gazing at us from over her stall door. "Happy birthday, Neeve."

"She's beautiful." My stepsister went up to the horse and held out her hand, palm up. The mare snuffled at her skin, then let out a satisfied snort.

I hung back, apprehensive.

"What do you think?" Lord Raine asked, glancing at me as though he'd just recalled my presence.

"She's... very tall." I couldn't keep the doubt from my voice.

"Perhaps a little," he said. "But Neeve is a skilled rider. She'll grow into those stirrups soon enough. What about you, Rose? Do you like to ride?"

Mama and I hadn't done much riding in Parnese. She preferred to be drawn about in a carriage, and I'd only ridden twice, both times while visiting a friend who lived on the outskirts of the city. It wasn't something I showed any aptitude for. I recalled that when the huge horse I was perched on broke into a trot, I'd been frightened almost to tears.

However, I could tell that horsemanship was a skill prized by the king and my stepsister, and so my answer was not as truthful as it ought to have been.

"I do, my lord," I said. "Though I haven't been on horseback for at least a year."

He gave me an approving look. "It's not a skill you forget. Perhaps you'd like to go out with Neeve on her morning rides. I'm sure one of the ponies here will do."

"Ah..." I glanced at my stepsister. She was leaning close to her new mount, but her skeptical eyes were on me.

"I believe Rose prefers to sleep until our lessons begin," she said.

"Hmm." Lord Raine's expression cooled. "Nonetheless, it should not be said that my stepdaughter is lacking in the skills necessary for a noblewoman. It's time you reacquainted yourself with riding, Rose."

"Yes, my lord." I bobbed him a curtsey, for what else could I do?

"It is rather dark in the mornings now, Father," Neeve said. "Perhaps we could ride directly after lunch. If it's not too much trouble for the stable hands."

"An excellent thought. Now, say good night to your horse. It's time to go in."

As we trailed after him, I shot my stepsister a look—half gratitude for setting the hour later, half annoyance that I'd been pressed into riding at all.

But there was no help for it. When the king commanded, his subjects obeyed—no matter how reluctant they might be.

CHAPTER 17

And so, my riding lessons began. I was given a dumpy white pony named Snowbell, who had to break into an undignified, lurching trot from time to time, just to keep up with Neeve and the long-legged Peerless.

At first we went around and around the paddock inside the castle walls. The dirt churned to mud, which clung to the horses' legs and the hems of our riding habits. On the second day my bottom was uncomfortably bruised, and by the fourth afternoon it was all I could do to cling desperately to the saddle and wish the torture was at an end.

"You're terrible at this," Neeve remarked in an even voice.

"I know," I said miserably.

"Maybe you should give it up."

"I can't." I was wise enough to know the king would be most unhappy if I failed to become any sort of horsewoman.

Neeve frowned down at me from her perch on Peerless's back. "Is there anything you're good at?"

"Reading," I said. "And I can play the harp."

Despite my maimed pinky. Luckily, that finger wasn't used to play the instrument at all—as I'd learned during the one and only lesson I'd been able to wheedle out of Mama.

"You don't even *have* a harp."

"I used to."

One of the Parnesian courtiers had given us a lap harp when I was young. It had been only decorative, adorning our mantel until I'd taken the notion to play it. I'd plucked about on the strings for nearly three years. Sadly, the harp had broken when one of Mama's friends, clumsy with drink, had stumbled against it and knocked it over.

I was not talented enough for her to replace it, she'd said. More to the point, we couldn't afford to, and I'd wished my mother had just admitted as much without adding extra insult to my sorrow. Bad enough to lose my instrument, but to be accused of a lack of musicianship stung.

Especially as it wasn't true.

"There's a harp in one of the unused parlors," I said, trying not to let Snowbell's jolting knock the teeth from my head. "I saw it there a few weeks ago. Along with a pile of other instruments."

"I didn't even know that the castle had a music room." Neeve sounded quite uninterested in the fact.

"It's rather dusty." Obviously, my stepsister was not the only one who didn't pay any attention to the music parlor.

I'd noted the harp with a sort of wistful melancholy, but had not thought I could do anything about it. I had no notion of where to procure strings for it, or who might assist me. Neeve's unkind question, though, caused sudden desire to flare up. Perhaps the harp could be salvaged. Then I could show her—show the whole castle—that I had at least *one* talent to my name.

"Ow!" I said as Snowbell lurched into another trot, wincing as my bruised backside slapped against the saddle.

Neeve laughed. "Don't hunch forward so. Sit back, with your spine straight. Let your body move with the horse's gait."

Biting my lip, I tried to do as she said, but it wasn't that simple—especially as my legs were burning with soreness.

I was grateful when the stable master beckoned for us to bring our mounts back.

"Keep trying," Neeve said. "You'll master it, eventually."

It was so unlike her to give encouragement that I sent her a startled glance. "Thank you."

She was busy with Peerless's mane, plaiting the coarse, dark strands into a braid, and did not meet my eyes or acknowledge my words. Perhaps she was feeling sorry for accusing me of having no talents whatsoever.

I resolved to change that perception.

At dinner that night, perched gingerly on my chair, I brought up the matter of the harp. Mama allowed that I was a passable player, and I tried not to glare at her for the faint praise. The king said he saw nothing wrong with my using it, and promised to dispatch someone to do any necessary repairs and deliver the harp to me.

I thanked Lord Raine, but didn't expect him to keep his promise in any kind of timely manner. Yet only two days later, to my surprise, a tall gentleman with a fringe of gray beard appeared at the door of the schoolroom, holding the little harp in his arms.

"I beg your pardon for interrupting," he said to Miss Groves. "I believe your newest student is in want of this instrument?"

Our teacher smiled and beckoned. "Don't stand out in the hall, Master Fawkes. Come in, come in. What a pleasure to see you. I take it you've returned to the castle for the rest of the winter?"

I listened wide-eyed, trying to piece together who, precisely, this fellow was. Neeve folded her arms and sat back in her chair.

"Good morning, Miss Neeve," Master Fawkes said, gently setting the harp down on the teacher's desk. "I hope you continued your studies on the flute while I was away."

Neeve mumbled something that sounded like assent, and I tried not to stare at her. I'd never heard my stepsister mumble, let alone tell something suspiciously like a lie. Laughter bubbled up inside me, along with the joyful possibility that I'd finally found one thing I could do better.

"Rose," Miss Groves said, "this is Master Fawkes. He is Raine's foremost bard, and spends much of the year traveling, playing and singing and gathering the news from all about Raine and the Continent. We are graced with his company from Yule until early spring."

I stood and made him a curtsey. "Pleased to meet you, Master Fawkes."

"Likewise," he said, giving me a slanted smile. "I'd like to hear your stories, Miss Rose. It was rather a surprise to discover the king had married."

For him and me, both.

"I'm free tomorrow afternoon," I said, grateful for the excuse to avoid jolting about the paddock on Snowbell's increasingly hard back.

Neeve gave a slight snort, but didn't say anything.

"Excellent." Master Fawkes tipped his head at the harp. "You can show me what you know on this instrument, as well."

"I've mostly taught myself," I said, suddenly shy about my abilities. What if I were not as talented as I'd thought? Would the bard take the harp away?

"Don't worry, Rose," Miss Groves said. "Whatever your skill, I'm sure Master Fawkes will be happy to teach you. He's a skilled musician on any number of instruments."

"Even the harp?" Hope fluttered in me like a newly lit candle flame.

"Yes," he said. "And the lute, and the vielle. I also sing, of course. And play the flute." This last was said with a pointed glance at Neeve.

"Would you truly give me lessons?" I tried not to sound too excited at the prospect, despite my anticipation.

While I loved to read, there was a part of me that was restless for something more, and not just the things I was learning in Miss Groves' classroom. No matter how interesting the subject matter—and at times, it truly was engrossing—it was still *school*.

Playing the harp would help fill the empty hours each afternoon when I pined for Mistress Ainya's garden and Thorne's company in the Darkwood. Even though I was a poor student of magic, and knew very little about the forest, I missed my summer adventures fiercely.

"You'll still have to learn to ride," Neeve said. "Even someone as clumsy on horseback as you are must master it eventually."

"I will," I told her. But the excuse of music lessons would spare my poor backside for at least one or two afternoons a week.

"Very good," Master Fawkes said. "Here's the tuning key for the harp. I'll see you in my tower tomorrow after luncheon."

He handed me the T-shaped piece of metal, and I guessed that putting the instrument properly in tune was the first test. This one, however, I felt more than adequate to, unlike trying to sort lentils and beans into two flawless piles.

"Where is your tower?" I asked.

"Neeve will show you." He glanced at my stepsister. "After Rose's lesson, I expect to hear how you've progressed on the flute, hm?"

"Yes, Master Fawkes," she said. Though her words were accommodating, there was a rebellious look in her eyes.

I wondered what trouble she was planning, and hoped it would not involve me too greatly.

CHAPTER 18

The next morning, before I was even fully awake, a ghastly noise filtered down the corridor and into my bedroom.

"By the Twins, what is that sound?" I asked Sorche, who had come into the room to poke up the fire and light the lamp.

I seldom swore, but the noise was dreadful—a shrieking squawk that sounded as though someone was murdering a chicken in the hallway.

The maid frowned. "It's Miss Neeve, practicing her flute."

"Oh dear." I burst out laughing, though there was a horrified edge to it. "She really is dreadful, isn't she?"

Sorche wound her hands in her apron. "It's not for me to say, Miss Rose."

Her voice was choked, and I couldn't tell if she was trying not to laugh at the sound, or holding back tears of pain.

It certainly was agonizing—and getting worse by the minute. I jumped out of bed, bare feet cold on the stone floor, and wrenched open my door.

"Quiet!" I yelled, little caring who heard me, as long as Neeve stopped mangling the air with the breathy shrieks of her flute.

Blessedly, the noise stopped. Then, down the hall, Neeve's door opened and she poked her head out.

"Good morning," she said placidly. "I thought we might perform a duet for the Yule Feast. I'll suggest it to Master Fawkes at my lesson today."

I gaped at her until she shut her door, questions crowding into my thoughts so quickly I could not give voice to any of them. What was the importance of the Yule Feast? Why did Neeve want to play a duet? Was she truly as tone-deaf as she sounded, or was she merely pretending?

"Come back inside, miss," Sorche said. "I've laid your dress out, and you ought to put on socks, at the very least."

"She can't be serious," I said, trudging back to my bedroom.

But I very much feared she was.

Both of us were distracted during Miss Groves' lecture that morning. Finally, the teacher raised her hands in exasperation and told us to choose whatever we wanted to do next, as long as it was somewhat scholarly. I happily dove back into the pages of the novel I was reading, and Neeve opened her sketchbook and began drawing plants.

After lunch, we walked back to the hallway housing our rooms.

"Give me a few minutes," I said, pausing at my door. "I need to make sure the harp is still in tune from last night."

It had taken nearly an hour to bring the two dozen strings to pitch. When I got to the highest ones, I'd gone extra carefully, for fear of breaking them.

"What a foolish instrument," Neeve said with a toss of her head. "My flute is much easier to tune."

I bit my tongue and refrained from pointing out that, the way she played, it didn't matter if her flute was on pitch or not. Nobody would be able to tell, when she began screeching away.

Luckily, the harp had stayed in tune—mostly. I tweaked the strings that had gone flat, then tucked the instrument under my arm and went to join Neeve.

She led me down a few corridors then opened a heavy door that had previously been locked. I glimpsed stairs winding up and realized we were at the east turret of the castle.

"Does Master Fawkes live in the tower?" I asked as we started up the steps.

"When he's at the castle, yes." Neeve led me up the circling staircase. "The rest of the time, his rooms are shut up."

At the top of the stairs was a wide landing and another of Castle Raine's ornately carved doors, propped open. This one, of course, depicted musical instruments. In the room beyond, I glimpsed plush carpets and an array of instruments: lutes of various sizes hanging on the walls, a vielle, an assortment of flutes laid out on a table, and a harp that could be the sister of the one I carried.

"Come in," Master Fawkes called.

I followed Neeve over the threshold, blinking at the clutter. Books were piled precariously along the curved edges of the walls, with pages of notes spread around them. His workbench was jammed with bits of wood, tangled metal, and various tools. The large desk to the right of the door was nearly hidden by stacks of paper, more books, writing implements, and a rather mangy stuffed owl.

The room smelled of leather and ink and the lemony scent of wood polish. I inhaled deeply.

"I would like to play a duet with Rose," Neeve announced, without preamble.

"Would you?" The bard looked at her, his mouth pinching at the corners.

"Yes. For the Yule Feast."

"Hmm." Master Fawkes turned to me. "Let's see what you can do, Rose, shall we?"

He moved a pile of music manuscripts off one of several straight-backed chairs in the room, and gestured for me to sit.

Trying to calm my suddenly galloping heartbeat, I settled on the woven rush seat of the chair and perched the harp on my knees. I leaned the top of the instrument against my right shoulder and plucked a tentative chord.

I shot a glance at the bard. Eyebrows raised, he nodded at me to continue. Beside him, Neeve crossed her arms, her flute case gripped tightly in one hand.

Pretend you're not here, I told myself, trying instead to imagine the light-filled parlor of our old apartment in Parnese. Slowly, my right hand moved over the strings, playing one of the simple melodies my mother had used to hum when I was little and couldn't sleep. I fumbled a few notes here and there, but the second time through the tune I felt secure enough to start adding some accompaniment with my left hand—a few bass notes, a light scatter of chords.

I played the melody twice more. Not perfectly, I thought, but well enough for someone who hadn't practiced the harp for over a year. When I was done, I looked up from the strings, hoping for Master Fawkes' approval.

"Good." He smiled at me and came to stand at my side. "Your technique needs work, but you've got the basic principles well enough. Now, put your thumb higher on the string, and try dropping your fingers down from that point..."

We worked on my hand position for a time, while Neeve sullenly looked on. Master Fawkes demonstrated a few rolling chords and a quick counterpoint, and I watched intently, trying to follow along.

"Have you got that?" he asked.

"I think so." I shook out my right hand, then tried to copy what he'd just shown me.

"Close enough." He gave me an encouraging nod. "Practice that, up and down the strings, for your next lesson."

"Will you teach me a new tune?" I asked. Exercises were all very well, but I was tired of rote drudgery in all my lessons. Lentils and beans, the succession of the Kings of Raine, and now musical scales. The dreariness was going to suffocate me.

The bard glanced at my stepsister. "Put your flute together, Neeve, and we'll determine what the two of you might play for the feast. Do you remember the 'Island Boat Song'?"

My stepsister laid her case on the cluttered table, opened it, and fitted the mouthpiece of her flute onto the body. A frown between her dark brows, she brought it to her mouth and blew.

A squawk emerged from the flute—joined by an affronted screech. The owl, apparently *not* stuffed, opened its gray wings and flew up into the rafters of the turret. Neeve stopped playing and the bird glared down at us, its eyes glowing orange from the shadows.

Master Fawkes let out a barely audible sigh, then turned to my stepsister.

"Try again," he said. "It would be best if you covered the entirety of the holes with your fingers this time."

As the lesson progressed, Neeve grew marginally better. Finally, something resembling an actual melody emerged from her flute. Biting my lip in concentration, I tried to pick out the notes of the tune on my harp. It was a challenge to distinguish the flow of the melody from Neeve's squeaks and halting pauses, but I did my best.

The result was very unmusical—as though a frog and a canary had been harnessed together to pull a tiny carriage, and were making a shambles of it.

"Good," Master Fawkes said after a time, though it wasn't. "We'll try again tomorrow afternoon. It is my hope we can prepare you adequately to perform for the Yule Feast."

"Um, when *is* the feast?" I asked, hoping we had at least a week to practice. Ideally, several weeks.

"Tomorrow night," Neeve said, taking her flute apart and shoving it back in its case.

I blinked at her, my heart contracting with apprehension.

"That soon?" We'd never be ready.

"Indeed." Master Fawkes gave me a pained look. "I'm certain the rehearsal tomorrow will go much better."

I doubted it.

CHAPTER 19

The Yule Feast was the first large celebration I'd seen at Castle Raine. Unlike the rulers of Parnese, Lord Raine did not seem to care much for hosting events. Since my mother and I arrived, there had been no balls, no feasts, no parties—which contributed to the dreariness of the castle even more.

Now, though, the great hall glowed with light. Lamps were placed around the room and on the feasting tables, and two huge chandeliers hung from the ceiling, studded with hundreds of candles. Tapestries covered the walls, depicting murky scenes of battles interspersed with nobles riding through a dark forest and feasting in a hall that looked very much like the one at Castle Raine.

There was no food on the tables yet. Before the meal began, the guests must be formally greeted by the king and his daughter. And apparently by his new wife and stepdaughter as well. The four of us were seated on a stone dais at the far end of the hall, Neeve and I placed to the side and slightly behind our respective parent.

I tried not to fidget, but it was difficult. The chair I perched on was hard, not softened by cushions as the king's and queen's were, and the procession of people coming forward barely glanced at me. I was hot in my new gown. The stiff brocade at the sleeves and neck itched my skin, and when no one was looking, I surreptitiously scratched my wrists.

It didn't help that Neeve seemed perfectly composed, her face serene, her hands peacefully clasped in her lap. Drat it—she had been raised to be a princess, while I'd never imagined myself in such a position.

The parade of strangers continued, most taking no note of me, while staring openly at Mama. I entertained myself by telling stories about them in my head, each one more foolish than the last, until I had to choke back my amusement. Neeve flicked her gaze to me, one brow rising in reproof. With great restraint, I managed not to stick my tongue out at her.

Finally, I saw a familiar face as Mistress Ainya came forward to bow to the king. She sent me a warm look, and for a moment I almost felt as though I belonged.

Master Fawkes was in the hall, too, along with Miss Groves. They stood in a line along the side wall with all the other people who served in the castle. Sorche was there as well. She met my eyes and gave me a little fluttering wave with her fingers. So, I was not entirely a stranger in the castle.

Finally, the last guest made his greetings—an emissary in an ornately fur-trimmed tunic, from the kingdom to the north. It was called Fiorland, I now knew from my studies with Miss Groves. Raine and Fiorland had been allies for centuries, and the kings respected one another's lands and rule.

In fact, Miss Groves had said it was not uncommon for the countries to exchange fosterlings—usually extra siblings who were not direct heirs to the throne.

"I don't have to go, do I?" I'd asked her, my heart thudding with fear at the possibility of being sent away to an even more remote country than Raine.

"Of course not." Neeve had given me one of her superior looks. "You're not of royal blood."

"Don't worry, Rose." Miss Groves had patted my shoulder. "If anything, the king of Fiorland will send one of his sons here. I understand he has a surplus. His youngest is, I believe, around the same age as you and Neeve."

"Then he wouldn't come for two years yet," Neeve had said. "Fosterlings must be fifteen."

"It's not certain he'd come at all. Now, let's look at those sums in your notebooks, shall we?"

I'd nearly forgotten that conversation, until seeing the Fiorlander emissary. Now I wondered, would he and King Tobin speak of a possible fosterling? If a prince came to Raine, would life in the castle be better, or worse? At least I wouldn't be the newcomer anymore. In principle, I decided I liked the idea.

The emissary bowed and left the dais, and the king rose to address his guests.

"Thank you, all, for coming to celebrate the turning of the year," he said. "You do your country, and your new queen, much honor. Now, let the festivities begin."

He clapped his hands, and servants bearing ewers of wine and platters of food began circling the tables.

I rose with a sigh and followed Mama to the places set at the head table for the royal family. It was going to be an evening of utter boredom—at least until the terrifying moment when Neeve and I were to perform our duet. In the meantime, I had no one to talk to. I was seated at the edge of the table, with Mama on my left. The king was beside her, and then Neeve on his other side. I never thought I'd miss my stepsister's company so much.

We faced the large room, presumably so that Lord Raine could look benevolently down upon his subjects. At least I had a good view of Master Fawkes and the small group of musicians he'd gathered to provide entertainment while the guests ate. They were seated in the musicians' gallery: a small balcony on the second floor, above and to the left of where we sat. Master Fawkes' fingers were nimble on his lute, accompanying the lilt of the vielle and the soft tap of a hand drum. I had to admit they were fine players, and their tunes drifted gaily through the air.

In comparison, Neeve and I were going to sound dreadful.

My belly clutched at the thought of the performance to come, and my appetite fled.

"Must we play tonight?" I'd asked at the end of the rehearsal that afternoon. Neeve and I had made no better progress, and the result of our duet was painful to listen to.

"I'm afraid so." Master Fawkes had given me a sorrowful look. "It's tradition that the king and queen's children entertain the guests at the end of the meal. It's supposed to be a showcase of their talents."

I'd glanced at Neeve. "What did you do last year?"

"I recited a poem I'd written."

"Why don't you do that again? I'd be happy to sit out."

"You can't sit out," Neeve said.

"Why not?"

"Because you are required to perform," Master Fawkes said. "Did no one tell you this?"

"No." I gritted my teeth, then glared at Neeve. "You might have said something."

I guessed Mama had been supposed to tell me, but she was too flighty. And no one else had seen fit to mention it.

My stepsister shrugged. "I thought you knew. Besides, I was helping you by offering to play together."

Helping? It was difficult for me to fathom that she couldn't hear how absolutely horrible our attempt at making music sounded.

"Can't we change?" I asked. "I can play alone, and you can recite another poem. Or something."

She shook her head. "You know as well as I that our parents are expecting us to perform together."

"That's only because you told them so at dinner last night." I set my harp down on the cluttered floor and crossed my arms.

Neeve gave me an exasperated look. "Because my father asked what we were doing for the feast. Really, Rose, you're making such a fuss out of nothing."

Now, I tried to swallow back the lump of apprehension in my throat. Humiliating myself in front of the entire castle wasn't *nothing*. I couldn't decide if Neeve truly was tone-deaf, or was aware that she was a terrible musician and simply didn't care. In either case, there was no escape from the dreadful performance.

And now the time was approaching. I stopped pushing my uneaten food about on my plate and sat back, trying to conquer my rising nerves.

My fingers were cold. I wound my linen napkin around them, threading the cloth around my hands and wishing I could disappear.

Finally, the plates were removed. My stomach knotted. Between the main meal and the dessert course was when the royal offspring performed. I wished I could sink beneath the table, hide there under the tablecloth and perform some spell so that everyone would forget my existence.

Lord Raine pushed his heavy wooden chair back and stood. It didn't take long for the guests to quiet. Once they did, he held his hand out, gesturing for Neeve to rise, then turned to me. Feeling the weight of everyone's stares, I stood up.

"We are delighted to present my daughter, Neeve, and her new stepsister, Rose," the king said. "They will now play a duet for your enjoyment."

Stiffly, I stepped to the space cleared in front of the head table. Neeve joined me from the other side, her face as pale and serene as usual.

A servant approached with my harp. For a fierce moment I hoped he would trip and smash the instrument, so that I might be saved. Unfortunately, he delivered it safely into my arms, then went to fetch me a chair. Another liveried fellow handed Neeve her flute.

As we settled, the great hall hushed. Neeve blew a breathy squeak into her flute in a semblance of tuning. I dropped my head, pretending to busy myself with the strings of the harp. Oh, this was going to be so painful.

I could tell everyone was wondering about me, and about my mother, of course—the beautiful foreigner who had managed to capture the king's hand so quickly in marriage. I imagined we weren't looked upon kindly by the general populace. My chance to make a good impression was about to be hopelessly ruined.

A kernel of anger stirred in my belly.

"Ready?" Neeve asked softly.

No. But I couldn't continue to sit there, pretending to tune the harp all night. I gave her a tight nod.

She counted, then began to play in a different tempo. Clenching my jaw, I plucked a chord, trying to match my timing to hers.

Perhaps she was nervous, for her playing was worse than ever. Over half the sounds Neeve produced on her flute were shrieks and breathy squawks. I heard someone smother a chuckle, and a high-pitched titter came from one of the far tables.

The heat in my stomach flared into outright rage, hot pressure building in my chest. My pinky stub throbbed in time with my heartbeat, aching.

How dare they laugh. These stupid denizens of Raine, with their horrible, dark winters and their dreary old castle!

I flicked my fingers hard, pulling the harp strings in an angry arpeggio. Neeve gave me a startled look over the top of her flute, but I frowned at her and yanked another handful of notes from my instrument. Why did Mama bring me here, only to ignore me? Why hadn't she left me in Parnese, where I belonged? I hated this place. Hated it with all my heart.

"Fire!" someone yelled.

I glanced around to see that the tapestries on the wall behind us were burning, flames leaping up the cloth. The acrid smell of smoke stung my nose, and I watched, aghast, as the fire reached for the timbered ceiling of the hall.

Neeve lowered her flute mid-phrase. "Rose, stop it!" she cried.

Her voice was lost in the general panic as guests overturned the tables and stampeded for the door. I stopped playing and leaped up, heart thudding. Should I run for safety, too?

Before my clamoring thoughts could decide, Neeve threw her flute aside and lifted her hands. They were outlined in blue fire.

"*Heleg!*" she shouted.

Impossibly, tiny shards of ice began to fall from the ceiling. Like snow, but thicker. The ice stung my upturned face.

Someone was chanting over the sound of a lute. White light flashed. The flames snuffed out, and the ice turned to blue petals dropping softly, like dry rain, over the shambles of the feasting tables.

I blinked. The people scrambling for the doors slowed, turned. Quiet music twined around every breathing soul in the hall. I could *feel*

it, soothing, calming. Shading the memory of what had happened. I
shook my head sharply.

"Honored guests," the king called, standing and holding up his
hands. "I'm sorry our little illusion this evening was a bit *too* convinc-
ing! Please, resume your seats. There is no fire, no cause for concern."
He gestured to the tapestries on the wall. They were singed around the
edges, the tops blackened, but he spoke truly. They were no longer
ablaze.

"The servants are about to bring out the dessert course," the king
continued. "Please, take advantage of my hospitality. The kitchens
have outdone themselves with the spiced pastry swans—and the honey
mead."

He gestured urgently to the liveried servants. Looking rather
dazed, some of them righted the overturned chairs and benches, while
the rest dashed for the kitchens. The guests milled about, finally
taking their seats again. Through it all, the calming music did its work.

Mere illusion, it whispered. *All is well. Sit. Feast.*

Numbly, I went back to my chair, still carrying my harp. In the
musicians' gallery, I could just make out Master Fawkes playing the
lute. His expression was strained. Mistress Ainya stood behind him,
her hands on his shoulders, and then I knew who it was that had put
the evening aright.

But how had it gone so dreadfully wrong?

The stub of my pinky throbbed, and I couldn't help feeling that,
somehow, I'd been responsible for the fire. But how could that be? I
had no power.

Beside me, my mother laughed at something the king said. There
was a brittle edge to the sound, and I glanced at her. She looked at me
then quickly away again, as if unwilling to acknowledge my presence. I
felt hollow inside.

The servants delivered plates of pastry to the head table, and I ate,
barely tasting the spices and sugar.

Finally, the Yule Feast came to an end. The king and my mother
stood near the door, bidding the guests farewell. Neeve and I were
excused from this duty. Gratefully, I turned to go to my rooms.

"Rose." Mistress Ainya hailed me as I went across the great hall, then beckoned me to join her.

I veered to where she stood beside the wall, next to Master Fawkes. Both of them looked weary beyond words.

"Thank you," I said to them. "I'm not sure what happened, but I know you set it to rights."

"Rather more excitement than we wanted," the bard said, his voice gravelly. He shot a glance at the herbwife, then back to me. "We'll be speaking with you about this soon. When you get back to your rooms, please set the events of the evening down in writing, in as much detail as you can manage."

I blinked at him. "But I didn't do anything."

He glanced at Mistress Ainya, then back to me. "It is exceedingly unlikely that you are at fault. But we would still like your impressions of what happened."

Mistress Ainya squinted at me. "There is a shadow of fate hanging over you, Rose. A pity I cannot read the shadows."

"Indeed." Master Fawkes patted her shoulder. "Come—I'll see you back to your cottage. We all need a bit of rest. Good night, Rose."

"Sleep well," I replied.

I returned to my rooms, wrote down what I remembered from the night's events, then went to bed. But despite the muddled exhaustion in my head, it took a long time for slumber to find me.

CHAPTER 20

The next day, Castle Raine was quiet. Miss Groves looked tired, and assigned us to doing sums, then reading history chapters for the entire morning.

"No need to give me that frown, Rose," she said. "It will settle your mind."

More like put me to sleep, I thought, despite my aching hand. It seemed I'd pulled a muscle in my left palm while playing, and the dull pain made me feel muzzy and irritable.

By the end of the morning, however, I did feel more clearheaded. The servants brought our lunch—stew and bread, as usual—and I was glad to put my books away.

"Did you enjoy the feast last night?" I asked Miss Groves, curious to hear her version of the evening's events.

Neeve slanted her gaze at me but said nothing as I waited for the teacher to reply.

"I did. We don't often get to see Master Fawkes perform illusion work—even though it went a bit awry."

"I wasn't sure if it was real or magic," I said. "In Parnese, nobody casts illusions."

At least, not any more. I shook my head, trying not to remember Pietro.

Miss Groves gave me a thoughtful look. "It's not spoken of widely, but for centuries the bards of Raine have created illusions through their songs and stories. Master Fawkes is one of the most talented bards we have had, if the histories can be believed. At the Yule Feast two years ago, he made a flock of doves fly through the great hall and disappear in a flash of golden light. It was lovely."

Interesting. I leaned forward and slurped up a spoonful of stew. If Miss Groves, whom I thought of as quite perceptive, didn't know that Neeve, and possibly myself, had been involved in the "illusion," then I supposed all was well.

"That reminds me," the teacher said. "I received word this morning that Master Fawkes will be resting for the next several days and has cancelled your music lessons. It takes a bit of energy to create illusions, as I understand."

And probably even more to put out flames and stop ice from falling from the ceiling. Not to mention soothing an entire hall full of feasters into thinking nothing alarming had happened.

"Just as well," Neeve said. "I cracked my flute when I dropped it on the floor last night. I'm afraid I won't be playing until it gets fixed."

She didn't sound very upset about it, and I wondered if her flute would stay broken forever. Honestly, I wouldn't mind if that were the case.

"Is Master Fawkes receiving visitors?" I asked Miss Groves.

She gave me an encouraging smile. "I don't know, but you can try."

LATER THAT AFTERNOON, I climbed the winding stairs up the turret to the bard's door. It was closed. I rapped softly with my knuckles, but no one came to answer, even after several minutes. With a sigh, I trudged back down to my gloomy rooms.

The next day, after lunch, I had better luck. Master Fawkes' door was slightly ajar. I peeked around it to see the bard sitting in his over-stuffed armchair before the messy desk. He looked tired, his face gaunt, his eyes shadowed. The owl, perched beside a stack of papers, swiveled its head and regarded me with its unblinking yellow gaze.

Master Fawkes, alerted by the owl, glanced up and saw me. "Rose. Come in."

I slipped into the room, hands twisted in my skirts. When I reached the edge of his desk I stood there awkwardly, unsure of what to say.

"I'm sorry you're not well," I finally managed.

He gave me a slight smile. "Thank you for your concern. Illusion work is tiring under the best of circumstances. And what happened at the feast was not, by any stretch, the best of circumstances."

The owl ruffled its feathers, as if in agreement, and I looked down at the floor. The events of that night were still swirling confusedly in my mind.

"Did you write down everything you recalled about the events of the feast?" he asked.

I nodded. "Should I bring you my notes?"

"Not just yet." He waved his hand wearily. "Later, when our lessons resume, I'll read them. Mistress Ainya told me you might have a bit of human magic. Perhaps, like myself, it is amplified through music."

Before Miss Groves had mentioned the power of the bards of Raine, I'd never heard of such a thing. Human magic enhanced by music? What would the followers of the Twin Gods make of such a thing?

"Ah, yes," he said, reading the confusion on my face. "I don't believe Parnese is acquainted with bardic magic—or, if it is, your musicians keep their secrets well."

"I don't know." The more time I spent in Raine, the less certain I was of everything—and I did not like it one bit.

"Then we shall see if you have a bent toward the bardic," Master Fawkes said, then let out a hollow sigh. "I must rest now. But as soon as I feel better, we'll make a comprehensive study of your playing and determine if you hold the power of both music and magic."

I nodded, a tickle of excitement shivering through me. If I'd awakened my power by playing music, wouldn't that be wonderful? Perhaps

I wouldn't have to wait until I turned fourteen to discover my magic, after all.

As soon as Master Fawkes felt recovered, I went eagerly to my harp lessons. Unfortunately, the next few weeks proved only that I was a good harp player—and nothing more. The bard set me a number of experiments while I played, including dwelling on my pent-up unhappiness at being forced to move to Raine. Nothing happened, except that I spent two days moping about in misery, with an aching hand and a headache from staring at tinder all afternoon and trying to light it on fire with my mind.

"I am sorry," the bard said a month later, after yet another unsuccessful attempt to spark magic from me via my harp playing. "You do not have the bardic power, Rose. If there's any magic in you, music is not the way to draw it out."

"Then what *is*?" I wanted to cry with frustration. I so wanted to have magic. To be special.

He shook his head. "I don't know. But you *do* have a musical touch, and our lessons will continue. Without, of course, any more attempts at magic."

I nodded blankly at him. My only hope to prove I had sorcerous talent now lay with Mistress Ainya, and the fast-approaching date of my fourteenth birthday. Either that, or perhaps the magic of the Darkwood would somehow seep into me, making me like Neeve and Thorne.

That was a vain hope, of course. The reality was that I was nothing more than an ordinary human girl, fated, according to the herbwife, to watch as great events unfolded around me.

Swallowing back salt, I bent my head to the strings of my harp. If I could not have magic, at least I had music.

It was a bitter comfort.

CHAPTER 21

After the excitement of the Yule Feast, the rest of the winter passed uneventfully. It seemed to rain constantly, and everyone in the castle grew snappish. Despite the fact that I was entirely lacking in bardic power, my harp playing improved. Sadly, my riding did not.

Neeve's flute was, indeed, cracked beyond repair. Much to my relief —and, I suspected, that of Master Fawkes—she declared her pursuit of music at an end. Instead, she spent many hours riding Peerless in the overcast drizzle outside.

By contrast, I spent much of my time curled before the fire, reading. The rest of the history of Raine proved to be rather interesting, although everything written about the Darkwood was annoyingly vague. And there was some mystery surrounding the *nirwen* flower. The pre-castle history of the country didn't mention it at all.

It had something to do with the magic of the Darkwood, of that I was sure. I could still close my eyes and recall the glowing golden petals Neeve and I had seen inscribed in the pool.

In addition to history and my beloved tales of adventure, I'd scoured the library shelves for books about magic, or the Darkwood, or both. Alas, my efforts proved unsuccessful. If there were such books, they were hidden away, perhaps under lock and key, where curious eyes could not find them.

At last, a morning arrived where the sun dawned from a clear blue sky. I stood beside my window as I dressed, letting the faint warmth of its rays soothe the chill from my cheeks. Perhaps the dark, gray winter would not, after all, last forever.

Miss Groves cut our lessons short.

"I've told the kitchens to send up a picnic," she said, her eyes twinkling. "It's much too nice a day to spend cooped up inside these cold stone walls. Take your lunch and go outside, the both of you."

We were glad to obey. Bundles of sandwiches tucked into our cloak pockets, Neeve and I hurried to the door in the wall beside the kitchen gardens.

"Must you come?" Neeve asked, her hand on the latch.

"I have as much right to go into the Darkwood as you," I replied hotly.

"You do not." She used the haughty tone I hated, as though she were so much better than I.

I pulled my sleeve up and thrust my tattooed elbow beneath her nose. "What's that, then?"

"It is permission," she said coldly. "But it is not birthright."

I glared at her. During the winter in the castle, I'd almost forgotten how superior she could be concerning the forest. And magic.

I'd also grown used to her odd coloring and aloof ways. But in the light of the sun, it struck me once again how strange my stepsister was. Strange and... not entirely human?

"Who was your mother?" I asked.

"Why does it matter to you?" Red spots rose in her cheeks. "Who was your father?"

"I don't know. I never met him." I held her gaze, daring her to answer me. "Did you know your mother?"

"I never met her, either." Neeve's voice was tight. "She died soon after giving birth to me."

"Oh." I pondered this a moment. "That's sad."

If forced to choose, I'd rather have Mama, foolish as she might be, over Neeve's remote father.

"Is your father dead?" Neeve asked.

She meant the question to be unkind, but it didn't bother me. I'd wondered the very thing myself when I was younger, and finally come to my own conclusion.

I shrugged. "Maybe. But it doesn't matter. Mama and I fared quite well on our own."

Until she married your father. I didn't say it aloud, however. Neeve was obviously still as unhappy about that fact as I was.

A crow cawed from the edge of the evergreens, and my stepsister looked away. Without another word, she pushed open the door and walked into the moat of damp grasses dividing the castle from the Darkwood. Despite the faint warmth of the sunlight flickering through the branches, an air of sadness clung to her, a black-haired girl in a black cloak. Maybe I shouldn't follow her this time, after all.

I hesitated at the wall, until she turned and gave me a sharp look.

"Are you coming, or not?" she asked.

Well then.

"Coming," I said, hurrying to close the gap between us.

When we reached the shadows beneath the trees, I was very glad to have made that choice. Thorne was there, his dark cloak blending with the cedar trunk he leaned against. His features were as lean and handsome as I recalled, and amber specks danced in the darkness of his eyes.

"The two of you took your time," he said dryly.

"Thorne!" I made a few quick steps forward, then halted. We were not friends enough that I could rush to embrace him in greeting.

Besides, Neeve was there first. He put an arm about her shoulders, as if sensing her sorrow, and then I wished I'd stayed behind after all. Whatever affection lay between the two of them, it was not mine to have.

He glanced over at me. "I hear you caused quite a stir at the Yule Feast."

"Neeve was part of it, too," I said, wanting him to turn that disapproving look on my stepsister.

Neeve lifted her chin and stepped away from him. "I've performed many times at the feast without calamity."

One of Thorne's elegant brows rose. "Calamity? I'd like the first-hand story, if you please."

I didn't ask how he knew about it. Perhaps a sparrow had brought the tale to his ear, or one of the villagers. Or even Mistress Ainya herself.

"It was Neeve's idea," I said.

She sent me a narrow-eyed glance. "I'd no idea it would cause so much trouble. Nothing like that happened in rehearsal."

"Nothing like what?" Thorne asked.

"We might have set the great hall on fire," I admitted.

"*You* did," Neeve said. "I just tried to put it out."

"With useless shards of ice!"

Thorne raised his hands. "Calm down, both of you. I understand that Mistress Ainya and Master Fawkes managed to pass it off as an illusion that went awry. But Neeve, you should know better than to use magic in front of others."

"I had to do *something*," she said. "I couldn't let Rose burn the castle down."

"As to that." Thorne turned to me, his dark eyes piercing. "Did you cause the fire?"

"I..." I bit my lip. "I don't know. I mean, I can't do magic—Mistress Ainya could tell you as much. But when I was playing, and the duet was just so horrible, this sort of scorching feeling came over me. And then the tapestries caught fire."

"Hmm." His expression grew thoughtful. "Have you been able to duplicate that feeling?"

"No. And Master Fawkes and I tried for *weeks*."

"I expect you did. A pity it wasn't a success."

Neeve scowled. "You sound as if you *want* Rose to have magic."

Thorne turned to her, his expression solemn. "During my time... away, I met with the Oracles. Strange things are afoot, Neeve. Things that threaten to bring upheaval and imbalance to both our worlds. You and Rose stand at the center. If she has a hidden power, it might make all the difference in the conflict to come."

My stepsister grew even more pale, if such a thing were possible. "Do you mean... war?"

Thorne shook his head, more in sorrow than negation. "I don't know. Nobody does, except perhaps the Oracles, and they will not say."

"War with whom?" I asked. "What do you mean, both our worlds? Why won't you tell me *anything*?"

"I know it's difficult." Thorne turned to me. "But you're young yet, and untried. The time will come when all shall be revealed."

"We remember the last time you tried to tell the Darkwood's secrets," Neeve said, much more bluntly. "We can't trust you."

"You can!" I protested. "I won't say anything—I know that if I try, I'll get struck down."

"Which is why I've removed that condition of the spell," Thorne said.

Neeve frowned mightily, though she kept her red lips closed on the arguments I saw rising in her eyes.

"You did?" I turned to Thorne. "When?"

"When I heard you'd fallen ill, and guessed that the binding spell had some unintended consequences."

"Very well." I folded my arms. "But if I knew your secrets, who would I tell? Neeve already knows everything."

"I understand that your mother is cousin to the Parnesian royalty," Thorne said. "Does she correspond with them, or anyone from your home country?"

"I... don't know." There was so little I knew about my mother's life of late.

Sadness sifted through me at how distant we'd become. Not that she'd shared every detail when we dwelt in Parnese, but at least she'd been there, woven through the fabric of my everyday life. Now I was alone, except for Neeve. And Thorne.

Very well—and Miss Groves, and Master Fawkes, and Sorche, and Mistress Ainya, if summer would ever come. I shook off my self-pity.

"Mama might very well be writing letters back to Parnese," I admitted.

"One word in the wrong ears could spell disaster," Thorne said. "I'm sorry, Rose, but for the safety of Raine, and my entire people, it is vital you not learn our secrets. Yet."

I wanted to scream in frustration. I wanted magic to burst like flame from my fingertips, to prove I was worthy. I wanted Thorne to wrap his arm around my shoulders the way he had with Neeve.

Instead, a drop of rain plummeted from the branch overhead and trickled down the back of my neck, as cold as the knowledge that I was, and would ever be, just Rose. Not a sorcerer. Not a mysterious, pale-skinned beauty who might or might not be mortal. Just me—a clumsy, ordinary human girl.

I swallowed back my misery and managed to nod at Thorne. For now, there was nothing I could do except wait. And watch. Every now and then he or Neeve let something slip, and I would pounce upon every scrap of knowledge they carelessly let drop.

Someday, sooner than they might guess, I vowed I'd discover all the secrets of the Darkwood—and who, or *what*, Thorne really was.

CHAPTER 22

With the advent of spring, our afternoons in the forest resumed. They were not nearly as pleasant as in the summer and early fall, since it still rained frequently. Often Neeve and I had the choice to go out into the drizzle and return with sopping cloaks and squelching shoes, or remain inside the castle, bored but dry. Despite the rain, we usually chose the forest.

As the days grew longer, so too grew my anticipation for my upcoming birthday. In less than a month, I might awake and discover the power of magic burning brightly within me.

I was sorry to see Master Fawkes pack up his lute and clothing and take to the road once more. He promised he'd return the next winter, and urged me to continue my study of the harp. Although I was sad to see him go, I was secretly glad to trade his presence for Thorne's.

As the days passed and the weather improved, I returned to my twice-weekly lessons with Mistress Ainya. She quizzed me at length about the Yule Feast fire. When she could determine nothing in me that confirmed I'd started the blaze, she sighed and set about teaching me to spin.

I didn't see what spinning had to do with magic—other than the mundane transformation of wool to thread—but I took up the task with only small complaint. Meanwhile, Neeve was allowed to concoct interesting brews, and once even managed to create the illusion of a white moth. It careened crazily about the cottage for a few moments before turning to dust. The ashy particles drifted to the floor, and I knew it would fall to me to sweep them up. As usual.

A week before my birthday, the castle finally began to feel less clammy. It was sunny more often than not, and it was remarkable how much a difference that made to my mood. The cold, dry winters of Parnese had at least been filled with light. Living in Raine felt like we'd been in a disused cookpot with a lid clapped over the top for the last several months.

But now the lid was off, and I was about to turn another year older. Life felt momentous.

"It's my birthday tomorrow," I reminded Neeve as we took our places in the schoolroom that morning.

She gave me a sour look. "I know. You told me about it two weeks ago. And last week. And the day before yesterday."

"Well." I glanced down at the scratched surface of the table. "I didn't want you to forget."

Her response to that was a haughty sniff.

"Since you've mentioned it, Rose," Miss Groves said, "I think we'll postpone the start of class tomorrow by one hour. What do you think of that?"

"That would be grand," I said.

Though I'd grown accustomed to the early schedule of my life in Raine, I still didn't like it. On the two days a week we weren't required to appear in the schoolroom, I often lay abed until nearly noon, relishing the chance to wake, and doze in the warm blankets, and then wake again at my leisure.

Of course, I didn't imagine I'd sleep late the next morning—especially if, as I hoped, I awoke to newfound magic.

That afternoon, as Neeve and I went through the Darkwood on the way to Mistress Ainya's cottage, there was no sign of Thorne. I recalled that he'd given my stepsister her birthday gift early, and tried to hide the bite of disappointment that he had not done the same for me.

Neeve wore her pendant daily. She tucked it away beneath the neckline of her dress, but I noted the fine silver chain about her neck, and knew what it was she concealed.

"So, Rose," Mistress Ainya said to me as we carded wool at her kitchen table. "Tomorrow you turn fourteen."

"Yes." I tried not to squeal the word.

The herbwife gave me a long look. "You do understand that coming into magic is not necessarily a simple thing. You might wake and feel no different in the morning, or the morning after that, or the one after that. For some, it creeps up on them."

"I understand," I said, certain that would not be the case with me.

"And remember, it might not be this year. Or any year."

I tried not to scowl, and clung instead to my hopes. Neeve still seemed to believe that I'd started the fire during the Yule Feast, but she couldn't explain why she thought so.

If my stepsister thought I had magic, though, then I chose to believe her.

That night, the eve of my birthday, I lay wide awake with my mind afire, the way one does when falling asleep is the wisest course. My thoughts clattered around my brain, hope and worry grappling with one another.

What if I had magic?

What if I did not?

Finally, in the darkest part of the night, I drifted to sleep.

Fire. Blood. Searing pain in my left hand.

I was trapped in a windowless room, smoke pouring in under the door. Panic thundered through my veins as I pounded my fists against the heavy iron door. No escape.

"Let me out!" I cried, over and over, until the words were nothing more than a croaking rasp in my abraded throat.

My hands bruised and aching, my face wet with tears, I slumped down in one corner of the cell. I was going to burn alive.

Horrific images thrust themselves into my mind—Ser Pietro's flesh sizzling, Neeve striking at me with an icy sword that bit deep into my side with a searing howl, Mama holding me tightly against her while a frightening, yellow-eyed woman raised her huge knife...

"No," I moaned, covering my head with my arms and trying not to inhale the dense air.

Smoke. Shadows. Death.

"Wake up." The voice was urgent. "Rose—you must awaken. Concentrate."

The pain in my left hand receded, replaced by a fierce itching midway up my arm.

I lifted my head and saw the leaf tattoo inside my elbow glowing a fierce, bright green. The smoke swirled away from that light, and I gulped in an untainted breath.

"Who is it?" I whispered. "Please, let me out."

"You must escape on your own. You're trapped inside a nightmare. Now, *wake up!*"

The shouted words made me start, and my eyes flew open.

It took a long, shaking moment for me to realize I lay in my bed at Castle Raine. No smoke filled the room, only the faint pearly light of approaching dawn filtering from behind the curtains. No one lurked in the corners, ready to attack me with sword or knife.

I was safe, despite my racing heartbeat and clammy skin. I was awake. And completely alone.

Belatedly, I realized the voice I'd heard had been Thorne's. Had he truly been there, in my terrible dream, or had I simply imagined him out of my desperate need for a rescuer?

My throat was parched. I threw back the covers and reached for the glass and pitcher of water on my nightstand, only to freeze when I saw my left arm. The leaf tattoo was glowing, ever so faintly. As I stared at it, the light faded until the leaf had returned to ordinary ink.

I blinked. Had I imagined it, carried over some afterimage from the intensity of my dream?

I didn't think so.

Clumsily, I poured water into the glass, spilling some on my nightdress. I gulped half the contents, welcoming the blessed coolness on my desert-burned throat.

There is no fire, I reassured myself. No danger. The coals on the hearth had burned out. Still clutching my glass, I stood and carefully went to the windows.

The light outside was growing stronger. I twitched one of the curtains back, then sucked in my breath. Three small, glowing lights darted above the trees across the meadow. As I watched, they dipped and circled, then sank below the branches of the Darkwood and were lost to sight.

What did it all mean?

I finished my water and returned to perch cross-legged atop the bed. Had my magic manifested, causing such dreadful nightmares and strange portents?

As morning crept over Raine, I stared unseeing at the rosy bed hangings. Was I any different? I stretched my toes and pulled in a deep breath, searching for anything that might feel like newly awakened power. The stub of my pinky throbbed in time to my heartbeat. The leaf at my elbow was quiet.

Other than the sweat drying on my forehead and the damp spot on my nightdress, I felt the same as any other morning.

Please, I thought ferociously. *Please, let me be magic.*

Nothing stirred within me. No spark, no awareness.

I sat for a long time, yearning, searching.

Maybe it would come later in the day, I told myself, after I awoke for good.

Maybe.

Finally, with the chirp and twitter of birds welcoming the sun outside my window, I gave in to the press of exhaustion. Crawling beneath the covers once more, I let the sorrow-tinged heaviness of sleep claim me.

❧

"MISTRESS ROSE!" Sorche called. "Are you awake? I've brought you a tray."

Muzzily, I opened my eyes, conscious of a great sense of loss.

Then the memory of my nightmare washed over me, and I sat up.

"I'm awake," I mumbled, stuffing back my disappointment.

The maid bustled into the room. "Good morning, and happy birthday! Your mother thought you'd like a bit of breakfast in bed."

I summoned a tight smile for Sorche. "That would be lovely."

Even better would be seeing Mama herself, of course. I was too old to take shelter in her embrace, but oh, how much I wanted to. I needed comfort.

At least she'd remembered it was my birthday. I blinked back my foolish tears and resolved to take whatever scraps of her affection she remembered to toss my way.

I stuffed the pillows behind my back and applied myself to my breakfast—sweet rolls, milky tea, crisp sausages, and an apple. The fruit was withered from the cellars, and I felt a stab of longing for the bright oranges I'd so blissfully taken for granted in Parnese.

When Sorche took the tray away, I slipped out of bed. Despite myself, I couldn't help trying to feel *some* spark of magic. I drew in a trembling lungful of air, let it out.

Nothing.

I balled my hands into fists and resolved not to cry. Mistress Ainya had said these things took time. I'd been a silly girl, to think that turning fourteen would suddenly unlock a heretofore hidden door in my soul.

Trying not to dwell on my disappointment, I dressed and went to the schoolroom.

Neeve was already there. She nodded a greeting, but didn't treat me any differently than she had the day before. Clearly she sensed no change within me. That, more than anything, confirmed the fact.

Miss Groves kindly spent most of the morning in discussions of history and writing, and not mathematics, which I appreciated. After a quick, quiet lunch, Neeve and I made for the door in the castle wall.

For the first time all day, I felt a spark of hope. Maybe Thorne *had* been there in my dream. Maybe once I was in the mysterious, enchanted Darkwood, my magic would finally stir awake. And maybe Thorne had a birthday present for me, after all.

At least one of those possibilities—if not all of them—seemed likely, and I traversed the halls of Castle Raine with a renewed sense of optimism.

CHAPTER 23

I followed Neeve out the door in the castle wall, breathing deeply of the spicy scent of evergreens. The grass between the stone wall and the Darkwood was starred with white daisies. I plucked a handful as we went and tied them into a lopsided crown.

The moment my stepsister and I walked beneath the shadow of the trees, I spotted Thorne waiting for us. I tried not to look at him too eagerly.

He gave a brief laugh, the white of his teeth flashing in the soft light under the cedar boughs. Whatever had happened the night before, he seemed unaware of it. Unaware, or unwilling to show any sign he had visited my dreams.

"Rose, you are like a puppy," he said. "Come here, then, and get your gift."

I was torn between annoyance that he thought of me as a pup and gladness that he did *indeed* have a present for me. I hurried forward over the soft carpeting of needles. Neeve, one brow arched, followed more slowly.

Thorne drew a small, silk-wrapped bundle from the pocket of his cloak. The fabric was the bright blue of the sky at noon, and cool against my fingers as he handed it to me.

"May I open it now?" I asked, glancing at him.

He nodded, bright flecks of amusement still dancing in his eyes. "Yes."

Conscious of Neeve at my shoulder, of Thorne's gaze upon me, I carefully folded back the blue silk. Gold glinted inside. Barely breathing, I pulled out a necklace similar to the one he'd given Neeve.

"It's beautiful." I held it up.

Dangling from the fine gold chain was a pendant formed out of a circle of twined vines, sparked with blue. It seemed to glow in the shadows of the wood, the gold picking up glints of light. I brought it close, to see that the vines ended in perfectly crafted leaves, each one holding a tiny sapphire like a drop of dew. The workmanship was extraordinary. Careful not to snag my unruly hair, I fastened the chain about my neck.

"Who made it?" I asked, knowing I wasn't going to receive a satisfactory answer.

But it was my birthday. A surge of stubbornness combined with my disappointment, urging me to press harder than usual.

"My people," Thorne said, in his usual annoyingly mysterious manner.

"Yes, but who *are* they?" I wasn't going to let him get away with half-answers this time, if I could help it.

"You will learn, in time."

"No." I shoved up my sleeve and jabbed my leaf-marked elbow at him. "Isn't this enough?"

He glanced at the leaf, and I thought I saw regret flash through his eyes before he looked away into the shadows beneath the trees.

"That is enough to bind you to the forest, but the fate of my people is not something we take lightly." He suddenly sounded exhausted. "Please, Rose. Stop arguing."

I gave him a sharp look. "What else should I know about this mark?"

Like the fact it sometimes glowed.

"It will not harm you." Thorne still would not meet my eyes.

Conviction grew in me that he *did* know something of what had occurred in the night. I opened my mouth to insist he tell me more, but Neeve stepped forward.

"Stop with your questions," she said. "They're growing tiresome."

"If you would bother telling me anything, I wouldn't need to ask all the time." I scowled at her and shook my sleeve back down. Neeve didn't need to know that I suspected Thorne had performed magic in my dreams.

My annoyance wasn't all for her, of course. Despite being in the shelter of the forest, I felt no more stirrings of magic than I'd had since I arose. The Darkwood had disappointed my hopes.

As if reading my thoughts, Thorne turned to look at me once more.

"Do you feel any hint of power?" he asked carefully, as if aware that I would not have kept such news to myself, had I awoken changed.

"No." I scuffed the loam with my booted toe. "I feel exactly the same as yesterday."

Except for the lingering unease brought on by the nightmare, and the sense that he knew more about it that he let on.

"I'm sorry," he said. "But that doesn't mean you won't develop magic at some point, Rose. Remember what Mistress Ainya said. Sometimes it takes years to manifest."

I nodded mutely. There was no use in trying to jolly myself along. I was fourteen—and still distressingly unmagical.

Neeve set a hand on my shoulder, as if in apology, her touch as light as the brush of a moth's wing.

"Would you like to go deeper into the Darkwood?" Thorne asked, clearly trying to cheer me up.

I sniffed a few times and cleared my throat. Perhaps he was right—perhaps my power was not meant to appear on my fourteenth birthday. I clung to that thought. And, despite my mood, I would never turn down a chance to see more of the forest.

"Yes," I finally said, once my voice was under control. "I'd like that very much."

Thorne gave me a generous smile, which cheered me a bit more. "Come along."

Soft-footed, he strode along a pathway carpeted with evergreen needles and overhung with new ferns. I followed, my new pendant shining on my chest, and Neeve came behind. The shadows beneath the trees seemed lighter as we passed, as though the forest was brightened by Thorne's passing.

After a short while, we came to the stream with the boulder, and the meadow beyond, where Neeve and I had seen the White Hart. And where we'd rescued yet another hobnie.

"How many hobnies are in the forest?" I asked Thorne as we passed through the dappled light of a birch grove.

"Seven," he replied.

"It seems like each one is more sour-tempered than the last," I said, thinking back on my encounters of the previous summer.

"They don't trust mortals, and they dislike anyone to see them in a spot of trouble. They're too proud to be gratefully rescued."

"Well, that's plain." I shook my head, recalling the insults every hobnie had heaped upon me and Neeve.

Thorne glanced at me over his shoulder. "One day, they will repay your kindness. The Darkwood keeps a balance."

I recalled Neeve had said the same. "I don't help them because I expect to be rewarded."

The hobnies fell into the same category as the various creatures I'd mended and befriended in Parnese—and they seemed the only things in the whole Darkwood who ever needed my aid.

Thorne grinned. "That's precisely why you will be."

I had to believe him, though I surely didn't see what help any of the grouchy little hobnies could give me. Perhaps if I ever got lost in the forest, one could guide me out? But if that happened, I'd rely on Thorne. After all, he was the guardian of the Darkwood. The *Galadhir*.

The path led alongside the stream until it joined a much larger creek. The water broadened, the current rippling in lazy circles. I glimpsed a few spotted silver fish darting in the depths. Thorne followed the bank, and soon I heard a faint rushing sound that must surely be a waterfall. The forest grew brighter, small pink flowers blooming in the underbrush as the trees thinned.

"Step carefully," Thorne said as we emerged at the edge of a sudden drop-off.

I halted, taking in the view. Shades of green as far as I could see, and more trees than I could begin to count. Cedar and pine, hemlock and birch, the wind ruffling over them as though they were the fur of some gigantic beast.

The crash of the waterfall was loud, and spray drifted up to wet my face. Thorne was right to urge caution—the path was damp, edged with mossy, water-darkened rocks. Using my hands for balance, I followed him down the winding cut of the trail, Neeve at my back. Back and forth we went, the roar of the water growing thunderous as we descended.

Purple trumpet-shaped flowers bloomed, nodding as we passed, and the smell of crushed mint was sharp in my nostrils.

At last we reached the bottom, where the water fell in a white torrent into the basin of a large pool. The power of the Darkwood was obvious here in the surge and plunge of the falls, and I shivered to feel it. Had I been alone, I would have felt afraid. I pushed the damp frizz of red curls back from my face and took a moment to catch my breath.

Neeve halted beside me, showing no trace of exertion.

"Are you going to call the nixie?" she asked Thorne.

"I'm going to ask her to dance for us, if she's so inclined," he answered. "The nixie comes when she pleases. One cannot command the elementals of the forest, Neeve. You should know that."

Before I could ask any of the questions his words had raised, Thorne pursed his lips and whistled a series of lilting notes. Somehow, in a way I could not explain, they matched the crashing tone of the falling water, the dash of the spray, the gurgle of the creek as it regathered itself in the bowl of the pool.

Both he and Neeve stared intently at the surface of the water. I could see nothing but froth and foam. Then, slowly, a figure rose from the depths. Her webbed hands broke the surface, her hair swirled silver and black and green, like algae, and then her head emerged.

The nixie was beautiful and hideous all at once, with her wide, tilted eyes and slitted nostrils. A pink water lily was tucked behind one ear. Her lips were bluish green, and when she smiled at Thorne I glimpsed the serrated edges of her teeth.

"*Nenavale*." He made her a slight bow.

"Greetings, *Galadhir*," she said, the syllables sliding like water over stone. Her gaze moved past him to fasten on me, and her expression darkened. "Who is this mortal girl that dares breach the forest?"

I shivered under the force of her baleful stare.

Thorne held up one hand. "Rose is under my protection."

The nixie gave a long, slow blink, her eyelids gliding strangely over her dark eyes. "As you say, *Galadhir*."

She lifted her arms over her head, and I could make out the faintest sign of scales on her skin. Slowly she began to turn in place, her hair spiraling out in a fan around her pale body. She kicked, legs that blurred into a tail, and suddenly arced up out of the water in a graceful swoop and dive.

Droplets glittered, suspended in the air like a handful of diamonds, then fell back into the pool. The sun slipped out from behind a cloud, and suddenly there were rainbows everywhere, dazzling my eyes.

I stepped to the edge of the water, entranced.

"Rose," Thorne said, his voice urgent. "Stand back—"

His words were lost in a crash and a plunge, as the nixie's long, clammy fingers closed about my arms and she pulled me under.

The pool was dark and cold, the water shocking me into panic. I kicked, trying to reach the surface, but the nixie dragged me inexorably deeper. My lungs burned for air. I scrabbled at her fingers, but her grip was too strong.

Quench the ember, I heard, as she thrust me beneath the waterfall. *Drown the blaze.*

The water beat at me, shoving me so far beneath the surface that the world above was only a bright mote in my vision. The pool seemed to go down for miles as the waterfall pushed into the frigid depths, taking me with it.

CHAPTER 24

Dark and drowning. My mind clamored with terror as the last precious bubbles of air slipped between my lips. My final regret was that I could not say goodbye to Mama.

Then something wrapped around me, a coil of blue fire pulling me from beneath the waterfall's grasp. Up, and up.

And finally, *out*.

I broke the surface of the pool, crying and coughing. Whatever carried me deposited me on the shore, several paces from the deadly waters.

Thorne bent and pounded me between the shoulder blades. I coughed up even more water, hacking, my nose and eyes streaming, dimly aware of Neeve holding my hair back from my face.

"Breathe," Thorne said urgently. I heard fear in his normally calm voice.

I managed a ragged, gulping breath. The air sawed my lungs and my body shuddered with the influx of air, then relaxed as it realized I was not drowning, after all.

Exhausted, I slumped on the wet moss. Far more gently than I would have expected, Neeve wiped my face with a linen kerchief. Hers, I supposed, though why she carried a kerchief into the Darkwood, I couldn't fathom. It was all I could do not to lose mine the moment they emerged from the laundry.

Satisfied I was breathing, Thorne turned to the pool. I shivered and weakly tried to scoot further away from where the waterfall crashed down. One arm around my shoulders, Neeve assisted my retreat.

"*Nenavale*," Thorne said, his voice harder than I'd ever heard it. "Harm this girl again, and your place within the forest will be given to another. Do you understand?"

The nixie floated in the center of the pool, the top of her head and her eyes barely visible above the water. For a long moment, she did not reply. I wondered if Thorne was going to rip her out of the pool right then and there, and install some other creature in her place. The force of his anger seemed a solid thing, filling the air with sharp edges.

"Yesss," she finally said. "I understand. But bring her not to the water's edge again, *Galadhir*. My sisters will try to drown her."

"Then you must speak to them."

She shook her head, her long hair waving lazily about her in the water. "They mussst do as their nature bids. I cannot dictate to them, as you do to me."

"Warn them that it will not go lightly should they attempt to injure Rose."

"I shall warn them. I promissse nothing more."

Before he could speak to her again, she flipped over, her long, finned legs splashing in the air. Then she was gone, the pool empty but for the foam and flurry of the waterfall.

Thorne stared after her for several heartbeats, then slowly turned and came to where I huddled, Neeve at my side.

"I'm sorry." He knelt and took my hands. It was a measure of how cold I was that, for once, his touch felt warm. "I had no idea I was putting you in such danger."

"Why?" Neeve asked. "Why would the nixie do such a thing? She's never harmed me."

"Your heritage protects you," Thorne said, his voice full of self-reproach. "It was foolish of me to bring a foreigner so far into the Darkwood. Even though I am *Galadhir*, I cannot bend the creatures of the forest to my will—or change their essential nature. Nixies prey upon mortals. It is to my shame that I so arrogantly believed I could command otherwise."

"But you saved me." I squeezed his hands, hating the desolation in his eyes.

"I cannot forgive myself for such stupidity. I endangered you."

It seemed he was speaking of more than what had just occurred, and I wondered again about his voice in my dreams.

"You rescued me," I said.

He only shook his head sadly and unclasped my hands. "We must return you to the castle. Can you walk?"

"Of course." I spoke the words with a confidence I didn't feel—but I couldn't bear the desolate look in his eyes.

With Neeve's help, I rose shakily to my feet. I swayed a moment, then took a deep breath, resolutely keeping my gaze from the steep ascent beside the waterfall. One way or the other, I would manage— even if my stepsister had to pull and Thorne push me from behind.

To my relief, however, he led us directly away from the waterfall. The embrace of the trees around us felt welcoming as the thunder of the falls faded.

"A moment," Thorne said, when we could no longer hear the water.

He stepped away a few paces, waved his hands, and spoke under his breath. I glanced at Neeve with raised brows, but she only shrugged. Whatever Thorne was doing, she had no more knowledge of it than I.

Something rippled through the air—a sudden gust moving over us, but not from the wind. Thorne nodded, then motioned us forward to the path that suddenly opened between the trees. After just a few paces, I gaped in surprise as I recognized the familiar landscape.

"Why, we're almost to Castle Raine," I said, glancing about me. "This is the path we take back from Mistress Ainya's cottage."

"It is," Thorne agreed.

I looked at him, but he said nothing more. Whatever magic he'd used to shift us to the edge of the forest, it seemed to have tired him. His dark eyes were shadowed, his expression grim.

As soon as we came in sight of the gray stone walls, he halted.

"Make sure she changes into dry clothes and has some broth," he said to Neeve.

"I will." My stepsister took my elbow. "I'll make her a pot of restorative tea, as well."

"I'll be all right," I said. "I'm not a complete invalid, you know."

He gave me a grave nod. "Still, take care not to catch a chill. Farewell, to the both of you."

We left him standing there, shoulders bowed. There was nothing I could say to take the burden of blame from him.

Despite my show of confidence, I was glad of Neeve's support as we made our way to the castle. She passed off my wet state with some story to Sorche about how I'd stumbled into the stream—which I supposed was true enough. Shortly, I was in my nightgown and tucked between the covers, a mug of hot tea steaming on the nightstand.

"Rest," Neeve said. "And don't be angry with Thorne."

"I'm not angry with him. Why should I be?"

She regarded me steadily. "This is the second time you've nearly died because of him."

"I don't think he's trying to kill me," I replied. "And both of you have warned me of the dangers of the Darkwood often enough. I'll be more careful next time."

Brave words, but I did not feel nearly so certain of them as Neeve left me to recuperate. Though my stepsister didn't know it, this was not the second time the forest had tried to harm me, but the third— counting the incident on the journey to the castle.

How many more times would it try? And why? I apparently had no powers, and yet the Darkwood seemed to see me as a threat. Was it because of the shadow of fate Mistress Ainya said hung over me? If so, I could see no way to escape from it. These thoughts left me shivering beneath the covers, and it was a long time before I was finally warm enough to rest.

CHAPTER 25

The rest of the summer passed much like the one the year before, and without further calamity. Neeve and I rescued two more hobnies—one with his beard trapped in a rabbit snare of his own making, one with it hopelessly tangled in a briar bush —with the same, insult-laden results. Thorne did not invite me on any more excursions deeper into the Darkwood, and I was relieved by it, content to stay safely on the outskirts of the forest.

Much as I loved the forest, and the promise of magic it held, it clearly was dangerous to me, a foreigner to Raine. Thorne had made that clear enough.

I continued to the play the harp on my own, and became a proficient spinner. Mistress Ainya was patient, Miss Groves forced me to improve my mathematical skills, and Neeve seemed to be warming toward me. Or, at least, more accepting of my presence.

The two of us, along with Thorne, spent many quiet afternoons in the Darkwood near the castle. He told a few more stories of the forest, demonstrated how to walk silently among the trees, and taught my stepsister to spin illusions of light. I wished I had that talent, rather than the far more mundane one of turning wool to thread.

Halfway through the summer, the king went to visit Fiorland, and my mother decided to take dinner in her rooms while he was gone. I told myself it scarcely mattered that I never saw her.

When the king returned, so did our meals together in the grand dining room. I blinked in surprise when I saw my mother, who looked as though the intervening weeks had caused her to grow younger and even more beautiful. Neeve narrowed her eyes as she made her curtsey to the queen, and I wondered what she knew.

As we made our way back to our rooms after dinner, I glanced at Neeve.

"Did you notice anything odd about my mother?" I asked.

"No." Her answer was quick and cold.

"Are you certain?" I pressed. "She seemed somehow changed."

Neeve set her mouth and said nothing more, and so, as usual, I was left with a teetering stack of questions. One day, I feared they would tumble down and bury me.

The edge of autumn crept in, leaving the morning air crisp and berries ripening red on the bushes. With it came a change in Castle Raine—one that I didn't recall from the year before.

Servants conferred in the hallways, suddenly going silent when I passed. An air of anticipation hovered, and at dinner Lord Raine was preoccupied. He spoke with his advisors in vague terms, referencing trade supplies and extra labor.

"What is going on?" I asked Neeve as we waited for the dessert course.

She gave me a blank look. "I've no idea what you mean."

The next morning, Miss Groves assigned several chapters in the *History of Fiorland*—a much less interesting book than the *History of Raine*. Mostly, it seemed that the Fiorlanders liked to sail, and had a somewhat violent past raiding the coastal towns of the neighboring countries.

"Don't worry," Miss Groves said, correctly interpreting my resigned glance at the textbook. "There will be no class tomorrow, so you'll have time to read the entire assignment."

"No class?" I looked up from the heavy leather-bound book. "Why not?"

"It's a holiday for the whole castle," she said. "You may sleep as late as you like. Sorche will bring your meals from the kitchen."

"We're not dining with the king and queen tonight, either," Neeve said. "I forgot to tell you. The kitchens will send our supper up."

I trailed my fingers over the raised red lettering on the history book's cover and pretended that my nerves weren't quivering. Something was about to happen. Something I wasn't supposed to know about.

"It will be nice to have a little time," I said, pretending to an ease I didn't feel. "To catch up on my reading and such."

I thought about feigning a yawn, but that would be taking my nonchalance too far. Instead, I settled for a vapid smile.

Neeve gave me a sharp look, but Miss Groves nodded. "Excellent. I plan on turning in early myself."

Well, that was an obvious lie. Whatever was going on, Miss Groves obviously knew about it. She wouldn't cancel our classes lightly.

When our lunch was delivered, it was accompanied by mugs of sweet herbal tea instead of the usual cups of water. Neeve drank hers, but I sniffed mine suspiciously. Pretending to sip away, I managed to dribble most of it into my lap. My skirts grew uncomfortably wet, but the heavy wool absorbed the tea well enough that my subterfuge wasn't immediately obvious.

After we finished, I sat at the table, hoping I wouldn't drip too much when I stood.

Neeve yawned, then turned to give me a sleepy look. "I'm sorry, Rose, but I'm suddenly quite tired. Do you mind if we don't go into the forest this afternoon?"

I was supposed to be drowsy too, I guessed. Either Neeve had also been given the sleeping draught, or she was putting on a show. I let my eyelids droop and gave a complacent nod.

"A nap sounds just the thing," I said.

At least my false lethargy allowed me to rise slowly. A trickle of tea ran off my skirts and puddled under the table, where, I hoped, it would remain unnoticed until it dried. I paused a moment, palms flat on the table.

"Off to your rooms, girls," Miss Groves said briskly.

I sidled around the end of the table so I wouldn't have to risk facing the teacher directly and revealing my wet skirt, and obediently followed Neeve to the door.

We said nothing as we traversed the hallways back to the wing where our bedrooms were. Either my stepsister knew what was going on, or she didn't. If I said anything, I ran the risk of giving myself away.

When we reached my door, I mumbled farewell to Neeve and ambled into my rooms.

The moment the door closed, though, I raced to my bedroom. I had a sudden thought to wring out my skirts and try to feed the remains of the tea to Sorche, who would surely be set as my guard. But the wool had absorbed the liquid too well, and I gave that idea up as quickly as it came.

I changed into dry clothes and stuffed my wet ones in the back of the wardrobe, then sat beside the fire. To look quietly busy, I took up the drop spindle Mistress Ainya had given me and began to spin out a fine gray thread from the cloud of wool in my basket.

"Miss Rose?" Sorche tapped on the door.

"Come in," I called, my mind racing.

When the maid stepped in, I could tell from her expression that she was, indeed, there to check on me.

"How do you feel this afternoon?" she asked. "A little tired, maybe?"

She was terrible at dissembling, and I tried not to smile at her awkward questioning.

"Goodness," I said, setting my spinning aside. "Now that you mention it, I am rather sleepy. Might you bring me an extra blanket?"

She gave a satisfied nod. "Of course. But don't you think you'd be more comfortable lying in your bed? If you nap in a chair, you'll wake with a stiff neck."

"I suppose you're right," I said, playing along.

I summoned a false yawn, then let her remove my shoes as if I were a small child, and tuck me into bed.

She shut the curtains, then lingered a while in the parlor, tidying up the already tidy shelves. When her shadow came near the bedroom door, I closed my eyes and let my chest rise and fall in the long, slow breaths of sleep.

Finally, Sorche banked the fire and left, shutting the door quietly behind her. I lay rigidly beneath the blankets, listening for the snick of the latch. What if they locked me in? When I was sure she was gone, I sprang up and tiptoed out through the parlor.

Carefully, I tried the door.

Unlocked, thank goodness. I exhaled my held breath. I could hear people moving about out in the hallway, but I'd no way of seeing who they were or where they were going.

The only place I could spy what was happening was out my bedroom window. I hurried to the thick green curtains and, as slowly as I dared, pulled one back until I could peep out.

In the courtyard below were over a dozen people dressed for travel, with large baskets fastened on their backs. Someone shouted and waved an arm and the group moved away, turning the corner so I could no longer see them.

Where were they going?

To discover anything, I'd have to sneak out of my rooms.

Thinking furiously, I turned back to my bed and, as quietly as possible, dragged out the trunk stored beneath. Inside the trunk was a bright silk tapestry from my room in Parnese and a few childhood trinkets. Most importantly, tucked at the bottom were a pair of trousers and a heavy black coat, required attire for my skullduggery class.

Mama had not supervised my packing, other than to make sure I brought my good gowns and underthings and suitable shoes. I'd thought the other clothes might come in handy, however, and was glad of my foresight.

I changed into my skulking outfit, dismayed to find that the trousers were unaccountably short and too tight. I left the waistband unbuttoned, then pulled on heavy socks and my sturdy boots, which mostly made up for the gap at my ankles. I slipped on my belt, attaching the pouch containing a few coins, my scissors, the knife I'd filched from the kitchens at the beginning of the year, plus a dried piece of fruit I'd apparently overlooked from a few days before. Next I pulled on a warm shirt and the black coat—also a bit tight—and was ready.

But what if Sorche discovered I was gone and raised the alarm to look for me before I escaped the castle?

Luckily, my bed sported a ridiculous amount of cushions. I usually threw half of them to the floor when I slept. They came in handy, however, for making a girl-shaped lump beneath the covers.

The crowning touch, which I was rather proud of, was a red-fringed scarf pulled from the wardrobe. Balled up with a bit of fringe trailed over the pillow, in the dim light it almost resembled my hair.

If one squinted and didn't look too closely.

Hoping the mounded pillows would be enough to fool Sorche, I returned to listen at my door. The footsteps I'd heard previously were gone. I waited several minutes longer, just to make sure, but the hallway remained quiet.

Finally, scarcely breathing, I lifted the latch and pulled my door open a crack.

The castle was quiet. Strangely quiet. I fancied I could hear the lamp flames sizzling in the wall sconces. I glanced down the hall to Neeve's door. Was she in her room, fast asleep?

I couldn't risk taking the time to look. Either she was there and asleep, or she wasn't. Determining which would only delay my own departure.

Summoning my slightly rusty skullduggery skills, I slipped from shadow to shadow. At the head of the stairs I paused again, listening, but everything below was still. Heart hammering in my chest, I crept down the exposed length of the staircase.

No cries rang out. When I reached the bottom, I scuttled behind a half-open door and tried to catch my breath. Peaceful afternoon light slanted through the high windows overhead. No one and nothing stirred within the castle walls.

I recalled a tale I'd read, of an enchanted castle where everyone fell into a deep sleep. Had that happened here? Was everyone in the grip of a magical slumber?

But no—I'd heard and seen people moving about. Plus, there were no sleeping bodies of servants or courtiers slumped in the corners. Shaking off the notion, I continued on toward the great hall. At the arched entrance, I paused, straining my ears. Nothing.

I peeked around the edge of the stonework arch. The hall was empty.

I skirted the edges of the huge room and reached the entryway of Castle Raine. The tall doors were shut, but not barred. I paused, studying the entry. Maybe I should have chosen a less obvious exit— but it was too late now. Biting my lip, I eased the right-hand door open.

The stairs outside were empty, as was the cobblestoned courtyard below, but I saw evidence that a group of people had massed there recently. A scrap of paper fluttered down the steps, which were littered with discarded bread crusts, bits of straw, and muddy boot prints.

A few piles of fresh horse manure lay on the cobbles below, and I found it surprising that no one had yet swept them up. Usually the stable hands were quite efficient. Where had everyone gone?

Pulling the edges of my coat around me, I went down the stairs, crossed the courtyard, and slipped under the portcullis. Despite my continued wariness, I met no one. Outside the castle walls I found several sets of cart tracks converging. Instead of following the wide dirt road toward the village, however, the tracks veered to the left, toward the forest. The grass was flattened by the passage of many feet, and I wondered if the entire population of the castle—minus myself— had left on this mysterious journey.

I walked beside the wheel ruts as they rounded the castle, then halted, my breath catching. The tracks led straight ahead. Directly into the Darkwood.

I hesitated, the breeze ruffling my hair, and stared at the evidence before me. It seemed that everyone in Castle Raine had taken the mad notion to go into the forest. But why?

Why? Why? The question pounded in my chest.

I folded my hands into fists. Hopefully, they hadn't gone too deep into the dangerous reaches of the forest. But even if they had, I would willingly risk my safety for the answers I so desperately wanted.

Breath tight in my lungs, I walked alone into the Darkwood.

CHAPTER 26

The shadows beneath the evergreens enfolded me. The cart tracks managed to wind between the trees, though I would have sworn there was no possible way for carts and horses, and at least three dozen people, to move so easily through the Darkwood.

Somehow, though, they'd managed. Thorne must be involved—perhaps even using his magic to coax the tall cedars and hemlocks to shift out of the way, if such a thing were even possible.

But wherever the tracks led, I would follow.

As I made my way through the forest, I found it quieter than usual—strangely hushed and almost dormant. An occasional questioning chirp sounded through the trees, as if the birds shared my puzzlement.

It was easy to follow the ruts carved through the moss, and I was glad to note that, other than the tracks, there was very little damage to the forest. I saw no broken branches or torn bushes, no uprooted trees or upturned stones gashing the loam. Only the parallel marks of wheels and the trampling of many feet.

Curiosity—and a touch of fear—fired my steps, and I went at a brisk pace. Surely I would hear the people in front of me before I caught up to them, and would use caution then. Yet no matter how quickly I went, there was only the hush of the forest, shafts of sunlight filtering through the high branches. Once, a rabbit darted across the track, and I jumped back, startled.

Nothing looked familiar; not that the forest was terribly well known to me. I'd no doubt that Neeve would know precisely where she was within the Darkwood, but I had no sense of where I was in the vast reaches of the forest. Far from the edge, I'd guess. And getting farther.

I pulled my coat close around me and hoped that the quiet of the forest would continue—that sense that the trees had been charmed to let humans pass through without trouble.

At least I had a trail to follow.

After a time, hunger pulled at my belly. I thought about the dried fruit in my belt pouch and wished I'd thought to bring something more to eat. But how could I have guessed that this adventure would lead me so far into the forest?

My thirst was easier to satisfy. Neeve and I had drunk many times from the little streams threaded through the Darkwood. When the cart tracks passed near one such rivulet, I paused to scoop several palmfuls of cool, clear water to my mouth.

With mounting unease, I noted that the light filtering through the trees was fading. Twilight would come soon, and I was alone in the woods. A shiver gripped the back of my neck, but I pushed it away.

Surely I would meet up with the people I was following very soon. They couldn't be that far ahead—could they?

Darkness fell, turning everything the color of ash. I moved as quickly as I could, nearly running along the ruts embedded in the loam. My breath sawed harshly in and out of my lungs, but I didn't pause.

Where had the people of Castle Raine gone?

An owl hooted overhead, and I nearly jumped out of my skin. A whimper tightened my throat as something crackled in the underbrush.

Then light showed ahead, three small glimmers that at first I thought were the glow of lamps. With renewed courage, I hurried forward—only to find I could not catch up to the lights. They were too high for lanterns, I realized, and flitted through the trees. Were they the same bright creatures I had glimpsed before, floating over the silver tarn and dancing above the Darkwood?

Too busy looking up at them, I missed the moment the tracks veered away from the edge of a ravine. One moment I was striding along, the next, my boots encountered nothing but empty air.

With a shout, I tumbled down a steep slope. Brambles ripped at my coat and tangled in my hair. I flailed my arms and legs, trying to find purchase. Finally, I managed to dig my heels into the soil and wrap my scratched hands around the thin stems of a nearby bush.

Panting, I hung there a moment.

If only I could see! Below me was blackness, and I couldn't tell how deep the ravine was. If I let go, I might fall to my death. Above me, dark branches interlaced against the charcoal sky.

Then a flicker. A spark.

One of the glimmering lights floated over the edge of the ravine and traveled past me. It came so close I could have reached out to touch it, were my hands not knotted fiercely around a bush.

My fear transformed to wonder as I saw that the heart of the glowing ball was made up of a tiny, winged figure. As it drifted past, I squinted, but could only make out a head and body, arms and legs. And bright wings, beating so quickly they were almost a blur.

"Wait," I breathed as the little creature continued on down the slope.

It stopped, as if it had heard me. Belatedly, I realized that it had halted at the bottom. Which lay, to my utter relief, not that far below.

I let go of the bush and slid down the last bit of hill.

"Thank you," I said softly.

The spark bobbed up and down, then rose and hovered a few paces away. I slowly got to my feet, brushing the worst of the dirt and twigs from my clothing. A scrape on my cheek stung, and I'd be bruised on the morrow, but nothing worse than that.

Slowly, the ball of light began to drift away into the surrounding trees.

It was my only guide, and it did not seem to wish me harm. I pulled my coat to rights and followed.

The glowing spark led me along the bottom of the embankment. After a short time, I smelled smoke. Not the scent of danger, but that of a cooking fire where meat sizzled over the flames. My mouth filled with hunger again.

Soon after, I saw light through the trees—the warm shine of lanterns and the redder blaze of campfires. It was as though the creature made of light had freed me from some enchantment of wandering lost and alone through the Darkwood, forever.

I looked up to thank my guide, but it had disappeared, perhaps to join the winking multitude of stars that sprinkled the sky overhead.

"Thank you," I whispered again, just in case it could still hear me.

The sound of voices filtered from the encampment ahead. Although my first impulse was to rush forward, I hung back. If it was, indeed, the folk of Castle Raine, they did not want my presence. After all, I was supposed to be deep in a drugged sleep back in my rooms. As soon as I made myself known, I'd no doubt they would dispatch me back to the castle with all speed.

It might be another group entirely, and then what? Were there brigands this deep in the forest? Or—my heart thumped wildly at the thought—perhaps it was Thorne's mysterious people.

Pulse speeding, I crept as close as I dared, then carefully peered from behind the creased bark of a cedar tree.

Heart sinking slightly, I saw that the camp was filled with people I recognized from Castle Raine. The head cook brandished a ladle above a large iron pot hung over a cook fire. One of the grooms was hard at work brushing down the cart horses. I even caught a glimpse of Miss Groves in conversation with another woman.

Hurriedly I ducked back behind the tree. Well then. Nothing particularly interesting seemed to be happening, other than the population of the castle removing to the middle of the Darkwood. I'd settle in for the night, and see what the morrow might bring.

Surely an answer to why they were there in the first place.

I crept a few paces back into the forest—not too far, so that I could still see the comforting flicker of the fires and lanterns. After a little searching, I found a mossy spot at the base of a tree where I could lean my back against the rough, sweet-smelling bark.

At least the night was not too cold. I would be able to rest without much discomfort, though a blanket would have been nice. As would something more to eat. Should I devour my bit of dried fruit now, or save it for the morning?

I decided to wait, and pulled my coat closer about me. Next time I left the castle, I vowed to be better supplied. With a sigh, I leaned my head back against the tree, too tired to care that the nubbly bark poked the back of my head.

I must have dozed, but something brought me wide awake. Lifting my head, I scanned the trees. My heartbeat thumped against my ribs. Someone, or something, was watching me—I was sure of it. Slowly, I slid my hand to my belt pouch and fumbled for my purloined knife. It was a small weapon, but better than nothing.

The camp was quiet now, the fires banked, the murmurs of conversation stilled. If I yelled for help, would anyone wake and hear me?

"Who's there?" I whispered, my throat raw with fear.

A figure detached from the shadows beneath the trees and strode forward. I recognized that confident walk, the swirl of that cloak, and my tight grip on the knife eased.

"Thorne?" I asked softly, though I knew it was him.

"Rose." He came and knelt beside me. One long, cool finger traced the scratch on my cheek. "You're hurt. I'm sorry I wasn't here to sense you entering the Darkwood. I only recently became aware of your presence."

"Am I in trouble?" I stared up at him. He didn't *seem* angry. Weary, perhaps, and worried, but no temper sparked in his dark eyes. At least, none that I could see in the dimness.

"Trouble?" He settled cross-legged beside me. "That depends. You were lucky to avoid the dangers of the forest. And luckier still to find this place. It is not a simple thing for mortals to do."

"One of the sparks showed me," I said.

"Ah." He cocked his head thoughtfully. "Then you're here for a reason, although those who dwell in Castle Raine will not be pleased to find out you followed them."

I folded my arms around my knees. "Well, they should have just told me where they were going. It would have been far less bother than tracking them through the whole forest."

A half-smile teased his lips. "You're so very stubborn."

I couldn't argue with that. At least he wasn't furious with me.

"Where exactly are we?" I asked. "Other than deep in the Darkwood, obviously. What are the people of Castle Raine doing here?"

In the silence that followed my question, my stomach gurgled loudly. My cheeks heated with embarrassment, and I wished I'd eaten my fruit, after all.

"Since you are, against all expectation, here," Thorne said, "I will tell you what I may. And I suppose I must feed you as well."

He rummaged in his cloak and brought forth a small, round loaf of bread and a flask of water.

"Thank you," I said, grateful for even such plain fare.

Despite the simplicity of the food, or perhaps because of my hunger, the bread tasted delicious, and more filling than I would have guessed. The water was cool and refreshing, with a slight tingle upon my tongue. I wondered where it had come from, but decided that was the least of my questions. Curbing my tongue, I waited for Thorne to speak.

"We are near the very heart of the Darkwood," he said at last.

"It only takes an afternoon to travel to?"

"If you are meant to find it, yes. If you are not meant to come here, however, then you would wander lost in the forest for days, and never discover the heart of the woods."

"Oh." I took another bite of bread, swallowing it along with the information. "Is there anything here, besides trees?" I waved my hand at the towering evergreens.

He gave a brief, nearly soundless laugh. "Yes. But you'll see it in the morning."

"What happens then?"

"Patience, Rose."

I was too weary to reply as hotly as I wished. "Why must you be so evasive? Just tell me."

He only shook his head, the faint starlight shining on his dark hair.

Oh, he was maddening—but he'd said I would know more tomorrow. At least I was only one night away from answers. I supposed I could curb my impatience that long. And I was tired.

As if my body was only waiting for me to acknowledge the fact, I yawned widely.

"Do you have a spare blanket, by chance?" I asked Thorne.

In answer, he unclasped his cloak and whirled it over me. It was warm, and smelled of moonlight and strange flowers. I had a moment to wonder if he'd put a sleeping enchantment on me, but then sweet darkness pulled me into slumber.

CHAPTER 27

I woke once in the night to find I was lying beneath the tree, Thorne's cloak over me. I lifted my head and saw him still sitting beside me.

"Hush," he said softly. "All is well. Go back to sleep."

Reassured, I did.

The bustle of the nearby camp coming to life woke me: the clang of cooking pots, the sound of voices, the snap of sticks breaking to feed the fire. I lay a moment, comfortable on the soft mosses, and blinked up at the bits of fresh blue sky visible through the screen of evergreen branches. It was early, judging by the slant of the light—not much after dawn.

I stretched, finding I was not as sore from my tumble into the ravine as I'd feared. Finally, I sat up, sorry to find that Thorne was gone.

His cloak still covered me, though. Another loaf of bread, half wrapped in leaves, lay where he'd sat. The flask had been refilled, too, though with normal-tasting water this time, as I discovered when I took a sip.

Combing the needles and twigs out of my hair with my fingers as best I could, I thought about how to approach the camp. Or if I should.

Perhaps it was better to remain hidden and watch. At least until I knew what, precisely, was afoot. Standing, I slung Thorne's cloak over my shoulders. The dark green color would help conceal me as I crept closer to the camp.

The smell of frying meat drifted on the air, along with the raw smoke of newly kindled flames. I skulked from tree to tree until I saw the outline of tents ahead. Most were small, but a larger one rose in the center.

I guessed it belonged to the king. For a moment, I wondered if my mother were there, but quickly dismissed the notion. Either she was lying in a drugged sleep in the castle, or she knew what was happening and had chosen not to participate. Camping in the forest was not something Mama would willingly do. She preferred her comforts too much—as our journey to Raine had proven.

As I watched, Neeve stepped out of the big tent. I scowled at this proof of her treachery. Clearly she'd known all along what was going on, and had only pretended ignorance to lull me. She glanced around, and I faded back into the trees. If anyone had the power to discover my illicit presence, it was my stepsister.

It didn't take long for the rest of the tents to empty. I revised my estimate of the number of people present, as more men and women, and even children, joined those breaking their fasts around the camp-fires. The inhabitants of the village of Little Hazel must have joined the group, for surely Castle Raine did not hold so many bodies.

A bell clanged, and the few stragglers finished their meals and hurried back to their tents. In a few minutes, a line of people had formed on the far side of the camp. All of them carried baskets and bags, some on their backs, some over shoulders. Even the children held containers of some kind.

Obviously, the folk of Raine had come into the forest to collect something. As they filed away from the camp, I followed, as soft-footed as I could manage. The sound of conversations and laughter was a welcome change from my silent trek through the forest the day before.

The trees thinned, and ahead I glimpsed a wide clearing filled with people. When I grew close enough to make out their features, my steps halted, my chest suddenly filled with excited fire.

Every one of the figures standing in the clearing had pale skin and pointed ears, their dark eyes filled with strange light. Most sported intricate braids looped and twined about their faces, though not everyone had the jet-black hair of Neeve and Thorne. I spied some dark brown and russet plaits, and some with silver hair. Not one of them had bright red locks like my own, and neither did their hair frizz and curl, but fell straight and shining where it was not elegantly plaited.

Here, in the heart of the Darkwood, was where Thorne's people dwelt. Just as I'd suspected.

I had *finally* discovered the great mystery of the forest.

At the head of the delegation stood a hard-faced man wearing a silver circlet upon his brow. This was no mortal man, however. The planes of his face were even stranger than Thorne's, with a feral, almost jagged cast. Thorne stood slightly behind and to the left of the man, in the position of advisor. Or heir? Was Thorne a prince?

Lord Raine stepped forward, and I saw that he, too, had donned a crown. Clearly, this was a meeting between monarchs.

"Greetings, Nightshade Lord," the king said. "We offer peace and renewed prosperity to you and your people."

The lord inclined his head. "And to you, King Tobin. Is my niece among you this day?"

King Tobin gestured, and Neeve came to stand at his side, pale and serious. My mind whirled furiously, various pieces falling into place. As I'd guessed, Neeve was not entirely human. Her mother must have been one of these strange, graceful beings.

"Greetings, Uncle." Neeve dropped the Nightshade Lord an elegant curtsey.

He regarded her a moment, then gave a short nod. "I am pleased to see that reports of your wellbeing are accurate."

I saw her glance at Thorne. "They are, my lord. I am quite well."

"Still, I hear news of the castle that concerns me." The Nightshade Lord's voice grew cold. "King Tobin, you have wed a mortal woman from outside the borders of Raine. I must question the wisdom of such an action."

The king's shoulders stiffened. "You need not concern yourself with my kingdom. I would never place my people, or our alliance with the Dark Elves, in jeopardy. Your secret is safe."

The Dark Elves! At last, I had a name for them. And a fitting one it was.

"I hope you are correct." The Nightshade Lord's dark gaze swept the clearing.

I shrank back, heart pounding, and went to my knees on the soft moss. What would they do to me if they discovered a spy in their midst? I was living proof that the king was wrong, and an outsider was now privy to the fact of the Dark Elves' existence.

Not that *I* was any danger to them. Whom would I tell? And who would even believe me? This was the stuff of myth and fable, magic and wonder.

Thorne's cautions came to me then, and I recalled his concern that I might tell Mama, and that she would share the information with her friends in Parnese. It was a justified concern. My mother didn't keep secrets, not when sharing them could benefit her in some way. If she thought revealing the Dark Elves' existence would give her power or social standing, she would not hesitate to do so.

But I would never tell Mama, and thus she would never be able to share that information where it might do harm.

I couldn't name the danger, exactly, but I knew how people reacted when faced with a power they did not understand. The crackle of remembered flames sounded loud in my ears.

"I believe King Tobin has acted in the interests of his kingdom," Thorne said. "And the interests of his daughter. In my role as *Galadhir*, I have sensed little threat to the Darkwood."

"*Little* threat?" The Nightshade Lord's eyes narrowed.

"My lord, there is never complete safety," Thorne said. "You know that as well as I. Fate weaves its web, despite our petty strivings."

The Dark Elf lord's scowl eased, though he still looked displeased.

"For centuries, our people have met on the day of the *nirwen*'s blooming," King Tobin said. "You know as well as I that we only have a short time to gather the blossoms before they fade. Why waste time in useless bickering? Already the day is advancing."

"Very well." The Nightshade Lord strode forward. "I accept your peace, and offer you prosperity in return. For another turning of the moons."

The two rulers clasped hands, and I felt the forest shiver, then settle. The moment they parted, the clearing erupted in activity.

As the Dark Elves moved forward, I could see they'd been grouped around two tall stones rising in the center of the silvery grasses. Squinting, I could just make out mysterious runes carved along the granite sides of the stones.

Like the humans, the elves had brought a variety of baskets and sacks. As the sun rose higher, the first beams slanted down, touching the standing stones with light. Brightness sparked, the runes glowing gold.

The crowd let out a cheer, human and inhuman voices mingling. Then, before my astonished gaze, flowers began to open all across the clearing. Bright gold blooms, five petals like a star. In a ripple of light, the flowers sprang up, spreading in shining rivulets through the forest.

Dark Elf and mortal fell to picking the sudden bounty, but no matter how quickly they plucked the flowers, more opened to take their place.

One pushed up through the earth at my knee, the petals uncurling to shed a warm glow over me. *Nirwen.*

I knew it was magic.

I held out a tentative finger, half expecting to feel heat rising from the blossom. It was no warmer than the air, however.

Partially from curiosity, partially to keep anyone from coming over to pluck the bloom, and thus discovering me, I gently snapped the stem between my fingers. The *nirwen* didn't immediately droop or fade, I was glad to see. Carefully, I tucked the glowing flower into my belt pouch.

"What are you doing here?" The familiar voice was hard with suspicion and anger.

With an inward sigh, I swiveled to see my stepsister standing a few paces away, hands on her hips and angry color high on her cheeks.

CHAPTER 28

"Hello, Neeve," I said, trying to sound calm.

"I should have known." She stalked over to where I knelt. "You *do* love to follow people where you're not wanted, don't you?"

I got to my feet and glared at her, not budging one inch. "And I'm good at it. Besides, Thorne knows I'm here."

"He does?" Her eyes widened a fraction.

"Yes." I pulled his cloak around me with a dramatic swirl.

She stared at it, the scowl returning to her face. "That doesn't mean you're welcome here. How much did you see?"

"Everything. I know about the Dark Elves, and that the Night-shade Lord is your uncle. And that you're all here to pick *nirwen*, because it doesn't last very long." I was a little unclear on the last bit, but Neeve didn't challenge me on the point.

"Then you know too much." She stared at me a moment more. "If Thorne's aware you're here, I don't suppose I could convince him to take your memories away."

"I wouldn't let him," I said fiercely. Not that I could stop him, if he truly planned to do so. The knowledge made me shiver.

A haughty-faced elven woman walked by, the basket over her arm already half full of bright flowers. She glanced at us and sniffed, clearly implying we were shirking our duties.

"Come." Neeve grabbed my arm, her fingers hard.

"Where?" Was she planning to haul me in front of her father and the Nightshade Lord? I dug in my heels.

"There's a glade nearby where the *nirwen* grows. We can pick, and talk, undisturbed."

"Very well." I pulled out of her grasp. The last thing I needed was my stepsister dragging me about like a recalcitrant child.

"Here." She thrust the basket she was carrying at me. "I'll fetch another from the camp. Use it to shield your face if anyone you recognize comes close."

I was relieved that Neeve was willing to conceal my presence; perhaps because Thorne had already accepted me.

Luckily, the camp was deserted. My stepsister snatched a few sacks from a pile, then led me around the spread of tents and into the shelter of the trees.

Somehow, I was not surprised to see Thorne waiting for us there.

Neeve strode up to him, indignant.

"How can you allow Rose's presence?" she demanded. "Why didn't you stop her from coming?"

"Peace," he said, lifting his hands. "I cannot be all places at all times. The fact that Rose was able to follow the tracks through the forest shows she's meant to be here. And didn't you tell me you'd seen the *nirwen* blossom when you scryed in Airgid Tarn—and that Rose saw it, too?"

I threw Neeve a smug look.

"We shouldn't waste time arguing," she said, though she was the one who'd started it. "We only have a little time to harvest the blossoms."

"How much time?" I asked Thorne, as we followed Neeve through the underbrush.

"The blossom fades a few hours after sunset," he said. "We must gather as many as we can in that time. *Nirwen* is precious. And, for my kind, its essence provides an invaluable medicine."

"How often does it bloom?" I asked, wondering at his urgency.

"Once every three years," he said.

I halted in shock. "Every three *years*? And only for a day?"

"Less than a day," he reminded me.

"Hurry up," Neeve called over her shoulder.

I blinked away my surprise and hastened after her. The mass of people gathered to pick the flower suddenly made sense. Of course the entire castle and village would turn out, if they only had a short time to harvest as many as possible.

We came to the glade my stepsister had spoken of, a small dell filled with *nirwen* blossoms. I watched her bend and pick the flowers, snapping the stems the way I had plucked my first bloom.

"There is a tale about the *nirwen*," Thorne said to me as he walked carefully among the glowing flowers.

Neeve threw him a look. "Must you tell her *everything*?"

"It's her right," he said mildly. "Anyone at the harvest is entitled to know the story."

I nodded eagerly. At last, the answers I had craved for so long were falling upon me, like raindrops on parched earth.

Neeve pointedly turned her back and continued tucking flowers into her harvest sack.

"Centuries ago," Thorne said, "a prophecy was foretold. Great danger was coming, and only the union of a mortal maid and a Dark Elf prince could save my people. In the way of prophecy, however, it wasn't quite that simple."

"It seldom is," I said with a snort. "At least, in the stories I read."

"They have the right of it." Thorne plucked a flower and held it up thoughtfully. "The enemy was defeated, yes, but the prince was mortally wounded. He retreated, to die in peace. When his mortal wife learned of his injuries, she sought him, weeping. Where her tears fell, golden flowers sprang up. The strength of her love enabled her to save her husband. So powerful was her magic that the *nirwen* flower to this day carries healing properties renowned by my people."

"It's a pretty story," Neeve said from across the glade. "But I don't think it's true."

"Wait..." I looked at Thorne. "The mortal wife had that much magic?"

"Of course she didn't," Neeve said. "It's a fable. That's all."

"Some humans have power," I retorted. "Master Fawkes, and Mistress Ainya. So it's not *all* a fable. What do you think, Thorne? Was she magic?"

He looked uncomfortable, his dark eyes not meeting mine. "I cannot say. There is a long history of the people of Raine mingling with the Dark Elves. Some think our magic can pass through the bloodlines. Others insist that humans have a strange magic all their own."

I plucked a few flowers and thought on that. "So, Mistress Ainya and Master Fawkes' magic is because they have Dark Elf ancestors?"

"Perhaps," Thorne said, his hands busy with flowers.

"But if only the people of Raine have magic, what about the sorcerers in Parnese? What about the priests of the Twin Gods?"

"We don't worship them here," Neeve said coldly.

I'd known as much, although no one had ever said it quite so bluntly. But then, the countries to the north and west of Parnese were known to have barbaric pasts. Raine included.

"Why aren't more of your people here, Thorne?" If the *nirwen* was so important to the Dark Elves, it was strange that there were not hundreds of them present for the harvest.

"There are enough," he said. "And whatever is harvested is split evenly between my people and yours."

"No matter who picks the most? That doesn't seem fair."

"It's not a competition," Neeve said. "Everyone shares in the bounty."

"The balance is... complicated." Thorne glanced around our little glade, which we'd emptied of glowing blossoms. "Speaking of which, we need to find another patch."

We did, and when our containers were full to overflowing with blossoms, Neeve and Thorne took them back to the camp. We all judged it was better for me to remain hidden in the trees.

They returned with lunch—bread and cheese and fruit, and skins of cool water.

"The harvest is going well," Thorne said as we sat in a sunny patch of forest, eating. "This year, there is an abundance of *nirwen*."

"Will we be able to pick all the flowers before they fade?" I asked.

"No." Neeve brushed crumbs from her skirt. "We never do."

"Then why not bring more people?"

My stepsister glared at me, and Thorne let out a small laugh.

"Where, and how, the *nirwen* grows is one of the most closely guarded secrets of Raine," he said. "The fewer who actually set eyes upon my people, the better."

I bit into my apple, thinking. I supposed I was so used to Thorne's strange features that he seemed normal—but if I were not, I would have been shocked when I saw the Dark Elves. They were so otherworldly, there could be no disguising the fact that beings other than humans dwelt in Raine.

"Where do the Dark Elves live?" I asked. "Is your city nearby?"

Thorne and Neeve exchanged a quick glance, and then he shook his head.

"It's some distance still to reach Elfhame, and the courts."

I seized on this bit of information. "Elfhame? The courts? Nightshade isn't the only one?"

"There are seven courts," Thorne said.

"Is the Nightshade Lord the King of Elfhame?"

"You ask too many questions," Neeve said.

"There is no king," Thorne said, ignoring her sniping. "Each court's ruler sits in a convocation together, when there's need. Mostly the courts govern themselves. Now, enough talk. We have only a few more hours to gather as much *nirwen* as we can."

True to his word, Thorne worked us hard. We spread out through the forest, within earshot, but not so close that I could continue to ask the questions springing up inside me.

Which court did Thorne belong to? What were the other ones called? Was Elfhame the city of the Dark Elves?

Twice more Neeve and Thorne took our harvest back to the camp while I waited. Despite being left alone, I was too tired to be afraid. Besides, it seemed as though all the power of the Darkwood was focused on the harvest. One mortal girl could be overlooked for a time.

Finally, twilight fell. The shining beacons of the *nirwen* were easy to follow, but once plucked, we stood in the ashen dimness of the Dark-wood. My fingers ached from gathering flowers all day, and my shoulders were sore where the picking basket hung. The blossoms were not terribly heavy, but I wasn't used to carrying around any burden, let alone for hours at a time.

Thorne glanced at our overfull baskets and bags. "A good day's work."

Neeve nodded wearily. "Yes—but what are we going to do about Rose?"

"I don't particularly want to sleep alone in the forest again," I said. Maybe Neeve could commandeer a small tent and join me. Or Thorne could watch over me again.

"You won't." Thorne gave me a long look. "We must take you into the camp and bring you before the king and the Nightshade Lord."

"Or maybe I *can* spend the night under the trees," I said hastily. "It's not so bad, after all."

Thorne let out a sigh. "I must bring you forth. If you're discovered, it will raise too many awkward questions. And you cannot be left behind when everyone departs."

"Why not? I followed the cart tracks here. I could follow them back to the castle easily enough."

"No, you can't," Neeve said.

I opened my mouth to argue, but Thorne lifted his hand.

"Not that you're incapable of doing so," he said. "But the people of Castle Raine return via... other means. And the tracks you followed here have since disappeared."

"Oh."

I recalled how Thorne had used magic to transport us from the waterfall to the edge of the forest, and guessed he would do the same for the humans now present in the Darkwood.

"The *nirwen* must be processed," Neeve said. "We can't waste time returning to the castle the normal way. At first light, we strike the camp and depart."

"I must tell you, also, that after today you'll not see me again until spring," Thorne said, turning to lead us back to the camp.

My heart clutched a little in my chest. I had so few allies, I hated to lose him, even if he'd return in a few months.

"Why must you go?" I tried not to sound too forlorn.

"All hands are needed to help with the harvest—and most especially my own, due to my bond with the Darkwood. And then I will remain with my people, as I do every winter."

I could make no argument against that. Silently, the burden of flowers heavy upon my shoulders, I followed him and Neeve through the dusky shadows of the forest.

Campfires and the glow of lanterns glimmered through the trees. We'd reach the camp soon. My steps dragged, heavy with the fear of being presented to the imposing Nightshade Lord. Not to mention facing the wrath of Lord Raine into the bargain.

CHAPTER 29

I t was every bit as terrible as I'd feared.

I stood before a platform set up in the clearing, where Lord Raine and the Nightshade Lord presided over a makeshift court. My stomach knotted before their combined disapproving gazes. At least I had Thorne with me, hovering just behind my right shoulder. Neeve watched from a few paces away, though I didn't think I had her support so much as her grudging acceptance.

"This is your stepdaughter?" The Nightshade Lord looked from me to the king, clearly unimpressed. "She seems young to be wandering the Darkwood alone. I thought you took better care of your subjects— particularly the ones who dwell within your castle."

Lord Raine's mouth tightened. "I am not remiss in my duties, Nightshade. I understand that Rose is known to the *Galadhir*, and her presence in the Darkwood is permitted."

The Nightshade Lord's cold, dark gaze turned on Thorne. "What games are you playing, Guardian of the Wood? Remember, my niece's wellbeing is entrusted to you. Any breach of that duty, and you will pay dearly."

"My lord." Thorne stepped forward and bowed his head. "You know I'd never let Neeve come to harm. Rose presents no threat."

I tried to look small and unthreatening, which wasn't difficult. My hair was a tangled frizz of red (I hadn't thought to bring a hairbrush, and Neeve hadn't offered one), my clothing was wrinkled from sleeping in the forest, and besides, who would wear a too-small black outfit to meet a Dark Elf king?

My only solace was that Thorne had draped his cloak about me again, and I'd managed to smooth the hair back from my face. I was presentable, at a quick glance. The scrutiny of the two lords, however, made me feel like a tattered mouse facing a pair of sleek and deadly cats.

Lord Raine glanced at the elf lord, frowning. "I find it troubling that Thorne—your kinsman—allowed an outsider to discover our secrets. The *nirwen* harvest should not be so easily infiltrated."

"By a member of *your* family," the Nightshade Lord said. "I thought you had precautions in place."

"I assure you—"

"Please." Thorne raised his hands. "My lords, there is no need to argue. I accept the blame you both place upon me. But remember, the Darkwood allowed Rose to pass—which it would never have done if she was a danger to Elfhame. She is meant to be here."

That silenced the monarchs. The Nightshade Lord gave me a long look that made my toes curl in my boots. There was something predatory in his eyes—a sudden sharpness that made me feel all too visible. Conscious of my horribly disheveled state, I dropped my gaze to the ground and tried to seem like an innocent girl, haplessly caught up in the web of fate. After all, it was true. Even if my wicked little voice had urged me to uncover everything I could about the forest and its secrets.

"Very well," the Nightshade Lord said. "She is here now, and I suppose that is as the Darkwood wills."

I swallowed past the dryness in my throat, and tried to banish the fear running through me like a shadow in my blood.

Lord Raine nodded, but still seemed displeased.

"Rose," he said to me, "as a consequence of your disobedience, you will not be allowed out of the castle for the next several months."

My mouth was forming the word *but* when Thorne gave me a

gentle poke in the back, as if sensing my denial. It was a reminder that one did not argue with the king—especially not in front of another lord.

I gulped back my protest. Then I recalled that Thorne was going away, leaving the forest empty, and my rebellion died down to ashes.

"Yes, my lord." I bobbed Lord Raine a curtsey.

"Now that the matter is settled," Lord Raine said, rising, "let us begin the feasting. What do you say, elf lord?"

"I say it is past time for the festivities to begin, mortal king." The Nightshade Lord stood, and I blinked to see he was nearly a head taller than the King of Raine.

To my dismay, his gaze fell upon me again, weighing, considering. I took a step back and felt Thorne's reassuring presence at my side. The Dark Elf's eyes narrowed slightly. Then he turned to address the gathering. I pulled in a breath, feeling like a rabbit who'd just escaped the snare.

"Gentlefolk!" the Nightshade Lord called, his powerful voice filling the clearing and filtering between the trees. "Let us celebrate the conclusion of another successful *nirwen* harvest with food and drink, story and song!"

The assembled crowd of elves and humans let out a cheer. Music began, and I looked around, following the sound until I saw that Master Fawkes was there, in company with a slender Dark Elf lady. It shouldn't have surprised me to see him, as he was Raine's bard, yet it did. He strummed his lute, and she plucked a strange, round instrument with many strings. The resulting melody was ethereal and lovely, drifting like soft mist through the clearing.

With a wave of his hand, the Nightshade Lord caused long tables to appear, laden with platters of food. Dark Elves and mortals alike found places to sit on the chairs that had likewise materialized. A few humans circulated, carrying ewers of honey mead that I guessed had been transported from Castle Raine's cellars.

Lanterns shone around the perimeter of the clearing, and the two standing stones in the center glowed with a soft, pearly light. The tables sported lights, too—delicate, colorful fires dancing over silver structures that were not, quite, candelabra.

Overhead, the stars gleamed brilliantly. Several dozen sparks detached themselves from the firmament and grew larger, resolving into the flitting light-creatures I'd seen before. The bright lights swirled above the guests, bobbing and dancing. Thorne smiled up at them, and even Neeve looked faintly amused.

"What are they?" I asked.

"We call them glimglows," Thorne said.

"They helped me come here," I said. "Do they live in the forest?"

"I'm hungry," Neeve said, abruptly moving away. "Let's find a spot at the tables."

"An excellent thought," Thorne agreed.

It didn't escape my notice that neither of them had answered my question. But I didn't want to be accused of being pesterful yet again. With an inward sigh, I followed them to the end of one of the tables where there was plenty of room for the three of us.

An air of melancholy gaiety tinged the feasting. Dark Elves and humans smiled and ate, though they didn't converse much with one another. The music was happy, yet sad. The food was delicious, sharp and sweet flavors that mingled pleasantly on my tongue, followed by a refreshing drink of the same tingling water Thorne had given me the night before.

Thorne took a small cup of mead, but both Neeve and I shook our heads when it was offered. For me, the evening was too magical to dull my senses with alcohol—not that I had much of a taste for it. I wondered if Neeve felt the same.

I caught her looking to where the Nightshade Lord sat, surrounded by his elegant Dark Elf courtiers. Neeve's expression was filled with stark yearning, and I blinked to see it. It hadn't occurred to me that my stepsister, too, might want a life outside of the one she had.

"Do you ever visit them?" I asked.

"No." Neeve's gaze returned to her plate.

"Why not?" I persisted. "After all, he's your uncle."

"I'm not allowed to set foot in Elfhame," she said, her tone sharp.

"Neeve." Thorne set a hand on her shoulder.

She twitched away from his touch. "I know—it's necessary. But that doesn't mean I like the bargain my ancestors struck. Especially when *you* can travel freely."

"Don't be so upset—" Thorne began, but Neeve rounded on him fiercely.

"It's where my mother is from." Her eyes were bright with fury. "It's my *homeland*, Thorne, and I am barred from ever seeing it. Forbidden to be with my own people. I have the right to be angry about that—whatever you might think."

I watched this interaction, mouth open. Just when I finally received answers to my questions, a dozen new ones sprang up to take their place.

CHAPTER 30

A s the evening drifted more fully into night, the feasting came to an end. A sound filled the air, shimmering silver like the peal of some unearthly bell.

"Stand up," Thorne said, rising and taking my arm to pull me away from my chair. "The tables are about to be cleared."

He meant it quite literally. Between one heartbeat and the next, the table in front of us disappeared. The chair I'd been seated on was gone, as well. I tried not to stare like a gawky mortal unused to magic and miracles—even though I was one.

"What happens if someone's still sitting there?" I asked.

"They sprawl upon the ground when their chair is dispelled," Neeve said, sounding a bit as though she wished that had happened to me. She, of course, had gracefully gotten to her feet even before Thorne spoke. "I must go bid my uncle farewell," she continued, shaking out her already immaculate skirts. "Stay here, Rose."

"Wait... the Nightshade Lord is leaving now?"

"Yes." Thorne's voice was solemn.

I turned to him, trying not to sound bereft. "Does that mean you're going, too?"

"Not yet." He smiled crookedly, then went to Neeve and set his hands on her shoulders. "Do not let him bully you one bit, *Glosgwen-neth*. You have Nightshade blood running through your veins."

"I'm quite aware of the fact." She lifted her chin and strode off. I couldn't imagine anyone, even the frightening Nightshade Lord, getting the better of her.

As I watched my stepsister go, I realized a line of Dark Elves was forming across the clearing. They carried their baskets and sacks of *nirwen*, the golden glow of the blossoms illuminating their strange, haughty faces.

"What's going on?" I asked Thorne. "Are they going to just march away like that, into the night?"

"Rose," Thorne said, his dark eyes serious. "What you are about to see... You must promise never to speak of it to anyone who doesn't already know."

I stared up at him, my heart pounding. I'd thought the existence of the Dark Elves and the *nirwen* were the greatest secrets of the Dark-wood. Now, I realized I'd been wrong. Anticipation ran like fire just under my skin.

There was another secret—a much bigger one, judging from the look on Thorne's face.

"I promise," I whispered.

His expression stern, Thorne pushed up his left sleeve and gestured for me to do the same. Fingers trembling, I did. A flash of pain ran from my stub of a pinky to the tattooed leaf at my elbow. Was he going to perform another binding ceremony?

"Don't look so frightened," he said, his face softening as he clasped my hand in his. "I'm only reminding the forest that you have been marked by my blood, and Neeve's."

The leaf inscribed at my elbow throbbed in time with my heart-beat. Thorne's hand was cool and strong.

"Watch," he said quietly, not letting go of me.

I found his touch comforting, and hoped he wouldn't unclasp his hand anytime soon.

The line of Dark Elves reached from the forest's edge to the center of the clearing, stopping where the Nightshade Lord stood before the two upright stones. The bright sparks Thorne had called glimglows danced and swooped overhead. A faint breeze ruffled my hair, stirred the branches of the trees surrounding the clearing, then died down to stillness.

Slowly, the Nightshade Lord raised his hands. They were outlined in blue light, and the hairs on the back of my neck stood up to see the force of his power.

"Farewell, Raine," he said. "We shall meet again in three of your mortal years. Until then, keep the promises you have made."

"I will, Nightshade," the king said. "And you do the same."

The two monarchs tilted their heads toward one another in a measured goodbye. Then Lord Raine stepped back to where the rest of the humans stood, all but hidden in the shadows.

The Nightshade Lord, his long, dark hair crackling with blue sparks, turned to face the space between the two stones. The air shimmered, and I nearly gasped aloud when I understood what I was seeing.

A doorway, bounded on either side by shimmering granite.

The elf lord cried out, one of the strange words of his people, and blue light flashed, so bright I had to close my eyes. When I opened them again, I saw that the door had opened.

It was a portal between the mortal world and that of the Dark Elves—beyond anything I'd imagined. No wonder there was no city here, no sign of habitation. Thorne's people didn't live in Raine. They lived in the land beyond the gateway.

It was night in that land, too. Flowers grew beyond the gate, blooms glowing with soft violet light, and a swirl of warm air breathed out, scented with herbs I could not name. A huge moon lay low in the sky, the edge just brushing the feathery tops of the trees. Higher up, a second moon floated, a sharp slice of light dimming my glimpse of unfamiliar stars. The forest of the Darkwood extended between the worlds, though on the elf side it was even darker and more mysterious, thick with enchantment.

The elves began to file between the stones, bearing the bright flowers of the *nirwen*. It was uncanny, to see them step into that space and not emerge in the clearing beyond. Instead, one by one, they winked out of existence in the mortal world.

Finally, only the Nightshade Lord was left.

He glanced over his shoulder to where Thorne and I stood at the edge of the clearing. I shrank back from the intensity of his gaze, which seemed to see everything about me, despite the darkness that had fallen. Thorne held my hand tightly, though he said nothing.

Then, accompanied by a sudden scatter of glimglow sparks, the elf lord turned away and strode between the stones.

The glowing runes went dark, and the doorway to the other world disappeared with a sound like breaking stone.

I heard a muffled sob, and with a shock realized it was my stepsister. Sympathy rose full and fast within me. If my heart was near to breaking with the beauty of the Dark Elves' world and their magical disappearance, surely for Neeve it was a sorrow almost impossible to bear.

"What was that place?" I whispered.

"That," Thorne said, "was the land of Elfhame."

"I never knew... never would have guessed it." My mind whirled with what I'd discovered that day.

"Of course not." He let go of my hand. "We guard our secrets well."

I swayed as a wave of exhaustion pulled at me, and Thorne slipped a steadying arm around my shoulders.

"Tomorrow," he said, "I send you all home to Castle Raine, then follow my people into Elfhame. Now, come. Let us see if Neeve will share her tent with you tonight."

Stony-faced, my stepsister agreed. And if, in the dark before dawn, I heard her weeping into her pillow, I said not a word.

PART III

CHAPTER 31

The rest of the fall passed into the seemingly endless rains of winter. Lord Raine gave me a stern lecture, reiterating his command that I stay out of the Darkwood for the rest of the year, and reminding me to keep the gateway to Elfhame a close-held secret. I nodded and curtseyed, and he sent me on my way. Most days I didn't mind my enforced confinement within the castle walls, as I had nowhere else I might go—other than Mistress Ainya's cottage. And since I had no magic, it was painful to be there and watch Neeve, who was impossibly far ahead of me in all her studies with the herbwife.

Just when I thought I'd go mad from lack of anything to do but study and read—and jolt about on Snowbell's back in the muddy paddock—Master Fawkes arrived. Most gratefully, I took up my harp lessons again.

We did not speak of the *nirwen* harvest, but he did begin teaching me a beautiful, ethereal tune very similar to the music I'd heard him play in the Darkwood's enchanted clearing. The melody was simple and aching. When I played it, I thought of the longing on my stepsister's face as her people stepped through the doorway to Elfhame, leaving her behind.

I thought of Thorne, too, and every day I donned my golden

pendant. Like Neeve, I tucked it beneath the neckline of my clothing, carrying the secrets of the Dark Elves just above my heart.

Our nightly dinners with the king and queen remained much the same, although the news from Parnese was disturbing. Mama had received a letter from a cousin in the courts there—proof that she had not cut all ties, and that Thorne had been wise in his caution—and the king's advisors confirmed the rumors that the priests of the Twin Gods had seized a great deal of power.

"What does it mean?" I asked, worry twisting in my belly.

If the priest's influence could reach all the way to Raine, then the people I cared about were in danger: Thorne, Neeve, Master Fawkes, Mistress Ainya. And, of course, the entire populace of Elfhame. I did not think the Twin Gods would be kindly disposed toward magical, non-human elves dwelling just outside the mortal world.

"There is no reason for those meddling priests to come to Raine," Lord Raine said, his voice hard. "With the exception of our trade agreements, we stay out of the affairs of the Continent, and they stay out of ours."

My mother, looking pale and beautiful, reached for her goblet of wine.

"You have spies in Parnese, though, don't you?" she asked. "Just in case?"

The king glanced at me and Neeve, then back to my mother. "There is nothing to fear, Arabelle. We will speak more of this later. But I do have some welcome news concerning our neighbor in the north. The King of Fiorland is sending his youngest son here as a fosterling."

I set my fork down upon my plate with a clank and exchanged a quick look with Neeve. Her mouth was set, a hint of red staining her cheeks. Clearly the news displeased her.

For myself, I had to admit a certain anticipation. Even if the prince was an utter bore, any change, especially in the doldrums of winter, was welcome.

"When is the boy arriving?" my mother asked.

"He is coming with the Fiorland emissary, in time for the Yule Feast," Lord Raine replied.

Less than a moon's turning. My interest sharpened at the prospect.

"What's his name?" I asked, ignoring Neeve's scowl. She might not care for this news, but I was determined to gather up every scrap of information I could.

"Kian Leifson," Lord Raine said. "He will foster with us for four years, as is customary. I expect you to treat him as a member of the family."

"Yes, Father," Neeve said. Her voice was quiet, but I detected the note of rebellion beneath.

"Of course, my lord," I said, with much more sincerity.

Not only would I no longer be the newest outsider in Castle Raine, it was quite possible that Kian would be a friendly fellow. The youngest of several siblings—surely he would be jovial. Or at least have some interesting stories to tell.

My mother gave me a pointed look, then glanced at Neeve, and from this it was clear to me that Kian was there as a potential suitor for my stepsister. Certainly not for me, which didn't bother me in the least. I might be a princess by marriage, but Neeve was heir to the throne. The advantage of strengthening the political alliance between Raine and Fiorland was obvious.

I gave Mama a slight nod in return, my thoughts whirling. Where was Thorne in all of this? Clearly his affections lay with Neeve. It would break his heart to see her wed to a mortal prince. My own heart twisted in sympathy.

As for myself, I could privately admit that Thorne was dearer to me than a friend. But he was a Dark Elf, and I was a human girl with nothing more than the shadow of some unknown fate hanging over me. Our worlds might touch, but never join.

⁂

As the Yule Feast approached, the entire castle was distracted by the imminent arrival of Prince Kian. Even Neeve's fifteenth birthday went mostly unremarked. She grew quieter than usual, and took to spending every afternoon riding Peerless.

She certainly understood the implications of hosting the Fiorlander prince—and what that meant for her future—but every time I broached the subject, she turned the conversation away.

I was grateful that the castle's memories of last year's feast were thoroughly eclipsed by the bustle of preparing for the Fiorlanders' arrival. The royal seamstress was busy with a new wardrobe for Neeve, who was now as tall as my mother. I, too, was to receive new gowns, as I'd outgrown the ones from last winter. I was especially pleased with my new court dress, a soft red velvet decorated with glints of gold embroidery at the sleeves and neck. It reminded me of summer sun slanting through the Darkwood.

Which reminded me of Thorne. I sighed, and tried not to count the months until spring. At least the new prince would provide a distraction during the remaining weary months of winter.

Master Fawkes dissuaded me from performing my new Elvish-sounding piece at the Yule Feast, instead suggesting I prepare a jaunty rendition of a local ballad. I agreed with him that the Dark Elf tune was too mysterious, too strange to play before the Fiorlanders. Raine's secrets could not be hinted at, even in music.

Two days before the feast, Prince Kian and his companions arrived. Neeve and I were called from the classroom to the great hall as soon as word reached the castle of their imminent arrival.

"You have time to change before you greet the prince," Miss Groves said as we closed our books and put away our writing implements.

Neeve frowned and shook out her dark skirts. "I don't see the need."

Clearly, my stepsister was not interested in catching Prince Kian's eye. Not that she looked disreputable—but her new green gown would have helped her make a stunning first impression.

"Are you ready, Rose?" Neeve asked.

"Certainly." I wasn't the one destined to wed the prince, after all, and I was eager to meet our new companion.

We arrived in the great hall to find Lord Raine and my mother seated in the ornate chairs that served as their thrones. Smaller chairs for myself and Neeve were drawn up on either side, and we quickly settled ourselves as the front doors were pulled open.

"His Highness Prince Kian Leifson of Fiorland," the king's herald announced. "Jarl Eiric, emissary of the Fiorland court. And Herr Lund, manservant to the prince."

The three men stepped into the hall, with the prince in the lead. At least, I assumed it was Prince Kian, as I recognized the emissary from the year before, and the thin, quiet man at the back certainly didn't look like royalty—not to mention he was far older than fifteen.

Prince Kian was tall, with blond hair and a square jaw. He strode forward confidently and made a formal bow before the king and queen.

"Your majesties," he said, "I am delighted to be here in Raine, and thank you for your hospitality. I expect the next four years will greatly strengthen the ties between our countries."

He straightened and smiled, and I was glad to see that one of his front teeth was a bit crooked. Otherwise, he would have been too annoyingly perfect.

His gaze went to Neeve and then skipped over to me, and his smile deepened. Oh dear. I hoped he hadn't mistaken *me* for the princess of Raine.

"Prince Kian, welcome." The king rose, then held out his hand to Neeve. "Let me present my daughter, Princess Neeve."

Neeve stood, no warmth or greeting on her pale face.

The prince blinked, his blue eyes going back to Neeve, and his smile faltered. Despite the flash of surprise I glimpsed in his expression, he made her a flawless bow.

"Lady Neeve," he said. "The pleasure is mine."

She inclined her head, and said nothing. Goodness—even at her prickliest, when we'd first met, Neeve had at least *spoken* to me. It looked as though we might be in for an awkward four years. I wished I was standing close enough to my stepsister to prod her into speech, but alas, all I could do was give her a pointed look. Which she pointedly ignored in turn.

"This is my wife, Queen Arabelle," Lord Raine continued. "And her daughter, Lady Rosaline."

I stood and gave the prince my best court curtsey.

"Lady Rosaline." He inclined his head.

"Please, call me Rose."

His expression warmed. "I will, if that is what you wish."

Lord Raine cleared his throat. "Prince Kian, I'll have the servants show you to your rooms in the west wing. Don't hesitate to let me know if there's anything you need. Dinner will be served promptly at seven."

My breath caught a moment, as I realized that everything was about to change again—in ways I hadn't anticipated. Beginning with our dinners, which now would include the prince. Was he to join us in the classroom as well?

I'd been a fool not to consider what it would mean, having a foster-ling at the castle, or how it would upset my familiar routine. And what were we to do once summer came? Surely Neeve and I couldn't allow Prince Kian to follow us into the Darkwood.

The king dismissed us, and I caught my stepsister's eye as we filed out of the hall. She looked more grim than usual, and in truth, I couldn't blame her.

Once we had mounted the stairs and were alone in the east corridor, I touched her elbow.

"What do you think of him?" I asked.

"I don't," she replied shortly. "The sooner he's gone from Castle Raine, the better."

I stared at her. "He's meant to be here for four years, though. Do you have a plan to make him go? Wouldn't that cause a diplomatic incident?"

"I'm not going to force him to leave, Rose." Her tone carried an exasperated edge. "But I will certainly make it clear that I've no intention of agreeing to a marriage alliance with Fiorland."

I wanted to ask if she thought that was wise, but I didn't want to be on the receiving end of her temper. And there was time, surely, for her to change her mind—provided that an alliance was the desired outcome. Who knew what the king had planned for her future?

"Do you think Prince Kian will listen to you?" I'd already judged his character to be willful, though perhaps that was because he was a prince, and royalty was used to getting their own way.

She shrugged. "I don't care. My mind is made up. But you may go ahead and make moon-eyes at him all you like."

"I'll do no such thing!" Heat rushed into my cheeks.

While it was true I'd noted that Prince Kian was attractive, I wasn't going to *do* anything about it. I had no desire to marry and relocate to the wilds of Fiorland. By all accounts, the place was even colder and more uncivilized than Raine.

Besides, he was there for Neeve, not for me. No matter how much she might deny it.

She arched one dark brow and gave me a superior look. Fuming, I stalked to my door and pushed it open. The last thing I wanted was to be in the awkward middle, and I knew, clear as day, that Lord Raine would be most displeased if he thought I was setting my sights on the Fiorlander Prince.

Mama would probably take it more lightly; but then, it seemed she could do no wrong in her husband's eyes. That consideration did not extend to me. If the king thought I was trying to steal Neeve's suitor for myself—which I certainly had no intention of doing—he would not deal with me kindly.

The best course would be for me to smooth the way between Neeve and Prince Kian. Even if they didn't take to one another, no one could accuse me of standing between them if it was clear I'd been doing my best to matchmake.

I paced into my bedroom and went to the window. Although it wasn't currently raining, the silvery dome of winter clouds let not a sliver of sunshine through. A breeze stirred the dark branches of the trees, spreading like an ocean of blackish green as far as I could see. Setting my hands on the sill, I leaned forward until my forehead touched the cool glass.

Yearning coiled through me.

I wanted *magic*, not marriage. I wanted the Darkwood to accept me. And if I went anywhere, I wanted it to be through the portal into Elfhame, hand in hand with Thorne.

I squeezed my eyes shut, berating myself for such useless dreaming. The hot restlessness beneath my skin only made me miserable.

I knew it, and yet, I could not let it go.

CHAPTER 32

Dinner that evening was awkwardly formal. As usual, Neeve and I arrived punctually. A few moments later, a servant ushered Prince Kian and Jarl Eiric into the dining room.

The prince strode forward and made us a bow.

"Good evening, ladies," he said.

Neeve inclined her head, but gave him no reply. I wanted to shake her. She could at least pretend to be polite. To break the uncomfortable silence, I smiled at the prince.

"How are your rooms?" I asked. "Are you settling in?"

Prince Kian shot Neeve a baffled glance, then turned to me. "They're very comfortable, thank you. And what a view of the forest! I hope the king might take me hunting soon. I imagine there's all sorts of game in the woods."

"No," Neeve said.

The prince blinked at her. "There's not?"

"We don't hunt for pleasure here," she said. "The royal gamesmen provide what is necessary for the kitchens. But chasing hapless animals through the Darkwood is not a pastime anyone in Raine enjoys."

"Then you're the worse off for it," he said, a superior note in his voice. "Hunting is a wonderful sport, and useful besides. What else does your kingdom have to offer?"

Neeve turned up her nose. "I have no idea what might amuse you."

Oh, she wasn't even trying! I wanted to jab her with my elbow, but that would be too obvious. Instead, I settled for a quick poke in the back with my finger.

"The castle has an excellent library," I said. "And Neeve likes to ride."

The prince's expression warmed slightly. "Do you ride as well, Lady Rose?"

"Yes, but I'm not an accomplished horsewoman the way Neeve is. Perhaps the two of you can go riding together."

Neeve sent me a look as sharp as daggers, but the prince nodded.

"I'd like that, Lady Neeve," he said. "Anytime you're inclined to ride out, please let me know, and I'd be glad to accompany you."

Luckily, before my stepsister could snub the prince any further, Lord Raine and Mama arrived. As we followed them to the table, I noticed the emissary watching Neeve, his eyes narrowed. No doubt the jarl was taking note of everything to report back to his king. I decided I would kick Neeve under the table if she continued responding so poorly to the prince.

My stepsister's expression hardened to marble as the king seated Kian at his left hand, taking her place. I scooted down one more chair, and we all sat, Neeve as rigid as stone beside me. The Fiorlander emissary was across from her, and one of the king's advisors faced me. Not that I expected any conversation from that quarter. Whenever the king discussed the business of the kingdom at dinner, Neeve and I were all but invisible.

I knew that we were supposed to be taking in the conversation—or at least Neeve was, in preparation for her eventual assumption of the throne of Raine. I was the afterthought, and thus didn't pay as much attention as I probably should have.

Tonight, though, I listened as the king and the jarl spoke of trade agreements, with Prince Kian putting in an occasional word. Mama performed the role of hostess beautifully, drawing the prince out and helping put the entire table at ease. Well, everyone except Neeve, who remained sullenly withdrawn.

As soon as dinner officially ended, she stalked out of the dining room, and I had to hurry to catch up with her.

"It wouldn't hurt you to at least be civil to the prince," I said.

"Yes, it would." She gave me a cold look. "I don't want to encourage him in any way. Stop trying to push us together."

I didn't try to deny the accusation. "You can be kind, without promising to marry the fellow."

Although in truth, Neeve was not particularly skilled at kindness. Perhaps, for her, showing any amount of warmth was an admission of fondness. Which I supposed meant she cared about me—though really, it was so hard to tell.

"At least he won't be with us in the classroom every morning," she said. "I don't think I could stand to spend so much time in his presence."

We'd discovered at dinner that the prince's manservant also served as his tutor, and that most of Prince Kian's days would be spent in private study and weapons training. He would, however, join us one morning a week during our regular history lessons.

"Did you feel that way about me when I first arrived?" I asked, wondering if my stepsister had hated me quite so fiercely.

"No." Neeve glanced over at me, then away.

Well. I supposed I should be grateful for that. "Why are you so set against Prince Kian, anyway?"

She paced forward, and we were almost to my bedroom door before she answered.

"I don't belong in the mortal world," she said in a low voice. "I don't want to ascend to the throne of Raine, and I certainly don't want to be married off because I'm the heir. I have my own plans for my life, and they don't include an arranged marriage with some prince of Fiorland."

I blinked at the vehemence in her voice. "Your own plans? Like what?"

"Nothing." She set her mouth and glared at me, clearly sorry she'd let so much slip.

"Why can't you go into Elfhame?" I'd wondered ever since the *nirwen* harvest, but had known that Neeve would give me no answers. I'd planned to ask Thorne in the spring, but now my stepsister had given me the perfect opening.

For a moment, I thought she wouldn't answer. Then she let out a long breath, her posture slumping the tiniest bit. Which, for Neeve, was an admission of defeat.

She glanced down the empty hallway, then back at me.

"Let's go inside," she said, tilting her head at my door.

No one lurked in the halls, but I understood her desire for caution. With a nod, I led her into the warmth of my suite, then checked to make sure Sorche wasn't in the bedroom. Satisfied we were alone, we settled in the two chairs pulled up in front of the hearth.

"Hundreds of years ago," Neeve said, without preamble, "when the doorway to Elfhame first opened, a bargain was struck. In order to keep the portal between our worlds from closing completely, a human had to marry a Dark Elf noble and dwell in their land, or a Dark Elf had to wed a human royal and live here, in Raine."

"Wait." I studied her, trying to grasp this new information. "Does that mean there's a human living in Elfhame?"

"No. One or the other will suffice, though the bloodlines cannot be diluted more than three generations." She let out an unhappy breath. "Currently, I am all that is keeping the doorway open."

"But aren't you equally half elf and half human? Why can't you go into Elfhame? Wouldn't you count as a human there?"

"The inheritance is carried by the mother," she said. "The magic of the portal recognizes only her Dark Elf blood in me. If I were to step into Elfhame, the door would close between the worlds. Forever." The yearning and sorrow in her voice cut me to the heart.

No wonder my stepsister almost never smiled. At least I had the option of returning to Parnese once I was grown. She, however, was well and truly trapped in a world where she felt she didn't belong.

The fire popped, and I leaned toward its warmth. "Can't you go into Elfhame once you have children to fulfill the bargain? If you were to marry Prince Kian—"

"No." She folded her arms about herself. "My mother died soon after birthing me. It isn't easy for Dark Elf women to bear half-mortal children. Though my offspring would thrive—as I did—I can't expect to survive long enough to see my own children grown, let alone wed."

"Oh. That's terrible." I pondered a moment, staring into the flames. "How will the doorway stay open, then?"

She stirred uncomfortably. "If something happened to me, then the Nightshade Lord or one of the other nobles would select a mortal bride at a future *nirwen* harvest and take her into Elfhame to dwell. They are likely considering that possibility even now, to ensure the doorway remains open."

I wondered how willing that bride would be to give up everything she'd known in order to go live with the Dark Elves. Then I recalled the way the Nightshade Lord had looked at me, and could not help an involuntary shiver. Oh no—surely not. I was too young.

You'll be seventeen when next the portal opens, my treacherous mind said. Old enough to marry. Or be forced into marriage...

I thrust the thought away.

"Why worry so much about keeping the doorway open?" I asked. "Why not just let it close?"

Neeve let out another sigh. "I shouldn't tell you *all* our secrets, Rose."

"It's a bit late now," I said tartly. "You might as well."

She turned her head and regarded me, her dark eyes flecked with brightness that might have been tears. I tried not to hold my breath. It seemed Prince Kian's arrival had broken down a few more of the walls between the two of us, and for that I was grateful.

"It's because of the *nirwen*," Neeve finally said. "It only grows on the human side of the doorway. And though it's important for Raine, it's an essential medicine for those with Dark Elf blood, curing one of the illnesses that used to decimate the population. Without the flower, the disease would rampage, unchecked, through Elfhame."

In that case, it made sense why the Dark Elves were set on keeping the portal open. Indeed, it was a wonder that the entire burden currently rested on Neeve's shoulders. No wonder Thorne was her guardian.

"So that's why you're not allowed to step through the doorway."

"That is why." She rose. "I'm going to bed now."

I stood too and, before she could move away, pulled her into an embrace. She stood stiffly in my arms, and after a moment stepped back, face set. I ached for her, and for the fact that she could not take even the small, sisterly comfort I offered.

"Sleep well," I said, walking with her to my door.

"Thank you." She reached out and touched my shoulder. "It is good to have someone else who understands."

I nodded, and watched her go down the hall to her rooms. We were, both of us, shadowed by our fates—but at least I had a choice about whom I would wed and where I would dwell. Poor Neeve was bound so tightly, it was a wonder she could even breathe.

CHAPTER 33

T he Yule Feast was upon us in a heartbeat. While I was apprehensive about a repeat of last year's debacle, my worry over Neeve and fretting about how to encourage her to act friendlier toward Prince Kian distracted me from that worry.

I donned my new gown, wishing that Thorne might see me in it. Alas, there would never be an excuse for me to wear my court finery into the forest. I banished the foolish thought and resolved to put Thorne out of my mind. At least for the evening.

Sorche did her best to braid and tame my hair. When she was finished, I studied myself in the mirror.

"You look lovely, miss," the maid said.

I gave a slow nod. I didn't want to appear too fine, of course. Yet something was missing. I carefully pulled my Dark Elf pendant out from beneath the neckline of the dress. The gold was warm against my fingers and glowed softly against the green gown.

"What do you think?" I asked.

Sorche studied me a moment. "It's a lovely piece, and no mistake. But do you think it's wise?"

"Probably not." The necklace was a little *too* fine, and certainly would stand out for its workmanship. Better not to give any hint to

Prince Kian and the Fiorlander emissary that Raine had ties to a magical land filled with Elvish artisans.

I blew out a sigh and tucked the necklace back into hiding, then rose to fetch Neeve. Neither of us wanted to arrive in the great hall alone, though she said little as we traversed the hallways together. I wondered if she, like me, was worried about a catastrophe at the feast.

When we arrived, I saw that another chair had been placed upon the stone dais, presumably for the prince. It was set to the right of Lord Raine's, with Neeve's chair pushed nearly to the edge. She looked at the extra seat, her lips compressing into a line at the further proof of her displacement.

"Prince Kian is our guest," I reminded her in a low voice. "Of course the king will show him favor."

My stepsister looked as if she wished to argue with me, but the arrival of the king and queen, with Prince Kian and Jarl Eiric just behind them, stilled her words.

The prince made his usual courtly greetings to us, his eyes meeting mine a trifle too warmly as he bowed over my hand. I pulled back and turned to Neeve.

"Don't you think our princess is looking fair this evening?" I said brightly. "Green is a particularly becoming color on you, Neeve."

She narrowed her eyes at me. "It's too cheerful."

"And yet is this not a joyous time?" Prince Kian asked. "Tomorrow, winter's darkness will begin to recede. The promise of spring's new beginnings is on the horizon."

"That's very poetic," I said, thinking it sounded more like something the prince had memorized from a book than anything he might spontaneously say.

He had the grace to look abashed. "Actually, it's paraphrased from the *edda* I plan to recite this evening."

"You're going to perform?" Neeve gave him a cool look.

"Indeed." The emissary stepped forward and nodded to Neeve. "Our young prince is a member of your household now, and glad to participate in your traditions. As I recall, you and your stepsister performed at last year's Yule Feast. I presume you'll do so again?"

Heat flashed into my cheeks. I'd hoped—vainly, of course—that everyone had forgotten about the prior incident. But the jarl had attended last year.

"Yes," Neeve said shortly.

The jarl gave her a smile that put me in mind of a fox watching the chickens. I wondered how long he'd been the Fiorland emissary to Raine, and just how much he might know of our secrets.

"And are we to be treated to a repeat of your lovely duet?" he asked.

"Alas." Neeve's tone was dry. "I'm no longer pursuing my musical studies. Though I believe Rose will play us a song upon the harp."

"What will your performance be?" Prince Kian asked her.

I leaned forward, equally curious to know. When I'd asked my step-sister about it before, she'd been evasive. As usual.

I couldn't imagine that she was planning on performing a magical spectacle, not with Prince Kian so newly arrived. But what else could she possibly do—make a sachet of herbs? Display her botanical illus-trations?

Neeve only shook her head. "You'll find out."

"Take your places," the king said, gesturing to us. "The guests are arriving, and we must be ready to greet them."

I reluctantly turned and went the chair waiting on the far side of the dais, on the other side of my mother's. Too far to keep trying to smooth things between my stepsister and the prince—not that it seemed to be helping. I settled with a sigh and sent one last glance at Neeve, who was already pointedly ignoring Prince Kian. The next few hours were going to prove tedious.

The feast turned out to be not quite as dreary as I'd remembered. I recognized more of the guests: the seamstress who'd made my new gowns, the head groom, the family who dwelt down the lane from Mistress Ainya's cottage. Most of the castle staff was familiar by now, too, and I smiled and greeted them in turn. Even the king's advisors nodded to me, and I was glad to not be wholly invisible for one night, at least.

After the guests were seated we took our places at the head table, and servants brought out the meal. I was able to taste the food this time, without apprehension drying my tongue and withering my appetite. While I was still a bit nervous about performing, at least it wasn't the stomach-churning fear of the year before.

Whether I played well or poorly was entirely on my shoulders. I was confident I'd played through my song enough times to do a creditable job.

Master Fawkes was performing in the musicians' gallery, and I glanced up, knowing that he had faith in me. He saw me and nodded, his fingers never faltering on the strings of his lute.

In a heartbeat, and what also felt like an eternity, the main part of the feast was over. As the places were cleared, I glanced to where Neeve and Kian sat. He was unsmiling, and her pale cheeks were painted with temper.

Oh dear. I hoped they would not break into open hostilities—but surely they both had enough diplomacy to keep from fighting in front the assembled guests. I hoped.

The king stood and clapped his hands for attention. When the room quieted, he spoke.

"Welcome to another turning of the year. We have much to celebrate: a good harvest, fine health, and, this year, the newest member of the royal family, fostered from Fiorland. Please join me in welcoming Prince Kian Leifson to Castle Raine!"

The crowd broke into applause and scattered cheers as Lord Raine gestured for the prince to rise. Prince Kian did, and clasped his hands together at his chest.

"Thank you," he said with a slight bow. "It's an honor to be here in Raine. I look forward to four wonderful years among your people, and the many things I've no doubt I'll learn."

Neeve scowled at the reminder that he'd be underfoot for so long. The prince glanced her way, his expression tightening. Trying to ease the tension, I smiled at him. He caught my eye, and his lips turned up the slightest bit. Poor fellow, to be trapped between the king and my stepsister all night. No wonder he'd been looking grim.

"We are glad to have you," Lord Raine said, and my mother nodded her agreement. "Now, it's time for the performances. Who would like to begin?"

There was a moment of awkward silence, and then I jumped to my feet.

"I will," I said, my heart beating fast inside my chest.

Better to have it over and done with, I reasoned. Especially as neither Neeve nor the prince seemed eager to put themselves forward.

"I will go last," my stepsister declared.

Her father nodded with the air of someone who knew what she planned, and once again my curiosity sparked. What was she up to?

"Then I would be delighted to perform second," Prince Kian said, with an agreeable smile.

I descended to the cleared area in front of the head table. One of the servants met me, carrying my harp. Another brought a chair, and I settled.

After a quick tweak to bring the stubborn high string to pitch, I drew in a deep breath. Last year, Neeve had announced our duet, but she was not here to give the introduction.

"I'm going to play an arrangement of 'The Miller's Daughter,'" I said, trying to project my voice to the far tables. "I hope you enjoy it."

Praying nothing would catch fire, I set my fingers to the strings and began. The lilting melody rang out. I fumbled the first set of chords, then made myself concentrate on the music instead of my fear. I could see feet tapping beneath the tables as the tune went on—a good sign.

No hot pressure built up in my chest and neither did the tapestries suddenly ignite. I gave the head table a quick glance, glad to see my mother smiling. The king looked pleased enough, tapping his fingers upon the tablecloth, and Neeve wasn't frowning, which was akin to high praise from her. Prince Kian winked at me, and I quickly looked away, determined not to let him distract me.

I played twice more through the tune, ending with a flourish that reached up to the rafters. After a breath of silence, the crowd applauded. I sat back, feeling suddenly as wrung out as an overcooked turnip. It was over.

And nothing terrible had happened.

Cradling my harp in my arms, I stood and bowed, then handed the instrument back to the waiting servant and returned to my seat at the high table. From that vantage point, I saw Master Fawkes give me an approving nod. I sent him a weak smile in return.

Then it was Prince Kian's turn. He strode confidently to the space I'd just occupied.

"This evening, I will recite you a portion of the *Elder Edda*," he said, pivoting to address the room. "It is one of the great Fiorlander poems, and I'm happy to share it with the people of Raine. May it bring you pleasure."

He cleared his throat, and the room slowly quieted to just a few foot shuffles and a muffled cough.

"See how the darkness comes, full with snow." His voice rang out, strong and clear. "The fires of winter burn, the old gods sleep. The dragons wake beneath the stars. Even the sea stills under her blanket of ice."

I shivered. The poetry was lovely, but Fiorland seemed savage and cold, especially compared to Parnese. Kian continued, describing an ancient warrior doing battle with the Frost King in order to win back the sun.

There was a hypnotic quality to the verses, and I felt them wash over me. Warriors and quests, battles and intrigue—the heroic world of the past seemed close enough to touch. I wondered if the Dark Elves had any such poetry.

The torchlight flickered, gilding Kian's hair. I could imagine him as a lord of ancient lore striding into battle, and wondered if Neeve might see him in this flattering light, too. Under cover of taking a sip from my goblet, I shot her a glance.

She did not seem enthralled. Then again, she didn't seem to be openly despising, either. Perhaps there was hope.

Kian lifted one hand, his voice deepening.

"And now, in victory's wake, the sun slips free of the Frost King's grasp. Look! The raven's claws release the moon. Tomorrow Spring comes striding, combing out her long golden hair. Until then, warriors, bide. Until then, wives, spin. Together we toast to the heroes of old."

He held his pose a moment, silent, until it was clear his recitation was at an end. The applause that followed was wholehearted. Grinning, he turned and swept bows to all the tables, ending with ours. His gaze met mine, and belatedly I looked away, toward Neeve. *That* was where his bright blue gaze ought to be pointed.

To my relief, neither the king nor my mother seemed to notice Kian's attention toward me. Lord Raine beckoned the prince back to his place, then clapped him on the shoulder—a sure sign of approval.

As soon as Kian was seated, the king looked to his daughter.

"Neeve, are you ready?"

"Yes." She stood, brushing down her skirts, and I glimpsed her riding boots beneath.

"People of Raine," the king said, his voice carrying through the room. "My daughter will now give us a demonstration of her excellent horsemanship."

"Inside?" my mother asked, sounding a touch appalled.

I shared her reaction. Neeve was going to ride her horse? In the great hall? The feast was turning into a circus.

"Don't worry, my dear," Lord Raine said to Mama. "Peerless is well-mannered enough not to misbehave. And we can hardly ask the guests to go out in the rain, can we?"

"I suppose not." Mama mustered up a charming smile. "I'm sure you have considered it well."

The guests murmured amongst themselves, but did not seem unduly shocked. Indeed, there was a rising sense of anticipation. The Fiorlander emissary looked intrigued, and Prince Kian leaned forward, his interest clearly engaged as Neeve strode to the front of the hall.

That was a good sign. I would endeavor to get the two of them out on horseback together. Surely there was a mount in the castle's stables that would suit him. Snowbell would not do, of course. Even I knew that much. The image of Prince Kian astride my dumpy little horse almost made me laugh aloud.

The doors of the great hall opened, letting in a gust of cold, rain-laden air. And a groom leading Peerless.

The mare was brushed to a high sheen, her mane and tail braided with scarlet ribbons, the leather of her saddle and bridle polished. Neeve took the reins from the groom and leaned forward, her forehead resting against Peerless's for a moment.

Then, in one smooth move, she turned and gripped the saddle, lifted her foot, and was astride in a flurry of emerald cloth. Her court gown had been cleverly modified into split skirts for riding. Until that moment, I had not even guessed it.

I couldn't tell if the groom had assisted her with a boost into the saddle, or if she'd perfected the move on her own. Considering how much time she'd spent riding of late, I suspected the latter.

Her expression smooth, Neeve fastened the reins to the low pommel of her saddle. Hands at her sides, she nudged Peerless into motion. The horse trotted forward, weaving expertly between the tables. Unlike Snowbell's jolting, Neeve seemed to be almost gliding. I'd no idea how she managed it.

The guests nodded in approval. At last, their princess was exceeding expectations. No amateur sketches of plants or horrible flute squawks this year, but a demonstration of skill worthy of a royal.

When they reached the cleared space before the head table, horse and rider performed an intricate figure eight. Neeve leaned into the turns, her skirts fluttering. How was she even guiding her mount?

They halted and Peerless rose up on her back legs, front hooves pawing the air. My heart pounded—was this part of the performance, or was Neeve's mount trying to throw her?

With the faintest of smiles, Neeve kept her balance and lifted her arms into the air. The hall exploded with applause.

Part of her show, then. I swallowed back my anxiety and joined the clapping.

The moment her horse's front feet touched the floor, Neeve dismounted, light as a feather. She bowed to her father, and Peerless bobbed her head.

Then, without even touching her horse, Neeve turned and strode to where the groom waited. Peerless followed as though she was being led by a rope, though only the strings of affection bound her to her mistress.

It was an impressive showing indeed. The audience renewed their applause as Neeve patted Peerless, then came back to her place at the head table.

Prince Kian jumped up and pulled out her chair for her, his expression clearly admiring. For a moment, I thought Neeve might even show him a bit of warmth. *Smile,* I thought at her.

At the last moment she cast down her eyes and took her seat. It was close enough to flirting that Kian seemed happy, though I could tell she hadn't meant it that way.

Or had she? With Neeve, it was almost impossible to know.

CHAPTER 34

The winter dragged on, wet and dreary. I tried to hold on to my memories of Parnese: the golden light shining from the south, the smell of blossoms wafting through the graceful arches of open windows, the way the air was not a chilly enemy but a warm friend.

Alas, despite my best efforts, Parnese was fading. Compared to the drizzle and gray skies of Raine, it seemed far away indeed. I feared that in another year or two, my childhood home would be nothing more than a wispy dream.

"Mama," I said one evening after dinner, as we were preparing to exit the dining room, "might we not return to Parnese for a visit sometime?"

She was quiet a moment, her beautiful face pensive. Then she shook her head and gave me a smile, the corners of her mouth tight.

"Don't be foolish, Rose. This is our home now."

"So we'll never go back?" I'd known it, but hearing her say the words made my heart heavy.

"Homesick?" Kian asked, overhearing us. "I've felt the same during my travels, but don't worry—it will pass. There's so much of the world to see, after all!"

"I suppose." I couldn't explain my melancholy to myself, much less to him. "I just... I miss it."

"One should never be barred from the place they belong," Neeve said, her voice holding an undercurrent of yearning that matched my own.

She shot her father a narrow-eyed glance, and I knew she spoke of Elfhame, and her fierce desire to dwell there, among her own people. To be accepted and loved for who she was.

How well I understood. I touched her arm in sympathy and she did not immediately pull away.

"You are a princess of Raine," the king said sternly. "Your place is here."

"Forever," Neeve said bitterly.

Her expression cold, she stalked to the door and left the dining room without a backward glance.

Kian looked to Lord Raine in some confusion. "But surely Neeve can leave Raine? What if..." He paused, a flush reddening his ears. "What if she marries some foreign lord?"

"Whomever Neeve marries, they will take their place by her side. Here." The king's expression was as stony and unyielding as the granite walls surrounding us.

To avert the questions I saw building in Kian's eyes, I stepped forward and took his arm.

"I didn't know you were so well travelled. Tell me, what countries have you visited? Which were your favorites?"

Brow still furrowed, he looked down at me. I summoned my most charming smile—the one I'd seen Mama use when she wanted to flatter a courtier or bargain with a tradesman—and the prince's frown eased.

"I have been to Parnese," he said. "But I was just a boy at the time and don't remember it well. More recently, my father took me to Islo Puerto to help negotiate a trade agreement. The climate was too warm, but the wine was good. And I've been all around the kingdoms to the north of Raine, of course. Even Athraig, though they were not particularly welcoming."

I nodded, though the list of countries he'd visited made me feel a bit provincial.

As Kian escorted me from the room, he leaned close. "Is it true that Neeve is forbidden to leave Raine?" he asked in a low voice.

I blinked up at him in pretend puzzlement.

"Oh, I'm sure the king didn't mean that at all," I lied. "Only that she will be Queen of Raine after him."

"Well yes, obviously." He cleared his throat. "Are there any, um, alliances being discussed that you know of?"

"Trade alliances?" I asked innocently.

Of course, I knew he was actually asking if King Tobin was making any arrangements to barter Neeve's hand in marriage in return for military or economic advantage.

"Not exactly." He flushed. "Is Neeve promised to someone since birth, or anything of the sort?"

I struggled to frame an answer. One the one hand, I liked Kian well enough and didn't want to see him wed someone who held him in disdain. On the other hand, Neeve held *everyone* in disdain—and we all knew that fosterlings were usually sent to courts where they might make a match with the daughters and sons of neighboring kingdoms. I supposed Kian thought being King of Raine beside Neeve was a better fate than being last in line for the Fiorlander throne.

"There are no betrothal arrangements that I'm aware of," I finally said.

Neeve's heart was fixed on Elfhame, but she would never be able to dwell in that land, whether she married Kian or not.

He let out a sigh—not that of a frustrated suitor, but like someone trying to piece together a puzzle. "She's... not an easy person to get to know, is she?"

"No," I said.

"Not like you." He gave me a warm smile. "I enjoy your company, Rose. And aren't you related to the royal line of Parnese?"

Oh, no. This was dangerous territory. My pedigree was good, plus I was the stepdaughter of the King of Raine. To some, I would appear to be an eligible prospect. But for my own peace of mind, not to mention the politics of the castle, I must ensure that Kian did not see me as a possible wife.

"My mother is a *very* distant cousin to the old queen," I said. "But we have nothing in Parnese—no manor house, no lands. Our entire existence now is dependent upon King Tobin. I can't imagine what might become of me were I to suffer his displeasure or fall out of favor."

By doing something rash, like stealing the suitor meant for Neeve. Not that she wanted him, poor boy. If she desired to wed anyone, it would be Thorne.

The thought irritated me, and I slipped my arm from Kian's. We'd reached the branching hall where our ways parted, and I was more than ready to put the conversation to an end.

"If you want to know Neeve, go riding with her," I said, a bit curtly. "She's out almost every afternoon on Peerless, or hadn't you noticed?"

"I had." His voice was impatient. "I keep hinting, but so far she hasn't invited me along."

"Neeve isn't subtle." Except when it pleased her to be. "Don't ask for her permission—you'll never get it. Just arrive, mounted, and follow her if she tries to leave you behind."

That strategy had worked for me, after all.

He glanced at me. "Are you certain she won't slap me or order the footmen to hold me back?"

What type of royalty was Kian used to? I shook my head.

"She might be unkind, but Neeve doesn't abuse her position as princess. It will make her cross to have you join her, but you must persist."

"But—"

"I'm done giving you advice. Use it or not, as you please. Good night, Prince Kian."

I turned and left him standing in the hall, a pensive look in his eyes, and told myself I didn't care one way or another what he might choose to do.

I almost believed it.

You might still have him, the wicked part of me whispered. *Another few years and he would marry you and take you away to be a fine lady of Fiorland. Neeve is no match for you.*

Perhaps—but I didn't want to be a minor noble in a foreign court, reliant upon the whims of a king. That was not the future I aspired to.

What, then? the voice continued. *You can't do magic. Thorne will never be yours. Your mother cares naught for what will become of you.*

"Stop it," I said, slamming the door shut on the insidious thoughts.

They seemed to be growing worse the longer I was penned inside the castle, the voice whispering mischief in my ear at every turn.

To distract myself, I took to scouring the library for the types of banned tomes I'd collected in Parnese. Books about magic and sorcerers, of course, but I was also looking for something even more forbidden: accounts of the Dark Elves and the doorway into Elfhame.

The remainder of the Rainish history books were vague, which I supposed made sense. The kingdom's most closely guarded secret wasn't going to be written down for everyone to see. Recalling Thorne's story of the *nirwen*, I turned to the legends and fables. Perhaps there would be a grain of truth there, disguised as myth.

I found a fanciful tale about the powers of the *nirwen* restoring a young woman's beauty, and veiled allusions to the strangeness of the Darkwood, but nothing of any substance. Sighing, I closed the heavy book I'd been perusing and sat back into the wan shaft of sunlight sliding in through one of the library's high windows.

There must be a secret collection—a hidden room full of tomes concerning magic and the Dark Elves. Could I ask Miss Groves about such a thing?

Probably not. Although I'd witnessed the harvest and the departure of the elves back to Elfhame, I was still a newcomer.

Maybe Mistress Ainya would help me, come spring. If I was useless at magic, at least my eyes could see and my mind could learn.

I absently rubbed the stub of my pinky, my gaze roving over the rows of books in their shelves. They stuck out in even lines, each bank holding a specific subject or grouping of similar works. Beyond the ones containing my favorites of adventure and history lay drier subjects: masonry, brickmaking, mining. Then hearthcrafts like cookery and food preservation, and, oddly, poetry after that.

The bookshelves marched the length of the room, but for the first time I noticed a slight irregularity. The very last opening between the bays of shelves looked wider than all the others. Perhaps the architects of the room hadn't planned it perfectly, but it was worth investigating.

After glancing over my shoulder to make sure I was still alone, I rose and made my way to the last row in the library. As I'd suspected, that alcove was broader than all the rest—wide enough for me to stretch my arms out without touching the shelves on either side.

To my left were housed the books of poetry and classical philosophy. On the right were volumes in foreign languages, some in flowing script completely unrecognizable, others in letters that I could at least sound out. Between them, facing out, were shelves filled with what looked like ledger books holding the accounts of Castle Raine.

Dry stuff indeed.

But did they, perhaps, conceal hidden treasure? Holding my breath, I pulled out one of the red clothbound books and peeked behind it. Nothing—just the featureless dark wood of the shelf behind.

I replaced the ledger and stepped back to survey the extra-wide shelf. I'd have to be meticulous in my examination, starting from the upper left and working my way down. Depending on how much time I could steal away, the task might take me several weeks, but I wasn't too worried at the prospect. I didn't have much else to occupy myself, after all.

I would, however, need one of the ladders scattered around the library in order to reach the top shelf.

After finding one—and making note of its location so that I could return it once I was done—I began my task. It was dusty work, and a bit dreary, pulling out book after book, but I kept at it until dusk cloaked the library in shadows and my stomach tightened with hunger.

I didn't want to miss dinner, of course, and have my absence remarked upon. And really, it was too much to hope that I'd discover any secrets the very first day. Even if I knew what I was looking for, which I clearly didn't. A secret lever, perhaps, like when I'd found the hidden doorway in the herb shed. Or another shelf, concealed behind the dry account books. Surely there must be something.

Tiredly, I pushed the ladder back where I'd found it and went up to my rooms to wash off the worst of the dust and change for dinner.

CHAPTER 35

T he days marched on, each one growing a tiny bit longer as the winter receded. Kian had screwed up his courage and gone riding with Neeve. Since she hadn't ordered his head to be chopped off, or any such nonsense, he continued to accompany her a few afternoons a week.

I was glad of it, since it gave me uninterrupted time to continue searching the library.

Unfortunately, my quest was not successful. After a fortnight of searching, I reached the last book on the shelf. Heart quivering, I pulled it out...

Nothing. The shelves did not swing open, no secret cache of forbidden titles suddenly revealed to my hungry eyes.

Disappointment heavy in my chest, I sat back, the book in my hand, and tried to think of what to do next. I supposed I would have to find a new hobby instead of searching for secrets in the library. Perhaps take up the vielle, or attempt embroidery once more.

With a little more force than was necessary, I shoved the book back into place.

Click.

My eyes widened, and I scanned the shelves. There, midway down in the exact center, the shelf seemed to have popped forward. My pulse pounding like a drum, I stood. Carefully, scarcely breathing, I pulled the protruding shelf forward.

Delight danced through me as the small section pivoted out, revealing another shelf of books concealed behind it. I had been right!

"Rose?" someone called from the front of the library.

After a panicked heartbeat, I realized it was Neeve. Hands shaking, I slammed the shelf closed and prayed that it would open again the next time I tried.

"I'm here." I grabbed a random book of poetry off the shelf and stepped out of the bay.

"What are you doing back there?" Neeve strode forward, her dark eyes narrowed.

"Just picking out something to read." I brandished the book at her. "You should try it sometime."

She only sniffed in reply.

"Did you need me?" I asked, leading her back toward the main section. Upon consideration, it was unusual for Neeve to seek me out. Something must be bothering her a great deal.

"Yes." She glanced down at her hands, the dark fall of her hair sweeping like shadows across her face.

I set the unwanted poetry book down on a nearby table, then leaned against the edge and waited for her to speak.

"Well?" I demanded after several moments had passed in fraught silence. "What's the matter?"

Her head jerked up, her eyes narrowed in displeasure—but it seemed more a general glare than one directed specifically at me.

"Prince Kian," she said shortly.

"What of him?"

Telltale spots of red rose in her cheeks. "He kissed me."

"What?" I straightened, my feelings tangled into a knot of emotion.

It wasn't that I harbored dreams of the prince—well, not the way I did about Thorne. But still, did Neeve have to have *everything*? Magic, and Thorne, and Kian into the bargain? Not to mention being heir to the throne of Raine.

"What happened?" I asked, folding my arms and trying to keep the annoyance from my tone.

"We were riding outside the castle, and my cloak snared in the brambles and came off. He dismounted and freed it, and when I got down to put it back on, he clasped it about my shoulders. And then he leaned forward and *kissed* me." Her face tightened with aggravation.

"Well," I pointed out, "you are the Princess of Raine. It's why he's here, after all."

"I don't want it." She whirled and paced a few agitated steps. "I don't want an arranged match with a silly boy, or to rule Raine, for that matter. I want—"

She choked off the words, but I knew what came next.

"Elfhame," I said softly.

"Sh!" She rounded on me.

"What?" I glared right back. "We're in the library—nobody can hear us."

"I don't trust the jarl. Or the prince's tutor, for that matter. They would be all too happy to learn our secrets and use them for advantage."

"What advantage, though?" I uncrossed my arms. "I've been thinking about it, and what could another country actually *do*, even if they knew?"

"Invade," she said darkly.

"Invade Raine? Or..." I glanced over my shoulder, her caution now contagious. "That other place?"

"Both."

"The you-knows seem fairly fierce," I said. "Plus they have the Darkwood to protect them." Not to mention magic.

"If we were overrun here, we would lose control of the *nirwen* harvest. That would have a devastating result upon my people."

"How so?" I recalled Thorne mentioning that the flower made an essential medicine for the Dark Elves—but surely they could find another remedy?

"Without the *nirwen*, no children will be born," she said starkly. "My people will die out within a generation. It almost happened, centuries ago, until the gateway reopened and the flower bloomed for the first time."

"Because of a human girl with magic." I clung to that part of the legend.

I still believed there was a deeper tale surrounding the *nirwen*, and I wondered if the books I'd just discovered would contain some of that truth. It took great restraint for me not to glance down at the last bank of shelves.

Neeve pressed her lips together. "Perhaps. But the truth remains that without the *nirwen*, my people are doomed. And there is no guarantee they would be able to hold against a human invasion, even with their specific advantages."

I nodded. Now that Neeve had pointed out some of the dangers, I could see others: the invaders picking all the *nirwen* and using it to force the Dark Elves to surrender, or a smaller country, like Fiorland, discovering the secret and holding the threat of exposure over Raine in order to gain trade advantages or extort bribes.

Which led me to another thought...

"What happens if you marry Prince Kian? Or another royal foreigner, for that matter? Surely they must learn the truth at some point?"

Neeve gave me a pitying look. "Either they can be trusted, or they are sedated during the few days of the harvest."

"As I was supposed to have been." And perhaps my mother as well. The memory made my temper rise. "Not everyone is so docile. *I* followed you, if you recall."

"Because the Darkwood let you," she shot back. "And you were discovered, if *you* recall. Besides, the Nightshade Lord could easily have taken your memories if Thorne hadn't argued in your favor."

That cooled my irritation. I preferred not to think of the haughty Dark Elf ruler—or the way he'd looked at me.

"Very well," I said. "But what happens this summer, when we want to go into the forest? Surely Kian will be curious, just as I was? Especially if he's falling in love with you."

"Stop it." The color flared in her cheeks again. "He's doing no such thing—and if he is, I forbid it."

"You can't forbid people to have their feelings," I said with a touch of exasperation.

"Can't *you* make friends with him, instead?" Her voice was uncharacteristically pleading.

"Be your shield, you mean?" I let out an unamused laugh. "I don't think your father would look very kindly on me for trying to steal your suitor. Lord Raine is still a trifle angry with me about what happened at the harvest, I think."

"Please, Rose." Neeve reached out and took my hand.

The unexpected gesture took me by surprise, and I softened toward her. It took a great deal for Neeve to ask for help, and I was touched—and a little proud—that I'd earned so much of her trust.

"I'll do what I can," I said. "Although I won't try to shift Prince Kian's attentions onto myself." Even if I could, that was a course that could only end in disaster.

"What, then?"

"Resume riding with you, I suppose." I made a face. "Prince Kian will behave himself if there's a chaperone along. Even if it's just me."

She let out a sniff of displeasure and released my hand. "You and dumpy old Snowbell will only slow me down. I ride for pleasure, not to meander about at a slug's pace."

I crossed my arms again. "In that case, Prince Kian is *your* problem. I have better things to do, you know."

This time I couldn't help darting a look at the enticement of the far library shelves. Drat it. Why had I promised to help Neeve when this delectable new mystery was right at my fingertips?

"Better things? Like molder away in the library?" She gave a dismissive wave. "At least if you come riding with us you'll get some fresh air."

It was so like Neeve to change her tune without any attempt at apology, I almost smiled, despite my annoyance. Her words might be haughty, but I could still see the entreaty in her eyes.

"I'm not promising to come every day," I said, already wincing at the thought of the bruises I'd have to endure.

"Just help me keep the prince at bay for the next few rides," she said. "His interest will cool when I make it clear I have no intention of returning his affections."

I wasn't so certain. It was why Prince Kian was in Raine, after all, and I suspected even Neeve's cold disapproval wouldn't prove a lasting deterrent. Not if his choice was between being a penniless younger son, or sitting beside a queen and helping rule a kingdom.

Which also meant that, eventually, he must know the truth about the Darkwood.

That's years away, I told myself. *So much can change in that time.*

If only I could believe it.

"You ride out after lunch most days, don't you?" I asked, resigning myself to an uncomfortable few afternoons.

"Yes. Thank you."

The genuine warmth in Neeve's voice went far toward making me feel as though I'd made the right choice. And the mysterious shelf wasn't going anywhere, after all, no matter how much I burned to discover its secrets.

The gong for dinner echoed down the hall, and in a rare gesture of camaraderie my stepsister held out her arm. "Shall we?"

I nodded and slipped my elbow through hers. As we walked out of the library, however, the back of my neck prickled with frustrated anticipation. It was all I could do to let the heavy door close on the tantalizing discovery I'd made.

Once the castle bedded down for the night, however, I'd return. There'd be no sleep for me until I pulled open the hidden compartment and discovered what lay inside.

Tonight, I promised the secret shelf. *I'll be back for you.*

CHAPTER 36

I t was late in the evening before I could slip away from my rooms. I hurried down the cold, shadowy corridors of Castle Raine, trying not to appear too furtive. When I finally gained the library doors, my heart was thudding nervously in my chest. Looking first to the right, then the left, I grabbed the handle and pulled, ready to scurry into the darkened room.

The door was locked.

I bit down on a yell of frustration and forced myself not to stamp my foot in a temper. Locked! In my excitement, I'd forgotten that Miss Groves had told me the library was closed up at night.

Clenching my hands into fists, I stared at the door as if the force of my glare would make it swing open. But I was no Dark Elf, no magically gifted human, to make the world bend to my will. The library remained locked. And I was just ordinary Rose, frustrated with the world, my stepsister, Prince Kian. And myself, of course.

My mood was sour as I returned to my rooms. Absorbed in my discouraged thoughts, I reached the branching in the hallway—and nearly collided with Prince Kian. He was garbed in leather armor, his sword buckled at his side and sturdy boots on his feet.

"Rose!" He caught me by the arm as I stumbled in surprise. "What are you doing wandering the halls at this hour?"

"It's not that late," I said, although it was past the time I was usually in bed. "Where are you going, dressed like that? A surprise attack on the kitchens? Planning to slay some mice?"

He stepped back, an offended look on his face. "I'm off to train with the arms master."

"At this hour?" I ignored the fact that I'd just protested it wasn't late.

"Yes," he said gravely. "It's important to prepare for combat in various conditions. Not all battles happen in daylight."

"Oh." I blinked at him. "I've never really considered it."

"You should. Have you learned to use a weapon? Everyone in the castle, no matter their age or gender, should be prepared to defend against attacks."

I tried to hold back my laugh, but he heard it and gave me an affronted scowl.

"Attacks?" I tilted my head at him. "From what, pray tell—the weather? Although... if you could vanquish the rain clouds, I wouldn't mind."

"It's not a joking matter. If you were a Fiorlander, and not some pampered Parnesian, you'd understand." He dropped his hand to the pommel of his sword. "Even here in Raine, they don't take such things seriously enough. It's a good thing Fiorland is an ally, otherwise fire and blade would teach these people to fear."

I narrowed my eyes at him. "That sounds like a threat, Prince Kian. I'm sure Lord Raine wouldn't like to hear you saying such things within the walls of his castle."

He jerked his head, some of the intensity leaving his expression. "Of course not—I didn't mean to imply—"

"I'm sure you didn't," I said, in a cool tone that meant the exact opposite. "And I won't make a mention of it. Still, I think it might be better for everyone if you were less... ardent in your pursuit of Princess Neeve."

There. Let him chew on that. I was rather pleased how neatly he'd put himself in my power.

For a moment he stared at me, and then a sour look crossed his face. "She told you?"

"We're sisters," I said, smugly and somewhat misleadingly. It wasn't as though Neeve told me everything, after all. Far from it. But the prince didn't need to know that.

"I admire her," he said shortly.

My disbelief must have shown on my face.

"It's true." He lowered his voice. "She's a splendid rider, and will make a strong queen."

"For you to rule beside?" I couldn't help the sarcasm lacing my voice.

"Perhaps." He shifted uncomfortably, the tips of his ears reddening. "If she'll have me."

It was a surprisingly honest answer, and my estimation of the prince rose a tiny notch. Perhaps he did care for Neeve. Who was I to judge the strength of his affections? They didn't seem *entirely* motivated by ambition, in any case.

"If that's what you really want, stop pursuing her," I said. "Can't you see she's like a feral creature? If you chase her, she'll just run away."

"I know." He let out a breath. "I was just hoping..."

"That she'd find you irresistible and come tamely to your hand the moment you puckered up?" I raised my brows and made kissing noises at him.

"Stop laughing at me."

"I can't help it if you make yourself foolish." All my annoyance at him had faded, however. "You'd best be off to the armsman."

"Arms *master*," he corrected. "You are hopeless—you and your sister both."

I'd rather be hopeless than have him begin to wonder again about why I was in the hallways late at night.

"Enjoy your training," I said, already making for the west wing.

"Good night," he called after my retreating back.

I waved without turning, and was glad to gain the safety of my rooms without encountering anyone else. As I prepared for bed, I weighed whether I still must go riding with Neeve and Kian the next day, as I'd promised her.

The unfortunate answer was yes. Otherwise I'd have to explain to Neeve about meeting the prince in the night-hushed halls of the castle, which would lead to uncomfortable questions about what I'd been doing out and about at that hour.

I climbed between the sheets and pulled the coverlet up. From painful experience, I knew this would be the last restful night I'd have for several days. It would be difficult to sleep with the painful aches and bruises that jolting about in the saddle would bring.

With a sigh, I blew the candle out.

AFTER LUNCH THE NEXT DAY, I followed Neeve dispiritedly out to the stables. The morning drizzle had cleared, but the air was still thick with moisture and clammy against my cheeks. My itchy wool riding skirts flapped around my legs. I wanted nothing more than to retreat back to the library.

Prince Kian was already in the courtyard, standing beside a tall chestnut gelding. Next to him was a groom holding the reins of two other horses: Peerless, and a dappled mare whose coat was the same quiet gray as the clouds above us.

"Good afternoon." The prince made us a bow, then sent me a quizzical look. "I understand you're to come riding with us today?"

I frowned back at him. "Neeve asked me to accompany you. Occasionally."

Hopefully this once would suffice, now that I'd had my little chat with him. Provided he didn't do anything foolish, like try to kiss my stepsister again.

"I'm sure you won't mind if Rose comes along," Neeve told him.

"I'm sure I won't," he replied calmly. "I find her company quite entertaining."

I resisted the urge to stick out my tongue at him, and instead glanced about the yard. "Where's Snowbell?"

I supposed the gray horse was meant for me instead, but she was a huge beast. My little pony might be a laughable mount, but at least I wouldn't break my neck if I fell off her.

The groom handed Peerless to Neeve, then stepped forward. "Lady Rose, I've been instructed that you'll be riding Sterling from now on."

I set my hands to my hips. "Who told you this?"

"*I* did," Neeve said. "Really, Rose. It's high time you moved up to a real horse. My father agrees. Ponies are for children."

Well. How could I argue otherwise without seeming childish?

"You're not frightened, are you?" Kian asked, a hint of humor in his voice. "She's a docile mount, the groom tells me."

Docile compared to what? Some half-tamed stallion, like the king preferred to ride? Of course I was nervous, but I didn't want Kian to think me weak and fearful, for then he might not take my threats seriously.

"Let's go." Neeve swung smoothly up onto Peerless. "We've wasted too much time in talking already. It's going to rain again soon."

"Of course it is." The prince glanced up at the sky with a glum expression. "Doesn't it ever snow here? That's much more pleasant than this endless drizzle."

Neeve shook her head, not bothering to argue, and he mounted as expertly as she had.

Both of them astride, they watched me expectantly. With an inward sigh, I marched to the gray mare's side. She was as tall as a barn, and the stirrup was practically at chin level.

"Might I have your assistance?" I asked the groom.

He nodded and laced his fingers together for me to set my foot in. I grabbed the saddle, made an awkward hop and scramble, and somehow managed to gain my perch—thanks in no small part to a shove from the groom.

Sterling whuffled, as though surprised to have such a novice rider on her back, but at least she didn't sidle or stamp.

"Nice girl," I said, patting her neck and hoping she didn't mind.

Her ears swiveled, and I felt somewhat reassured. Still, I wished saddles came with belts. The cobblestones seemed very far away.

Neeve nodded to Kian, then wheeled Peerless and rode toward the gate. The prince was quick to follow. I snatched up my reins as Sterling followed. At least I wouldn't have to prod her into motion, as I had with Snowbell, but I wasn't sure how I felt about having an independent mount.

The horses' hooves clopped hollowly over the stone, echoing my heartbeat. As soon as we cleared the gate, Neeve guided her mount to the wet brown grasses edging the road and glanced over her shoulder.

"Ready to ride?" she called.

Kian's answer was a whoop as he leaned forward and urged his mount to speed. Peerless was off like a shot, though, staying in the lead.

Much to my relief, Sterling didn't immediately bolt after them. I felt her shiver with anticipation under me, and her ears swiveled back, as if awaiting my command.

"Very well," I said under my breath. "Please, don't let me fall off."

I grabbed the edge of the saddle with one hand, tightened my legs, and gave Sterling a gentle nudge with my heel.

She leaped forward, and I sucked in a breath through fear-squeezed lungs. After a sickening moment, as I tried not to notice how quickly we were going, I realized that riding Sterling was an entirely different experience than jolting about on Snowbell's back.

Other than her daunting size—or perhaps because of it—Sterling's gait was remarkably smooth, especially once we moved out of a trot and into the rocking motion of a canter. I leaned forward, feeling the strength of the creature under me, the wind against my face, the smell of moss and damp, and finally realized why Neeve loved riding.

It was freedom.

A different sort from the freedom I found between the pages of books, or in the notes of my harp, and slightly more frightening. More visceral. Which was probably why Neeve adored it.

To my surprise, I felt a grin stretch my lips wide.

Ahead, Neeve and Kian halted where the road curved toward Little Hazel. They turned their mounts and watched me canter toward them. I sat back and tugged slightly on the reins, and Sterling slowed to a bouncing trot, then back to a walk as we drew close.

"Well done." Kian nodded at me. "Neeve told me you were a wretched rider, but I see she misspoke."

I shot my stepsister an annoyed glance, but couldn't dispute the truth of her words. Former truth, at any rate.

"Sterling is a far superior mount to my old pony," I admitted. "I never thought there'd be such a difference."

"I told you so," Neeve said, smugly arching one brow. "But do try to keep up."

At least I now had a horse that would be able to, even if my riding skills were not particularly polished. As Neeve and Kian set off across the pastures at a more sedate pace, I rubbed Sterling's neck.

"Thank you," I whispered.

She bobbed her head, as if she understood. Then I nudged her into the fallow fields after my stepsister and the prince, grateful that the afternoon would not turn out to be quite the ordeal I'd feared.

CHAPTER 37

The next day dawned clear, one of those rare sunny days in late winter that reminded everyone that spring was actually on the way. The air held a touch of warmth, and even though I'd planned to beg off riding that afternoon, Neeve coaxed me into going out again.

"The prince is better behaved when you're along," she said. "And it's a perfect day."

"I'm stiff," I protested, which was the truth.

Happily, I was not as sore and aching as I'd been after an afternoon on Snowbell's back, and had managed a decent night's sleep.

"Riding today will help," Neeve said. "You need to stretch out your muscles and become accustomed to Sterling."

I didn't especially want to make a habit of daily rides—plus, the promise of the hidden bookshelf tugged mightily at me—but in the end I conceded.

And once again, my stepsister was right. After a few minutes atop Sterling, my muscles seemed to ease. Or maybe it was the sunshine warming my shoulders and the fresh scent of cedar in the air.

Prince Kian was in a jolly mood, and seemed to pay no heed to Neeve's narrow-eyed glances in his direction.

"I've been thinking," he said as we rode out through the castle gate, "I don't believe I've seen either of you working with the weapons master. You both should begin training in arms."

Careful to keep my expression blank, I glanced at him to see if he were teasing. No—he seemed to have meant the words quite in earnest.

"I don't believe that's necessary," Neeve said coldly. "Unlike your country, we aren't a land of barbaric warriors."

He grinned at her and pushed a lock of golden hair out of his eyes. "Raine could learn some things from Fiorland. It's always good to be prepared. Just in case."

"In case of what?" I demanded. "Raine has no enemies."

"Not at the moment." His smile faded. "But the world can turn on anyone like a rabid dog. Don't you have a history of trouble with the Athraig? As far as I can tell, your country is small and not terribly well defended."

"I'm not from Raine," I reminded him. "I'm from Parnese."

His expression grew even more shadowed. "You've heard the king's advisors at dinner. Parnese is unsettled. What if the Twin Gods' priests seize power and turn their eyes to conquering their neighbors?"

"Then we will repel them," Neeve said. "Raine is not as helpless as you think."

She nudged Peerless into a trot, clearly done with the conversation.

"I'm going to suggest it to your father, anyway," Kian called after her. "Every noble heir should at least be able to defend themselves."

Which Neeve could do quite handily—with magic. I bit my tongue on the knowledge, and shrugged at Kian.

"I don't think I need to be included in your schemes," I said. "I'm not the heir, after all."

He gave me a keen look. "You're pretty, Rose, and kind. And have ties to both Parnese and Raine. You'd make a good political alliance."

"Um. We ought to catch up to Neeve." I glanced ahead to where my stepsister rode, seeming not to care whether we joined her or not.

"If you don't agree to weapons training," he said, "I might have to mention that I encountered you skulking about the halls the other night. I had a good excuse. But what's yours?"

I blew an annoyed breath out between my teeth. "Very well, I'll train with the arms master. But I highly doubt Lord Raine will agree to the idea."

Unfortunately, I was wrong.

Kian broached the topic at dinner that evening, and the king seemed pleased that his fosterling showed such care for Neeve. I was, as usual, an afterthought. To my silent dismay, Kian managed to work in my inclusion, and the matter was settled.

Mama looked faintly horrified that we were discussing such things at dinner, although worse topics had arisen plenty of times.

"I'm not certain it's a seemly pursuit for princesses," she said, laying her smooth hand on the king's arm.

I refrained from mentioning my former lessons in skullduggery and basic knife work. Not that I'd been any good at the latter. Even though I carried a blade into the Darkwood, I didn't particularly have the skill to use it. Except in the freeing of hobnies.

"You worry too much, Arabelle." Lord Raine patted her hand. "I think the prince's advice is well taken. The girls will begin training tomorrow afternoon. I'll inform Sir Durum."

My mother made a small grimace. She and the captain of the guard were not kindly disposed toward one another. Whenever he joined us at dinner, he made it clear that he thought her nothing more than a useless ornament in the king's court.

What he thought of me, I did not know. Unfortunately, I was about to find out.

◈

THE NEXT AFTERNOON, in anticipation of training, I pulled on my most threadbare skirt and oldest tunic, and laced up my boots. My unruly hair consented to being screwed into a bun, though I had doubts about how long it would remain contained. I considered belting on my kitchen knife, but then decided that Sir Durum would probably laugh at my pathetic little weapon.

As it turned out, he laughed at me anyway, and not kindly.

"You look like a kitchen girl," he said, nodding to where I stood beside Neeve and Kian. "Are you certain you've come to the right room? The scullery is down the hall."

I swallowed, unsure of what to say. Sir Durum intimidated me, with his large, muscular frame, cold gaze, and sharp words. It didn't seem wise to reply tartly, so I scuffed my foot on the sawdust-covered floor and tried not to let his remarks sting.

The training arena was large, illuminated by enclosed lanterns and a dim filtering of gray light through high windows cut into the stone walls. It was enough to show Kian, wearing his leather armor, and Neeve, dressed in dark leggings, high boots, and a leather jerkin.

"This is Rose," Kian said mildly. "Surely you're aware of that fact, sir."

I shot him a grateful look for speaking up for me.

The arms master grunted, his gaze moving from me to Neeve. "At least you had the sense not to wear skirts, Lady Neeve. There's hope for you yet."

I glanced down at the tips of my boots. The only trousers I owned were my too-small black ones, which were now impossible for me to fit into.

Neeve matched Sir Durum's stare. "I'm here for weapons training. And you might consider diplomacy lessons in return."

I swallowed my sudden amusement, and Kian made a choked noise beside me. Trust Neeve to never be intimidated. I flicked her a grateful look, which she ignored.

The arms master seemed impervious to her comment. He set his hands on his hips and surveyed us with his usual dour expression.

"Do either of you girls know how to hold a blade?" he demanded.

I remained quiet, and Neeve shook her head.

Sir Durum made an impatient noise in the back of his throat, then stalked over to one of the racks of weapons lining the hall.

"Follow him," Kian whispered, nodding after the arms master.

Neeve and I exchanged a glance, then went to where Sir Durum waited. Kian followed, his footsteps light. The arms master glared at us, then turned to the row of blades.

"Lady Neeve, take that one." He pointed to a slender sword with a metal-wrapped hilt, watching closely as she stepped up to take the weapon. "No, no, one hand only. Point it up until you feel the balance. Now hold it straight, without wavering. Kian, help adjust her grip."

The prince moved to Neeve's side, and Sir Durum turned to me. He eyed me up and down, his mouth set in a grim line.

"Bows, for you," he said.

"Don't I get a sword?" I asked, stung. Was there some rule in Raine that only royalty could use swords?

"You can waste my time, and yours, mucking about with a long-blade if you choose. But I've trained many a warrior, and I know a sword wielder when I see one." He nodded to Neeve. "And when I don't." He gave me a hard look.

"I'll try one, anyway." I stuck my chin into the air, trying to feel brave.

"Foolishness," he muttered, turning to look at the row of swords again. Finally, he jabbed his finger at a short blade with a plain, leather-wrapped grip. "That one."

Mindful of his instructions to Neeve, I reached out with one hand to pick it up. Stars, but it was heavier than I expected. I gritted my teeth and held it upright, trying to keep my wrist from wobbling. Sir Durum grunted.

"Weak hands," he said. "You'll need to strengthen your grip a great deal. Try holding it in your left."

I switched the sword to my other hand, but the blade began wavering wildly. The arms master stepped out of the way, watched me with narrowed eyes for a moment, then reached and deftly snagged the sword from my awkward grasp.

"Still determined to use a sword?" he asked.

"Yes," I said—more out of spite than actual desire.

My hands were accustomed to holding books, not reins—to writing, not stirring up pots of herbal potions. No wonder Neeve was better at this than I. But I was too stubborn to admit defeat just yet.

Sir Durum gave me a sour look. "So be it."

He thrust the hilt at me, and I tried to grasp the sword with confidence.

"We'll work on form," he said, striding to the center of the room. "Kian, demonstrate."

"Single, or double?" the prince asked, pulling his blade from the scabbard at his hip.

"Single to start."

Kian brought the hilt to his chest in a brief salute, then lunged forward. His blade swept in a shining arc from right to left. He followed it, turning almost like a dancer, to stab behind him. I blinked, astonished by his dexterity. Clearly Prince Kian knew what he was doing.

I glanced at Neeve. Her eyes were shining, her cheeks lightly flushed—but I couldn't tell if it was because of the prince, or simply the sheer thrill of seeing someone wield a sword with such grace and fluidity.

"Ho!" Sir Durum shouted, rushing at Kian with a huge, two-handed sword.

I sucked in my breath, but the prince pivoted out of the way. He thrust at the arms master, and their blades met with a clang that seemed to shake the dust motes hanging in the air. The two of them circled, stabbed, parried, moving far too quickly for comfort.

Finally, they paused, blades locked together. I could see the sweat on Kian's face, though he was grinning.

"Enough," Sir Durum said.

The prince gave a quick nod, and they separated. Facing one another, they gave the salute with their swords that Kian had demonstrated at the beginning.

"Good," the arms master said, then set his massive blade aside and drew his sleeve across his forehead—his only sign of exertion.

"What did you think?" Kian asked, coming over to where Neeve and I stood, his grin still firmly in place.

"Impressive," Neeve said, which made his smile widen even more.

"How long have you been training?" I asked.

He gave a little shrug. "For as long as I can remember. Wooden swords when I was young, then steel once I grew older. I'm also skilled with the crossbow, lance, and knife."

Sir Durum let out a grunt, which I took as agreement.

"Is that all you did up there in Fiorland?" Neeve asked. "Train with weapons?"

"I had regular school lessons, too," he replied, sounding a little insulted.

I wondered if, being the youngest of seven, he'd had to defend himself against his rambunctious older brothers.

"You're very good," I said. "I don't think I'll ever be able to do that."

"You won't," Sir Durum said. "You're starting too late, for one thing."

And have no aptitude for it, for another. I could read his unspoken words in his face.

Perhaps he was right. But I wasn't going to admit defeat without trying my best to prove him wrong.

CHAPTER 38

I f I'd thought riding made me stiff and sore, it was nothing to the rigors of weapons training. Sir Durum, after that initial selection, equipped both Neeve and me with wooden swords and started us on a strength and dexterity regimen. By dinnertime, I was scarcely able to bring my fork to my mouth without my arm trembling with exhaustion.

In addition to arm and wrist exercises, the weapons master had us dart and lunge, twist and roll. At the end of training each day, my scalp was scratchy with sawdust and my clothes sticky with sweat. It was not a pleasant combination.

Kian assisted, and sometimes demonstrated. I couldn't help thinking, rather uncharitably, that he'd come up with this plan so that he could show off his skills. They were remarkable, I had to admit, though I tried not to admire his fluid, muscular sparring when he faced off against Sir Durum.

Neeve was equally impressed, I could tell—though she did her best not to show it. Certainly Kian couldn't tell, despite his frequent glances in her direction whenever he demonstrated a strike or parry.

Our training was broken only by afternoons of riding. It was maddening.

Every morning I vowed I'd find time to sneak off to the library—and every night I collapsed, exhausted, into bed, no closer to exploring the mysterious bookshelf than I'd been the day before.

Finally, a day came when Sir Durum decreed we had the afternoon off, and the weather was too wretched to ride. Though I was tempted to return to my rooms after lunch and ask Sorche to draw me a hot bath, the lure of the library drew me on.

Pretending I was going to spend the afternoon reading and napping, I left the schoolroom and made my way down to the ground floor of the castle. To my relief, the library door was unlocked. I slipped inside and drew in a deep breath rich with the scent of leather and paper and candle wax.

I was halfway to the back shelf when I realized I wasn't alone.

"Greetings, Lady Rose," a smooth voice said.

I jumped a little, and squeaked like a startled mouse. Jarl Eiric sat at one of the long tables, a partially unrolled scroll propped open before him.

"My lord." I dipped him a quick curtsey.

It hadn't ever been made explicitly clear to me whether I outranked a jarl of Fiorland, but I preferred to err on the side of politeness. Especially as Prince Kian's advisor reminded me of a raptor, with his jutting nose and sharp, beady eyes that watched everything intently. It always seemed he was waiting to pounce, talons extended.

"What brings you to the library?" he asked mildly, though his expression was intent as he watched me.

I let out a little laugh, hoping it sounded carefree. "I need another novel to read."

One brow rose. "Something frivolous, I expect."

I blinked at him, then decided to play the fool. If Jarl Eiric underestimated my intelligence, all the better.

"I'm halfway through the Summerland series. Do you know it?" I barely gave him time to shake his head before continuing. "It's the most delightful tale about the crown princess of the Summerland, who is cruelly switched at birth with a hapless orphan. Luckily, she can speak to animals, and has the dearest little creatures as her friends. Oh, and she owns a pastry shop!"

As I spoke, I went to his table and settled in the chair across from him. Ignoring his frown, I carried on describing my fabricated book series, making sure it was as lighthearted as possible. He assumed I was frivolous, did he? I prattled on, making sure to put in the most ridiculously charming elements I could imagine: animal companions, delicious baked goods, misunderstandings, sunrises, roses, tea parties, choruses of emotion, kisses like spun sugar—

"It sounds delightful." He shoved back his chair and stood. "But I'm afraid I must be going."

"Are you certain?" I gave him an innocent look. "I haven't even gotten to the best parts yet. You see, there's the most enchanting white horse—"

"Perhaps another time." He made me a curt bow, then scooped up the scroll.

"It would be my pleasure." I clasped my hands together and gazed up at him. "You're a wonderful listener, my lord."

He cleared his throat. "Good day, Lady Rose."

"Ta!" I wiggled my fingers at him, trying not to burst into laughter at the panicked look on his face. Or the speed with which he exited the library, which was closer to a run than a walk.

As soon as the door closed, I allowed myself a few satisfied chuckles. I'd likely deflected Jarl Eiric for a good several months, if not more. But as I considered our encounter, my mirth faded, replaced with a faint sense of unease.

Not at the trick I'd played on him—I was completely unrepentant on that score—but at the contents of the scroll he'd been perusing. I hadn't gotten a good look at it, but just before he'd rolled it up, I caught a glance at the contents.

It appeared to be a diagram of Castle Raine's outer walls, with height and thickness noted. Perhaps the secret door that Neeve and I used was indicated as well. I didn't like it. What would the jarl want with such details? The only reasons I could think of were nefarious.

Perhaps I could casually ask the prince if he and his man were surveying the castle for a possible invasion? I shook my head at the notion. I supposed I could approach the king, but I had only unfounded suspicions and circumstantial evidence. Still, I resolved to be wary around the jarl, and alert for any other oddities in his behavior.

Those unpleasant thoughts had clouded my anticipation, but as I approached the last bank of shelves my excitement leaped up again. I paused at the opening of the book bay and peered in all directions to make sure no one else was lurking unexpectedly in the corners.

The library was reassuringly empty.

My heartbeat suddenly hammering in my throat, I went to the back shelf and pulled out the book at the end of the bottom row. It was a quiet weight in my hand—a key waiting to be turned.

I bit my lip, and pushed it back into place.

Click.

To my intense relief, the middle portion of the bookshelf swung open as it had before. I grabbed the smooth wooden edge of the shelf, my hand trembling, and pulled it wide.

A dozen book-sized cubbies occupied the hidden space, though only a few of them were filled. Directly in front of me was a thick tome bound in pale leather. I wiped my sweaty palms down my skirts, then carefully slipped the book out.

On closer examination, I realized the volume was actually covered with a thin sheet of tree bark—birch, perhaps. On the font, in faded gold script, were the words *Elfhame: A Studie of the Dark Elves and their Wayes.*

Yes! I wanted to leap and shout with victory. Instead, grinning fiercely, I opened the book.

My elation dimmed as I realized that the entire thing was written with the same archaic spelling and phrasing as the title. Most of the words were familiar, or close enough that I could puzzle them out— but this wasn't going to be a simple thing to read. Still, it was what I'd hoped for, and I shouldn't be picky about the fact that the book appeared to have been written centuries ago.

I set it back into its cubby and pulled out the next book, although to call it a book was generous. It was more of a leaflet. I opened it, dismayed to find that the entire thing was written in a strange dotted and curling script, in a form that looked like poetry.

I saw faint notes written in the margins, but these too were in a language I couldn't read, although most of the letters were familiar.

The third book was, thankfully, written in a language I could understand, judging by the title on the red cloth cover: *Recipes*, it said. I opened it and skimmed the contents, noting that the pages were made of very thick parchment.

At first glance, the book seemed to contain a series of household concoctions, complete with lists of ingredients. Whether one simmered or baked or whipped vigorously was made very clear, as well as how to store the result.

Yet the more I looked at the recipes, the more my conviction grew that this was no ordinary book. I turned page after page, trying to guess what each recipe was for. Some called for culinary spices, others used herbs, but just as I was coming to the conclusion that it was a cookery book, the next recipe incorporated ground carnelians and riverbank clay.

Beauty products, perhaps? I scanned, but found no mention of *nirwen*. Other unfamiliar names caught my eye, and though I had only the most passing knowledge of the language, I thought some of the terms were in Old Rainish. If so, there were dictionaries in the library I could put to good use.

It wasn't until I neared the end of the book that it gave up its secrets.

The top right-hand corners of the final pages were discolored, as though they'd gotten wet. In one instance, the parchment seemed to be peeling apart, which was odd.

I picked at the edge, then looked more closely, my heart pounding.

Where the recipe page had stripped back, a different book was revealed, layered between the mundane lists of ingredients and preparations. I pried delicately at the thick parchment with my fingernail, trying not to tear the paper, until finally I had enough of the page uncovered that I could read what had been hidden.

Unlike the precise lettering of the recipes, the writing was angular and jagged, and a little difficult to decipher. Biting my lip, I held the book up to catch the light, and read:

...unless the priests discover my subterfuge. Even then, this account of their

sorcerous explorations, and my own initiation into the mysteries of the flame and sword, shall stand as witness to the dangers of such power. Although the calling of fire is not a simple thing, and the results are often meager at best, I fear that in the future the red priests of the Twin Gods may unlock greater abilities. Heed this warning, Your Majesty, I beg you. All precautions must be taken to ensure...

The page ended, and I'd have to pry apart the next layer to discover more. Slowly, I lowered the book, belatedly realizing that my hands were trembling, my pulse beating like wings in my throat.

The red priests. Sorcerous flame.

When had this book been written, and by whom? I turned it back and forth in my hands, then carefully opened it once more. The account had been set down some time ago, judging by the archaic wording here and there—but not so far in the past as the *Studie* of the Dark Elves. As to who had written it, the answer probably lay closer to the beginning of the hidden pages.

Did the king know of this book? Did Thorne?

I ought to tell them, and yet...

Learn what you can, my little voice whispered. *This is your secret. If you give it up, unread, you lose the chance to discover everything. Everything.*

The book had languished in its hidden cubby for decades, if not longer. Surely another month or two wouldn't matter, I reasoned. Besides, someone would have to go to the effort of separating the pages. It might as well be me.

Although I was reluctant to put the book away, I set it in its place. Rocking back on my heels, I studied the three titles. The leaflet was no use to me. But the other two were treasures. I wanted to devour both of them.

Not here in the library, though. I couldn't risk discovery, which would certainly result in the books being taken from me. They were best read at midnight by the light of a single lamp, with the curtains closed and the doors locked.

I'd take them back to my rooms and devise a hiding place; some-where Sorche wouldn't discover. Yet I was reluctant to leave the cubbies glaringly empty. Luckily, I was in a room packed with books.

I held my hand up beside the white-bound tome, judging its height and thickness. Surely in this whole immense room full of books, I could find one that looked the same. And a red one, as well.

It took longer than I wanted, and every little noise made me jump, but I finally collected an armful of books that might suit. Returning to the hidden shelf, I chose the closest matches, putting them in place of the *Studie* and the recipe book filled with secrets.

Next, how to get them back to my rooms? I couldn't openly carry such forbidden tomes around the halls, and now that I'd found substitutes, I didn't want to leave them in their cubbies. I scolded myself for not bringing a satchel along, or even a spare scarf. My only option was to wrap them in a corner of my underskirt and tuck the whole bundle under the waistband of my dress. It made an ungainly lump, but I could carry a larger book in front, and my hidden cargo wouldn't be too obvious. I hoped.

Waddling slightly due to my bunched-up skirts, I replaced all the pale and red-bound volumes I'd gathered, and then chose the largest book I could find: an illustrated compendium of catapults. Thus burdened, I stepped out of the library just as the dinner gong sounded.

Drat it. I didn't want to do anything to draw attention to myself—including being late to dinner. Feeling like an overweight duck, I made what haste I could up the stairs.

Unfortunately, Neeve was waiting for me in the corridor outside my rooms.

I halted, checking my panicked impulse to retreat.

"Whatever are you doing?" Neeve eyed me up and down.

"Um. Just bringing up a book from the library." It was true, after all.

"But what is wrong with your skirts?"

I cast about for a plausible answer. "I... tore the hem of my underskirt and had to kirtle it up to keep from tripping."

Her brows rose, dark slashes against her pale skin. "How clumsy of you."

"Yes, well. You know I'm not the most graceful of girls." I gave her an apologetic smile and sidled toward my door. "Let me change, and we'll go down to dinner."

"Hurry." She held my door open for me, the skeptical expression never leaving her face.

At least she didn't press for answers. It wasn't her way, and for once,

I was grateful for her lack of curiosity—yet another area we completely differed. I never stopped asking questions, and she never started. I often thought she was too restrained, but today her reticence worked in my favor.

My lie about my torn underskirt meant that I had to race to conceal the books before I threw on a new dress. I tucked the *Studie* and recipe book at the bottom of my trunk—a temporary hiding place —then pulled on the nearest gown and shoved a pair of decorative combs into my unruly hair as a finishing touch.

When I stepped back into the hallway, Neeve gave me a quizzical look, but didn't remark upon my appearance. What would she say if she knew I'd discovered a book about her homeland?

Tell her, the wicked voice urged.

No. Not yet. Once I'd puzzled out what the *Studie* contained, then I might consider doing so. Or I might simply return the book to its hidden shelf. A secret shared was always a risky thing.

CHAPTER 39

As I'd suspected, the *Studie* of Elfhame was difficult going. It didn't help that I was trying to decipher the faded writing by flickering candlelight late at night. Or that the archaic language had me puzzling out every other sentence.

I alternated this frustrating pastime with prising open the pages of the recipe book. Unfortunately, this proved even more aggravating. For every tantalizing page I was able to peel apart, two others stayed stubbornly glued together. After a mishap where I tore some of the writing entirely away, I proceeded very carefully.

With trial and error, I discovered that I could gently dampen the page, wait a day, and have a bit more success with my peeling attempts. I made agonizingly slow progress, however, and when my impatience got the better of me, I'd go back to reading the *Studie*.

Or, in some cases, I'd abandon both books entirely and gratefully dive into an uncomplicated tale of love and adventure. It was a relief to lose myself in stories where the heroes always succeeded, despite impossible odds.

Over a handful of weeks, I was able to tease out bits and pieces from the little red book. It was a series of letters, written by someone who'd infiltrated the sect of the red priests of the Twin Gods.

Wardens, they were called, and the spy had been sent to Parnese some-time in the past—perhaps a hundred years ago or more—to investigate rumors that the priests were dabbling in magic.

It made sense that the rulers of Raine would be alert for such things, given their connection with the Dark Elves and their magic. I found the letters fascinating, especially when the spy described the rites of the priests and their attempts to draw forth sorcerous power. The author had even witnessed firsthand a flicker of flame dancing on the palm of the head Warden.

Better yet, the spy had set down the particulars of the rituals and incantations used by the red priests. I devoured these accounts, pulse racing. Finally, *finally*, I'd found what I'd been searching for, what had been hinted at in the scraps I'd collected in Parnese.

One night, when the castle had quieted into the dark hours after midnight, I made my attempt. As silently as possible, I rolled back my heavy carpet, exposing the slate flagstones. With a bit of charcoal I'd fished from the hearth, I inscribed sigils on the floor, painstakingly copied from the book.

Circles bisected with jagged runes I didn't recognize, half-moons balanced on their sides, and in the center, the sword and flame of the Twin Gods.

When it was done, I stood back and, book in hand, compared my work to the diagram set down on the pages. I'd forgotten a rune on the left-hand side, so quickly filled it in, my fingers smudged with soot, then examined the result once more. The inscription on the floor seemed identical to what was depicted in the book—or as close as my efforts could make it.

Anticipation rippling through me, I set my charcoal aside and scanned the incantation, silently mouthing the strange syllables. *Esfera to quera, firenda des almar.*

It was not the language of the Dark Elves, I could tell that much. Truthfully, I didn't much care what language it was, as long as it worked.

Breath trembling, I stepped into the center of the inscription, careful not to smudge any of the lines. Then, hands raised, I chanted the words.

"*Esfera to quera, firenda des almar. Esfera to quera, firenda des almar.*"

Over and over. With each repetition, I felt something building. The stub of my pinky ached in remembered pain. The leaf on my inner elbow flared.

Yes. This was the moment. The room wavered, as if the air were full of heat. My knees weakened, and I swayed, fighting to remain upright.

"*Esfera to que—*"

"Rose!" My bedroom door flew open, though I was certain I'd locked it. Neeve stood there, her eyes wide in an expression of half fury, half panic. Her hands were outlined in blue light.

"Stop it," she said, her voice choked.

I already had—her interruption had halted the flow of the chant, blunted the power I thought I'd felt building. A blinding headache crashed over me, and I staggered, smearing the charcoal inscription. The room cooled. The glow around Neeve's hands faded, and I crumpled forward into her unwilling arms.

"What are you doing?" she asked, hauling me over to the bed. "What is this?"

She sent a scathing look at me, then at the charcoal-marked floor.

"I just wanted magic," I mumbled through the exhaustion stunning my senses.

"This is dangerous." Neeve pushed me between the covers, then went to rub out the rest of my markings with her bare foot. "You're only a mortal. You're not supposed to have power."

"*They* have it," I said, groping for the red-bound book on my nightstand. "The priests of the Twin Gods—and they're human, like me."

Neeve snatched the book from my hand and flipped through it, bending close to the light of the candle. A heavy silence filled the room, but I didn't care. I closed my eyes, trying to time my breathing so it didn't escalate the pulsing pain in my head.

"I'm confiscating this," Neeve said after several moments. "Thorne needs to see this book—and you need to stop meddling in things you don't understand."

"But I'm the one who found it," I protested weakly. "You can't just take it."

Thank all the stars the *Studie* of the Dark Elves was still hidden, or my stepsister would have stolen that from me, as well.

"Sleep," she said, and I was too tired to argue, though I wanted to weep in defeat.

It wasn't fair. It was never fair...

THE NEXT MORNING, my head still hurt and I was in a bleak mood. Once again, my discoveries had been snatched from my fingertips. Neeve, pale and composed, said nothing as we went to the schoolroom, and breathed not a word after lunch. It was only as we made our way through the chilly halls on our way to the dining room that she spoke.

"I've given my father the book," she said. "He'll share it with Thorne. You should've brought it to the king as soon as you realized what you had. That knowledge is essential to the safety of Raine."

I scowled. "Everyone knows the red priests have fire sorcery. I don't see that reading old letters about it will make any difference."

"Where did you find it?" She sent me a piercing look.

"In the library." My gaze skittered to the floor, then back to her. "If you'd ever set foot in there, maybe you would have discovered it yourself."

Her lips pressed together and she made no answer.

"When you came in last night," I said, a bit sullenly, "how did you know?"

"I felt a tug on my wellspring," she said. "Just like that time at the Yule Feast—when you swore you had nothing to do with it."

"I didn't do anything," I replied. At least, not that time. How could I have? "Are you saying you have some kind of ability to sense magic?"

"I suppose I may," she said coldly. "Rose, you must stop meddling."

"But what if I have power?" I cried. "I felt something last night, I swear it! By your own admission, you wouldn't have come in if you hadn't felt something."

She narrowed her eyes at me. "Both Thorne and Mistress Ainya agree you don't possess any magic."

I stopped in the middle of the hallway and stared vehemently at her. "Then why do you keep accusing me of it? Either they're right, and I'm powerless, or you are, and I *do* have magic."

She grimaced and shook her head. "I don't *know*, Rose. Believe me, if the answer were clear, I wouldn't have kept it to myself."

"What are you keeping to yourself, anyway?" I stepped closer to her, until we were scant inches apart. "What do you know, that you aren't telling me?"

Her nostrils flared as she stared at me a long moment. "Nothing."

Pale sparks danced in the darkness of her eyes, a reminder that she was half Dark Elf. Not entirely human at all.

"I don't believe you." I clenched my hands into fists.

She held my gaze and lifted one shoulder in a shrug. "Believe what you want. I'm going down to dinner."

With that, she whirled and stalked away, her hair flying like dark strands of spider's silk. Scowling, I watched her go.

I have magic. I clung to the thought, despite all evidence to the contrary. But if that were true, why hadn't it manifested? Why was I left to constantly clutch for something just out of reach?

CHAPTER 40

Lord Raine made no mention of the little red book, or the secrets it contained. I assumed that Neeve had made some kind of excuse and claimed she'd found it herself, as the king's manner toward me remained unchanged. Although the thought rankled, I let the matter lie.

Neeve kept herself aloof, and I told myself I didn't care. I didn't want to be friends, anyway, not after she'd taken the book—the one thing that could have unlocked the power I'd always craved. Winter bled into spring, and I stubbornly continued my reading of the *Studie*, spending long hours with the archaic text.

A picture of the Dark Elves' world slowly took shape in my mind: the star-strewn sky, the intricate customs of the courts, the strange flora and fauna of Elfhame. And, of course, the wonder of their magic. The Dark Elves moved in a mysterious world full of power and shadow. The more I learned of it, the more I pined to see it.

And the angrier I grew at Neeve for taking away the key to my own understanding of human sorcery.

The days lengthened. My muscles ached from riding and clumsily wielding a wooden practice sword. My brain ached from working on the *Studie* and from too little sleep. At least my harp playing was going well, although Master Fawkes was soon to depart the castle.

My sadness at this fact was mitigated by the knowledge that I'd see Thorne again soon. Although, with Kian accompanying Neeve on her rides so often, how would we manage to keep the prince from coming into the forest with us?

It seemed Lord Raine was aware of the problem, however.

"I will be away for much of the summer," he announced at dinner one evening.

I shot a glance at Mama, who seemed resigned to the news. While she and Lord Raine did not seem unhappy, the first glow had worn off their marriage. She, however, looked as young and radiant as ever. I worried at my bottom lip with my teeth, hoping she wouldn't do anything foolish while the king was away.

Then she reached and laid her hand on his arm, and I could see the genuine affection in her expression.

"We'll miss you, Tobin," she said. "And the prince as well."

Kian glanced up, a startled look in his eyes. "I'm going with you?"

"Indeed," Jarl Eiric said from his place across from Neeve. "We are both accompanying the king on his diplomatic missions this season."

"You might have told me," Kian said, his brows drawing together. "Perhaps I prefer to stay here."

He shot a look over the table at Neeve. It was clear he still fancied himself in love with her, although he'd been more circumspect since our little chat in the midnight hallways.

The faintest hint of pink flushed her cheeks, proof she was aware of his regard. I fidgeted with my napkin beneath the table, glad that the king had found a way to keep the Fiorlander's prying eyes from the Darkwood. At least this summer.

"We will be journeying to Fiorland for a few weeks," Lord Raine said calmly. "And then down to Parnese. Disturbing rumors are reaching my ears about the state of the government there."

The jarl nodded, his eyes hooded. For my part, I was careful to conceal my reaction. Surely this must have something to do with the red book, and the growing number of sorcerers among the Twin Gods' priests.

"Is it safe?" Mama asked, worry clear in her voice.

"We'll take Sir Durum and a cohort of my best soldiers." The king patted her hand where it rested on his arm. "Don't fret, my dear."

"When do you leave?" Neeve asked.

Her father glanced at her. "Before the first of May."

A tiny nod passed between them, and from this I understood that the king had planned his schedule specifically to keep the prince and Jarl Eiric away from the secrets lying at the heart of Raine.

I did not point out they would miss my fifteenth birthday. I was barely a princess, after all.

◈

THE DAYS PASSED, the rains lightened, and, true to his word, in mid-April the king set off with his retinue. Most of the castle turned out to bid them farewell. I stood beside Neeve and Kian on the damp cobbles. The courtyard was silvery with misty morning air, and for a brief moment my heart bumped with envy.

I wanted to go off into the world and have adventures. And to see Parnese again! I'd told Kian to look for my old friends, and given him Marco's address, although I'd no idea if it was still current. Unlike Mama, I had no contact with the friends I'd left behind.

I'll see Thorne soon, I reminded myself, and the jealousy receded.

The waiting horses shifted, impatient with the foolish farewells of humans. Or maybe it was my own wish to see the travelers off, so that I would not be so full of yearning to join them.

Lord Raine kissed Mama on the cheek, then mounted his horse—the signal that it was time to depart.

"I'll miss you," Kian said. Although he glanced at both of us, I knew he meant the words for Neeve.

"Enjoy your travels," she said, without an ounce of extra warmth.

The smile in the prince's eyes dimmed, and a grudging sympathy moved through me. I had a notion of how it felt to be enamored of someone who did not return that regard. It wasn't a pleasant feeling.

"We'll miss you, too," I said to Kian, and gave my stepsister a jab in the back.

She stiffened, but nodded to the prince. "We shall."

His expression easing, he swung up into the saddle. "I'll bring back gifts. For both of you!"

The subdued air of the courtyard was suddenly transformed with bustle and motion, last-minute goodbyes, the clop of hooves over stone. Kian turned and waved one more time as the group passed under the portcullis.

I lifted my hand in farewell, and hissed at Neeve to do the same. With a stubborn look on her face, she gave a halfhearted wave, then pivoted and made for the front doors.

"You could be kinder," I said, following at her heels.

She shot me a glance. "It's good that he left. Don't you want to go into the Darkwood tomorrow? Or have you become such a delicate flower that you prefer to remain penned up behind the castle walls?"

"Just because I can't wave a sword about doesn't mean I've become some kind of cosseted court lady," I replied hotly. "At least we don't have to keep training, now that Sir Durum has gone off with the king."

My inability to master the rudiments of blade work was frustrating, to say the least. Sir Durum, never the most patient man, had taken to grunting at me when we arrived for training, shoving a practice sword into my hand, and then working with Neeve.

Kian had tried to help, but I was hopelessly clumsy; slicing where I should block, parrying when I was supposed to be on the attack. The blade never went where I wanted it to, and it was a good thing I was still relegated to a wooden weapon. More than once I'd accidentally hacked at my own legs, and even dropped the sword point-first onto my foot. That bruise had taken weeks to heal, and I'd limped grumpily about the castle, wishing Kian had never mentioned weapons training to the king.

"Even though the weapons master is accompanying my father," Neeve said, "I'll continue to train."

"You will?" I grimaced. The thought held no appeal to me. "With whom?"

"The under-captain of the guard, Lem. Sir Durum suggested it. He said I shouldn't let my natural talent languish."

He'd said no such thing to me, of course. Mostly, I was grateful for the reprieve. Although it was never pleasant being the worst at anything.

"I don't plan to join you," I said, somewhat snappishly.

"I didn't think you would." There was no hint of censure in her voice.

"When will you train, though?" Between morning classes with Miss Groves, afternoon jaunts into the Darkwood, and working with Mistress Ainya, I couldn't imagine when Neeve would find the time.

"I have permission to absent myself from the schoolroom two mornings a week."

I blinked at her. I'd grown used to our routine, and to Neeve's company. Even though I was still angry with her about the book, I didn't like the fact she was abandoning me for the dubious charms of the training arena.

"Do you think that's wise?" I asked, not bothering to keep the edge from my voice. "I mean, the heir of Raine needs to be well educated."

"It's only twice a week," she said, with a hint of exasperation. "Besides, I've learned nearly everything I need to know. Did you think we were going to stay in the classroom forever?"

"No, but..." In truth, I hadn't considered it. The pattern of our days had been only slightly changed by Kian's arrival, and I'd simply assumed that things would continue as usual until— Well. Until we were fully grown, I supposed. "What if you miss an important lesson?"

It was a weak argument, and I knew it.

"Miss Groves has taken that into account." Neeve tossed me a superior look. "There are plenty of subjects where I'm ahead of you, and this will give you a chance to catch up. You needn't sound so upset about it."

I was, though. Once again, my stepsister was singled out for being better at something than I was. My only ally, Master Fawkes, had departed for his summer travels as the Bard of Raine, and I was back to being ordinary, untalented Rose.

One day, my little voice promised, *you'll be so much more—and then you'll show them.*

I couldn't help the sigh that escaped my lips. Perhaps. Or perhaps not. That voice inside me had led me astray enough times that I knew not to trust it, no matter how much I might want to.

CHAPTER 41

My bleak mood didn't last long, as the next afternoon Neeve and I made for the Darkwood.

Though the air was cool, the clouds overhead had lifted into a high pewter dome. Black-winged birds cawed from the branches of the cedar trees as we stepped out of the door concealed in the garden shed.

Beyond the walls, the brown grasses were wet. The hem of my skirt darkened with moisture as we strode to the line of trees. My heart thumped unreasonably loudly in my chest, and I told myself that it was only anticipation at setting foot in the forest again.

I was lying to myself, of course, and not very well.

In truth, I couldn't wait to see Thorne. Through the dark winter months, thoughts of him had flashed almost constantly through my mind: his serious eyes flecked with gold, how he'd covered me with his cloak that first night of the *nirwen* harvest, the way my hand had felt clasped in his as we watched the Dark Elves step through the portal back into Elfhame.

Foolish yearnings, and I knew it—but I couldn't help myself. That bittersweet longing flared even more strongly as I puzzled out the information scribed in the Dark Elf *Studie*. I could envision Thorne moving through the elegant courts, and wondered what his standing was as *Galadhir*. As far as I could make out, the Dark Elves had an intricate web of protocol among the nobility.

I scanned the shadowy tree line as Neeve and I approached. Would Thorne be waiting?

Of course. There he was, slender and as still as the cedar tree he stood beside. Our eyes met, and I grinned at him.

"There's Thorne," Neeve said a moment later, veering toward him.

"Yes." I didn't tell her I'd spotted him first, but hugged that knowledge to myself.

For once, I'd come out ahead.

It doesn't matter, my little voice said. *You'll still never have him. No mere mortal can pair with the Guardian of the Darkwood.*

I shoved the words away, though the truth of them spiked deep into my heart.

But today was fresh and new, and the future didn't matter, even when Thorne embraced Neeve in greeting. Then he turned to me and held out his arms, and the pain blew away like ashes.

"Well met again, Rose," he said.

He enfolded me in his embrace, and all the blood in my body seemed to rush to the surface of my skin, so quickly I felt dizzy. He smelled of evergreens and starlight, and I wanted nothing more than to lean into him and never let go.

But Kian's unrequited behavior around Neeve was fresh in my mind, and after two precious heartbeats, I pulled away. I didn't want Thorne to look at me with bemused pity, the way my stepsister regarded the prince.

And so, since it was no use showing my feelings, I plastered a cheerful smile on my face and hoped my coppery skin hid my blush.

"Hello, Thorne," I said. "Did you know that Neeve is becoming a swordswoman?" Deflection was always a useful skill, as I'd learned in my long-ago diplomacy class.

Brows slanted up, Thorne glanced at my stepsister. "You are? Is that wise?"

"Why wouldn't it be?" Neeve frowned. "Rose is just jealous because she's useless with a weapon."

"Have you forgotten your vision?" Thorne's tone was somber. "In it, you wielded a sword against Rose."

Oh. I took a step back. It hadn't occurred to me that perhaps all of Neeve's lessons might be turned on *me.* And, as she'd said, I was hopeless to defend myself.

Neeve was not one to roll her eyes, but she gave Thorne an exasperated look. "You've told me time and again that scrying visions are almost never to be taken literally. As if I would attack Rose!"

"*Almost* never," Thorne said quietly. "But every vision contains a seed of truth."

Neeve sniffed. "I think it highly unlikely."

"It's too nice a day to squabble," I said, although the afternoon wasn't particularly lovely. "Are we to visit Mistress Ainya?"

"That was my intent." Thorne pushed his intricately plaited hair behind one pointed ear. "I plan to give her my regards, and I'm certain she'd like to begin lessons again with both of you."

Another summer of sorting lentils and sweeping the floor. It would grow tiresome, but for the moment I was pleased at the thought of returning to Mistress Ainya's cottage. Despite Neeve being the better student, I'd had some warm and happy times in the herbwife's kitchen.

As Neeve and I followed Thorne through the forest, I felt the same sense of unwelcome that I'd had the first time I'd trodden that path. Although no branches reached out to scratch my skin, and no cloud of gnats bedeviled me, there was a cold edge to the shadows.

Neeve didn't seem to notice, but partway down the overgrown trail, Thorne halted and held up his hand.

"Rose," he said, turning to look at me, "has anything strange occurred since I've seen you last? More tapestries set afire or odd scryings you ought to tell me about?"

"Well... I have a new mount, and, of course, Kian arrived." I was curiously reluctant to admit that I'd attempted the rites of the red priests.

Neeve whirled and gave me a narrow-eyed look. "Tell him."

"Tell me what?" Thorne took a step toward me, expression severe.

"I... Well. Do you know about the book?" I glanced at Neeve pleadingly. She tilted her head and said nothing, leaving me to answer on my own.

"The book," Thorne said flatly. "The only book of note I'm aware of is one the king recently shared with me."

"That's the one." I swallowed. "With the spy in Parnese, and the red priests. The letters were hidden between pages of odd recipes."

"Yes." Thorne's brows drew together. "I hadn't realized you'd seen the book, Rose."

"I'm the one who found it," I said, a touch defensively. "Hidden in the library."

"It was wise of you to bring it to Lord Raine's attention," Thorne said. "The descriptions of human sorcery were of great interest to the Oracles."

"*She* didn't tell the king about it," Neeve said. "I did. And I only found out about it when Rose attempted to perform one of the fire-calling rituals."

Thorne looked at me, his expression both stern and despairing. "Of course you did. Rose—when will you learn that fire will burn you? Such things aren't to be trifled with."

"I'm human!" I replied hotly. "Neeve has Dark Elf magic—why can't I have sorcery? And something happened that night. Neeve, you felt it!"

"Just because the flame-summoning ritual has power, doesn't mean *you* do," my stepsister said. "Why do you think the priests forbid knowledge of sorcery? Because anyone with the proper tools can perform it. My wellspring stirred because the incantation was taking effect. That's the only reason."

I folded my arms and stared at her with a sense of betrayal. Why couldn't she just tell Thorne I had a spark of power? I could have spent more time with him and Mistress Ainya, and this time, maybe a closer look would prove I had some kind of long-buried human magic.

Instead, Neeve had to go and ruin everything.

Tears pricking my eyes, I looked down at the ground, staring at the mossy loam stitched with twigs and pine needles.

"Don't be upset." Thorne set a hand on my shoulder. He stood so near I could smell his subtle aroma—fresh rain, wild herbs. "Perhaps, once the Oracles have finished studying the book, they will agree to let you try once again. With proper supervision."

I knew a scrap tossed my way when I saw one, and resolved to take no hope in it.

"When might that be?" I looked up at him.

He regarded me silently for a moment. "I couldn't say. The Oracles take their time about such things, and time between—" He cut himself off, and exchanged a glance with Neeve that made me want to stamp my foot.

"Prince Kian tried to kiss Neeve," I said, looking for a way to break the camaraderie between them.

"What?" Eyes widening, Thorne lifted his hand from my shoulder and turned to my stepsister. "That's unacceptable. Neeve, you must tell me at once if you are in any danger."

My stepsister scowled at me, then looked back at Thorne. "I'm not in danger from an attempted kiss. I can fend perfectly well for myself."

"Nonetheless, you must take care. As the heir—"

"Yes, yes." She brushed her hand through the moist air, as if his words were annoying insects she could wave away. "Don't worry. Rose is helping me."

Thorne looked at me. "Explain."

If I'd thought his face was stern before, now he'd all but turned to granite.

"It's nothing," I said hastily, sorry I'd brought it up. I'd meant to cause trouble for Neeve, not upset the *Galadhir*. "I'm just there to keep Kian from trying anything."

"Has he tried to kiss *you?*" Thorne's eyes glittered dangerously.

"Of course not," Neeve said, in a tone that stung. "She's not the Princess of Raine."

Just for that, I wished I'd led Kian on a bit more. *You should have,* my wicked voice said. I ignored it and shook my head.

"He hasn't," I said. "Tried to kiss me, that is."

Thorne's expression eased. "You are, the both of you, too young to be kissing boys. Or girls either, for that matter."

I knew that some women preferred the company of their own

gender, having seen such pairings in Parnese, but Neeve blinked at him.

"Girls? Truly?"

"The heart loves where it may," he said. "Such unions are not unusual among my kind. But for now, you are not old enough to concern yourself with these matters."

He sounded so prim, my sullen mood broke and I couldn't help laughing at him. "Really, you make yourself out to be so ancient! Humans are often betrothed at seventeen, you know."

"And you are some years yet from that age," he replied stiffly.

"Not that far," Neeve said, something thoughtful in her expression.

"At what age are Dark Elves handfasted?" I asked.

"It depends," he said. "But we've wasted enough time in talk. Mistress Ainya is waiting." He turned and began striding down the path once more.

I shared a look with Neeve and she slanted me a half-smile, clearly amused by Thorne's obvious evasion when we turned the tables.

The birds began to chirp around us as we continued through the Darkwood. I wondered if the *Galadhir* had just had a private word with his forest, for the threatening edge I'd felt earlier had disappeared.

We passed the familiar moss-covered stump at the curve in the path, walked through the grove of white-barked birches, and shortly arrived at the clearing holding Mistress Ainya's cottage. The herb garden by the front gate was already green, lush with mint and rue and thick-leaved comfrey plants.

A curl of smoke drifted from the chimney, and the purple bells of wood hyacinths lined the path. Just before we arrived at her weathered front door, it swung open.

"Come in!" the herbwife said, her smile as merry as I remembered, her eyes crinkling at the corners. "Well met, *Galadhir*. I was expecting you to arrive any day. And Rose and Neeve, how well both of you look! I declare, you've each grown several inches... or perhaps I've been shrinking. Come, sit, sit."

Thorne bowed over her hand while Neeve and I settled at the familiar table. I drew in a deep breath of lavender-scented air, and glanced up to see the rows of dried herbs overhead. It was a comforting sight.

"How was your winter, mistress?" Thorne asked.

"Oh, my bones ached a bit now and then," she answered, going to fetch her teapot. "Nothing a bit of willow-bark brew couldn't remedy, however. How is it with you?"

A shadow crossed Thorne's face, and he gave the herbwife a somber look. "The Oracles are troubled. Something is brewing in the mortal world."

Mistress Ainya paused in her tea making and gave him an intent look. "What sort of trouble?"

"The Oracles will not say. Only that their visions are full of fear. And fire."

With that, he glanced at me. I couldn't help the little shiver that ran up my spine. His harshness over the book made more sense now, though I wished he'd explained himself earlier.

Mistress Ainya poured boiling water over the herbs she'd sifted into the teapot and gave a shake of her head. "It's best not to worry overmuch about such things, but go forward as we may. And as to that, are you ready to begin your summer lessons, girls?"

She set the teapot down and looked from me to Neeve.

"Yes," I said.

Neeve hesitated, and the herbwife's gaze sharpened.

"I won't be able to come as often," Neeve said, keeping her eyes fixed upon the wooden planks of the table.

"And why not?" Mistress Ainya asked, her voice mild despite the sharp look in her eyes.

My stepsister raised her head. "I'm training in sword work."

"Are you now?" Mistress Ainya's brows shot up and she turned to me. "And what of you, Rose? Are you becoming a warrior as well?"

"No," I said, trying not to sound too wretched about it. "I've no talent for weapons."

She set her wizened hand on my shoulder and gave it a squeeze. "Hm. I wouldn't fret about it, my dear. There are plenty of other paths you can take."

I couldn't think of a single one, but I tried to smile as if her words cheered me. "I'll have plenty of time to study with you, at least."

"That you will. Now, tell me all the news of the castle—and this new fosterling. Kian, is it?"

"He's good with weapons," I said. "And riding."

"Is he kind?" Mistress Ainya directed this at Neeve.

My stepsister gave a small shrug. "I suppose. We haven't really gotten a chance to know him."

"And now he is off with the king for the summer," Thorne said, sounding not unhappy at the fact.

"A good plan." Mistress Ainya poured out four cups of tea. "Best to keep foreign eyes turned from the Darkwood. Especially if the Oracles are disturbed."

"Kian can't go off with the king every year, though," I said. "What will happen next summer?" Or, more importantly, the one after that, when the *nirwen* harvest arrived?

"Each season in its own time," the herbwife said. "And speaking of such, I believe your birthday is soon, Rose, is it not?"

"In two weeks." I wasn't nearly as excited about turning a year older as I had been the previous year. But still, I had to admit to a tickle of excitement. Despite what Neeve might say, I still felt the experiment I'd done with the red priest's rite showed I had a thread of magic in my blood.

"We shall make a celebration of it," Mistress Ainya said. "I'll teach you how to bake rose cakes, and we can open the first bottle of last fall's honey mead."

She was clearly trying to make me feel better, and it worked. Neeve didn't get to have a birthday celebration at the cottage, after all.

"I'd like that," I said, then couldn't help glancing at Thorne. "Will you come?"

"Of course." His dark eyes were steady on mine, and my heart gave a ridiculous flutter as I stared back at him.

Foolish, foolish, my inner voice whispered, but I paid it no mind.

It was spring, after all, the air soft with promise. Winter would come, I knew, but for now, I would heed Mistress Ainya's advice and take each day as it came.

CHAPTER 42

As it turned out, I did not get to celebrate my birthday with a small, convivial party in Mistress Ainya's garden after all.

Instead, the night I turned fifteen I was racked with pains and fever. *I'm not well,* I thought, waking in misery in the thick darkness of my room. Then the sickness had me in its jaws, shaking me fiercely, and I cried out in pain. My bones burned as though lined with coals, and my left hand throbbed, an explosion of agony with each heartbeat.

The inside of my elbow felt raw and seared, as though the leaf tattoo had been branded into my skin, sizzling with power that ate at my flesh.

I was dimly aware of Mama coming in, her face illuminated by a flickering candle. I stared at the flame, feeling as though I were the wick, and the heat was consuming me, burning me up until there'd be nothing left but ashes...

Mama frowned and placed her cool hand against my cheek, then gasped.

"Fetch cold water, quickly," she snapped at someone—probably Sorche.

"Mama," I whispered.

"Hush," she said, fear in her eyes as she stroked my sweat-matted hair from my face. "Hush, my child."

I flared in and out of consciousness—now shivering, now burning, but always the ache thudding through me. Light outside my window, then dark. Neeve's grave face as she coaxed me to sip an herbal tisane she'd made. Sorche spooning thin gruel into my mouth.

Slowly, the periods of awareness grew longer. My body hurt, but not with the racking pains that had shaken me earlier. I was parched—I could not drink enough to slake my thirst, and my skin felt dry and papery, as though I'd been too long in some desert land.

At last I revived enough to speak, though it strained my throat to do so.

"What happened?" I asked Sorche, who sat vigil near my bed.

"You were so sick, miss," she said, her voice quavering. "We didn't rightly know if you'd survive."

"I did." The words felt like sand hissing through my teeth. "How long?"

"A full nine days. Would you take a bit of porridge now?"

I nodded weakly, and she fed me, gave me more water to drink, and tucked the covers about me as I drifted back into an uneasy sleep.

⚜

AS THE DAYS PROGRESSED, I was able to rise, to walk a bit about my room, to finally don more than just a nightdress, and make an appearance in the dining room.

It was odd, having dinner without Lord Raine in attendance. Mama sat at the head of the table, as serene and beautiful as ever, though when I looked closely I could see a tightness about the corners of her eyes. She was not as at ease as she appeared—but I was probably the only one who could tell.

One of the king's advisors sat at Mama's right hand. He'd given me a quick greeting, then gone back to discussing judicial matters with my mother, who was helping run the kingdom while her husband was away.

Neeve sat across from the advisor, and I was next to her.

"Are you well enough to be here?" she asked, observing the shaking of my spoon as I brought it up to my mouth.

"If I stay in my rooms a moment longer, I'll go mad." I tried to keep the utensil steady, and concentrated on not spilling soup all over the pristine white tablecloth.

My fever had left a strange clumsiness in its wake. Sometimes I felt normal, but other times my limbs were gripped with strange shudders, heat flashing over my skin. Good thing I wasn't training with weapons at the moment. The compounded awkwardness would have surely resulted in injury to myself and anyone else who happened too near.

As soon as I'd recovered a bit, I'd peeled back the sleeve of my nightdress to study the tattoo on my left arm. Despite the memory of it sizzling against my skin, it looked no different—an innocuous green leaf, not blackened around the edges or curled up from the heat.

I gingerly touched it with the tip of my finger, relieved to find that, while the spot was tender, it was no different from the whole rest of me. Although my memories of it burning into my skin were disturbing, the tattoo hadn't actually seemed to damage me. I prodded at it for a few moments, and then Sorche bustled back into the room and I hastily tugged my sleeve back down to hide the mark.

The only positive thing about my enforced bed rest was that I had plenty of time to read the *Studie*. I pored over the book, going back over the confusing sections, building the world of the Dark Elves in my mind.

I memorized the names of the courts mentioned most often— Nightshade, Hawthorne, and Rowan—and then the others: Cereus, Moonflower, Ash, and Birch. The author even provided a few sketches of Hawthorne and Nightshade. The palaces featured tall, gracefully arched doorways and windows, fluted columns, and rambling gardens. I even saw what I guessed was a depiction of a glimglow, a smudged, winged form hovering in the corner of the page.

It was more difficult to get a clear picture of the Dark Elves' garments from the written descriptions of their flowing clothing and elaborate jewels. At least I knew the gorgeous workmanship of their jewelry.

Every so often I'd take my pendant out and turn it to catch the light, marveling at the delicately worked gold, the tiny sparks of blue sapphires. I could imagine the elves moving about their courts, beautifully adorned with precious metals and twinkling jewels, their hair bound up in intricate braids, feasting and laughing while the glimglows fluttered overhead.

The book was not only a happy account of court life, however. It seemed the Dark Elves' politics were as complex as their jewelry. The author wrote of intrigues and machinations, of manipulative, cold-hearted mothers and lovesick courtiers. I supposed it was no different from any mortal court, but still—I would not want to be thrust into that fierce world.

Of the Oracles, the book said very little. I gathered that any time a child was born to the elves, a prophecy was spoken over them, but other than that, almost no mention was made.

I wondered if the same were true of half-blood children. Did Neeve have an oracular foretelling, proclaimed into the hushed air of Elfhame at the moment of her birth?

There was no one I could ask, except Neeve or Thorne. But then I'd have to explain how I even knew to inquire about such things, and this secret was my own.

As I read, I couldn't help thinking of my stepsister, and how deeply she would treasure this knowledge of her people. Still, this was not a book to be freely shared. If I were ever to tell Neeve—which I rather doubted—I'd have to be very careful about how I went about it.

CHAPTER 43

The summer was well advanced by the time I felt strong enough to join Neeve for an afternoon in the Darkwood. When I asked how she'd been spending the weeks, she shrugged.

"Weapons training, riding, schoolwork..." At this she made a face. "It's quite boring without you in the classroom. Some herbcraft with Mistress Ainya. And lessons with Thorne, of course."

Of course. In magic.

No need to say the words aloud. I glanced up at the canopy of green over our heads, wondering if the forest listened to our conversations.

"Will Thorne join us today?" I kept my voice casual, as though it didn't matter to me one way or the other.

"No." Neeve offered no explanation, and I couldn't ask again, for then my show of nonchalance would be revealed as a lie.

Despite Thorne's absence, though, I fancied I could sense his presence in the cool shadows beneath the trees, feel his touch in the breeze brushing my cheeks.

I picked up a twiggy branch and swept it over the tops of the bracken ferns growing beside the path. The smell of damp soil and evergreens permeated the air. I'd missed that scent, cooped up as I'd been in my rooms. Opening the window brought a faint hint of it to my nose, but the cold stone of the castle overwhelmed any trace of wildness.

As we walked through the forest, Neeve and I did not speak but fell back into the same companionable silence we'd shared in times past. Even through my illness I'd noted that since Kian had left the castle, my stepsister's mood had improved. When he returned in the fall I hoped he wouldn't go back to mooning about after her, which would only cause her edgy irritation to return.

Neeve and I meandered a bit beside a cheerful stream, and I thought I recognized the overgrown trail we followed. When we turned a corner, my guess proved correct: ahead loomed the boulder where Neeve and I had seen the White Hart. Instead of climbing the hunk of stone this time, my stepsister led me past it. Blue harebells and pale pink columbine lined the edges of the streamside path, and the smell of mint teased my nose.

"Where are we going?" I asked.

Neeve only shrugged. I didn't press her. It was a pleasant enough stroll, and lovely to be outside the castle after being pent up so long within its gloomy stone walls. With a pang, I thought of the vanished weeks of summer, the lost chances to spend time with Thorne before he returned to Elfhame for the winter.

I wondered if he missed me at all, or if tutoring Neeve and his duties as *Galadhir* filled all his time, leaving no thought for a mortal girl. I let out a gusty sigh, trying to blow my melancholy thoughts away.

The trail curved away from the stream and the path grew steeper, white-barked aspen now lining the way. I was about to ask Neeve to stop so I could catch my breath, when she halted.

"Look," she said, turning to point through the thinning trees.

At first I couldn't see what she was pointing to, but after a moment realized it was a view of Castle Raine. It seemed strangely distant, nestled in a hazy blue valley, the turrets rising gracefully from the dark fur of the forest below.

I shaded my eyes with one hand and peered down at the castle. "Are we really so far away?"

"Probably not," Neeve said. "This hill isn't always here."

I nodded slowly, recalling I hadn't ever seen a rise of this height when I stared out the windows. Perhaps it wasn't visible from the castle at all, even when it chose to appear in the Darkwood.

"What else can we see?" I stood on tiptoes, as if that would give me a better vantage point.

The road wound out from the other side of the castle, and I caught sight of the buildings of Little Hazel tucked into the trees beyond. I squinted, but couldn't see Mistress Ainya's cottage.

As for the rest of Raine, the Darkwood seemed to take up most of the view, with a few fields and scattered copses of trees, and the distant silver shine of a river. Or maybe it was the sea, but surely we were too far to see the shore from here.

The air was cooler at this height, sharpened with the scent of pine. I felt small compared to the immensity of the forest—just a girl, measured against the wild mystery of the Darkwood. Despite myself, I shivered.

"Let's go back," Neeve said, as if she felt it too.

I glanced at her, and glimpsed the fierce longing she normally concealed. It shone from her dark eyes, drew her brows up and softened her mouth, and in that moment she looked beautiful. No less odd, but lovely all the same.

The impulse to tell her about the *Studie* rose in me, fierce and almost overwhelming. I bit down hard on my lip to keep from speaking. Such knowledge would only hurt Neeve, even though it was her birthright.

As we skidded down the steep trail, a faint call for help reached my ears. I halted and cocked my head.

"Did you hear that?" I asked my stepsister.

She waved one hand impatiently. "Another hobnie."

"We should go help it."

Eyes narrowed, she glanced at me. "We don't *always* have to rush to their aid, you know."

I felt otherwise, of course. But instead of wasting time in fruitless argument, I struck out across the hillside in the direction of the cry. The footing was uneven and rocky, and I stumbled a few times, but soon heard the hobnie again.

"Help, help," the hoarse and petulant voice called, much closer this time.

"I'm coming," I cried. "Where are you?"

"Right here! Hurry up," the hobnie replied. "And mind the edge."

The edge?

I frowned, and then gasped as the hillside gave way beneath my feet. For a sickening moment I fell through nothingness, before landing with a jolt on my hands and knees on a narrow stone ledge. To one side was the rocky soil of the hillside, and to the other, nothing but air and fog.

Huddled at one end of the ledge was a hobnie wearing an orange cap and soiled tunic. He scowled at me. "What a mess you've made of things, you clumsy, whey-faced girl."

"Rose!" Neeve shouted from somewhere above. Her voice was strangely muffled. "Where did you go?"

"Here," I called, carefully scooting away from the sheer drop-off until my shoulders were pressed against the dirt. "Be careful—the hill-side ends in a cliff."

The ledge was a precarious resting place. One wrong move, and I might tumble over the edge into that gaping abyss. Fear pounded through me, snagging my breath and hurtling through my blood.

Thorne, I thought urgently. *Galadhir—we are in trouble. Help!*

I held out no hope that he might actually hear me, of course.

"I've found the edge," Neeve called. "But I can't see you—or any way down."

"I don't suppose you brought a rope?" I meant to sound cheerful, but the words came out forlorn and scared.

"No. I could go back to the castle—"

"Don't leave us!" the hobnie screeched. "The drake is coming, and you must help battle for our lives."

Oh, that did not sound at all good.

I looked over at the hobnie. "What's a drake?"

"Scales and wings and teeth and claws." The little fellow shivered.

"If I'm lucky, it will devour you first and decide it's had enough, and fly away."

"That's rude," I said, more frightened at the thought of being a monster's dinner than angry at the hobnie. I'd learned not to expect courtesy from his kind.

"I should have brought my sword," Neeve said, clearly able to hear us, even if she couldn't see us.

"At least you have your magic," I said. But would it be enough?

"It comes!" The hobnie scrunched down into a little ball and threw his beard over his face, as though it would keep him from being seen.

My throat dry with fear, I pulled the kitchen knife from my belt and scanned the foggy curtain of air before us.

I heard the drake first—the rhythmic whoosh of huge wings, a hollow drumbeat in the strained silence. The stench came next, a waft of rotten meat and rank leather.

Then it was suddenly upon us, looming out of the fog, twice the size of a horse. The drake's sinuous neck and body was held aloft by enormous, batlike wings. It darted its head forward, jaws wide and lined with dagger-sharp teeth.

The smell was overpowering. Breathing shallowly, I held up my knife. We were woefully outmatched.

Above us, Neeve shouted something in Elvish, and a ball of glowing blue light struck the drake's head.

It reared back, screeching. I wanted to shout encouragement, but the monster recovered almost immediately. It darted back in, raking the ledge with a taloned claw. I yelped and twisted away, but the drake's swipe caught me across the side of my calf.

For a moment, I felt nothing. Then heat and pain cut across my senses. With a sharp cry, I pressed myself as far from the edge as I could.

"Are you all right?" Neeve cried.

"Yes," I answered, although I wasn't certain. "Kill the blasted thing if you can."

Her reply was another spate of Elvish, and shards of ice flung like spears at our opponent. The drake seemed more enraged than harmed by her attack, and soared higher to meet this new threat.

With the help of my knife, I tore strips of cloth from my skirt and, gritting my teeth, tied a makeshift bandage just below my knee. My leg was sticky with blood, and I tried not to look too closely at the ragged gash torn through my skin and muscle.

Overhead, I could hear Neeve's voice growing hoarse. Flashes of blue lit the foggy air. She seemed to be holding her own, but the drake remained uninjured.

The hobnie peeked around his beard, then ducked his head down again.

"It's the end for us," he squeaked.

My left hand ached horribly, and a rush of anger filled me. *No.* I refused to die this way, victim of a monstrous attack in the Darkwood.

Where was Thorne, anyway? Wasn't the *Galadhir* supposed to be guarding Neeve with his life?

I rose to my knees, hand clenched around the handle of my knife as something fierce and smoky stormed through me. My lungs were on fire, my head ached, my vision blurred.

The drake dipped low again, its scaly black body twisting toward me. Death lurked in the yellow glint of its eyes.

"*Thorne!*" I yelled, and threw my knife right into its eye.

The blade lodged there, point first.

Neeve screamed.

Then the drake exploded, engulfed in flame. I gagged and covered my face as hot blood and gobbets of singed flesh sprayed through the air.

"*Quilda-ri!*" a strong voice called, and I slumped in relief. The *Galadhir* had finally come.

A cool breeze swept the air, clearing out the oily haze left by the incinerated drake. I leaned my head against the stone, empty and exhausted.

From somewhere above, Thorne and Neeve were speaking, his voice urgent, hers subdued. I was too tired to make sense of their words.

The stone beneath me shuddered, and the hobnie let out a screech of dismay.

"Hold fast," Thorne said. "I'm coming."

Dirt crumbled at the far edge of the stone, tumbling over the precipice. A path formed as I watched, magically cut into the soil of the hill. The hobnie jumped to his feet and barreled up it, and I heard Thorne make an annoyed sound.

A moment later, the *Galadhir* appeared, and I wanted to sob with joy at the sight of his severe face.

"I'm sorry," I whispered, though I wasn't sure why.

"Hush." He bent and gathered me up, expression going grim when he saw the blood soaking my skirts. "Rose—you're hurt?"

"Yes," I said. "It swiped my leg."

My calf—in fact, my entire body—felt numb.

Thorne carried me up the newly made path to where Neeve stood at the top of the hillside. She looked even paler than usual, her normally red lips now a pale pink, her dark eyes empty of all brightness.

"Is Rose all right?" she asked as Thorne set me gently on the trampled grasses.

He made no reply, but peeled my bloodied skirt away from my leg and, with nimble fingers, loosened the bandage.

Pain growled at me like a feral dog crouching to attack, but Thorne spread his hands over my wounded calf.

"*Envinya*," he murmured.

The hurt receded, washed away by a tide of healing. I sighed and closed my eyes briefly.

"What happened?" he asked, his voice gentle, though there was steel beneath.

"Neeve killed the drake," I said, opening my eyes.

At the same moment, my stepsister said, "I didn't kill the monster —but I think Rose did."

I looked from her to Thorne, bewildered. "I just threw my knife and hit its eye. Does that make drakes explode?"

"Not usually." Thorne stared at me, his mouth set in a firm line.

"Surely you felt it?" Neeve asked him. "Rose might have struck the drake's eye, but magic delivered the final blow. And it was not mine."

"Was it the hobnie?" I asked weakly.

"Some strange power stirred here just before I arrived," Thorne said. "Hold still, Rose."

As if I could do anything else.

Still kneeling beside me, he placed one hand on my forehead and the other on my chest. I held my breath and stared up at him.

"What are you doing?" I asked softly.

"Checking you for power." He narrowed his eyes and hummed an Elvish syllable under his breath.

I fancied I could feel a tingle moving out from where his hands rested on me, though maybe that was just my natural reaction to being so close to him. Intently, I watched his face, hoping for a moment when his eyes would widen with surprise and he'd leap to his feet, declaring that I did, indeed, possess a deep well of power.

Sadly, that didn't happen. Thorne's expression remained troubled and a bit perplexed, even when he lifted his hands.

"Well?" Neeve asked.

He shook his head, sending a thin braid to swing down beside his cheek. "Rose possesses no magic—as both I and Mistress Ainya have confirmed in the past."

I frowned, though heavy acceptance moved through me at his words.

"But—" Neeve began.

Thorne held up his hand. "I know. It is a mystery—but the Dark-wood is full of things even I don't quite understand. Now, however, is not the time to delve for answers—your wellspring is dangerously dry, Neeve, and Rose is still bleeding."

It was true—Neeve didn't look well. As for myself, I very carefully kept my gaze away from the ragged wound on my lower leg.

Thorne took my hand in his, then reached for Neeve. "Hold on tightly."

As soon as Neeve clasped his fingers, he spoke a short phrase in his own language. The world tilted and blurred, and with a wrench we were suddenly in the courtyard of Castle Raine.

CHAPTER 44

To my surprise, Thorne made no effort to conceal himself as servants bustled to help us. He carried me into the castle and up the stairs, all the while giving instructions. One fellow was dispatched for the doctor, a maid was sent to ask the queen to attend us in my rooms, and still others went to fetch hot water and bandages. Neeve stayed close beside us, quiet and pale, and even with the throbbing pain in my leg, it worried me to see how drawn she looked.

When we reached my rooms, Sorche threw open the door. Still carrying me, Thorne strode through the sitting room and to the bed. A trail of servants followed us inside, carrying the items he'd requested.

"But the blood," I protested, as he laid me down. "I don't want to ruin the covers."

He shook his head. "It doesn't matter."

"Truly," Sorche said. "Don't fret, miss. It will wash out."

Neeve sank into the chair beside my bed, and one of the servants brought her a small glass of amber liquid—brandy, by the smell of it. She took a sip and made a face, but continued to drink.

I watched her, trying to distract myself from the unpleasantness of my own injury and the nausea surging through me. I yelped as Sorche gently peeled my skirt away from the wound. Thorne's healing had stemmed the worst of the bleeding, but a quick glance confirmed that blood still oozed from the jagged gash running down my calf.

"It'll need to be stitched," Sorche murmured to Thorne, who sat cross-legged at the foot of the bed. "Lucky it didn't slash her heel."

My mother rushed into the room in a flurry of pale skirts and perfume. The servants scrambled to attention. Thorne rose from his place, and I was sorry when his weight left the mattress. Having him within reach made me feel safer.

"Who are you?" Mama demanded, looking at Thorne. Then she saw me lying on the bed and let out a gasp. "My darling girl! What happened?"

"There was an accident," Thorne said quietly. "But Rose is not too badly hurt."

I looked at him, then blinked in surprise. His face had changed. Although he was still striking to look at, his features were blunter, his eyes suddenly a deep hazel instead of amber-flecked black. The tips of his ears had rounded, and although his long hair remained loose, held back with elaborate braids around his face, Thorne now looked human.

Seeing my surprise, Neeve surreptitiously poked my shoulder. When I glanced at her, she shook her head, the smallest gesture. Clearly, Thorne had used his magic to appear mortal. It seemed a wise precaution. How much did the queen know of the Darkwood, and the secret world that lay within?

She swept the room with her gaze, taking note of the gathered servants.

"We'd best discuss this in private," she said, gesturing to the door.

The servants took her meaning and hurried out, though Sorche held back and gave me a worried look.

"I'll be back as soon as they fetch the doctor from his rounds in Little Hazel," she said, before stepping out and closing the bedroom door behind her.

Mama drew in a deep breath, her gaze going from me, to Neeve, to Thorne.

"Explain, sir," she said, her voice clipped. "Who are you?"

Thorne made her a small bow. "I am the warden of the forest, Thorne Windrift. Perhaps the king has mentioned me?"

"He told me a hermit dwells within the woods. I take it you are that person?"

"Yes, Your Majesty."

Mama's gaze sharpened. "My husband also told me it is your *particular* duty to safeguard the princesses when they roam about the forest."

Interesting. Despite the king concealing the Dark Elves' existence from her, my mother was more aware of what transpired outside the castle than I'd guessed. Perhaps Lord Raine hadn't been foolish to leave her in charge over the summer, after all—although she was mistaken about one thing. Thorne's job was to keep Neeve safe. I was simply an afterthought, no matter how much Mama wanted to believe I was a real princess.

Thorne winced slightly at her words, but kept his head high.

"You are correct, Your Majesty—their safety is my charge. I can only say that certain... difficulties kept me from this most important task. For that, I must beg your forgiveness."

He dropped gracefully to one knee and bent his head, his dark hair falling like an obsidian waterfall about his face and shoulders.

Mama made the little sniff that meant she was mollified. "I think you ought to beg Rose and Neeve to forgive you, as they were the ones injured by your absence." She stepped past him and came to lay her hand upon my cheek.

"I'm only a little tired," Neeve said. "In another day or two, I'll be perfectly well."

Thorne raised his head, his expression solemn. "Nonetheless, the queen is right. I failed you. It will not happen again."

Despite my fondness for the *Galadhir*, I wasn't as eager to pardon his absence. Leaving us to face the drake alone had felt like a betrayal, especially as I bore a serious injury from that encounter.

"Where were you?" I asked him, uncaring that the words came out a bit peevish.

His lips tightened, and for a moment I thought he wouldn't answer. Then Mama arched one brow.

"I, too, would like an answer to that question," she said.

He glanced to Neeve, then back to my mother. "I will tell you, but I beg that you keep it a secret between us."

"Understood," Mama said. "I will, of course, inform the king."

"Of course." Thorne sounded unhappy about it.

He was lucky Lord Raine was away, and that my mother had a weakness for pretty manners and a handsome face. I didn't think the king would have gone nearly so lightly with the *Galadhir* for failing in his sworn duties.

"The Darkwood is under attack," Thorne said, his voice strangely calm.

Mama's eyes widened in alarm and she put her hand to her chest. "Attack? By whom? Do we need to muster an army?"

"It is not a physical assault," he answered. "Rather, some kind of sorcery is prowling about the edges of Raine, trying to sniff its way into the forest."

"Sorcery." Mama's face grew pale. "Are you certain?"

Thorne gave her a grave look. "It is some type of magic, I know that much. I've a small understanding of such things."

A small understanding was rather an understatement. At least I was on the inside of this particular secret. Although his words had given me a shiver of guilt. Had my attempt at the red priest's rite called attention to Raine? But how could it? As Neeve was fond of telling me, and Thorne had just confirmed, I had no power.

"Is the sorcery dangerous?" Neeve asked.

Thorne hesitated a moment too long before answering. "No. But it is worrisome. Because of its interference, I didn't sense the drake's attack until it was upon you."

"Then it *is* a danger," Mama said. "Are you incapable of meeting this threat head-on, hermit?"

Thorne's expression remained calm, but there was an edge in his voice when he answered. "The best course is not to confront it directly. Whatever it is, whoever is directing it, it seems to be *seeking*. Thus far, I have given it nothing to find."

"How?" I asked.

"By holding up a mirror of the forest," he said. "Showing it only trees and valleys, villages and deer and birds. Nothing of interest."

No wonder he'd been preoccupied of late. I wondered if the

Oracles or other Dark Elves were helping him, or if, as *Galadhir*, the work fell entirely on his shoulders.

"I do not feel easy about this." My mother frowned. "The king must be summoned home immediately. How long has this been going on?"

"Since shortly after Lord Raine's departure," Thorne said.

"Are the incursions growing more frequent?" Mama asked, a flash of fear in her eyes.

"No," Thorne said, but he did not meet my mother's eyes.

"Perhaps we needn't send for my father quite yet," Neeve said.

I glanced at her in confusion, then recalled that the king's return meant Kian's as well, and that Neeve had been enjoying his absence.

"Do as you see fit," Thorne said, bowing to my mother. "I have lingered here too long, and must return to the Darkwood. Send word if either Rose or Neeve do not recover promptly."

Send word? Was there some kind of secret message system between the castle and the Dark Elves? Creasing my brow, I looked at Thorne.

He ignored my expression. "Rest well, Rose. The doctor has just arrived, I believe, and you will be in good hands."

"But..." There was so much I wanted to ask that the words jammed in my throat. *Why can't you heal me?* was foremost, followed by *When will I see you again?* and *What if the king returns and forbids us to go into the forest?*

None of these could be asked aloud, so I swallowed the questions.

Thorne gave me a crooked smile, almost as if he could sense my thoughts. Then he turned to Neeve and urged her to rest, bade farewell to Mama, and was gone—quiet as a shadow.

CHAPTER 45

Despite the healing magic Thorne had performed on my leg, I was slow to recover. To make matters worse, Mama had, indeed, sent for Lord Raine to come home. Time was running out, the last of the golden summer slipping by outside my window like honey dripping from a jar—a little more gone each morning, and I could not taste its sweetness.

Every day was a frustrating battle between my desire to go back into the Darkwood to see Thorne, and my stupid leg, which had a tendency to suddenly buckle if I stood for too long. Sorche brought me a crutch, which helped, but I felt as though my normal clumsiness was increased sevenfold as I hobbled around the castle.

Finally, I could bear it no longer.

"I'm going into the forest today," I told Neeve as we left the schoolroom.

She had taken to slowing her pace, accompanying me as I limped about. It was a kindness, and I was grateful for the company, though the one time I'd tried to thank her, she'd frowned and brushed off my gratitude.

"Nobody wants to see you fall and crack your skull," she'd said. "Then you'd be even more work to take care of."

But although she pretended it was duty, I knew she truly was concerned for me. For her part, she'd seemed to recover within a few days of our encounter with the drake. I tried not to be jealous, reminding myself that she hadn't taken a physical injury as I had.

At my declaration I intended to go to the forest, she shot me a glance. "Into the Darkwood? This afternoon?"

"Yes," I said stubbornly. "Your father and Kian will be back any day, and who knows what will happen then?"

She gave a slow nod and spoke the words we both knew were true. "The forest will be forbidden."

I was relieved she didn't try to dissuade me from what was probably an unwise attempt. At any rate, I didn't plan to go far into the Darkwood. Just enough to see Thorne. *And tell him goodbye for the season,* my little voice added.

The thought made my chest tighten. It seemed that the older Neeve and I grew, the harder it was to spend our summers rambling in the forest. I'd barely seen Mistress Ainya all season, and while I knew she couldn't teach me magic, I still missed her pleasant cottage and warm company.

Not as much as I missed seeing Thorne, of course. However foolish and one-sided my feelings might be, I couldn't help the flutter in my chest whenever I thought of him.

"I'll help you put on your boots," Neeve said, which was kindness indeed.

It took double our normal time to traverse the castle gardens and duck out through the small door in the wall. My steps were ungainly as I clumped across the grassy stretch separating Castle Raine from the Darkwood. My crutch made awkward divots in the soil, and the still-healing gash on my leg throbbed in time with my heartbeat. Although the doctor had stitched it up neatly, I would bear a scar; a permanent reminder of our battle against the drake.

We stepped into the coolness beneath the evergreens, and I drew in a deep breath of the damp, cedar-scented air. Strange, how comfortable the Darkwood had become to me—even with its dangers. If I felt this way about the forest, how much stronger was my stepsister's connection? I glanced at Neeve, whose eyes had brightened, lips parted in a slight smile.

"Is Thorne coming?" I turned in a small circle, balancing my weight on my crutch.

Neeve looked at me. "He is. But Rose, surely you know..." She trailed off, a hint of pity in her expression.

"Know what?" I could feel heat rising in my cheeks.

"Thorne is a Dark Elf. And *Galadhir*." Her voice was quiet, but I felt the trees vibrate as she spoke.

"I'm aware of the fact." I folded one arm across my stomach and gripped my crutch tightly. "It doesn't mean we can't be friends."

"Friends, yes. As much as a mortal and one of my people can be."

"*Your* people?" I scowled at her. "That's a silly thing to say—you're only half Dark Elf. Besides, you and I are close."

She brushed my words aside. "That's different."

"Didn't your mother marry Lord Raine?" I pressed.

"Because she had to!" Temper sparked in her eyes.

"So there was no love in their union? Do you truly believe that?"

"I don't know. She died."

"That is true," Thorne said, striding from the concealing under-brush. "But I can tell you, Neeve, that she and your father shared a true depth of affection."

My stepsister whirled to face him. "That makes it worse. Were you spying on us?"

He looked affronted. "Of course not. The Darkwood is my domain."

"How much did you hear?" I asked, embarrassment crawling through me. Did he guess how I felt about him? Did he pity me for it, too?

"Enough to know that Neeve is mistaken. But we shouldn't spend our time here bickering." He gave me an intent look. "How is your leg healing?"

"Slowly," I said, glancing down at it.

"Hm. Show me."

He gestured to a fallen, moss-covered log. I hobbled over and perched upon it, then drew up my skirts to reveal the wound. My exertions had caused it to redden, the scar a swollen line down my calf.

Thorne crouched down and let out a breath, the air hissing between his teeth. "As I feared—a trace of the drake's poison still lingers in the wound."

"Poison?" Alarm squeezed my chest. "Am I going to die?"

"No." Thorne put a reassuring hand on my ankle. "I drove most of it out on the day you were hurt. Only a residue remains, and you would have eventually overcome it—though it's better if I eradicate it now." He glanced up at me, a hint of apology in his eyes. "This might hurt a bit."

I braced myself against the log. "I'm ready."

He murmured the words of healing, and I yelped as searing cold flooded my leg. It hurt, no question. And not just *a bit*. I blinked back tears and clenched my jaw.

After a horribly long moment, the agony receded.

"I'm sorry," Thorne said, his long fingers still wrapped about my ankle. "Does it feel any better?"

"I can't tell." I cleared my throat. "My whole leg is numb."

Except for the place he touched me.

Slowly, warmth spread through my calf. I bent to inspect my injury, catching a whiff of Thorne's bark-and-amber smell. *Don't move*, I thought at him, trying to inhale deeply without being obvious.

"That's much improved," he said, tilting his head and regarding my leg.

He was right. The angry wound had closed, replaced by a smooth white line, slightly puckered along the edges.

"Try standing," Neeve suggested.

I didn't want to move away from Thorne, but he let go of my leg and stood in a smooth motion. Gripping my crutch, I pulled myself upright. Then, carefully, I shifted my weight so that I balanced on both feet.

My injured leg felt a trifle shaky, but sturdier than before. I bent my knees and then straightened, relieved to find that I didn't teeter sideways and collapse in an ungainly heap at Thorne's feet.

"That's better." I smiled at him. "Thank you."

Don't forget, you were hurt because he neglected his duties, my wicked voice pointed out.

Speaking of which...

"Is the sorcerous attack on the forest still happening?" I glanced at the trees as if I could see the foreign magic sniffing about the edges like a hungry wolf.

Thorne's expression hardened. "Still intrusive, but no more troublesome than before."

"That's not reassuring," Neeve said. "When will we be safe again?"

"I cannot say." He looked unhappy about the fact.

"Doesn't the forest have its own protections?" I asked.

It had been some time since I thought of my first journey through the Darkwood and the suffocating tendril of silver that had nearly choked me.

And the bear who'd saved me.

"It does," he said, "but the magical wards in place need strengthening. During the dormant winter months, I plan to work with the Oracles to craft an impenetrable shield about the Darkwood."

I didn't ask if that would work. It seemed clear the Dark Elves had never met a threat of this type before. I hoped that whatever protection they crafted, it would be sufficient.

A raven squawked and took flight from a high branch overhead, and Thorne looked up, his gaze unfocused for a moment.

"The king arrived at Portknowe early this morning," he said. "He will arrive at the castle soon after dark."

"Oh." Neeve's voice was flat.

"I suppose..." I swallowed to keep my voice steady. "Will we see you again, before spring?"

Thorne gave me a look tinged with sadness. "This is our farewell for the season, as you've already guessed. Be well and safe, the both of you."

With a soft cry, Neeve flew into his arms. I watched, jealousy bitter in my mouth.

"I wish I could go to Elfhame with you," she said, her voice muffled against his shoulder. "Just once."

"I'm sorry, *gwanur*." He stroked her hair gently. "I know it's difficult —but for the sake of both our worlds, you know it cannot be."

She pulled her sleeve across her face, erasing the tears I thought I'd glimpsed. When she straightened, her face was composed, her eyes hard.

"I know." The words sounded like a gate clanging shut on all her dreams.

I bit my lip, unwilling sympathy moving through me. We both desperately wanted things that were out of reach.

"Come," Thorne said, taking Neeve's hand, then reaching for mine.

I stepped forward and let him enfold my fingers in his cool clasp. It felt as though my entire heart rushed forward to nestle in my palm, beating hot and furious just under my skin.

Sunbeams slanted through the feathery evergreens, and the forest stilled, listening.

"We are not so far away from each other," he said, his voice serious. "The months will pass quickly, and before you know it, spring flowers will be blooming and the forest will be yours once more."

"Not *that* quickly," I muttered.

"Does time move differently in Elfhame?" Neeve asked.

Thorne glanced at her. "Where did you hear such a thing?"

"My father mentioned that the next *nirwen* harvest would seem to be only two months away for your people, while three years passed in our world. Is it true?"

He looked uncomfortable, as though he wished not to answer.

"Is it?" I pressed.

He sighed. "Yes—time moves differently in Elfhame. But we don't have days and months as you do here, so it is a difficult comparison to make."

"Why not?" I asked. "Doesn't the sun rise, as usual?"

"Elfhame has no sun."

I blinked at him. "No sun? Then it's night always? How dark it must be!"

Neeve gave me a sour look, and I realized the stupidity of my words. Dark. As in *Dark Elves*. No wonder their skin was so pale, their eyes so strange. Suddenly, entire passages of the *Studie* made much more sense, and I scolded myself for not seeing it sooner.

"We have two moons," Thorne said. "My world is not daybright, but it has its own illumination."

I thought of the glimpse I'd had of Elfhame through the portal: glowing flowers, a star-streaked sky, and the floating brightness of the glimglows.

"It must be beautiful," I said, then checked my words, recalling Neeve's pain.

She grimaced, and returned to her original question. "How long will it seem for you, between now and next spring?"

"It will feel, roughly, as though a dozen of your mortal days have passed."

"Only a dozen?" I exclaimed. "That's unfair." Neeve and I must slog through months while Thorne would have to wait less than two weeks.

"Fairness has nothing to do with it," he said. "Where realms meet, the normal rules don't apply."

"What if something happens to the forest during that time?" I glanced at the trees surrounding us. "Is it safe for you to leave it?"

"My connection with the Darkwood crosses the boundary between our worlds. I can work with the Oracles to strengthen the protections, even from within Elfhame. Now, enough of this talk. The castle is stirring in preparation for the king's return, and you two will be wanted."

Well, Neeve would, at any rate. And I supposed I ought to bathe and change, now that my leg was better.

Thorne let go of our hands, and my palm felt cold and empty, matching my plummeting spirits.

"Goodbye," I said, unable to keep the forlorn note from my voice.

"I will see you soon," Thorne said, and I tried not to envy him for it.

Without speaking, Neeve and I trudged back toward the castle, the walls rising gray and solid in the last of the warm fall sunlight. Next spring felt like an eternity away.

But at least Kian would be back with tales of his travels, and perhaps that distraction would help soften the stone of sadness in my heart.

CHAPTER 46

As Thorne had predicted, Lord Raine, Kian, and their retinue clattered into the courtyard an hour past sundown. The castle had learned of their return in advance, either through a messenger bird or fast rider, and so the servants were ready, the travelers' rooms warm and waiting.

Neeve and I were summoned to the great hall to greet the king, and arrived just as he strode through the tall doors. He was followed by Kian and the jarl, and Sir Durum with his cohort of soldiers, everyone looking dusty and travel-worn.

"Welcome home, darling," Mama said, going to kiss Lord Raine's cheek.

He greeted her, then beckoned for Neeve to step forward.

"Are you well, daughter?" he asked, searching her face.

"Yes," she said. "I'm glad of your safe return."

"And you, Rose?" he asked, nodding at me. "I hear you had a misadventure."

I dropped him a curtsey. "Indeed, my lord, but I've fully recovered." Thanks to Thorne.

The king gave a short nod, though something in his eyes told me it wasn't the end of the matter. He'd want details of the drake's attack later, in a less public setting, I was sure.

"Welcome back, Prince Kian," I said, poking Neeve with my elbow.

"Welcome," she grudgingly echoed.

At our greeting, his eyes lightened, the tiredness lifting from his face. "Rose, Neeve, it's good to see you."

"I hope you'll share stories of your travels with us," I said.

A shadow darkened his eyes. "I will—but it was not all fun and frivolity."

"You must be tired," Mama interrupted. "Come, gentlemen, let the servants show you to your rooms. The kitchen has prepared trays to send up, and I'm sure you'd like to wash the road dust away. Tomorrow will be time enough to regale us with tales of your journey."

"An excellent plan," Lord Raine said. "These last few days have been taxing. Once we received your communications, my dear, we made all haste to return. A rest would not go amiss."

I imagine they had pushed hard. Reports of a magical attack on the kingdom would be enough to summon any ruler back to their throne immediately.

Dismissed, Neeve and I trudged back to our rooms.

"At least your father didn't tell us not to go back into the Darkwood," I said.

She shot me a dark look. "That will come soon enough, I'm sure."

⚜

INDEED, my stepsister proved correct. As we finished our lunch the next day, a servant arrived, summoning us from the schoolroom to a meeting with the king.

My heart pounding, I pushed aside the remainder of my food, smoothed my hair—a useless gesture, as it sprang back immediately into a curly red riot—and followed Neeve to Lord Raine's study.

"At least he didn't make us meet in the throne room," Neeve said under her breath as we approached the heavy oak door carved with leaves and crowns. "We're not in desperate trouble."

I bit my lip, hoping she was right.

She knocked, then pushed the door open when Lord Raine bid us enter. The king stood before a large, multi-paned window that looked out on the Darkwood. To my surprise, Kian was there, as well as the jarl and the arms master.

"Come, sit." Lord Raine gestured to a semicircle of chairs arrayed near the large hearth. "We have business to discuss."

Everyone politely waited until the king sat in the middle chair, then took their own places. I was at one end, with Neeve next to me and Sir Durum between her and the king. Kian was on his other side, with Jarl Eiric beside him.

Glancing at the prince, I realized he'd grown taller and broader across the shoulders while he was away. His usually lighthearted expression was missing, his blue eyes somber.

"Neeve," the king said without preamble, "tell us of the drake's attack."

My stepsister glanced at the Fiorlanders, one brow raised. Correctly interpreting her expression, her father waved his hand.

"You may speak freely. Kian and Jarl Eiric have proven their trust-worthiness. Whatever is threatening the Darkwood, they are in my confidence."

Kian nodded his agreement, but I did not like the hint of a smirk about the jarl's lips. Still, it was Lord Raine's choice, and certainly not for me to argue with.

Neeve briefly described how we'd heard the hobnie's cries, I fell over the edge of the hill onto the ledge, and how the drake came, appearing out of the fog like a shadowy nightmare. She did not, however, mention magic—either her own or the strange power that had ultimately killed the creature.

"Rose flung her knife and struck it in the eye," she said. "It was a telling blow. Then Thorne came, the drake was dispatched, and he took us back to the castle."

Sir Durum glanced at me with surprise. "You scored a direct hit with a knife? I'd never considered you for knives, or thrown weapons. Do you think you could repeat it?"

"I don't know," I admitted. Probably my accuracy had been blind luck. Stars knew, I didn't have much talent for weapons.

Lord Raine's stony gaze fell on me. "I understand you were hurt during the encounter."

"The drake clawed my leg open," I said. "I bear a scar, but the wound has healed."

"Fully?" the jarl asked. "I understand such creatures bear poison in their touch."

For a foreigner, he was rather well informed. "Do you have such beasts in Fiorland?" I asked sweetly.

His eyes narrowed. "We have legends and tales, Lady Rose. The fact that such beasts now freely roam Raine is worrisome."

"The guardian of the wood believes the power now prodding at the Darkwood woke the creature," Lord Raine said. "He assures me that precautions are being taken to ensure nothing more of this nature will occur."

I wondered when Thorne had met with the king. Last night, probably. Had the *Galadhir* come into the castle, or did the king wrap himself in his cloak and go out to the forest? Probably the former. Thorne wasn't the king of a country, after all—he would be at the monarch's command.

"The forest isn't safe," Sir Durum said. "I'd advise you give the command for everyone to stay out of it for the time being."

"Wise advice." Lord Raine glanced at his daughter. "That includes you and your stepsister, of course."

"But—" Neeve began.

"No. Until the guardian can assure me the Darkwood is secure, you and Rose are forbidden to set foot in the forest. Do you understand?"

She dipped her head, spots of color high on her cheeks, but ceased her argument.

The king's cold eyes moved to me.

"Of course, my lord," I said hastily.

"Good. We must take care—Raine is not the only country dealing with a foreign attack."

"It's not?" I blurted out.

A tense silence fell, and then Lord Raine glanced at Kian.

"Prince Kian," he said, "you have my permission to speak of what we saw this summer."

"Thank you, my lord." Kian cleared his throat. "In our travels, we discovered that the priests of the Twin Gods have extended their influence beyond Parnese. The sect has seized power in a number of smaller nations, taking control of the government, the military, and the trade channels."

"What does that mean for us?" Neeve asked, clearly grasping the political ramifications before I did.

The king's expression grew harder than the granite walls of his castle. "These new puppet governments refused to honor our previous trade and travel agreements. We were forced to accept new terms disadvantageous to Raine."

"How could they enforce such a thing?" Neeve asked.

"Fear," the jarl said shortly. "Any town who resists them is burned to the ground. The city of Karta is nothing but a charred ruin filled with refugees."

"That's terrible!" I exclaimed. "What do they have to gain by such tactics?"

"Power," Lord Raine said.

"Wealth," Kian added.

"Control," Sir Durum said. "Some men crave such things, and when they get a taste, it spurs their desire for more."

"What about the government of Parnese?" Neeve shot her father a concerned look. "Can't the king and queen control the priests?"

"Too late," he answered. "The high priest of the Twin Gods commands the army of Parnese now. The royal family is under house arrest, and the council is run by agents of the church."

"It's good we returned early, and in haste," Kian said. "They were beginning to restrict sea travel. If we hadn't left when we did, we likely would've been trapped on the Continent."

"The situation is serious," Lord Raine agreed. "The danger extends far beyond the castle walls, and it's imperative that everyone remain as safe as possible. That means no going into the Darkwood."

I swallowed, worry circling my thoughts. What of my old friends in Parnese? Were they in danger under the priests' rule?

"Yes, Father," Neeve said. "We understand." This time, there was not a hint of rebellion in her face.

"You may go." Lord Raine gestured to me and Neeve. "Say nothing of what you've heard here today."

We murmured our assent, curtseyed to the king, and left his study, both of us silently wrapped in our own grim thoughts.

PART IV

CHAPTER 47

F all slid grimly into winter. The entire castle was subdued. Footsteps echoed hollowly in the hallways, and the servants moved nervously, as though they expected an attack at any moment.

Master Fawkes did not return. When I asked Miss Groves about his absence, she told me he was traveling beyond Raine, gathering information for the king. I was quite sorry to hear it—not only because I was concerned for his safety, but because, without the excuse of harp lessons, I had no reason to skip weapons training.

It was no hardship for Neeve, whose swordsmanship had improved during her lessons over the summer, or for Kian, as talented with weapons as ever. But since hearing that I had successfully flung a knife at the drake—even with as poor a weapon as a kitchen knife—Sir Durum was determined to discover if I possessed any other overlooked skills.

The weapons master took away my practice sword, which I was glad of, and replaced it with a blocky wooden mace, which I was not.

"Mayhap you'll do better with this." He pointed a thumb to the straw-stuffed dummies at the end of the training arena. "Go bash on one of those for a bit."

I did, with little success; missing more often than I connected and whacking myself several times, hard enough I was sure I'd sport bruises on the morrow. Watching me inflict blows on myself, Sir Durum grunted in disapproval.

"You've no need of an enemy to toughen you up, Rose. You're doing that well enough on your own. Adjust your grip—hands lower."

Changing my grip, and my stance, and my swing, did nothing to improve my handling of the mace. After three days of practice, the weapons master plucked it from my weary grasp.

"Not the mace," he said. "Tomorrow we'll try staves."

I was no better with staves, or polearms, or javelins. Indeed, one of my wild, wobbling throws managed to lodge a javelin in the rafters, where it hung precariously for the rest of the training, threatening everyone below. Kian and Neeve skirted the space beneath without mishap, but I kept glancing up at the javelin, expecting it to come down upon my head at any moment.

"I'd have thought thrown weapons," Sir Durum said dourly. "Ah well. Tomorrow, lances."

As anyone might have guessed, lances were not my ideal weapon either. After jabbing at the target several times, I managed to splinter the shaft of my weapon and deliver a blow to my own chest that drove the breath from my lungs. With a sour look, Sir Durum took the ruined lance away and bid me sit out the rest of the session on one of the hay bales scattered around the edge of the arena.

Glumly, I sank down on the scratchy bale and watched Neeve and Kian dance around one another, blades flashing, until the practice came to an end.

"Don't worry," Kian said encouragingly as he wiped down his blade. "You'll find the right weapon."

Neeve racked her sword, then glanced at me.

"Kitchen knife," she said, without a hint of mockery.

"That's not a real weapon," I protested.

"You did well enough with one when you fought the drake," she said.

"That was just luck." Wasn't it?

Sir Durum, overhearing our conversation, came to stand before me, arms crossed.

"I'd hoped you could wield something useful," he said. "Knives are no good. A short blade is ineffective against larger weapons, and hopeless against trained soldiers in battle."

Kian nodded, and even I could see the truth of it. Glumly, I toed the sawdust scattered over the floor, making a little circle with my boot. It seemed I was destined for failure in this, too.

Sir Durum cleared his throat and looked at the three of us, expression dour. "The Yule Feast is approaching."

We waited for him to continue, but he said nothing more. Neeve and I shared a confused glance.

"It is," Kian said after a moment. "Is there a reason you've mentioned it?"

"Aye." The weapons master's grimace pulled his lips down even further than usual. "The king has requested a demonstration of arms from my students."

"Oh." I suddenly understood why Sir Durum had been trying so hard to find something I could wield. "I won't reflect well on you, will I?"

Would my inability to use a weapon cost him his position? Guilt twisted in my chest at the thought—but surely the king wouldn't punish Sir Durum for my failings.

"Bows?" Kian suggested. "Maybe Rose could—"

"I don't want loose arrows flying about the feast," Sir Durum said. Which, given my general aptitude, or lack of it, was a wise choice. He heaved a sight. "I suppose it must be knives."

"Rose's aim was true," Neeve said.

"It was only the once," I reminded her, wincing at the thought of the accidents that might befall if I started tossing blades around.

"You'll not be throwing your knife in the arena," Sir Durum said gruffly, as if reading my thoughts. "Only in the most controlled circumstances, and not where others might be injured. We'll work on basic hand-to-hand bladework. A thrown blade is an assassin's weapon, and a dishonorable one. Not to mention that if you toss your knife at someone and miss, you're unarmed afterward and facing an enraged enemy."

That was a good point. I supposed I could carry two knives around, but anything more would feel a bit absurd. Of the three of us, Kian was best suited to sporting a bristling array of weapons, but he preferred his sword. For the first time, I wondered if he had any other blades concealed on his person.

I picked at a loose straw jabbing my trouser leg. It would be my luck that we'd finally found the one thing I could do, and it was useless and without honor in Sir Durum's eyes.

"I suppose we start tomorrow?" I asked.

At least a knife would pose a smaller danger to myself and others than the larger weapons I'd been trying to handle.

"Hmph." He looked me up and down. "Aye, we'll give you a dagger —and we'll add a buckler."

I smiled weakly. Of course. The weapons master wouldn't allow it to be as easy as waving a small knife about. No, I'd have a small shield strapped to my arm, as well. The possibilities for bashing myself in the face had just increased tenfold.

At least a dagger sounded more dignified than a kitchen knife. Even if it was practically the same thing.

After practice, I washed the dust and sweat away, then retreated to my bedroom and pulled out the *Studie*. By now, I was on my third time through the book and the archaic language no longer slowed me down. I was eager to soak up every detail, especially with my new under-standing from Thorne that no sun rode the starry skies of that world. Only two moons swirling overhead in different orbits, weaving a graceful dance of light and shadow over the enchanted realm.

⚜

THE NEXT AFTERNOON, Sir Durum thrust a small, round shield at me. I slipped it onto my left arm, and he helped me tighten the buckles. He didn't give me a blade, and I knew that asking for one would only earn me one of his glares. A dagger would appear when he deemed me ready, and not a moment before.

For the rest of the session I worked on raising and lowering my arm, blocking imaginary strikes. When the weapons master finally declared us finished for the day, my left arm was aching. I let it hang limply by my side and joined Neeve and Kian as they put away their weapons.

"Shield work today, I see." Kian grinned at me. "You can be our wall of defense in battle."

"Not with the tiny thing Sir Durum gave her," Neeve said. "That buckler would hardly deflect a pea, let alone a sword."

"It was heavy enough," I protested.

"You'll get stronger," Kian said without a trace of sympathy. "When are you getting a blade to go with it?"

I shrugged. I didn't pretend to know what the weapons master was thinking.

As it turned out, at the start of our next training session, Sir Durum handed me a dagger. I saw Kian swallow a laugh. Glancing down at the blade, I had to admit it was basically a glorified kitchen knife. Neeve nodded at me with a superior air.

I resolved to ignore them both, and hefted the dagger thoughtfully in my hand. The entire thing, from handle to blade tip, was the length of my forearm: short enough that a stray swipe wouldn't take anyone's hand off, but long enough that I might be able to inflict damage on an adversary. Or at least poke a few holes in their armor.

Now that I was finally outfitted, the training for the Yule Feast began in earnest. Neeve, Kian, and I had only a handful of weeks to choreograph a mock battle that would impress the king.

The two of them had already begun working out an elaborate sword fight. They would sweep up and down the length of the great hall with much impressive clanging of blades and agile leaping about. I glanced down at my knife and wished I could crawl away into some corner until after the year turned.

"Perhaps Rose could rush in at the end," Kian said.

"And impale myself on your sword?" I asked sourly.

Sir Durum grunted. "We'll come up with something."

After two hours, the only thing we'd accomplished was to make me look like the court jester, comic relief bouncing between two skilled opponents. None of the ideas to have me join them in battle were working, and at last the weapons master called a halt.

"It's terrible," I said, pushing my hair off my sweaty face with the back of my wrist. My left arm trembled with the effort of holding my shield up.

"You have to at least *try*, Rose," Neeve said, sheathing her blade with unconscious grace.

"I am," I said between gritted teeth, trying not to hate her in that moment.

"Tomorrow will be better," Sir Durum said as we trooped out of the arena, but I didn't believe him.

Kian left Neeve and me at our landing, and I stomped down the hall, furious with the world. Bits of straw itched my skin, my hair was a frizzy tangle, and I felt like my bones had been replaced with overcooked noodles. It was dark already, the sconces on the walls shedding too little light. Rain hissed on the windows outside.

"Rose, wait." Neeve hurried after me. "I'm sure that with a little more practice—"

I whirled on her. "Some people have to struggle, you know, instead of being handed everything on a golden platter."

She halted, dark eyes sparking with temper. "Are you referring to *me?*"

"Princess Neeve," I said mockingly. "Can't you see that you get everything you want, and hardly need to lift a finger?"

"Not everything," she said, her voice bitter.

"Everything that matters," I shot back. "If you're too stupid to see it, that's not my fault."

Her cheeks went scarlet. "I thought you, of all people, understood."

"Oh, I understand. Instead of noticing what you have, you waste your days pining for a foolish dream, and trampling everything else underfoot."

"Elfhame is my birthright—"

"And so is being a princess, and using magic, and excelling at riding and wielding a sword, and having Kian hang on your every word." I set a hand theatrically on my chest. "What a terrible burden."

"Is this about Thorne?" Her lips flattened into a thin line.

"It's about *you*," I shot back. "I'm utterly weary of your pretentious claim to tragedy while the world lays itself at your feet."

Hurt shone in her eyes, and I had a flash of satisfaction at the fact that I'd wounded her. For once, she could feel what it was like to be *me*.

"If you truly feel that way," she said, her voice cold, "then you needn't spend any more time in my company."

Without a second glance she stalked past, her spine very straight.

"Good." I made a face at her retreating back. "And good riddance."

She reached her rooms and slammed the door behind her. I did the same, hoping she could hear the angry thud of my own door closing.

But I already felt a little ashamed at the cruel words I'd hurled at her. Standing alone in my parlor, I crossed my arms and tried to regain my sense of righteous fury.

"She deserved it," I muttered.

Though she didn't—not really. It wasn't Neeve's fault that she carried Dark Elf magic in her blood, or that she was the Princess of Raine, or even that Thorne cared deeply for her.

Nor was it any fault of my own that I compared so poorly with her in every way. It was simply the truth of the world, difficult as it might be to swallow.

CHAPTER 48

Relations between Neeve and I were strained the next day. She did not wait for me to walk with her to the schoolroom, and we sat in tense silence as Miss Groves gave her lecture. Our studies had turned to the Continent, and the role of religion and government in shaping policies.

Dry stuff, on the surface, but given new urgency when we considered the events transpiring beyond Raine's borders.

Lunch was a terse affair. Afterward, Neeve did not even glance at me as we went back to our rooms to dress for our weapons training session.

Very well—I could pretend she didn't exist, in turn. Without acknowledging each other's presence, we entered the arena.

"What is the matter with you two?" Kian asked, immediately noticing that something was wrong.

"Nothing," I said.

Neeve only turned her back on him and went to fetch her sword.

Despite the tension—or perhaps because of it—training went well that afternoon. Sir Durum had hit upon a new idea, based, he said, on the sword-dancing practice he'd once seen a troupe of desert dwellers perform.

At the end of Neeve and Kian's sword battle, I was to step in, knife and buckler raised to catch their respective blades. I viewed the steely look in my stepsister's eyes with worry, but she allowed her sword to be arrested on my small blade.

Revenge was not her way, and for that I was grateful. At least, not the kind of revenge that would leave me obviously bleeding.

"Good," Sir Durum said. "Hold the pose."

He came forward and made some small adjustments: nudging Kian's shoulder forward, tapping Neeve's leg to straighten. My arms shook, especially the one holding my shield overhead, where Kian's sword rested.

"Don't look so pained," Kian told me, grinning. "You've just triumphantly interrupted our battle to the death, remember?"

"Right," I said, trying to unclench my jaw.

"Count to three," Sir Durum said, "and then each take a step back and bring your weapons in front of you, thusly."

He demonstrated, his own sword held perpendicular in front of him.

"One, two, three," Kian said, and we dropped our pose.

I stepped the wrong way, and Kian's blade almost sliced across my arm. I yelped and dived back, stumbling against Neeve. She gave me a distasteful look, as though she'd encountered a slime-covered worm, and put more distance between us.

"No." The arms master frowned at us. "Rose, stay in the middle—and place your shield under your blade, face out. Group up a little closer."

I shuffled into the center, Neeve and Kian flanking me.

"That's where you need to end up," Sir Durum said. "Try again."

We did, over and over, and finally achieved a passable transition from the end of the fight. I was uncomfortably aware that, without my clumsy presence, Neeve and Kian would have mastered the choreography almost immediately.

Sir Durum took up his sword again.

"Now, the blade dance. Mirror my movements." He raised his blade in salute.

I did my best to follow his sweeping steps and precise weapon placements. To my surprise, I wasn't dreadful—perhaps because it *did* feel more like a dance than a fight. Kian, Neeve, and I moved in concert, and although the effect wasn't as exciting as a mock battle, it had a certain pleasing symmetry.

At least, I hoped Lord Raine would think so when we performed it at the Yule Feast.

***

THE STONY SILENCE between Neeve and I continued. Sometimes I'd glance at her and see her watching me, a wounded look in her eyes.

I didn't think I'd had the power to hurt her so deeply, and with every passing day I felt worse about what I'd said. But by now, a simple apology wouldn't be enough to mend things between us, and I deeply rued the argument. If I could, I'd reel time back and leave all those hurtful words unspoken.

Finally, on the eve of her birthday, I had an inspiration.

Don't do it, my voice whispered.

It won't do any harm, I answered. At last, I'd hit upon the one gift that would bridge the unhappy gulf between us.

I bolted my bedroom door, just in case Sorche came up, then removed the Dark Elf *Studie* from its hiding place in the mattress. For a moment I held the pale-bound book, leafing through the pages with a sense of melancholy. I was only halfway through my reread, but it was my third time. And truly, there was no better gift to bestow upon my stepsister.

Elfhame was her birthright.

I held the book against my chest, bidding it farewell, then wrapped it in a dark blue scarf. The hall outside our rooms was quiet with the lull between dinner and bedtime. I padded to Neeve's door and knocked.

"Who is it?" she called.

"Rose."

There was a silence, and for a wretched moment I thought she wouldn't bother opening the door.

Then it cracked open, not wide enough for me to step inside, and my stepsister peered out.

"What do you want?" Her voice was cold.

"I, um." I glanced down at the scarf-wrapped bundle in my hand. "I brought you a birthday present."

"I don't need any gifts from you." She made to close the door, but I slipped my foot against the jamb.

"Please," I said. "It's important."

She regarded me levelly, unmoving. I counted three heartbeats pulsing in my ears before her she let out a breath—half exasperation, half acceptance.

"Very well." She opened the door. "But you're not welcome to stay for long."

Her parlor was warm, a blanket tossed over the chair near the hearth, as though she'd been sitting there staring into the flames when I knocked.

"Here." I held out the book. Explanations could come after she unwrapped it.

She took it gingerly, as though it might bite her, and slowly unwound the scarf. It was facedown when she finished, and with an impatient twitch of her mouth she flipped it over to see the title.

And froze.

The scarf fluttered, forgotten, to the floor.

The firelight caught the gold letters of the title, and they seemed to flare with new light as Neeve slowly traced the words.

"Where did you *find* this?" she finally asked, her voice low with wonder.

"In the library." I didn't elaborate as to where, precisely. "I thought you should have it. And what I said to you... I was wrong, and it was cruel of me. I'm truly sorry."

She looked up at me, stricken. "Oh, Rose..."

Astonishingly, tears glistened at the corners of her eyes. Even more surprising, she took a step forward and engulfed me in a hug. I returned her embrace, the tight knot inside me easing. I'd hated being so at odds with her.

"I'm sorry, too," she said, stepping back. "I've missed you."

I gave her a wry smile. "Being at odds wasn't any fun, was it?"

"No." She shook her head.

Then her gaze went back to the book, and her expression softened. It was clear she wanted to start reading it immediately.

"I'll just leave you with your gift," I said. "I've read it already, so if you want to talk about it…"

Neeve didn't berate me for being first to crack open the pages, or for keeping it a secret for so long. It seemed the wonder of her new acquisition outshone any questions or concerns. For the time being, at least.

"I will." She turned her smile on me, a rare sight indeed, and I was extraordinarily glad that I'd chosen to give her the *Studie*.

I knew, too, that I needn't caution her to keep it hidden. My step-sister was even more careful about such things than I. This time, I'd wager she wouldn't go running to the king with it, either.

"Good night," I said, going to the door. "And happy birthday."

"It is." She hugged the book to her chest. "It is, indeed."

The glow of our restored friendship warmed me as I went back to my rooms—almost erasing the niggling doubts that, perhaps, giving Neeve the book had not been a wise thing to do.

CHAPTER 49

The Yule Feast arrived, along with a sudden cold snap that left the castle chilly and the inhabitants irritable. I sat at the head table, picking at my food and trying to contain my mounting nervousness. Finally, as the second-to-last course was served, Neeve nodded at me.

It was time to prepare for our demonstration of arms.

I re-folded my napkin, placed it on the table, and quietly left. Neeve followed, and we headed to a nearby storeroom so we could change. Fighting a mock battle in our best gowns would be foolish. Without much talk, we quickly traded silk and satin for trousers, boots, and sturdy leather jerkins.

We met Kian in the corridor just outside the great hall. He gave us a jaunty smile, no sign of worry on his open face.

"Ready?" He unsheathed his sword. "This will be fun."

Not the term I would have used, but I nodded all the same.

Neeve peered into the hall, waiting for Lord Raine to announce the performance. Once he did, she and Kian would enter.

The king stood and made his usual speech. As the applause died down, Neeve danced backward through the doorway, her blade held high. Kian followed, teeth bared in a fierce grin.

From my place in the shadows, I watched as she and the prince leaped and spun, parried and attacked. The clang of their swords echoed in the huge room. The guests alternately gasped and murmured their appreciation, especially when Kian made a particularly spectacular dive to avoid Neeve's swing, ending with a somersault and vaulting back to his feet.

All with a naked blade in his hand. I admired his agility. I would have cut myself to ribbons had I attempted such a move.

The opponents worked their way down the hall, then back up. When they reached the head table, it was my cue to dash out and intercept their swords. I wiped my sweaty palms on my trousers, checked to make sure my shield was firmly in place, then drew my knife.

At the appointed moment, I ran into the room, praying I wouldn't trip over my own feet. Sliding between Neeve and Kian, I struck the pose we'd worked so hard to perfect. My heartbeat pounded in my throat, and sweat prickled along my hairline.

Thud. Kian's blade came to rest on my buckler. I braced myself as Neeve's sword descended to meet my little knife. For a panicked second, it seemed her blade wouldn't stop at the hilt, but slide off, cutting deep into my arm.

At the last second, she wrenched her sword to a stop. Her eyes met mine, apology shining in their depths.

The crowd applauded and cheered, and we held the pose until my arms burned. Then Kian counted to three under his breath. We stepped back, saluted, and began the sword-dancing portion of the demonstration.

All was going well, and I let myself relax—until a wayward swing of my sharp little blade slashed across Kian's wrist. He winced, but didn't drop his sword, thank goodness. I froze, staring at the blood beading along his skin.

"Rose," Neeve hissed.

"Keep going," Kian added from between clenched teeth.

I jerked my head and tried to fall back into the moves Sir Durum had drilled into us. Ruby droplets splashed down upon the flagstones as Kian raised his sword, and I desperately hoped no one else noticed.

We continued, Kian surreptitiously wiping the trickles of blood away by brushing his wrist close to his body whenever he could.

Sweating, I took great care to control my knife and shield as we completed the choreography. If my movements were blocky and ungraceful, so be it. The last thing I wanted was to backhand Neeve with my shield, or slice Kian again.

We finished and bowed, and I peeked cautiously at the head table. The king was smiling, and everyone looked pleased. Except for Sir Durum, but I couldn't tell if his dour expression was any different than usual.

Kian blotted the cut with his sleeve, and I was glad to see that the bleeding had slowed to a sluggish trickle. Thank heavens I hadn't sliced a vein open. The thought of the catastrophe narrowly avoided left me shaking.

The servants gathered our weapons, and the three of us trooped back to our places.

"A fine show of swordsmanship," Lord Raine said, nodding to Kian and Neeve. "And Rose, I'm glad you found a weapon to suit your abilities. I commend you, and Sir Durum, for your hard work."

"Thank you," I croaked.

Faint praise, perhaps, but at least he'd been kind. I was grateful he hadn't realized how close I'd come to creating a diplomatic incident.

For her part, Mama smiled at me and patted my hand, then congratulated my stepsister and Kian. As soon as her attention turned away, I dropped weakly into my chair. I was seated too far from Kian and Neeve to converse, and in truth, I wanted to skip dessert altogether and slink off to bed without having to speak to anyone.

Finally, the feast ended. Lord Raine stood and bid his guests farewell, and I was quick to rise as soon as we were dismissed. I hurried toward the door, but just as I was leaving, Sir Durum caught my eye and beckoned. There was no use pretending I hadn't seen him. With a heavy sigh, I went to join him where he stood near a frayed tapestry.

"A good fighter keeps her wits about her," he said. "No matter what."

I bit my lip and braced for a scolding. "I understand."

"Good." He clapped me across the shoulders. "Well done, to all of you."

With that, he gave a brisk nod and strode away down the hall. I blinked after him, astounded. Apparently he'd seen the accident and didn't think worse of me for it.

"Are you well?" Neeve asked, coming up to where I stood rooted by confusion.

Kian followed close behind. It seemed to me in that moment that the two of them moved together in perfect accord. Their work with the mock duel had given them a new ease together, and I wondered if they were aware of it.

"Yes." I gave her a befuddled look. "Sir Durum praised me for not losing my focus. Although I have the two of you to thank for that."

"Warriors watch one another's backs," Kian said with a wink.

"How's your wrist?" I asked.

"Perfectly fine." He held out his arm, pushing the sleeve back to reveal the red slash. "That paring knife of yours doesn't inflict much damage, I'm glad to say."

Neeve looked dubious, and I held my tongue. Neither of us pointed out that, had the cut been any deeper and closer to the center of his wrist, the performance would have ended in blood and disaster.

"At least the demonstration went well," I said. "I think the king was pleased."

"I wonder what Sir Durum will set us to next?" Kian sounded far too cheerful about the prospect of more training.

"Resting," I said. "He gave us the week off, don't forget."

"You don't want to lose your conditioning," Neeve said. "I plan to spend a little time at the arena every day."

"I'll join you," Kian said.

"Don't either of you want to relax?" I gave Neeve a pointed look. "Read some books?"

"There is time enough in the day," she replied. "Remember, Miss Groves has granted us a holiday, too."

"Suit yourselves." I glanced about the mostly empty hall. "I'm going to have a bath, and then go to bed." And try to forget that I'd almost killed a prince of Fiorland.

"A good thought," Kian said. "May I escort you two lovely princesses up to your rooms?"

I snorted. Despite our serviceable garb, Neeve looked composed and lovely, but my head was itchy with drying sweat, my hair springing from where I'd tied it back to riot frizzily around my face.

"I'm not saying a bath wouldn't improve things," Kian added, then dodged the elbow I threw at him.

We parted in good company, bidding one another good night in the hallway outside my bedroom door. Though I watched Kian closely, it seemed the last of his awkward infatuation with Neeve was finally gone.

Replaced, perhaps, with a steadier regard and respect, but I couldn't fault him for that. All three of us were growing older, the mantle of adulthood hovering over our shoulders, whether we were ready for it or not.

CHAPTER 50

Without the discipline of lessons with Master Fawkes, I only played my harp occasionally. I had no more secret books to read, since I'd decided to leave the incomprehensible leaflet in its hiding place. No one had seemed to notice the missing titles, and I presumed the secret shelf had been forgotten over the years.

Rose and Kian trained together frequently, and her manner continued to soften toward him. I tried not to feel excluded when they discussed specific weapon techniques, or shared a laugh over some obscure reference I didn't catch, but sometimes it was difficult not to sulk.

Not that either of them were deliberately excluding me, but loneliness closed around me like a cold fog, increasing as the winter wore on.

My training with dagger and buckler was going adequately, though no matter how much I asked Sir Durum to let me practice throwing my knife, he refused.

"Outside, when spring comes," he said, and I had to admit I saw the sense in it.

The afternoons I didn't train, I haunted the library, searching in vain for more books about sorcery. Finally, I had to admit that the shelves were empty of any such knowledge. At least there were still romances and adventures to read, though even those sometimes failed to entertain me.

Almost imperceptibly, the days lengthened and the weather warmed. As the first soft green of spring settled over the land, I wondered what Lord Raine's summer plans might be. Unlike the previous year, he didn't seem inclined to whisk the Fiorlanders away from the newly awakening Darkwood and its secrets.

Had Thorne and the Oracles been successful in shoring up the forest's defenses? There was no way to know, except to ask him. As the rains subsided, my anticipation of seeing the *Galadhir* grew, until some days I could scarcely breathe around the bubble of longing in my chest.

"Neeve," I said one afternoon, as we returned from the classroom to our wing of the castle, "what are we going to do about Kian?"

The Fiorlanders now knew about the strange creatures inhabiting the forest, and the *Galadhir*. But the gateway hidden in the center of the forest was another matter, and certainly must remain concealed from them.

Neeve looked at me, unsmiling. "What do you mean?"

"Spring is here." I waved at the stone walls. "We'll be going into the Darkwood soon."

"Yes." Her expression clouded. "Let me discuss matters with my father."

"Surely he won't allow the prince to come with us?"

"I don't know," she said. "But Father trusts the Fiorlanders now. They've spent enough time in Raine. And perhaps Kian ought to know our secrets, if..." She paused, the rest of the sentence hanging heavy in the air between us.

"If he's to marry you," I finished for her.

Color sprang to Neeve's cheeks. "That's not what I meant. I'm not planning to wed Kian."

I raised my brows. What else could her words mean?

"I wish you two joy," I said tartly.

"You're impossible," she snapped, then lengthened her stride down the hallway.

I refused to run after her, and so was left with a jumble of irritated thoughts for company. I only hoped Lord Raine would see the sense in keeping Kian from the Darkwood.

As it turned out, the king did—but only by forbidding *all* of us to go into the forest; an announcement he made at dinner two nights later.

"What?" Neeve asked, her eyes sparking with anger. "But I always spend time in the Darkwood—every summer as long as I can remember. You can't forbid it!"

"I must." Lord Raine sounded weary. "Despite the efforts of the forest warden, it isn't safe. The magical incursions have been repelled, but I understand the balance is precarious. Not to mention that strange and dangerous creatures still roam the forest."

"Then we should mount a hunt and vanquish the beasts," Jarl Eiric said with relish. "I've killed plenty of boar, and even a bear or two in my time."

"No." The king's voice was hard. "The Darkwood is not ours to hunt. And you know nothing of the beasts that dwell within. They are not... ordinary."

The jarl glowered at being so quickly dismissed, but said nothing more.

I wanted to sob, or scream, or both, at the thought of being denied the chance to see Thorne. Instead I took a careful sip of water and looked over at Neeve. From the rebellious set of her jaw, I knew she wouldn't meekly accept her father's orders.

It wasn't wise to disobey a king. But if Neeve was determined to go into the woods, she'd find a way. And I would be right at her heels.

❧❦❧

ONE WEEK PASSED, and then two. I watched Neeve closely, but she made no move toward the forest, instead immersing herself in training and riding—but never too far from the castle walls. Usually, Kian went with her, and one or two soldiers, no doubt detailed to keep a close watch on the prince and princess. Sometimes I accompanied them, but not that often, as I was *finally* allowed to practice throwing knives.

Sir Durum had commandeered a disused corner of the castle

gardens and set up a hay bale target. Before we started, he explained that at first I'd learn a straight throw.

"Rotations increase your range," he'd said. "But hitting your opponent in the chest with the handle of your knife isn't good. In combat you won't have time to judge your distance and plan how your blade will land. A point-first strike is the best attack."

The first day, however, he refused to even let me draw my dagger.

"Footwork first," he said. "Your body must learn the moves."

So for two afternoons, I drilled.

Step back. Lift my hand to my forehead. Pivot forward, miming a forward throw. Over and over, until my arm burned and the grass beneath my feet was churned to mud.

"Extend your arm," the weapons master said. "Point at the target where you want the blade to fly. Good. Again."

Finally, satisfied with my bladeless throws, he let me try with the dagger. When my first several throws fell short of the target and instead thwacked into the muddy grass, he shook his head.

"Weak," he said. "If you want to hit your opponent from more than a pace away, you'll have to strengthen your arms."

I blew out a breath but couldn't argue with his assessment. Although I'd managed to strike the drake in the eye, that had been a throw borne by desperation. So every morning and every evening I performed the arm-strengthening exercises Sir Durum prescribed. As the days passed, I improved, albeit slowly, and the weapons master gradually increased my distance from the target.

My skill with the knife improved, and my birthday drew ever closer, but still Neeve made no move toward the Darkwood.

Finally, as we went to the schoolroom one morning, my stepsister shot me a look. "You turn sixteen tomorrow," she said, something secretive in her eyes.

"Yes." I stretched my ever-aching arms. "What of it?"

"I have a birthday present for you."

"Do you?" My heart leaped at her words, though I tried not to show it.

A small smile curved her lips. "Something you want, in return for the gift you gave me. After class today, be ready."

I was so distracted by the thought of seeing Thorne I could scarcely pay attention to a word Miss Groves said. At last she threw up her hands in exasperation.

"I declare, the both of you are barely present," she said. "Neeve, do try to focus. And Rose, I know that tomorrow is your birthday, but it doesn't excuse you from attending to the lecture."

"I'm sorry." I dipped my head. But it was impossible to follow the particulars of Continental sea trade when the trees of the Darkwood beckoned so enticingly outside the window.

Finally, the teacher closed her book. "I can see there's no getting any knowledge into your brains today. You are both excused. I'll tell the kitchen to deliver lunch to your rooms."

I jumped up, smiling. "Thank you, Miss Groves! I promise I'll do better tomorrow."

"Consider it an early birthday present," she said. "But I do expect you to pay better attention, next class."

I nodded, then practically skipped out of the room, Neeve right behind me.

"Isn't it perfect timing?" I asked her. "We'll have all afternoon for... whatever it is you have planned."

She looked calmly back at me. "Wear your boots."

We parted ways in the corridor outside my bedroom door. Once inside, I hastened to don my trousers and boots, then belted on my pouch and dagger.

A servant brought up lunch—a tender spring salad, along with a hearty hunk of bread and smoked cheese, which I devoured immediately. Even taking the time to plait my hair back, I was ready and waiting a good quarter hour before Neeve knocked at my door.

"Are we going into the forest?" I asked, slipping into the hall.

She pressed her finger to her lips. "Follow me."

We went down to the kitchens, and then the cellars beneath. The route she took was different from the one leading to the trapdoor, and I guessed that Lord Raine had our usual exits to the Darkwood guarded—whether to keep us in, or danger out. Probably both.

In a musty root cellar, Neeve shifted several bags of onions, revealing a hole barely big enough for us to crawl through. I regarded it dubiously, but thoughts of Thorne kept me from protesting. I'd brave any number of dank, worm-infested tunnels to see him.

Luckily, it wasn't as horrible as I'd imagined. After the initial squeeze through the wall, we could easily go on hands and knees. Neeve conjured a faint blue light, and I followed in her wake. The earth was damp and cold beneath my palms, and I knew the knees of my trousers would be stained with ground-in dirt, but such things were trivial. We were going into the Darkwood.

It seemed we crawled for a very long time. My back was aching and my mouth gritty by the time the tunnel began sloping upward.

"Almost there," Neeve said. Then, a moment later, "Stay back."

I did, and heard the rustle of leaves, the crack of a branch breaking. Neeve's light faded, replaced with the glow of sunshine slanting through foliage.

"Come up," she called softly.

I did, emerging in the middle of a bush. I pushed through the branches and tumbled forward onto the soft green mosses carpeting the forest floor. Quiet with awe, I glanced about to see that we were in a small clearing within the shelter of the Darkwood.

Just barely in the forest—I glimpsed the castle walls beyond the grassy sward at the edge of the trees. But we'd made it unobserved. I let out a small laugh.

"However did you know this tunnel was here?" I asked, rising to brush the worst of the dirt away.

"The hobnie told me." Neeve sounded very matter-of-fact about it.

"Which hobnie? When?" I frowned at her. "And how did you even know to ask such a thing?"

She waved her hand. "It was the second one we rescued—Codlatach, I think his name was. And the hobnies know all the secrets of the Darkwood. I asked him last summer, when you were recovering from your illness."

"You might have mentioned it to me."

"They are sparing with their favors," she said. "Even though we saved his life, it was difficult to get him to tell me about any other passages from the castle to the forest."

What else might the hobnies reveal, if asked? My mind lit with a million questions, and I knew I'd have to ponder which ones were most important—later. Anything concerning Thorne and the gateway to Elfhame took priority, of course.

As if my thoughts had summoned him, the *Galadhir* strode into the clearing. The greeting on my lips died at the thunderous look on his face.

"What are you two doing here?" His voice was taut with anger.

I glanced mutely at Neeve. Thorne in a temper was formidable indeed. He seemed taller, his features sharper, and I could almost sense his power rolling off him in waves.

Neeve lifted her chin. "We always come to the forest in the spring. You know that."

"Not this year," he said. "I believe the king has expressly forbidden it. Has he not?"

He whirled and pinned me with his gaze. Heat washed over me, but I went to stand shoulder to shoulder with Neeve.

"It's my birthday tomorrow," I said, which I knew was hardly an excuse.

"And what good will that do if you're eaten by a dire wolf today?" His eyes narrowed. "The forest is a danger to you both, now more than ever. You must not come here again until I say it's safe."

"Will you deny me my birthright?" Neeve asked, her voice stubborn.

"If you're to survive to claim it, yes."

The corners of her lips trembled with grief, and Thorne's expression softened.

"It won't be forever. I promise. The Oracles and I just need a bit more time. Once we're successful, I'll deal with the upheavals the sorcerous incursions have caused, and then you may freely roam the forest once more."

"What if it takes years?" I asked.

"It won't. The summer after this is the *nirwen* harvest, and nothing must threaten that."

I gave a slow nod, trusting that the Dark Elves would do everything in their power to ensure that the harvest was uninterrupted. Though it wouldn't be in time for Neeve and me to roam the forest this summer.

My heart twisted. I didn't know if I could manage another winter cooped up in Castle Raine without fresh memories of Thorne to sustain me.

"We miss you," Neeve said, voicing the words I could not say.

"I miss you too." For a moment, the mantle of *Galadhir* dropped from him, and he looked young—and a little afraid. "But you must trust me in this, Neeve."

Neeve. Always Neeve. My throat tight, I dropped my gaze to the moss beneath my feet, counting the strewn cedar needles to distract from my pain.

"And you too, Rose." Suddenly he was before me, lifting my chin with gentle fingertips.

I glanced up, meeting his gaze, and was lost in a night sky full of stars.

He stilled, and I thought I could hear his heartbeat in the quiet between the trees, echoing my own.

In the distance, a long, wavering howl sounded. The hunger in that hollow cry sent a shiver up my spine.

Thorne dropped his hand and took a step back, expression shuttered.

"The wolves have scented you," he said. "It's time to go."

"Which way?" Neeve asked, glancing at the castle walls rising beyond the trees. "Back through the tunnel?"

Thorne cocked his head, listening. His lips tightened, as though he did not like what he heard.

"No. Through the door in the wall—quickly. I'll make sure it's unlocked."

Even as he spoke, he was hurrying us toward the boundary of grass separating the Darkwood from Castle Raine.

I glanced back to the clearing, marking its location in my mind.

"Don't even think of coming back," Thorne warned. "I'll be sealing up the tunnel as soon as you're safe within the castle walls."

Another howl sounded, much closer this time. It was echoed by other cries, and the hair on the back of my neck prickled. The wolves were closing quickly.

"Hurry." Thorne grabbed our elbows and hauled us across the grass.

I didn't even get a chance to gasp out a goodbye as he flung open the small door in the wall and thrust us inside, to safety.

"Thorne—" Neeve began, but he slammed the door in her face.

With a clunk, a bar I'd never noticed before fell across the weathered door. I was tempted to lift it, but the sound of snarling just outside chilled my blood.

Stricken, I turned to my stepsister. "Will he be all right?"

"He's the *Galadhir*," she said, though her face was etched with fear. "Even enchanted dire wolves are no match for him."

I desperately hoped she was right.

An immense roar filled the air, followed by the thudding sounds of a fight.

"We should go to the castle," Neeve said, but neither of us moved.

More growling, and then a high-pitched yelp. It occurred to me that I hadn't heard Thorne invoke any of his Elvish magic. What was happening on the other side of the wall? My hand fell on the sturdy bar crossing the door.

My stepsister sent me a panicked look. "Don't."

I let my hand fall away.

There was such a thing as curiosity, and then there was sheer stupidity. Opening the door was certainly the latter.

The sounds of the fight moved away, the growls and snapping growing fainter. Neeve and I huddled in silence, until, at last, a forlorn howl echoed through the air. I took it as a sign that Thorne had won. He must have. Surely the forest would not let its champion be defeated.

Neeve let out a low breath and jerked her head toward the castle. Silently, we trudged to the kitchen door. The air was cool with impending evening, and full of shadows.

Just before we stepped inside, I sent a glance at the dark tops of the trees visible over the castle walls. A cold premonition moved over me that it would be a long time until I set foot in the Darkwood—or saw Thorne—again.

CHAPTER 51

A solemn mood gripped me, persisting through dinner and casting everything in a melancholy light. After I readied myself for bed that night, I went to the window and rested my hand against the chilly glass.

"Thorne," I whispered, hoping he might somehow hear me, "be well."

The black expanse of the Darkwood made no reply, the salting of stars overhead bright and unwinking. With a sigh, I crawled beneath my covers and waited for sleep to take me, so that I might awaken a year older than when I'd closed my eyes. I was too wise now to hope for a sudden awakening of magical powers. Such dreams were for children, and I was a young woman now, on the cusp of my sixteenth year.

Crackling flames. Pain.

I groped myself upright up in my bed, agony burning through me. The castle was on fire! Weakly, I opened my eyes—to see that my bedroom was dark and quiet. No flames raced through the room.

And yet I felt the heat upon me, scorching my flesh, singeing my bones. My left hand felt like it had been plunged into the white-hot center of a furnace.

"Help!" I cried, but the word came out a scratchy whisper.

Nonetheless, there was an answer.

"Rose?" My mother cracked open the door between my bedroom and parlor, letting in a slice of light.

"Mama," I croaked. "I'm hot."

Even that took too much effort, and I collapsed onto the pillows, trembling. My vision blurred, as though a haze of heat waves rose between me and the world.

Mama rushed to my bedside. Her cool hand touched my forehead, and I heard her suck in a breath. She moved away, and a moment later returned, urging me to sit up and drink the glass of water she'd brought.

I couldn't. Hungry coals lodged under my skin, and I screamed.

"Hush, darling, hush," my mother said. "I'm going to fetch help."

I wasn't aware of her leaving. Only the fire writhing through my flesh. Scraps of conversation floated above me.

"...cold compresses."

"She's getting worse."

Broken sobbing.

"She might die! I beg you, let me take her..."

Day and night pulsed outside my window. The light hurt my eyes; the darkness fanned the flames.

Neeve's pale features, fear in her eyes.

My mother, crying, pleading.

The fire consumed me. Soon there would be nothing left but ashes.

Then a change: fresh air on my skin, sunlight stabbing me so that I cried out through a throat raw from screaming. A cart. Trees overhead, blocking the sky. My left arm a cinder, but for the tendril of green scribed upon my elbow. It grew ten feet tall, fending off the silver strands the forest sent to suffocate me.

A bear roared in the distance.

Kian saying, "...I'll kill it."

The smell of salt. Rocking up and down.

"She's opening her eyes. Rose. Rose, can you hear me?"

I pried open lids crusty with tears and saw Kian hovering over me, concern etching his features. He sat at my bedside, but I was in a room

I didn't recognize. Cramped walls and low ceiling, a porthole for a window. A boat.

"Yes," I whispered.

"Thank the snows!"

"Thirsty," I managed to say.

He turned, and I heard the clink of pitcher to glass. He brought it to my lips, and I swallowed, the water like shards of ice sliding down my throat—excruciating, yet wonderful at the same time.

"Where?" I moved my head the slightest bit, indicating the little cabin.

"On a ship for Parnese. We're halfway across the Strait now."

"Mama?"

He nodded. "Yes, and Sir Durum and I are accompanying you. She insisted you were dying, that it was a relapse of a sickness you had once before, and only a special doctor in Parnese could heal you." He smiled, relief glowing in his eyes. "But you're recovering on your own. We'll turn around the moment the ship resupplies in Parnese, and get you back home."

I wanted to protest that Parnese *was* home, not Raine, but flames licked at my arms, and I could not muster the strength.

Fight it, Rose, I thought grimly to myself. *You must...*

CHAPTER 52

When I finally regained consciousness, I felt as though my insides had been scoured with razor-sharp sand, my skin flayed and then inexpertly stitched back on.

But I was no longer burning.

I opened my eyes to a room full of brightness and the smell of lemons. *Parnese,* I instantly thought. The air of Raine did not feel this way—dry and citrus-scented. The sunlight lay across the tile floor in a warm beam, and gauzy blue curtains fluttered beside the half-open windows. I let out a deep sigh.

Not of contentment, but of immense relief that I breathed, and blinked. And lived. The pain I felt now was distant compared to the agony I dimly recalled.

I turned my head on the clean white pillow to see a silver hand bell on the bedside table. Shakily, I reached over and managed to lift and give it a shake.

A clear tone rang out, and a moment later, Mama hurried into the room.

"Rose." Her voice caught on a sob. "Thank goodness."

She came to my bed and enfolded me in a violet-perfumed hug. I could feel the wetness of tears on her cheeks.

"Mama," I whispered.

After a moment, she pulled back and looked at me intently. "How do you feel, my darling?"

"Terrible." I tried a smile, but my lips barely twitched. "What happened?"

She glanced to the window, then back at me. "You fell horribly ill, with the same sickness that struck you down when you were seven. The physicians in Raine could do nothing for you, and I begged Lord Raine to let me bring you back to Parnese, to the same doctor who helped you once before."

I blinked, absorbing her words. "The king let you go?"

"Yes." Her expression was grave. "You would not have survived otherwise."

I shivered, thinking how close to death I'd been. "He must love you very much. Parnese is dangerous."

"Yes," she said. "But it is also home."

I managed a nod. Something eased in me as I felt the warm air, heard the lilting of songbirds just outside the window—yellow and blue-feathered ones that never darted under the gray skies of Raine.

"Prince Kian will be glad to hear you've finally awoken," Mama said. "And Sir Durum will begin pressing us in earnest to return, but I refuse to set foot from here until you're well enough to travel."

I dared not guess when that might be. At the moment, I felt completely hollowed out. Even the brief conversation with Mama had sapped my strength. Despite myself, my eyes began to close.

"Rest now." She patted my shoulder. "But first, drink a bit."

With her help I managed a few sips of water, then lay back, unconsciousness pulling me down into its black embrace.

WHEN I NEXT ROUSED, it was to the sounds of argument in the next room.

"Certainly not," Mama was saying. "Would you court a relapse of Rose's health and undo everything we've risked to come here? She isn't ready. She hasn't even risen from her bed!"

"We are in danger of discovery." Sir Durum's voice was gruff. "We must leave soon."

"Perhaps we can agree on a compromise." It was Kian, speaking with surprising diplomacy. "I agree with the queen—Rose must regain some of her strength. But, Your Majesty, you must admit it's unwise to linger too long in Parnese. So far, we've escaped notice from the priests, but that can't last forever."

I heard the clack of Mama's pacing footsteps, a sure sign of her agitation.

"Another few weeks," she said, her steps halting. "We will depart before the autumn storms make sea travel hazardous."

"I'm glad you see the sense of it." Kian's voice was warm. "Do you agree, Sir Durum?"

The arms master grunted. "Best get the girl up and on her feet as soon as possible. Build up her strength."

"At least she's regained consciousness," Kian said. "In fact, I'll look in on her now."

I didn't bother closing my eyes as he appeared in the arched doorway. He gave me a crooked grin, as though he'd guessed I'd been awake and listening.

"Rose." He drew a chair up beside my bed and took my hand.

I found his warm clasp reassuring—something to hold on to, to keep from slipping back into sleep.

"I'm glad you're here," I said, my throat dry with disuse.

"I insisted." His blue eyes grew serious. "Lord Raine wanted to accompany the queen, but that was foolish. Raine couldn't allow its king go into such danger. I offered to come in his stead, since I'm familiar with the situation in Parnese. Sir Durum agreed, and here we are."

"How long?" I glanced groggily around the room. "I heard Mama mention the autumn storms."

"We arrived in port"—he cocked his head, calculating—"nearly three months ago."

"Three months?" The knowledge made my stomach clench. The longer we stayed, the greater the danger of discovery.

I recalled hearing that the members of the Parnesian royal family were under house arrest. Mama surely counted as such—but worse than that, she was married to the King of Raine. And Kian was a Fior-lander prince. If we were found, they were ideal hostages, leverage that the priests could use against both kingdoms.

I was in complete sympathy with Sir Durum's insistence we leave as soon as possible. Unfortunately, although my mind agreed, my body was horribly weak.

"Help me sit up," I said.

Kian frowned, but didn't argue. He slid one arm about my shoulders and lifted. As I sat, the room spun. Sudden nausea gripped me and sweat sprang to my forehead. I must have made a sound of distress, for he gently laid me back down again.

"Too soon, I think." The look he gave me was full of concern.

I managed a weak nod, my skin clammy, my insides churning.

"Rest now," Kian said. "We'll try again tomorrow."

TOMORROW TURNED INTO A WEEK, which turned into a fortnight. Slowly—excruciatingly slowly—I began to regain my strength. But the days were growing colder. Rain blew in most afternoons, not the soft, unceasing drizzle of Raine, but hard, diamond drops spattering against the windows, glazing the streets with water.

It did not help matters that I couldn't keep solid food down, only broths and tisanes. My bones stuck out, knobbly at my wrists and hips, and when I finally looked in a mirror I was shocked to see the gaunt-ness of my face. Hollow-cheeked, dark bruises beneath my eyes. Even my hair was subdued, lying flat and listless against my head.

Through it all, Kian was my most patient companion. Mama tried, but it pained her too much to see me in such a state. I caught her staring at me with haunted eyes, wincing when I stumbled. When I told her that I preferred Kian's help, she seemed relieved instead of hurt, and quickly withdrew.

I told myself it was for the best.

And I was glad of Kian's constant company. He coaxed me to sit, then, finally, to stand. He held my hands, moving slowly backward and guiding me about the room as I relearned the art of walking. When I felt able to move without help, he hovered, ready to catch me if I fell.

Which I did, fairly often. Every little dip in the tile seemed enough to make me lose my balance. If he hadn't been there, I was certain I would have broken a bone or two, maybe even cracked my head open.

But he caught me, every time.

"I'm sorry," I said, my words muffled in his shirt as he carried me back to bed.

He smoothed my hair. "Don't worry. Every day you go a little farther."

It was kind of him to say, but it wasn't precisely true. Some days I only managed to stand beside my bed for a few moments, swaying, before dizziness overcame me.

"I haven't come far enough," I said. "It's storm season now."

Indeed, though he said nothing, Sir Durum had taken to stalking about our apartments with a deep frown etched upon his face. I feared it was too late for us to leave Parnese.

The knowledge made me more relieved than frightened. I didn't think I could endure days at sea followed by the journey to Castle Raine. The mere thought of the carriage ride from our rooms to the port of Parnese left me dizzy and sweating.

I'd settle for the ability to navigate to the bathroom by myself, sit at the table to eat—all the daily things one took for granted until they were gone. I thought back to the days I'd limped around with my crutch, after the drake's attack. How sorry I'd felt for myself—and how mobile I'd actually been, without realizing it.

The fall descended upon us, filled with sudden squalls. I knew without asking that no boats would take us to Raine. The Strait was dangerous, and every autumn there were more tales of ships lost to the treacherous waves.

Mama said as much to Sir Durum, one afternoon when the wind rattled the rooftops. I lay in my bed, half dozing, as they spoke in the other room.

"We may not be safe here," she said, "but the possibility of being found out is better than the surety of drowning at sea."

"Besides," Kian added, "the priests haven't discovered us yet—and you'd think they would have by now, if they were going to."

"A fallacy," Sir Durum said. "A careless word, someone glimpsing you at the window and recognizing your face—there are too many ways to be found out."

"We've been taking every precaution," Mama said. "Now we must simply bide until the weather lifts."

The weapons master only grunted in reply.

Being cooped up in our set of rooms was wearing on everyone, however. Two servants had also come from Raine—Mr. and Mrs. Cresset—and they had to do all of the shopping and errand-running, as Mama, Kian, and even Sir Durum ran the risk of being recognized, having been in Parnese before.

The apartments Mama had rented contained five bedrooms, one for each of us. There was a small kitchen, two bathrooms, and a long room divided into living and dining spaces.

Most days after lunch, while I rested, Kian and Sir Durum rolled up the rugs and commenced training. Mama would come sit with me, bringing a book to read, or simply staring out the window. She was present if I needed something, but quick to rise and fetch the prince once I was ready to move about.

I slowly grew stronger, my appetite returning and my dizziness abating. Kian no longer needed to shadow my every step. Though I was glad of my increasing ability, I missed the feel of him bearing me in his arms, his steady heartbeat under my ear.

But I was able to hold conversations now, and sit up regularly, and he still spent most waking hours with me. My hands trembled if I held a book for too long, and so he read aloud to me and we entered the stories together, laughing at the comedies and discussing the more serious works at length.

Mrs. Cresset bought a battered chess set at the nearby market-place. Kian set it up at the table in the main room, and we played together for hours, sipping cups of tea and arguing over our moves. At the start of every game, I laid claim to the white pieces and he never protested my choice, though it meant he must always go second. Despite my fragile health, I was content.

And one day, as our eyes met and held across the checkered board, I realized I was growing fond of Kian. Exceedingly fond.

What about Neeve? my little voice asked, always stirring up trouble.

She's not here, I answered. *Be quiet.*

Still, the question added an edge to my every interaction with the prince. I was aware of the sweetness of our time together, but the sharp bite of our eventual return to Raine hovered, ever-present in the background.

CHAPTER 53

Our precarious existence shattered one afternoon when a knock came at the apartment door.

Mama gestured for Mr. Cresset to answer, then nodded at Kian and I to go back to my room. Chess game abandoned mid-move, we went, but I left the door open a crack so we could peer out.

Mama retreated into her own room, and Sir Durum strode across the living area to snatch up the sword he kept in the corner.

"Who is it?" Mr. Cresset asked, without opening the door.

"A friend. I'm alone."

"One moment."

Quietly, Sir Durum came to stand just beside the threshold, blade at the ready.

"I should have grabbed my weapon," Kian said softly, frustration in his voice. "What if it's the priests?"

I reached over to squeeze his hand. "Sir Durum can occupy them while you dash for your sword." Maybe.

For the first time, I wished for the weight of my old dagger at my hip. The blade was still in my rooms at Castle Raine, abandoned like the rest of my life there.

Slowly, Mr. Cresset unlocked the door and pulled it open a mere crack. Fear pounded in my throat. Had we been discovered?

I couldn't see who was outside, but the tense set of the servant's shoulders eased.

"Malabey," he said. "Come in—quickly."

A thin man scuttled into the room, and Mr. Cresset closed the door behind him. I stared at our guest, whose limbs were even spindlier than my own. He was garbed in a tattered assemblage of once-colorful scarves layered over a long tunic, worn to dingy hues by time and too much washing.

"What is it?" Sir Durum demanded. I noted he did not sheathe his sword.

The man called Malabey eyed the blade and skittered sideways a few steps.

"My mistress, Madame Caplata, has been arrested," he said in a brittle, birdlike voice.

"When?" my mother asked, stepping out of her room. "Today?"

"Less than an hour ago," Malabey said. "They'll be after you next."

Mama's eyes widened, one hand going to her throat. My ears rang with the panicked echo of his words. *They'll be after you...*

Our time had run out.

"We must go," Sir Durum said, sheathing his blade. "Immediately."

"Don't forget my pay." Malabey stretched out a long-fingered hand. "Eight golden coins. You promised."

"I'll give you ten," Mama said, though her voice shook.

She ducked back into her room and returned a moment later with a clinking pouch. Malabey snatched it from her hands and opened it. I could see his thin lips moving as he counted.

"It's all there," Sir Durum said, pushing Malabey toward the door. "Now go."

The man darted a beady look at Sir Durum. "Unkind."

"Thank you for coming to warn us," Mama said in a soothing tone. "You are a faithful servant of your mistress. When she is released, I know she too will reward you."

"If," Malabey said. "If indeed. Unless she burns."

I shuddered at the words, and Kian put a steadying arm around my shoulders. I leaned gratefully into his strength.

"You'd best find a safe spot," Mama said to our visitor. "Keep yourself from harm."

"Yourself as well, majesty." He dipped her a bow, looked to the left and right, then dashed for the door.

Mr. Cresset managed to fling it open before Malabey crashed into the solid wood. We all stared after him, a last glimpse of dingy scarves fluttering down the hallway.

"Close that," Sir Durum said. "We leave within the quarter hour."

"It's not enough time," Mama protested. "I can't pack everything."

"Then we leave it behind. But we must go."

"Is that wise?" Her gaze darted to my door.

"Wiser than waiting for capture." He pivoted. "Cresset, gather provisions for travel. Everyone, don serviceable clothing, pack a small bag, and do not delay!"

I jumped at his barked command.

"Don't worry," Kian said, squeezing my shoulders. "You're strong enough now."

I had to be. There was no other choice.

❦

IT TOOK MORE than a quarter hour, but not by much, for us to be ready. Mama was the last one out the door. She paused at the threshold, sending a glance back into the room: the books on the shelves, the abandoned chessboard on the table, my queen poised for a rout that would never come.

"I don't like leaving anything," Mama said. "Should we burn it?"

I stared at her, aghast. She wanted to set the apartments on fire?

Sir Durum gave a quick shake of his head. "Chances are, the priests don't know our whereabouts—but firing our rooms would tell them. Even if they can read what we've touched, it won't do them any good. We'll be halfway to Raine."

I tried to puzzle out what he was saying, but fear throbbed through me, waking my dizziness. It was all I could do to stay on my feet.

As we left the building and hurried down the street, the cold wind pulled at our cloaks and the first spatter of rain stung my cheeks.

"Another storm," Kian murmured.

He left unsaid the fact that it would be next to impossible to find a captain willing to take us across the Strait.

At the corner, Mama hailed a carriage, and the six of us bundled inside. It was tight quarters. I was squeezed in beside Mrs. Cresset, who carried a basket reeking of smoked cheese and onions, and Mama, who cast frequent, anxious glances out the window.

No one seemed to be following us, but Sir Durum kept his hand to his sword, even as the carriage rattled over the cobblestones of Parnese. I caught glimpses of the sea, dark silver, and the red-tiled roofs as we passed. The few pedestrians walked quickly, cloaks drawn tight. Half the inns were shuttered, the marketplaces nearly deserted.

My heart squeezed with homesickness—but not for this hushed and shadowed city. No, I ached for the Parnese that was warm and vibrant, bustling with music and cheer. Not the city as it was now, closed in on itself and shrinking with fear of the red priests. I feared the home of my childhood was gone forever.

But what did that leave me?

The smell of the sea grew stronger, even as rain lashed the sides of our vehicle. When we reached the harbor and disembarked from the carriage, the strength of the wind nearly brought me to my knees.

The storm pounded down on us. I gritted my teeth and staggered along as best I could. The satchel of clothing I carried pulled at my shoulder, but I'd refused to let anyone else take it. Their hands were full with their own belongings.

"Here." Sir Durum jerked his head toward a disreputable-looking pub.

When we stepped inside, the wind slammed the door shut behind us. The place smelled of sour ale and unwashed bodies, but at least it was better than the deluge outside. With one hand, I wiped the water from my face.

"We need a ship out, across the Strait," Sir Durum called, surveying the room. "Will any of you take us?"

It didn't look promising. Only a few of the tables were occupied, the hard-faced men and women clearly more interested in nursing their ale than setting foot outside. Most of them hunched their shoulders and didn't bother looking at us, let alone answering.

"What? Now?" a man asked, and his companions guffawed.

"Better luck becoming a red priest, and conjure yourselves wherever you like," a woman said, then cackled uproariously at her own words.

Mama stepped forward, lowering the hood of her cloak. Even in the greasy light, she looked beautiful, her golden hair shining, her eyes wide with entreaty.

"Please," she said. "For the sake of the old queen. Our lives are at stake, and we must flee the city immediately. Won't any of you help us?"

The room was silent for a heartbeat, and I leaned forward, willing someone to say yes.

Then one of the drinkers clunked his empty glass on the table, calling for more ale, and the moment was gone.

"We'll pay handsomely," Sir Durum said.

He was ignored, the babble of conversation and click of dice rising to cover his words.

"It's no use," Mama said, a catch in her voice. "We must try somewhere else."

"There isn't anywhere else," Sir Durum said. "Other than begging ship to ship."

"I'll go," Kian said, turning toward the door. "I'll find us passage, I swear it."

"Wait." The voice was low and throaty, and came from a woman seated in the corner nearest the door.

She wore dark gray, and all but blended with the shadows. When she rose, I was surprised we'd overlooked her, for she was nearly as tall and broad as Sir Durum.

"Smuggler," the arms master said under his breath.

"Aye." The woman gave him a crooked-toothed smile. "Which means I know a dozen ways out of the harbor. You'll pay for passage, you say?"

"Will you take us across the Strait?" Mama asked.

The smuggler shook her head. "My boat's not fit for such—but I know someone up coast who can."

My mother exchanged a look with Sir Durum. It wasn't the ideal solution, but it seemed the best we'd get under the circumstances.

"Ten gold," the weapons master said in a low voice.

The woman gave him an open-mouthed grin. "Twenty, and we've a bargain."

"Done—but we must go now."

"Aye. Storm's not getting any quieter." She shrugged into an oilcloth overcoat, then led us back out into the spattering wind and rain.

To my surprise, she turned away from the harbor and into a series of twisty alleyways. Once, she froze, then hastily motioned us all back. We crowded into a recessed doorway, my heart hammering with fear. One street over, I glimpsed a flash of red cloaks as a group of men hurried past.

Priests of the Twin Gods. Searching for us? I glanced at Kian, and he sent me a grim look in return. He was a skilled warrior—but what could he and Sir Durum do against sorcery?

"That's no good," the smuggler said, staring after the priests. "Right then. This way."

We continued on until we came to the most run-down area of the port—an area I'd always avoided as a child. I clenched my teeth, summoning my last reserves of strength. Surely we were almost at our destination, I told myself. Just a little farther...

The smuggler took us into a derelict building. Sir Durum grunted, half drawing his blade as the woman led us to a narrow stairwell descending into a cellar. Except this was no ordinary cellar. The bottom seemed *very* far down, the stairs disappearing into darkness. I could hear the faint lap of water on stone, and smelled the sea.

"My pay." She held out a grimy hand.

"When we're free of the city," Sir Durum said.

"You're a hard one." She didn't sound too upset by it, but simply pulled a lantern from behind a broken paving stone and lit the wick with a quick strike of her flint.

By the flickering light, we made our way down the salt-worn steps. I stepped cautiously, Kian holding my elbow to keep me from teetering over the edge. As we descended, a sea cave opened around us, and I could hear the distant crash of waves.

Water surged into the cave through an arched opening barely visible in the dimness, curtained outside by sheeting rain. At the bottom of the stairs lay a small landing, barely big enough for the seven of us, and, tied to a mooring, the smuggler's boat.

Also barely big enough for the seven of us. I eyed it doubtfully. It was a glorified rowboat, with two sets of oars, three benches, and sides that didn't look high enough to keep the waves from swamping us.

We might easily end our journey at the bottom of the bay. I swallowed back hopelessness. Surely Sir Durum would not let us set out into the jaws of certain watery death.

"Will we fit?" Mrs. Cresset asked, her voice trembling.

"No one stays behind," Sir Durum said.

"In you go." The smuggler began untying her boat.

The weapons master handed Mama in, then me. The vessel swayed and rocked, and vertigo threatened to pitch me over the edge. Only my mother's steadying grip enabled me to clamber over and sink down beside her on the wooden bench at the prow.

Mrs. Cresset squeezed next to us, then her husband and Kian took the middle bench. Every movement sent the boat rocking. Sweating and cold, I battled back nausea.

There was a commotion high above us, at the top of the stairs.

"There they are!" someone cried, echoing through the cave.

"Get in," the smuggler said, frantically pushing Sir Durum into the boat. "No time for swords, idiot. Take an oar."

Orange light blossomed overhead. Heart racing, I watched as three priests began descending the stairs, flames at their shoulders, though they held no torches. In the lead was the red-haired man I remembered from Ser Pietro's burning. Warder Galtus Celcio, now the most powerful man in Parnesia.

At my side, Mama gasped and huddled into herself, pulling her cloak over her head.

"Halt!" the warder cried, his voice booming off the stone.

"Go," the smuggler screeched. She pushed us off the rickety dock, leaping into the boat at the last second.

Kian and Mr. Cresset were already rowing desperately for the cave mouth, and Sir Durum hastily grabbed his oar.

The priest raised one hand. Flames licked from between his fingers, steadily growing into a ball of fire overhead. In his other hand, he held something small and white. A bone?

Heat built around us. The black water shimmered with the reflection of fire. The sensation in my chest built, and I shook violently, gagging.

We were going to die.

CHAPTER 54

T he fiery sphere pulsed over the priest's head, an evil sun
hungry to consume us. The water was lit with scarlet, the
rock walls washed with reflected flame.

"Stop!" the warder called. "Or I'll attack."

We didn't stop.

The frantic splash of our boat's oars sent salty droplets to glaze my
lips and sting my eyes. On the seat in front of me, Kian breathed hard,
and Sir Durum grunted as he plied his oar. My stomach turned and
twisted, and I heard a roaring in my ears—the crash of waves surging
into the sea cave, or my own panicked heartbeat, I couldn't tell.

Our rowboat was halfway to the rain-lashed opening. Once past the
rocks, we'd be safe. But it was too far. We couldn't possibly escape.

"Give me the girl, and the rest of you can go free." Galtus Celcio's
voice was coaxing, reasonable, as if a ball of flame wasn't hovering
above his head, ready to destroy us. "I know she's with you."

He held up the white object in his hand. I squinted, horrified when
I recognized it—the white queen from the chess set Kian and I had
spent hours playing.

Hidden in her cloak, Mama sobbed.

My whole body shook—with fear, with pain, with a deep-seated hunger I could not name.

"Your last chance." The priest's voice was no longer sweet.

Sibilant whispers raced around the rough cave walls: *grab the girl, flame ward, the rest can scorch...*

The ball of fire pulsed. Once. Twice. The priest drew his hand back, then shot his palm forward, releasing the fireball. It rushed toward us, the heat flaying my skin.

Something inside me gave a vicious wrench.

"*Esfera to quera, firenda des almar!*" I screamed, raising my left hand to shield my face.

The ball of flame stopped as though it had met a wall of glass. It hung in the air, crackling and straining. The priest shouted a furious denial.

I panted, nearly retching, then gasped the chant again, those words overheard by a long-ago spy, stolen from the red priests themselves.

"*Esfera to quera, firenda des almar.*" Somehow, they gave me mastery over the flame.

I dropped my hand and *pushed* with all my might, ignoring the heave of my stomach.

The sphere of fire quivered, then plunged, sizzling, into the sea. A gout of steam rose as the fireball submerged beneath the waves. The light of it faded—from white-hot, to orange, to sullen red.

An ember, sinking. Then gone.

A cry of pain in the dimness. I hoped it was the priest.

Silence, but for the surge of the waves. I bent forward, head touching my knees, and trembled on the hard bench of the rowboat. Beside me, Mrs. Cresset laid a hand on my back. Mama was still hidden in the folds of her cloak.

A huge swell lifted the boat, propelling us toward the storm-lashed waters outside. I raised my head at the motion, hope jangling through me. The priests remained on the stairs, a straggling flame illuminating the slumped form of their leader. His red cloak puddled like fresh blood as his followers gathered around him.

"Row," the smuggler urged under her breath.

Kian and the others bent to their task, oars slashing the water as the wave pushed us to the mouth of the cave. Something swirled in the sea beside us—white and eerie as bone. I looked at it, and shivered.

The singed shape of a chess piece: the white-crowned queen dissolving to ash as I watched.

EPILOGUE

O ne week later, we stepped off a merchant vessel and onto
the soil of Raine.

The smuggler, true to her word, had taken us to where
we could arrange passage across the Strait. That captain had refused to
sail, however, until the storm abated. We spent three miserable days
waiting, jumping at shadows and expecting the priests to arrive at any
moment.

They did not, and Sir Durum speculated that the leader had been
gravely injured during his attempt to capture us, throwing the priest-
hood into disarray. Face tight, Mama said nothing.

None of us spoke of what had happened in the cave.

Sometimes, I thought I'd dreamed it—the certainty that, for a
moment, I could force that ball of flame to do my bidding as I thrust it
deep beneath the waves.

Only Kian seemed willing to talk, and only in the few stolen
moments we found for ourselves. The captain hosted us in his spacious
home, and on the second day Kian and I managed to sneak out to the
stables, where we could speak unobserved.

We found a pile of straw to sit on, and he wrapped his cloak around
both our shoulders. I leaned against his warmth, and for a treacherous

moment wished we weren't returning to Raine. For several heartbeats we sat there in silence, breathing in the comforting smell of hay, leather, and horse.

"Was it you?" he finally asked. "With the fire and the wave?"

"I don't know." I let out a long sigh. "I've been wondering the same thing. But how could it have been?"

"Sorcery." His voice was grimly thoughtful. "The red priests truly possess it. If I hadn't seen it with my own eyes, I wouldn't have believed it."

What would he think when he met the Dark Elves and saw their magic? I shook my head.

He turned to gaze into my eyes. "Rose. Do you possess... magic?"

Would you hate me if I did? Would you love me?

I pressed my lips together, debating how much to tell him. Enough, I decided—but not too much.

"I don't," I said. "At least, as far as those who know about such things can determine. And I trust their judgment."

"Those who know about such things?" His eyes narrowed, and I could see his mind working, connecting bits of the puzzle. I knew the feeling, as I'd done much the same during my first year in Raine.

I breathed out, waiting for his next question. It didn't take long.

"The Darkwood is full of strange creatures," he said. "And I've heard about its guardian, yet never met him—which I find odd. Who is the warden of the forest?"

"His name is Thorne Windrift." I hadn't spoken his name aloud for months. The shape of it against my tongue sent a wave of longing through me.

Kian's gaze sharpened. "And this Thorne fellow, he's a fire sorcerer?"

"No." I shook my head, then plunged forward. "His magic is of a different kind."

"But he *does* have magic."

The leaf tattoo on my elbow buzzed, as though I was about to poke a nest of hornets. I was sorry to have spoken of it after all.

I blinked at Kian, trying to look innocent. "According to Neeve, yes."

Since she wasn't there to answer, I only felt a little guilty about shifting the knowledge onto her shoulders.

"Neeve?" Kian's brows rose. "How many blasted secrets does Raine hold, anyway?"

"Too many." I could say that much with complete honesty. "Nobody ever tells me anything."

"I am a prince of Fiorland," he said, with a touch of arrogance. "They will answer to me."

Perhaps. Though I thought it doubtful. Raine's secrets had been held from more than the likes of a king's youngest son, fosterling or no. When Lord Raine was ready, he would tell Kian what he wished the prince to know—and not before.

Now, though, as we stood waiting in the damp morning fog for the coaches to arrive and bear us through the Darkwood, I could see questions springing anew to Kian's eyes.

"Be careful of what you ask," I cautioned him.

"I'm trained in diplomacy," he said, lacing his arm through mine. "Don't worry."

I did, though.

The balance had been upset, and not just in Parnese. Things were shifting: magic, and alliances, and dangerous secrets. I feared that something was going to break.

I leaned against Kian as a cool wind ruffled the cedar boughs just ahead. Deep within the forest, I fancied I heard the distant roar of a bear, quickly covered by the brighter sounds of birds waking. The soft breeze carried the scent of wildness, Of hope, and pain.

Lifting my face to the misty air, I closed my eyes and let the Darkwood welcome me home.

_*_

The adventures of Rose, Neeve, Kian, and Thorne continue in BLACK AS NIGHT, coming Fall 2021, and conclude with RED AS FLAME, due out in early 2022.

ACKNOWLEDGMENTS

I don't remember which of my parent's friends gifted me the Andrew Lang Fairy Books when I was young, but thank you for opening a forever door for me into mystical and magical worlds. This story is inspired by the classic Snow White & Rose Red fairytale, with additional helpings of the better-known Snow White tale.

Particular thanks to my early readers on this book: Laurie, Chassily, and my newest beta, Cathi. Your feedback is, as always, incredibly helpful and keeps me out of all kinds of authorial trouble. Thank you.

A sweeping bow to the copy editing of Arran - ever dependable - and Ginger the typo-catcher extraordinaire.

Finally, I'd like to acknowledge the work of Leonard and the wonderful folks who compiled Parf Edhellen, a free online dictionary of Tolkien's languages. The Dark Elf language is deeply inspired by Sindarin, with many thanks to this excellent resource. www.elfdict.com

ABOUT THE AUTHOR

-USA Today bestselling, award-winning author of fantasy-flavored fiction -

Growing up on fairy tales and computer games, Anthea Sharp has melded the two in her award-winning, bestselling Feyland series, which has sold over 150k copies worldwide.

In addition to the fae fantasy/cyberpunk mashup of Feyland, she also writes Victorian Spacepunk, and fantasy romance featuring Dark Elves. Her books have won awards and topped bestseller lists, and garnered over 1.2 million reads at Wattpad. Her short fiction has appeared in Fiction River, DAW anthologies, The Future Chronicles, and Beyond The Stars: At Galaxy's edge, as well as many other publications.

Anthea lives in Southern California, where she writes, hangs out in virtual worlds, plays the fiddle with her Celtic band Fiddlehead, and spends time with her small-but-good family.

Contact her at antheasharp@hotmail.com or visit her website – www.antheasharp.com where you can sign up for her newsletter, Sharp Tales, and be among the first to hear about new releases and reader perks.

Anthea also writes historical romance under the pen name Anthea Lawson. Find out about her acclaimed Victorian romantic adventure novels at www.anthealawson.com.

OTHER WORKS

~ THE DARKWOOD TRILOGY ~

WHITE AS FROST

BLACK AS NIGHT

RED AS FLAME

~ THE FEYLAND SERIES ~

What if a high-tech game was a gateway to the treacherous Realm of Faerie?

THE FIRST ADVENTURE - Book 0 (prequel)

THE DARK REALM – Book 1

THE BRIGHT COURT – Book 2

THE TWILIGHT KINGDOM – Book 3

FAERIE SWAP - Book 3.5

TRINKET (short story)

SPARK - Book 4

BREA'S TALE - Book 4.5

ROYAL - Book 5

MARNY - Book 6

CHRONICLE WORLDS: FEYLAND

FEYLAND TALES: Volume 1

~ THE DARKWOOD CHRONICLES ~

Deep in the Darkwood, a magical doorway leads to the enchanted and dangerous land of the Dark Elves~

ELFHAME

HAWTHORNE

RAINE

HEART of the FOREST (A Novella)

~ VICTORIA ETERNAL ~

Steampunk meets Space Opera in a British Galactic Empire that never was...

PASSAGE OUT

STAR COMPASS

STARS & STEAM

COMETS & CORSETS

~ SHORT STORY COLLECTIONS ~

TALES OF FEYLAND & FAERIE

TALES OF MUSIC & MAGIC

THE FAERIE GIRL & OTHER TALES

THE PERFECT PERFUME & OTHER TALES

COFFEE & CHANGE

MERMAID SONG